THE LEGACY

THE LEGACY

Craig Lawrence

FireStep
Publishing

FireStep Publishing
Gemini House
136–140 Old Shoreham Road
Brighton
BN3 7BD

www.firesteppublishing.com

First published by Firestep Press, an imprint
of Firestep Publishing in 2015
A Unicorn Publishing Group company
www.unicornpress.org

ISBN 978-1-908487-43-8

This is a work of fiction. Names, characters, businesses,
places, events and incidents are either the products of the
author's imagination or used in a fictitious manner. Any
resemblance to actual persons, living or dead, or actual
events is purely coincidental.

A CIP catalogue reference for this book is
available in the British Library.

Cover by Ryan Gearing
Typeset by Vivian@Bookscribe

Printed and bound in the UK by Berforts, Stevenage

CHAPTER 1

The assassin moved slowly through the undergrowth. Flat on his stomach and with so little moon, it was unlikely that anyone would see him even if they came within a few feet. He reached the edge of the woods and stopped, slowing his breathing and listening. He could hear nothing other than the nocturnal sounds of woodland animals. He inched forwards, slowly parting the long grass that grew on the edge of the track. He thought of all the times he had done this before. Northern Ireland, Bosnia, Kosovo, Iraq, Afghanistan, he had served everywhere the British Army had been deployed over the last twenty years. A paratrooper by profession and master sniper by trade, he had ended lives on behalf of the British Government for over two decades. And he was very good indeed at his trade. So good that it had been easy to find a job when he left the Army. But this job was particularly important. It was, he hoped, one of his last. If it went well he would soon be able to retire to his native Scotland with enough money in various bank accounts to ensure that he never had to work again.

The villa had been built in the early twenties. White, sprawling and very private, it sat in nearly half an acre of prime real estate on the southern slopes of Montgo, the mountain that dominates the small fishing town of Javea on Spain's east coast. Its owner, Diego Velasquez, had chosen it deliberately. He had been a drug dealer on the Costa del Sol for many years and whilst this had made him rich, it had also made him a fair number of enemies. He believed that the low profile seclusion his villa provided kept him safe and, so far, it had. As the assassin watched, the perimeter gates slid quietly closed behind a big, black Mercedes saloon. The car sat low on its suspension; it was clearly armoured. It came to a standstill in front of the floodlit villa and Velasquez started to get out unsteadily.

'Open the door,' he shouted as he lurched towards the front step. 'Come on, open it, I need another drink.'

The assassin recognised Velasquez immediately. He'd been following him for over a week, discretely watching his every move, probing for a weakness that he could exploit. He'd found it a few days ago. He'd particularly enjoyed the build up to this kill. He'd seen enough of Velasquez over the last seven days to know that the world would be a better place without him. But there was still an element of risk. Velasquez's men were highly professional. They took few chances and, if the assassin made a mistake, he knew he would most likely pay for it. The trick with any kill was to minimise the risk by hitting the target when he least expected it. The element of surprise was crucial. But achieving surprise was difficult, not least because the people providing the protection had usually done the same training as the people trying to kill the target. They knew how to spot vulnerable points and they knew the importance of avoiding routine. But sooner or later, everyone makes a mistake. It's just a question of being patient. The assassin knew that every Friday evening Velasquez had supper with his brother in a neighbouring town. The time he arrived home varied from week to week and his driver always selected the route at random. But sooner or later, Velasquez always came home and the villa was always well illuminated when he did. The bright lights and cameras would deter the gangs of armed burglars that worked the Costas in the summer months and they would also make it difficult for anyone to place an explosive charge near the villa. But they were a godsend for a night-time shoot.

Conscious that his boss was at his most exposed as he left the car, Velasquez's long time driver and bodyguard came round to the rear passenger door. 'Boss, wait, get back in the car until I've got the door open and then I'll get you a drink.'

Ramon turned away from his boss and ran up the steps to unlock the front door of the villa as quickly as he could. Velasquez started to follow him up the steps, lurching slightly from side to side.

The assassin watched Velasquez leave the safety of the car and move towards his bodyguard. He shifted the rifle slightly until Velasquez's head filled the optical sight. He slowed his breathing, expelling the last of his air as the cross hairs lined up just to the right of Velasquez's right temple. He pulled the trigger. The rifle kicked back in his shoulder but he held his position.

Ramon heard a sharp crack and then his boss fell at his feet. He reached down 'Come on boss, get up, we're nearly in,' but as he looked at his boss he could see that Velasquez wasn't going anywhere. Half of his head had disappeared. The left side of his face was a bloody pulp. Ramon, who had handled his fair share of silenced weapons in his time, noticed the entry wound just below the right temple and realised what had happened. He pulled out his pistol, dived behind one of the pillars flanking the door and started to scan the darkness beyond the villa's garden in the hope of seeing someone to shoot at.

In the wood line, the assassin slid slowly back on his stomach. When he was a good twenty metres inside the woods, he sat up and started to check that his equipment was all there. He didn't want to leave anything behind that could lead anyone to him, although he doubted that his fire position would ever be found. He was nearly a kilometre from the villa. It had been a superb shot. The ground fell away and there was a slight wind, adding to the difficulty. He felt no regret at having killed Velasquez, just a quiet satisfaction at a job well done. He finished checking his equipment, confirmed that he had put the expended case in his pocket and did a final sweep of the area. He then leant against a large tree stump, opened his mouth and turned his head on its side to give his ears and eyes the best chance of detecting any human sounds in the woods around him. He stood perfectly still, slowing his breathing and straining to hear anything unusual. After five minutes, he stooped into a crouch and jogged the two hundred metres to the kitbag he had hidden behind a fallen tree. Quickly, he changed out of his black combats and into jeans, check shirt and loafers. He stuffed his combat kit into an old rucksack, put on his baseball hat and started to walk towards the rental car that he had parked at the side of the main road. His rifle was hidden inside a long bag with fishing rods sticking out at the end. Should he be questioned, he intended to claim that he was looking for the Cap de Verde lighthouse as he had fancied a bit of night fishing. An hour later, he was sat at the bar of the Club Nautico in Denia drinking San Miguel beer, flirting drunkenly with the barmaid – just another middle-aged foreigner enjoying his holiday.

Things had livened up at the villa. Alerted by Ramon's frantic shouting, Velasquez's men had come running out of the house and, having eventually doused the floodlights, were frantically scanning the hillside around the villa. Ramon was on his mobile talking to Velasquez's brother. 'I don't know who the fuck killed him. One minute he was telling me to get him a drink, the next he was dead. Must have been a silenced rifle. I didn't hear a thing. Yes I am sure he's dead. No I didn't give him mouth to mouth. Why? Because he doesn't have a fucking mouth left.'

The brother told Ramon to stay put, he was on his way. Ramon wasn't worried. He'd known Tony since they were both kids. But he was sad. Whilst he wouldn't say that he and Velasquez had become friends, he'd been with him for nearly ten years and he had enjoyed the job. The money was good and, whatever Velasquez's faults, he treated those loyal to him with respect. He was also a bit worried about the future; the demand for bodyguards who let their bosses get killed wasn't strong.

CHAPTER 2

Charles Highworth looked what he was: a formidably successful merchant banker. At forty-six years old, he was now at the height of his power. Tall and immaculately groomed, his slight paunch was well disguised by the cut of his beautifully tailored suit. His thick, lightly greying hair was swept back from his tanned face, revealing a slight scar on his forehead and clear green eyes. He was still ruggedly handsome but years of corporate lunches and a love of fine wine were slowly beginning to take their toll. His jaw was becoming less well defined and his once heavily muscled shoulders were now less impressive than they had been when he'd played rugby for Oxford. But he was still a big man and what he'd lost in physical size, he'd gained in the presence that comes from being hugely wealthy and successful. Utterly ruthless, he'd made millions over the last twenty years, accumulating vast amounts of money for the select clients that invested in his hedge fund, International Valiant. This last year had been particularly profitable. At a time when most were urging caution, he had invested heavily in the emerging markets of China and India, achieving an average increase of thirty-five percent in the value of his very significant investments.

As he sat in his office on the top floor of his company's Canary Warf office building, he started to smile. The headlines on the wide screen TV opposite him announced the best possible news: 'Tokifora's new processor set to end Intel dominance.' He knew this news would cause Tokifora's shares to skyrocket in value, and this was particularly gratifying as it would push his annual return way beyond thirty-five percent. Over the last eight months, his fund had gradually become the single biggest owner of Tokifora shares to the extent that he now had a forty-eight percent stake in the company. He had taken a risk investing such significant amounts in a single company but it had been a calculated risk. He had used his wide network of contacts and a fair amount of money to help Tokifora assemble a winning team of experts over the last two years. Not everyone he approached had been keen to join the team and there were occasions when he'd had to resort to what he called 'robust measures' to achieve his desired outcome. These measures involved coercion, bribery, blackmail and, on two particular occasions, murder. The illegality of these actions didn't bother him in the least – the end always justified the means, particularly if the end in question was him getting richer.

His PA, an attractive and highly efficient woman in her early thirties, came into the office and carefully put a cup of black coffee on his desk. 'Get Richards for me,' he snapped at her.

'Yes Sir,' she replied, leaving the room as quietly as she'd entered it.

His phone rang. 'Mr Richards is on the line,' she told him before connecting the call.

'Richards, I need to see you this evening. I'll meet you at the usual place, at the same time as last time.'

Highworth was a cautious man. He worked on the assumption that his phone was bugged and that his e-mail would probably be read by other people. He wasn't worried about any of the Government's covert agencies trying to keep tabs on him – why would they? – but he knew that other banks and newspapers would try. His success was so striking that he knew people wanted to find out how he managed to achieve such startling results given the current state of the global economy. And he had no doubt that despite the *News of the World*'s demise, newspapers would still resort to illegal means to obtain information if they felt the benefits outweighed the risks.

He thought about Richards. He didn't really like him but he had a healthy respect for his talents. An ex-Special Forces soldier who'd been forced to resign for reasons which he kept to himself, he had demonstrated his ability to fix even the most delicate of problems over the years. He was discrete, effective, absolutely reliable and comfortable operating on the wrong side of the law. Highworth was confident that he'd be able to resolve the issue that had been worrying him for the last week or so.

Having spoken to Richards, Highworth phoned his wife, Caroline. She was at home, a magnificent Queen Anne house on the edge of a small and very smart Surrey town called Farnham. She had married her husband ten years ago at the age of thirty-five when, recognising that she wasn't getting any younger, she set out to find and then seduce the most eligible of her brother's acquaintances. Eligible in her book meant rich, handsome and respected – love was of secondary importance. She knew her husband for what he was when she married him but she was equally tough. In many ways they were a perfect match and the marriage soon settled into a comfortable routine based on mutual respect and a shared desire to enjoy the lifestyle that significant wealth brings. With no children and with plenty of time and money to enjoy herself, she had a wide circle of friends and an active social life, both with and without her husband. Her own father, now long dead, had also been an accomplished banker, knighted for his services to charity towards the end of his life, and she now delighted in organising the same kind of charity balls and dinners that she had so enjoyed as she grew up.

'Darling it's me, I'm afraid I'm going to be late this evening,' said Highworth when his wife answered the phone. 'I need to meet someone to sort something out but I should be back before midnight.'

'Don't worry,' his wife replied easily, 'I promised mother I'd go round and help her plan the changes she's making to her garden. I'll stay a bit longer and persuade her to let me stay for supper.'

Highworth put the phone down and smiled. His wife was his chief ally and he recognised what a good team they made. Although she was now in her mid forties, she was still striking. Slim, elegant and always beautifully dressed, she never failed to turn heads. Although she looked like the typically well bred trophy wife of a rich banker, she was bright, perceptive and extremely well connected. She could read people with remarkable accuracy, something her husband had found extremely useful when considering whether to invest in particular companies. She was also good fun, completely loyal to her husband and, for someone of her background and position, wickedly mischievous in bed. She didn't know all of the underhand methods her husband employed to maintain his edge but, even if she did, he suspected she wouldn't mind, squaring any moral misgivings she might have by considering how many charities benefited from the wealth his activities created.

CHAPTER 3

Lucy Masters walked out of the main entrance of the International Relations Department and headed into town. Now coming to the end of her postgraduate studies, she'd just submitted the final draft of her PhD dissertation. She realised that she needed to think seriously about what she was going to do next. She hoped that her hard work would pay off and she'd get the doctorate without the need to revisit much of the work she'd already done. A bit of re-drafting would be fine but if those assessing her work felt that there was nothing original in what she was saying, then she might have to spend most of next year doing the further research necessary to strengthen her arguments. But she hoped this wouldn't be the case; her supervisors had been very positive about her performance and even her tutor, a notoriously grumpy man called Dr John Walker, had been upbeat when she'd seen him earlier in the week. Three weeks until the results were formally published on the Palace Green notice board and then she'd know for sure. A PhD from Durham University would open a lot of doors, not just in the City but also in the Foreign Office or DFID, the Department for International Development. She liked what she'd seen of the people in DFID having spent a fair amount of time with them whilst doing research for her thesis. There were one or two whose motives she sometimes doubted, but the majority had come across as hard working, professional and committed to trying to make the world a better place. She felt that she could do a lot worse than work with people whose values she shared.

At 5ft 10in Lucy was taller than most of her friends. She was also striking to look at with piercing blue eyes, long strawberry blonde hair and a body toned from years of hard physical exercise. She ran almost every day and whilst she enjoyed rowing – one of the reasons she'd chosen Durham in the first place – her real passion was climbing. She spent most of her holidays in the mountains somewhere, mainly on expeditions. During term time, she spent her weekends either in the Lake District or up in Scotland tackling some of the more challenging routes that Skye's Cuillin Ridge has to offer. Easily the best female climber at Durham, she was also better than all but two of the men. Her expedition work was earning her a widening reputation as a hard working team member who could lead the most difficult of routes with confidence. Some men found this difficult, particularly as she had a habit of telling them to 'man up and get on with it' whenever their nerves started to get the better of them. But she worked hard to maintain her edge. After her morning run of four to six miles through the Durham countryside, she would always end up in the gym, pushing herself through a rigorous routine of press ups, sit-ups, dips and heaves that even the fittest of the University rugby team would have struggled to complete.

As she headed into town, she thought of what to do next. Her father had sent her a text asking whether she had decided what she was going to do after she'd got the PhD. She hadn't replied. She knew that she really needed to get on with finding a job and starting a career but, until she knew whether she would have to re-do parts of her thesis, she didn't see much point in making any firm plans. For the moment, she'd saved enough money to spend the next few months climbing in Nepal and this was her immediate focus. A mini-expedition, the plan was to spend a few days in Kathmandu sorting out their equipment before travelling west to Pokhara and then trekking up into the Annapurna basin to climb the two highest peaks. Thereafter, she intended to spend another week in Kathmandu in order to enjoy the Dashain celebrations. Her best friend and fellow PhD student, Isobel Johnson, was going with her.

Lucy saw Isobel as she entered the cafe. 'Hey loser,' she called out as she approached Isobel's table.

'Hi, where've you been? I've been waiting for hours,' Isobel replied.

'No you haven't, I saw you just come in ahead of me.' The two girls laughed. Whenever they met they spent the first few minutes giving each other a hard time, normally about the other's latest male admirer. They had been best friends since the age of twelve when they had found themselves in the same dormitory on their first day at boarding school in York. At the time, both of their fathers had been serving abroad in the Army and they soon discovered that they had a lot in common. Both were only children, with the absence of siblings strengthening their friendship. They were athletic, bright and keen on outdoor sports, though Isobel preferred skiing to climbing. Slightly shorter than Lucy, Isobel nevertheless turned heads wherever she went. Her thick blonde hair was cut into a fashionable bob and her full lips and wide brown eyes always seemed to be smiling. She was attractive, intelligent and fun, with a mischievous streak that frequently got her into trouble.

'I've been thinking about Nepal,' Isobel said as her friend sat down and ordered a cappuccino. 'I think we should spend longer in the west after we've cracked the Annapurna peaks rather than head back to Kathmandu. Either that or we should trek out east as far as Everest Base Camp and spend a week or so there chilling with the climbing "fraternity".' She said the last word with heavy irony, using her hands to sign the parenthesis. She was always disparaging about groups of climbers, considering them to be amongst the least hygienic and the scruffiest of people. This was one reason she preferred skiing: the people were so much more fashionable and they generally had more money with which to enjoy themselves! 'What do you think of my plan?' Isobel asked.

It would be fun thought Lucy. As she hadn't yet decided what she was going to do next and as there were no pressing deadlines to meet, she agreed.

CHAPTER 4

At seven-thirty, Highworth left the office and started walking towards the Embankment. He was deep in thought. As the day had progressed the price of Tokifora's shares had continued to go up. Having started the day at 113 pence per share, they had reached 150 by the time the market closed. He was set to make an absolute killing but, whilst this pleased him, he was already thinking about his next venture and the dossier his team had given to him that afternoon. They'd spent two months doing the detailed research that Highworth always insisted on before committing significant sums. He thought about what was in the dossier. Bubble.com was an information technology company that had grown exponentially over the last few years. Current city rumours had it that the social networking capability it was developing would rival Facebook and Twitter. The research suggested that the company would need another six months or so of development and testing before the application could be rolled out but, when it was, his information suggested that it would be hugely popular. Highworth thought about this. He had faith in the research. He'd learnt long ago that time spent learning everything there was to know about a company was seldom wasted. As a result, he'd assembled a research team that few rivals could match. They were very well paid as individuals and they had a significant budget with which to obtain information. He'd also been watching the share price slowly increase over the last year. He knew that this was partly because of the success of Bubble.com's recently introduced web browser but also because city rumours about the social networking capability – known as Mymate – were starting to gain traction. But he also knew that software projects were notoriously difficult to bring into service. No matter how thoroughly tested an application might be prior to going on sale, there were always bugs. Usually, these were relatively easy to fix but if there were too many of them, people quickly lost confidence, particularly if the media started to pan the application. Once public support had been lost, it was notoriously difficult and expensive to re-position the application, even if all the bugs were eventually eliminated. From Highworth's perspective, Bubble.com's share price was entirely dependent on how much confidence the city had in the company's ability to bring the application to the market place without any significant flaws – and this is where Highworth had spotted a real opportunity.

The Chief Executive Officer (CEO) of Bubble.com was a flamboyant character called Peter Fairweather. Loud, arrogant and a prodigious self-publicist, Fairweather was the current darling of the dot com world. He spent huge amounts of money financing expeditions designed to catch the public's imagination and ensure that he ended up in a suitably heroic pose on the front pages of the newspapers. Thirty-two years old, tall, blond, articulate and outspoken, the television stations loved him and none were in any doubt that it was his personal energy that drove Bubble.com forward. But Highworth knew differently. His research team had identified that the real brains behind the company's success was a quiet, unassuming but brilliant software engineer called Colin Pearson. Though Pearson owned forty percent of the company and was therefore already a wealthy man, he shunned the limelight. He had no social life to speak of and preferred to spend his time working on Mymate with his team of programmers and designers. Provided Pearson remained at the centre of the project, Highworth was in absolutely no doubt that Mymate would be spectacularly successful.

Highworth walked past Charing Cross Station and turned down into Villiers Street. He liked this part of London and he was particularly fond of Gordon's Wine Bar. It claimed to be the oldest in London having been established in 1890 and it had a particular atmosphere. Going down into the cellars, he found a quiet table in the candlelit gloom and ordered a bottle of Pinot Noir and two glasses from a passing waitress. Although it was reasonably busy, she returned a few minutes later with the wine. She poured a small amount into a glass and stepped back from the table. Highworth looked up at her. 'I'm sure it'll be fine,' he said, smiling.

The waitress returned his smile and half filled his glass. She appreciated the fact that he hadn't made a show of tasting the wine. It amused her that so many people pretended to know what they were looking for when she poured them a taster from a newly opened bottle. She'd never seen him before but he looked to be above that sort of charade. Highworth took a sip of the wine and nodded his thanks to the waitress. She smiled again and left the table. He watched her walk back towards the bar and noticed Richards ducking his head as he entered the cellars. He poured the second glass of wine and handed it to Richards as he sat down opposite him. 'How are you?' asked Highworth.

'I'm fine,' replied Richards 'but keen to know what's happening that you needed to meet so quickly.'

Highworth wasted no more time on pleasantries. 'There's a company called Bubble.com that I'm interested in,' he said. 'The CEO is a man called Peter Fairweather. I need him to have a fatal accident within the next week or so.'

Richards thought for a few minutes. 'I've seen him on TV. Nice looking chap. Very full of himself. Does lots of publicity seeking stunts. Likes the ladies.'

'That's him,' said Highworth, used to Richards' habit of summarising people in a few short sentences.

Richards sipped his wine and looked at Highworth. He didn't care why Highworth wanted Fairweather dead and he wasn't remotely worried about the prospect of arranging for someone to be killed. He was thinking more about the complexity of the job and therefore how much it would cost. Having someone like Fairweather killed wouldn't be as expensive as knocking off a politician but it would still take time and effort, particularly if it needed to look like an accident. 'How badly does it need to be an accident?' asked Richards.

'Very badly,' replied Highworth. 'There can't be any suspicion otherwise it won't have the effect I want.'

Richards finished his wine. 'OK, I'll make a few calls and confirm the price but I would say that we're looking at eighty to a hundred and twenty thousand given the timeframe, less if you can wait,' said Richards.

'I can't. It needs to be before the end of the month,' replied Highworth.

Richards smiled as he got to his feet. 'I'll be in touch,' he said as he turned and left the bar.

Highworth watched him go thinking, as he always did, that you can't judge a man by his appearance. Richards looked ordinary. His suit was a middle of the range, off-the-peg number from a high street retailer. His shoes, tie and shirt were nondescript and even his face seemed to blend in with the surroundings. He looked middle aged, comfortable and harmless. If you met him for the first time and were asked to guess his occupation, you would probably say that he was an accountant or a sales manager for a multinational. But Highworth was in no doubt that he was the most dangerous man he had ever met. Not only was he a conduit into the murky world of contract killing, but he was also a very hard man himself. During one of their similar meetings a year ago, two local toughs, irritated by Highworth's cut glass accent and obvious wealth, had deliberately pushed him over as he walked back from the bar with two glasses of wine. Highworth went sprawling, crashing into a table and spilling his wine over the occupants. As he looked round to see who'd pushed him, he saw Richards move in quickly and smash one of the men's heads onto the bar so hard that the man collapsed with blood pouring from an open wound. The other man threw a massive punch but Richards rolled back on the balls of his feet, easily avoiding the blow. He then stepped quickly inside the man's arm, turning as he did so to land a powerful elbow strike into the bigger man's neck. The man hit the ground like a felled tree, struggling to breathe through a crushed trachea that only surgery would repair. Richards then walked calmly over to Highworth, helped him to his feet and quietly suggested that they try a different bar in a more upmarket part of town.

CHAPTER 5

The assassin was now back in his flat in Edinburgh's New Town. He liked the city and had been particularly pleased when he'd been able to buy the flat a few years ago. It had taken him months to find something suitable and this flat ticked all the boxes. It was in the centre of the city and was on the fourth floor of an old Georgian town house overlooking George Street. It had been sensitively renovated before he bought it, retaining many of the period features that he admired. It had high ceilings, large sash windows and polished wooden floors. It was furnished sparsely with rugs from his travels and a few antique chairs and tables that he hoped would appreciate in value. Original paintings from some of Edinburgh's exceptional galleries adorned the walls, giving the flat an elegant feel. A casual visitor would note the mountain theme linking the pictures. A more knowledgeable eye would admire the two paintings by Alfred de Breanski Senior and the three by Richard Ansell. All five were painted in the late eighteen hundreds and, though not hugely valuable, each would fetch between ten to thirty thousand pounds at auction.

The assassin sat at an old partners' desk drinking black coffee and checking e-mails on his laptop. His eyes were drawn to one that he knew was from Richards. Though it looked like yet more spam offering Viagra at a reduced rate, the inclusion of the numbers four, six and nineteen in the e-mail's title told him that he needed to read on. The e-mail having been sent on the seventh of the month, he read every seventh word in the main body of the message. The instructions were clear: 'Stay at home. Urgent we meet. Will find you on Thu.' The assassin didn't reply. Richards would assume the message had been received and would track him down on Thursday. They had done this so many times before that both trusted the other implicitly.

He finished his coffee, put on an old t-shirt and cotton shorts, laced up his trainers and left the flat. Ten minutes later he was running along the path that follows the Water of Leith on its journey from the centre of town to the sea. He was deep in thought. Leaving Spain had been easier than he'd expected. The police were slow to react when the shooting was eventually reported and, although they had gone through the motions of taking statements and looking for evidence, their heart wasn't in it. Velasquez was well known in the area and had been implicated in a number of police killings in Madrid. The tit for tat killing of a drug dealer with links to unsolved police murders was not something the police were going to get excited about. But this wasn't why the assassin was thinking so deeply. Richards was a cautious man who usually gave several weeks notice of any meeting. The urgency of this most recent request was therefore unusual and the assassin's pulse quickened at the prospect of a new job. 'If it pays sufficiently well,' he thought to himself as he ran, 'it could well be one of my last.'

CHAPTER 6

Heathrow was crowded as Lucy Masters headed towards the Air India check-in desk. She was dressed in skinny jeans, climbing boots, polo shirt and blue micro-fibre fleece. Her hair was tied in a ponytail and threaded through the gap at the back of her baseball cap. Her sunglasses were hooked into the V of her polo shirt but kept falling to the floor as she struggled to push the trolley containing her enormous North Face climber's bag towards the neatly dressed girl at the check-in. She'd made the decision to wear the boots because they were heavy and she was worried about her baggage allowance. She was regretting it now as she realised that she'd have to take them off to go through security. Isobel was already in Nepal and had been texting her repeatedly, telling her about the people she was meeting in the hotel she was staying in. Lucy couldn't wait to join her. An hour later, she was bracing herself as the airplane accelerated down the runway and lifted off for the thirteen-hour journey to Nepal.

'Excuse me,' she said to a passing stewardess when the seatbelt lights had gone off and the cabin crew had started to move around the aircraft. 'Please could I have a bottle of water?'

The Nepalese stewardess smiled at her. 'Of course,' she said, disappearing off into the galley. She returned a few minutes later and gave Lucy the water.

'Thank you,' said Lucy, looking up at the stewardess just as the blond head of a man disappeared into the toilet a few rows ahead. She hadn't noticed him before. The struggle with her bag had been all consuming and she was only now taking in the people around her.

A few minutes later the man reappeared from the toilets and started back towards his seat. She could see him clearly as he stepped over the legs of a middle aged man to get to his chair. He looked to be in his late twenties or early thirties with blond straggly hair and a tanned, unshaven face. She couldn't see the colour of his eyes but she did notice a recent scar that ran across his right cheek. He was wearing a grey t-shirt and faded old Levis held up with a Kenyan beaded belt. He braced against the back of a seat to lift himself over the man's legs and, as he did so, Lucy noticed the well developed muscles of his arms and shoulders tense with effort. And then he was gone, sinking down into his seat three rows ahead. 'I wonder where he's going,' thought Lucy with a smile. Her last boyfriend had lasted nearly a year but they had broken up eight months ago and she'd not met anyone she really liked since. Several well meaning friends had asked her to dinner to meet similarly aged single men but she could see why most of them were still single. 'I suspect people say that about me,' she thought to herself. The problem, as she saw it, was that most men were not good at treating women as equals. They wanted to be admired by a lesser being and seemed to find it difficult dealing with someone who wasn't really very impressed by whatever they had done. For the sake of her friends, Lucy made an effort to be interested in what these potential boyfriends had to say but, most of the time, they were just very dull and rather full of themselves. Lucy's only real concern was what her friends must think of her if they felt she would be a good match for any of the endless succession of men that they arranged for her to meet.

After twelve hours the pilot announced that they were beginning their descent into Kathmandu International Airport. As she strapped herself in, she looked up and caught a glimpse of the straggly blond man as he reached up to put something in the overhead locker. His movements were fluid and his stomach, when the t-shirt lifted up, looked flat and hard. 'Probably a climber,' she thought to herself, 'wonder if he's going to Annapurna?' She was lost in thought as the plane came to a standstill. She looked out of the window and could see the mobile stairs being positioned against the side of the aircraft. A few minutes later, passengers were thanked for travelling with Air

India and were asked to leave the plane using the front and rear exits. Lucy collected her belongings and walked towards the front of the plane and then out onto the top of the stairs that had been attached to the exit. As she started down towards the tarmac, she squinted her eyes against the bright sunshine and breathed in deeply. The smell of the Kathmandu Valley was distinct and just as she remembered it from her last visit twelve months ago. She loved Nepal. The people were friendly, the mountains were just incredible and the food was fantastic. She'd been five times in the last ten years and she was starting to pick up some of the language, enough at least to order a beer and find the nearest toilet.

'Namaste,' she said in greeting to the Nepalese official at the passport desk.

'Namaste,' he replied, smiling as he handed her passport back to her, 'Enjoy your stay'.

Lucy smiled back and went to reclaim her luggage. The blond man was standing by the carousel waiting for his bag to arrive so she stood back, waiting to see whether he collected a rucksack or a suitcase. If the former, then she might go over and strike up a conversation with him; if the latter, then she would go to the other end of the carousel to wait for her bag. After five minutes, the man bent down to pick up a bag similar to hers. Lucy started to smile as she watched him lift the big bag easily onto his shoulder and then turn and start walking towards the main exit. Lucy was keen to follow but her bag didn't arrive for another ten minutes. By the time she'd picked it up and walked out to the front of the terminal, the blond man had gone. Lucy sighed for what might have been. Kathmandu was a bustling city with a population of nine hundred and ninety thousand people. The chances of bumping into the man again were slim indeed. A taxi pulled up and Lucy climbed in, dragging her bag after her. She gave the driver the address of Isobel's hotel and sat back to enjoy the journey through one of the world's most interesting cities.

CHAPTER 7

It was Thursday morning and the assassin had just showered after a long run round Arthur's Seat. He never tired of the view from the top of the mountain. It overlooked the Palace of Holyroodhouse and the Royal Mile as it climbed its way up towards Edinburgh Castle. He pulled on jeans, a t-shirt and old loafers and headed out of his flat and into the street. He knew Richards would be in Edinburgh by now and that he was probably watching him to make sure that the meeting hadn't been compromised. He had learnt that the best thing to do was to go about his normal business, knowing that Richards would contact him as and when he wanted to. The assassin therefore went into the Costa Coffee on Queen's Street and ordered a black Americano and a Danish pastry. He found a table overlooking the gardens at the foot of the castle and sipped his coffee as he watched the world go by.

After fifteen minutes, Richards pulled out a chair and sat at the table with his own coffee. 'Good to see you,' he said. 'I'm glad you're back home and not up in the hills.'

'I was planning to head up to Skye tomorrow,' replied the assassin, 'but there's a particular painting being auctioned by Sotherby's on Saturday that I'm keen to try and get before heading up North.'

Richards smiled. The assassin was without doubt the most proficient killer that Richards had ever met. Cold, efficient and utterly professional, it seemed odd that such a man would have a passion for nineteenth century Scottish landscapes. But it takes all kinds thought Richards as he contemplated his own passion for the exquisite young Bolivian woman he had recently met. She was about half his age and was married to a junior diplomat at the Bolivian Embassy. The unfortunate man clearly believed his job was more important than appeasing his sexually insatiable wife. Richards didn't care. She was young, pretty and extremely adventurous in bed. Married women always appealed to him. They were less likely to develop an emotional attachment to him and this suited him just fine. Indeed, it had been one such relationship that had led to him having to leave the British Army.

Richards spoke softly but quickly, explaining who Peter Fairweather was and briefing the assassin on the additional research he had been able to do since he'd seen Charles Highworth earlier in the week. He explained about the need for urgency and that Fairweather's death had to look like an accident.

'He lives in St James' Square, near Piccadilly Circus,' said Richards. 'This Saturday, he's supposed to be watching his team take part in a polo tournament at the Guards Polo Club in Windsor Great Park. I'm not sure what time it will finish but he usually goes out for supper after these sorts of events, normally somewhere in London near his home.'

'Go on,' encouraged the assassin, listening intently.

'The only event he's got in his diary for Sunday is an invitation to a private viewing of a new collection at the National Portrait Gallery. He'll be with people all weekend and I suspect it will be difficult to get him alone. He hasn't got a regular girlfriend at the moment but, if his usual form is anything to go by, he'll spend Saturday night with someone he meets during the course of the day. Whether she stays over Sunday night depends, I suspect, on how she performs on Saturday night.' Richards handed over a thick manila envelope containing the detail he'd been able to amass. Though time had been short, his extensive network of contacts had served him well and the product was impressive. 'In terms of the price, I was thinking of something like eighty K,' said Richards.

The assassin smiled. Whilst he wouldn't describe Richards as a friend, he had known him a long time and he knew that the first price, which was rarely generous, was always subject to negotiation.

'What worries me about this,' said the assassin, 'is that I have no time to watch Fairweather before making the kill. Even if I leave for London this afternoon, I'll only have a few days to observe him before I have to finish him. As you know, this increases the risk significantly, particularly if it has to look like an accident.'

It was Richards' turn to smile. 'I thought you'd say that,' he said. They discussed the price for a further ten minutes and eventually agreed on a figure of a hundred thousand pounds, fifty percent payable now, fifty after the event. This suited the assassin. The first fifty thousand would allow him to buy the picture he wanted, even if the bidding went to twice what was expected. The assassin gave Richards the number of the offshore bank account into which the money was to be transferred. Richards left the cafe and took a taxi to the airport. Once there, he sat in one of the departure lounge's cafes, turned on his laptop and transferred the first fifty thousand to the assassin's offshore account. The game was on.

The assassin went back to his flat and began packing. Excited by the challenge, he started to think through the best way of killing Fairweather. The tricky bit was making it look like an accident. He had Fairweather's address in St James' Square and he knew the area well enough to know that he could easily hide in the shadows near the house or in the Square's central garden and wait for an opportunity to get close to Fairweather as he either entered or left the building. It would be relatively straightforward to pretend to stumble into Fairweather as he walked past him, inserting the blade of a knife between the ribs and into the heart as their bodies came together. This would kill him almost instantly. If he wore dark jeans, a dark hoodie and kept his head down, there would be little chance of him being identified from CCTV footage after the event. But the problem with this approach was that it wouldn't look like an accident. St James' is an exclusive part of town and home to lots of expensive London clubs. It is reasonably busy at all hours and well patrolled by the police because of the importance of some of the people using the clubs. It is not the sort of place that people are routinely mugged and killed and any such murder would merit investigation by the police. He had to come up with an alternative plan.

He continued to think through the problem as he drove down towards London the next morning. He always preferred to drive if he was working in the UK as it meant that he could avoid public transport and the thousands of cameras that were now a feature of every train station, airport and bus depot. He'd stolen the car, a five-year-old silver Citroën, the night before from one of the rougher parts of Edinburgh, replacing the number plates with a set that he'd made himself early in the morning with a machine that he'd stolen years ago. The new set were exact copies of a number plate he'd seen on a similar vehicle the previous night. This vehicle had been parked in the drive of a smart looking house near the Botanical Gardens, one of Edinburgh's most expensive residential areas. His rationale for copying this car's number plate was that people living at such an address were no doubt wealthy enough to pay their road tax and to keep their car insured and road legal. It would therefore be unlikely that this number plate would attract attention if randomly checked by the police, although he was only too aware that he didn't know the name of the vehicle's owner and he would therefore struggle if stopped and questioned in detail. To avoid drawing attention to himself, he drove carefully, keeping to the speed limit all the way into London.

CHAPTER 8

Highworth sat in his office reading the *Financial Times*. Tokifora's shares had gone up again from 150 pence per share to 154. This was clearly good news but he sensed that they would soon start to plateau and then probably start to dip. If asked to explain why he felt this, he would probably say that the gradual acquisition of large volumes of shares by his fund would have led other speculators to start investing in the company. This would have created an unusual level of demand which would have inflated the price of the shares beyond their realistic worth. The dipping would represent nothing more than the shares settling at what he and others would consider to be a fair price. But he was not really interested in owning shares that had stabilised, particularly when he would need a fair amount of money readily to hand to start buying Bubble.com shares shortly. He called in his PA. 'Tell the team to start selling Tokifora. Nothing drastic but I would like to have reduced our holding by twenty percent by Monday evening.' She nodded and left the office to issue instructions.

Highworth was an autocrat. He was rude, arrogant and, whilst charming to those he considered his peers, he bullied those who worked for him. His behaviour was tolerated because he was so successful at making money and because he paid his staff very well indeed, well enough for them to put up with being abused, at least for a few years. He was happy to be challenged by people when discussing investment proposals, particularly by members of his research team, but, following dinner with an old army friend, he had recently taken to telling his staff to defer to what he called 'the hierarchy of wisdom'. This slightly Delphic utterance had been taken by his staff to mean that as he was at the top of the hierarchy, he clearly had the most wisdom and they should do what he told them.

He was using all of his hierarchical wisdom to work out when the best time to start buying Bubble.com shares would be. He was clear that their current price would drop rapidly once Fairweather had died. They were currently trading at 545 pence per share, having risen by over a pound in the last six weeks as the market's confidence in Mymate grew. The confidence was in part fuelled by Fairthweather talking the application up at every opportunity, even guaranteeing that, once launched, it would only be a matter of a few years before it had a greater market share than Facebook. The first part of Highworth's plan to make a killing was to 'short sell' two million of Bubble.com's shares. Early next week he would enter into a contract agreeing to sell these shares in one month's time at a price of 450 pence, over 95 pence below their current value. The price had been carefully selected. It was sufficiently low that those looking to invest in the company would be keen to buy but not so low that the regulatory authorities would start to take a real interest in the offer. Billions of shares were short sold every day and he knew there would be plenty of takers given the current price. With the charismatic Fairweather dead, Highworth was effectively betting that the market would fast lose confidence in Bubble.com's ability to complete Mymate as planned and the share price would drop like a stone. He thought it would bottom out at about 250 to 300 pence per share within a week or so of Fairweather's death, allowing him to buy his two million shares at a knock down price before then honouring his contract to sell them for 450 pence. He hoped to make several million pounds almost overnight doing this, but the second part of his plan was where the big money would be made. He intended to buy several million more of the shares once their price had dropped because he knew from his research that provided Colin Pearson stayed with the company, Mymate would be delivered on time and the share price would eventually soar to an all-time high. He smiled. Short selling was a gamble. Indeed, in 2010, concerned about the impact of short selling on market behaviour, the US Securities and Exchange Commission had introduced a number of restrictive rules to try and constrain speculator opportunism. But the UK authorities hadn't, and provided you could influence events, the potential profits were so huge that the benefits far outweighed the risks.

Highworth's plan was beginning to fall into place. He picked up the phone and issued instructions to start short selling Bubble.com's shares. His team didn't demur. Whilst they might snigger about more wisdom cascading down the hierarchy, his track record was so remarkable that they simply did what they were told.

CHAPTER 9

Lucy and Isobel sat on their beds, wrapped in towels in the twin room they'd rented at the Sagarmatha Hotel. Clean, relatively cheap and with lots of hot water – a rare thing during the day in Kathmandu – it was better than its three stars suggested. It was ideally located for visiting the main tourist attractions but also close to the secondhand mountaineering shops they needed to visit to complete their kit before they set off for Pokhara and the Annapurna Basin.

'Shall we go out for dinner tonight?' asked Isobel, glad that her friend had eventually arrived. 'I've been living like a monk on my own, trying to save money for when we go west. But now that you're here, I need to go out!' Isobel smiled as she said this. She was looking forward to a few beers at one of the climbers' bars near the hotel followed by a curry at a local restaurant she'd found called the Rato Hatti. Literally translated this meant the 'Red Elephant' but it was known locally as the Pink Dumbo on account of a faded mural on one of its inside walls. Hidden down a back street, the food was excellent and the clientele was a mix of local Nepalis and ex-patriots, with very few tourists.

Lucy was also looking forward to a night out. The hot shower had reinvigorated her after the flight and her excitement at seeing Isobel was matched by her keen desire to immerse herself in the vibrant night life of Kathmandu. She stood up, pulled her jeans on and slipped a t-shirt over her head. 'Let's go,' she said to a still half dressed Isobel.

They left the hotel and walked towards Kathmandu's Durbar Square, passing the Kumari Ghar, the palace inhabited by a young girl said to be a living goddess. The bar they were heading to was called 'Rum Doodles' and was a particular favourite amongst mountaineers and trekkers. Although still early, it was reasonably busy and they had to force their way through to the bar. Lucy looked around her. It was just as she remembered it from her last visit and she felt comfortable to be back amongst people who shared her passion for the mountains.

'I'll get the beers, you go find a table,' ordered Isobel, squeezing between two huge Americans to catch the barman's eye. Lucy found a table in the furthest and darkest corner of the room. She wasn't being anti-social, she just wanted to sit back and take it all in for a while without being chatted up by unshaven twenty somethings who'd already had a few beers.

Isobel appeared a few minutes later with two ice cold Kingfishers. 'Cheers,' she said, flopping down into the old leather chair next to Lucy and taking a huge swig from her beer. 'I've missed you Luce. I've been busy but travel is so much more fun when you've got your best friend there to share it with.'

Lucy felt the same. She smiled and squeezed her friend's hand. 'Well I'm here now so let's have some fun.' They fell into animated conversation, catching up on each other's news and planning their expedition.

A few hours and several beers later, the two big Americans she'd seen earlier came over to their table and sat down. 'Hi girls, my name's Pete and this is Andy,' said the blonder of the two. 'Mind if we join you?' He had clearly drunk too much. Lucy detected a note of menace in his slurred voice and decided it was time to leave.

'We're just going actually,' said Lucy, 'weren't we Isobel?' Isobel nodded and started to get up.

Pete pushed her down into her chair. 'Not so fast,' he said. 'We're just starting to get acquainted.' Lucy stood and tried to push past Andy but he stuck his leg out and, looking up at her with a drunken grin, ordered her to sit down.

Lucy was used to dealing with drunken men at university and she stared hard at him before speaking slowly and deliberately. 'Move your foot and let me past or I'm going to scream.'

Andy smiled again, infuriating Lucy even more, but as she opened her mouth to scream, Pete stood up behind her and put his hand over her mouth, clamping it shut. This was getting out of hand, thought Isobel, rising from her seat to grab at Pete's arm. Lucy reacted quickly, raising her heel and driving it down on Pete's foot. He let out a loud shout and released his hold. 'You bitch,' he snarled, pushing her away from him. Lucy fell onto the table, knocking their beer glasses flying. As she stood up, Pete balled his fist and started to throw a punch at her face. She ducked instinctively but the punch never landed. Someone grabbed Pete's arm and, with remarkable speed, twisted it away from Lucy and up behind his back. 'Calm down big guy,' said the man who had hold of Pete's arm. 'My girlfriend doesn't want to talk to you. Why don't you guys go and have another beer and we'll just leave.'

The arm lock hurt like hell and Pete turned to look at the man, boiling with rage. Equally as tall as Pete himself, the man returned Pete's stare evenly. Though Pete was angry and drunk, he wasn't stupid. He recognised the man's formidable strength from the arm lock that was lifting him onto his toes and the calm look in the man's eyes started to unnerve him. There was something dangerous about him. Pete couldn't put his finger on it but he reminded him of a coiled snake, tense and ready to strike if provoked further. 'Yeah, OK, didn't know she was your girlfriend, sorry,' said Pete. The man released Pete's arm. Pete nodded to Andy and the two sauntered off towards the bar, muttering under their breath.

Lucy smiled at the man. 'Thank you,' she said, recognising him as the blond man she'd seen on the plane. 'I had it under control but I appreciate your help.'

'Sure you did but it gave me an excuse to introduce myself,' he said, smiling in an infectious and friendly way.

'Let me buy you a beer,' said Isobel, 'you've definitely earned it.' She went off towards the bar, avoiding the two Americans who were now heading towards the exit.

'My name's Harry Parker,' said the man, holding out his hand.

Lucy shook it and introduced herself, smiling at him and inviting him to sit down.

'I saw you on the plane,' she said, 'you arrived today.'

'I did,' he replied. 'And I also saw you on the plane, you were sitting a few rows back from me.'

Lucy watched him closely as he spoke. He was in his early thirties and ruggedly handsome, the long scar on his cheek and his straggly blond hair adding to his appeal. 'What brings you to Kathmandu Harry?' asked Lucy.

'I've got a flat here and I'm between jobs at the moment,' replied Harry, 'so I thought I'd come back for a month or so over Dashera and catch up with friends.'

Lucy was intrigued. Harry's accent was English and whilst he sounded very much like he had been educated at a good public school, he looked more like a Californian surfer. Just as she was about to ask him what he did, Isobel arrived with three more Kingfishers. She put the beers on the table and sat down between Harry and Lucy, introducing herself to Harry. 'Thank you for coming to our rescue,' said Isobel. 'You arrived just in the nick of time. If you hadn't come, we'd have had to hurt them!' She laughed as she said this.

Harry wasn't sure whether she was joking. Isobel looked perfectly capable of dealing with most things, including a few drunken and lecherous Americans. Without trying to appear too obvious, he looked closely at her hands as she held her beer glass. He could see calluses on her knuckles and also along the edge of the hand closest to him. 'Martial arts,' he thought to himself, 'I wonder what sort?' He was about to ask her when she started to tell him what they were doing in Nepal. They talked for about an hour, explaining their plans before Harry stood up and announced that he was starving. The girls looked at each other and then invited him to join them at the Pink Dumbo. He agreed.

The three of them left Rum Doodles and walked down the street towards the restaurant. As they passed a side street, the two

Americans stepped out from the shadows. Harry noticed that Pete, the smaller of the two, was armed with a wicked looking knife while Andy had what appeared to be a club.

'We owe you,' said Pete. 'Nobody fucks with us and gets away with it,' snarled Andy as he walked towards them, raising his arm ready to strike. As Harry was thinking what to say to try and calm the situation down, Isobel stepped forward and spun round backwards, raising and extending her right leg as she gathered speed so that her heel struck Pete's head. Pete fell to the ground instantly, dazed by the force of the blow. Isobel landed next to him with the agility of a cat and punched him twice in the face with real force.

Andy, shocked at the speed of Isobel's reactions, froze and Harry, seizing his opportunity, kicked the knife out of his hand and then landed a crushing punch to his stomach. Andy doubled over and Harry hit him with an uppercut on his chin, lifting him off his feet and leaving him in a crumpled heap next to his friend.

Isobel laughed. 'Well done tough guy. You beat me to him.' Harry was amazed at her reaction. He'd met a lot of tough women in his time but Isobel was something else.

'She likes fights,' said Lucy simply, kicking the knife away from the groaning Americans.

'Where did you learn to fight like that?' asked Harry, struggling to keep the awe out of his voice.

'Here and there,' said Isobel, smiling shyly. 'Buy me a beer sometime and I'll tell you all about it.'

Harry was about to ask her another question when he heard footsteps approaching at speed. He looked round to see two policemen running down the alley towards them, clearly attracted by the noise of the fight. Harry turned to them and spoke quickly in fluent Nepali. They nodded, asked a few questions, took his details and then handcuffed the two Americans as they were starting to rise to their feet. 'Dinner,' said Isobel, leading the way towards the Pink Dumbo.

CHAPTER 10

The assassin entered St James's Square from the Mall and walked past the Army and Navy Club with its dull sixties exterior and towards the British Library. At the opposite corner stood the old Libyan Embassy, now another club. On 17 April 1984, it became one of the most notorious buildings in Britain when a Libyan sniper opened fire from the building killing WPC Yvonne Fletcher. He'd stopped and looked at the small monument erected in her honour on previous visits. This time he was more interested in Fairweather's tall, white Georgian townhouse that stood sixty metres away. One of a row of similar houses that formed one side of the square, it was beautiful in its simplicity. Five storeys high and immaculately maintained, it looked out across the manicured communal gardens in the centre of the square. He noticed the secure looking windows, iron railings to the front of the house and CCTV cameras under the eaves. In the middle of the house were six steps leading up to a dark blue door with a large brass handle at its centre. It was the sort of house you would expect to see in a period drama. It stood for understated wealth and establishment respectability. The assassin walked past the London Library and stooped as if to tie a shoelace in front of the house. Looking up he could see that the first floor had French windows that opened onto small, ornamental balconies. The top floors had smaller windows that he suspected wouldn't open fully. He stood up and kept walking, crossing one of the five streets that led into the square. He continued on until he stood next to Yvonne Fletcher's monument and then turned back to look at the house. The building behind the house was having its façade re-plastered and a network of scaffolding led from the pavement up to the roof. 'Interesting,' he thought to himself. He walked back towards the house and then turned right up Duke of York Street, stopping opposite the scaffolding. He looked up at the roof line and saw that the scaffolding extended across the roof and along to a chimney stack that was shared with Fairweather's house. The makings of a plan began to form in his mind. If he could get onto Fairweather's roof, he could probably remove a few of the slates and get into the loft space and then down into the house. He'd done this before when mounting covert surveillance in the Army. He knew it was easy enough to do provided you were sheltered from a casual observer whilst removing the slates. 'Bingo', he thought to himself, 'we have a plan.' With that, he turned and started to walk up Jermyn Street, pausing to look in the windows of the numerous shirt shops that seem to have adopted this part of London as their own.

An hour later, he was back in his hotel room. He was pleased with what he'd discovered. All he needed to do now was to work out when Fairweather would be home and decide how best to kill him. It needed to be an accident and this limited his options, but he thought he'd seen how to do it. He changed into running kit and headed back outside. It was nearly five and the streets were starting to fill with people beginning their journey home. He jogged slowly through the crowds, making his way towards the Thames. He crossed the river and turned along the Embankment, increasing his pace as the pavement widened and the number of people reduced. By the time he reached the Houses of Parliament he was moving fast, enjoying the sensation of his body working hard whilst his subconscious considered the problem of how best to kill Fairweather. When he returned to the hotel, dripping with sweat and breathing hard, the plan was sufficiently refined that he felt it had a reasonable chance of success. There were one or two areas that still concerned him but provided he was able to achieve complete surprise when he confronted Fairweather, he felt the risks were manageable.

CHAPTER 11

Lucy and Isobel opened the door of the restaurant and walked towards the bar. It was busy and noisy. Lots of different languages were being spoken by people from at least a dozen different countries. The dim lights and overpowering smells of incense and spices created the comfortable warmth that Lucy needed after the violence outside. She lacked Isobel's matter of fact hardness. Where Isobel seemed to accept violence as a part of everyday life, it always unsettled Lucy, leaving her feeling churned up and jittery. But she felt herself relax as a smiling Nepalese man with perfect teeth came over, put his hands together and welcomed them with 'Namaste ladies'.

'My name is Gopal,' he said. 'Welcome to the Rato Hatti'. He looked beyond the girls and his face lit up when he saw Harry. 'Harry, how are you?'.

Harry smiled when he saw him. 'Gopal, I am very well, how are you?' The two shook hands warmly before Gopal led the three of them to a table at the back of the restaurant.

'I'll get you some beers while you think about food,' said Gopal before he disappeared off towards the bar.

'Are you a regular here?' asked Lucy.

'Not really,' replied Harry. 'But I've known Gopal a long time, we were in the Army together.'

'The Army?' said Lucy quizzically. 'You don't look like a soldier.'

'I'm not,' said Harry. 'Not anymore, but I was.'

The girls were intrigued. Harry seemed reluctant to talk about his background but over several beers and a superb curry, they managed to prise a fair amount out of him. Harry explained that he was the youngest of four brothers. By the time he was eighteen, he'd already decided that he was going to do something different to his brothers and to what his parents expected. Both his parents were doctors and, of his three brothers, two were doctors and one a dentist. Medicine was a family tradition and had been for generations. It wasn't that Harry despised the idea of becoming a doctor, just that he knew from an early age that he wanted to do something more adventurous. After school and still unsure of what career to follow, he spent a year travelling round the Far East. He developed a passion for scuba diving and, within six months of leaving school, he had qualified as a Dive Master and found a job working as a dive guide with a small company in the Philippines. The pay was poor but he racked up hundreds of dives and met some fascinating people. One of these was an officer in Britain's Brigade of Gurkhas. Just married, he was on holiday with his new wife. Whilst she was keen to sunbathe and read the latest bestsellers, the husband wanted to dive so Harry spent a fair amount of time paired up with him as his buddy. After two weeks of talking to his new friend and listening to his adventures, Harry decided that he too wanted to join the Gurkhas.

Harry kept trying to steer the conversation away from himself but the girls were fascinated by their new acquaintance's background. They had spent the last five years working in a rather dry academic environment and Harry was so different to the people they routinely met that both were captivated by his story. They asked frequent questions, laughing at his self-deprecating humour and wry perspective on life. Lucy ordered more beer and persuaded him to continue. Harry sighed, realising that, for the moment at least, he had little option but to continue his story. In truth, he was flattered by their interest. It wasn't every day that he found himself the centre of two such intelligent, attractive and fun girls' attention. So he explained that he was accepted by the Royal Gurkha Rifles and, after completing the year-long commissioning course at the Royal Military Academy in Sandhurst, he was sent to a Gurkha Battalion in Brunei. He served for a total of ten years. During that time, he completed three tours in Afghanistan, two with his own Gurkhas and one with a special operations unit comprised largely of Afghans. He explained that he had quickly mastered both Dari and Pashtu, the key languages in Afghanistan, and that, because of this and his obvious ability as an Infantry officer, he had been selected to work with the special Afghan unit.

Harry became thoughtful and distinctly more self-conscious when the girls asked him why he'd left the Army. 'I loved working with Gurkhas and I felt that, in my small way, I contributed to making Afghanistan a better place', he said. 'But I've seen some horrid things and I wanted to try and give something back, to make more of a difference than I could in the Army.' He then explained that when he left the Army, he worked in Africa for various charities. He'd done this for a few years and found that the organisational and man management skills he'd learnt in the Army were an asset to aid agencies, particularly those working in more austere conditions. His gift for languages also helped him develop strong relations with the indigenous people he was trying to help. He'd deliberately chosen to work in the most dangerous and inhospitable regions because, in his experience, this was where the need was greatest and yet very few agencies were prepared to put their people at risk by sending them there. His last two six-month assignments had been in Somalia. Harry rubbed the scar on his cheek as he explained that during his first assignment, he'd ended up in a fight with a Somalian pirate.

'He came home to his sister's tent to find me bending over her,' explained Harry. 'He thought I was trying to rape her and attacked me with a knife.'

'What happened?' asked Isobel.

'Well,' replied Harry, 'eventually, his sister calmed him down by explaining that I was trying to treat a nasty infection that she'd developed in a cut on her thigh. But by then, he'd already given me this permanent reminder of Somalia!'

'So what are you doing now?' asked Isobel.

'I'm between jobs,' said Harry. 'I live here in Kathmandu and I'm going to spend a few months catching up with friends, doing some trekking and a bit of climbing and generally having a rest. Then I'm going to look for another six-month contract in Africa.'

Harry and the girls continued their animated discussion whilst a waiter cleared the table. Another waiter poured them each a cup of coffee and placed a small shot glass in front of them. Harry smiled, knowing what was coming next. Gopal returned with a bottle of rum shaped to look like a Kukri, the Gurkhas' famous curved fighting knife. Gopal poured the rum into the glasses. 'On the house', he said. Harry and the girls thanked him and started to sip the rum.

'So what about you two, what are you doing tomorrow?' asked Harry.

'Nothing too strenuous,' replied Lucy. 'We need to get a couple of new ropes and some other stuff but we're pretty much free for the next few days until we head out west to Pokhara at the weekend.'

'OK,' said Harry. 'Why don't I give you a resident's tour of Kathmandu tomorrow morning? If you come to my place at, say, ten o'clock, I'll give you proper coffee and then I'll show you all the sights you won't see unless you go with someone who lives here.'

Lucy and Isobel agreed. They had nothing better to do and this sounded fun. 'You're going to have to forgive me,' said Harry, 'but I have to get back to phone one of my brothers before midnight. It's his birthday today and if I don't phone him and wish him Happy Birthday, he'll give me a hard time for the rest of the year.'

'That's fine,' said Lucy. She was feeling tired having only arrived that morning. 'You go, we'll have another coffee and then get the bill,' she said generously.

'No need – already done,' said Harry as he got up and left. Lucy and Isobel watched him disappear out of the restaurant and into the street.

'What do you think?' asked Lucy. 'Very nice, in a rugged, outdoorsy sort of way,' replied a slightly drunk Isobel. 'But not my type.'

'What do you mean?' asked Lucy.

'I don't like blonds,' replied Isobel. 'At least not this week!' Lucy laughed. Isobel's last boyfriend had been a less athletic version of Harry. The relationship had started off well but she'd eventually tired of his vanity and, in particular, the amount of time it took him to get ready to go out.

'Do you know,' said Isobel, 'it used to take him over an hour to get his hair just right before he'd go to the pub with me! And once a month, he used to sit in the bath with a shower cap on colouring his hair. It was more like going out with a girl than a man.'

Lucy laughed out loud. Isobel's boyfriend had been a cause of constant amusement to Lucy over the last year. His insistence on looking just right before he went out meant that Isobel was always late. And when she did arrive at parties, she was normally so angry with her boyfriend for making her late that she couldn't enjoy seeing her friends. Arm in arm and laughing at the shared memories of their lack of success with men, the two girls left the Rato Hatti and headed back to their hotel.

Chapter 12

The assassin arrived at Guards Polo Club just as lunch was being served in the majority of the marquees. It was a big tournament and there were several thousand spectators present. It was therefore relatively easy to move amongst the crowd and find a spot from which to watch Peter Fairweather. The assassin hadn't seen a polo match before and he was surprised at how civilised it was. As well as the hospitality tents and private marquees, there were lots of families and groups of friends having picnics in the grass car parks that formed two sides of the pitch. The four wheel drive vehicles that the majority seemed to own had their rear doors open, allowing lavish hampers to be unpacked and spread out in the luggage areas. Folding seats and collapsible tables arranged around the open rear doors made for a comfortable lunch in the sunny splendour of Windsor Great Park.

Fairweather appeared to be enjoying himself. Bubble.com sponsored one of the teams playing in the tournament and, so far, it was doing well. It had already won two of its games and it looked like the third was also going to be a victory. His team were all professional players and whilst they and their strings of ponies cost the company a fair amount of money, Fairweather thought it a worthwhile investment. He enjoyed the recognition that went with owning a highly successful polo team and he felt that rubbing shoulders with the rich and famous, as well as Royalty, was good for his own image, as well as that of Bubble.com. As the third game entered its last chukka, he was holding forth with a group of corporate investors, which included Charles and Caroline Highworth, in the private marquee that he had hired for the day. Corporate entertainment had its detractors but hosting some of the people who had funded the company's recent expansion was, at least to Fairweather, an enjoyable way of ensuring that he retained access to the resources that these people controlled.

Highworth moved closer to Fairweather to ask him how Mymate was progressing. 'Brilliant,' replied Fairweather. 'The testing is going better than expected with fewer problems than the team anticipated. We should be able to launch the product early next year as planned.'

Highworth smiled. 'If only you knew,' he thought to himself. Ever reliable, he didn't doubt that Richards had put the contract in place and that Fairweather now only had a few days to live. He enjoyed the irony of talking to a man about the future knowing that the man would be dead within a few days at his, Highworth's, behest. That he disliked Fairweather, considering him to be vulgar 'new money', only added to his pleasure.

Though he didn't know him, the assassin saw Highworth talking to Fairweather. He neither approved nor disapproved of Fairweather's obvious wealth. He was simply watching the target to try and learn something more about him. He was reassured that Fairweather didn't appear to be with a partner. Two or three attractive and well dressed women came over to him to talk or to give him a new glass of champagne, but in his expert view none of them exhibited the body language he would expect of a lover. 'Easier if he's alone tonight,' thought the assassin. Ordinarily, and though he tried to avoid unnecessary deaths, he would have no compunction in killing whoever came between him and his target. But, because this had to look like an accident, he would prefer it if Fairweather didn't have a woman in his bed on this particular night. The assassin continued to watch from the far side of the pitch. Though his attention was focused on Fairweather's marquee, he kept moving his binoculars as the ball was hit around the pitch. He doubted he was being watched but, if he was, he wanted to give the impression that he was taking a keen interest in the ebbs and flows of the game.

The last chukka came to a close. The Bubble.com team triumphed again and a delighted Fairweather joined his team as they collected the trophy from a smiling Prince of Wales. Fairweather ensured that the photographers took lots of pictures of him and the team's captain next to Prince Charles. He was keen to ensure that this month's *Hello* and *Grazia* magazines contained at least some pictures of him and being snapped with Royalty was one way of ensuring this. The Prince gave a short speech of congratulations and then, following a quiet word with Fairweather, he left the pitch and was whisked away in his official Jaguar limousine.

The assassin continued to watch the Bubble.com marquee from the far side of the pitch. Fairweather was in no rush to leave. He was clearly enjoying the moment, savouring the comments of his guests as they congratulated him on his victory and thanked him for his hospitality before leaving to begin the journey home. The assassin noticed that one of the three women he had seen in the afternoon had stayed behind to talk to Fairweather. In her late twenties, she was stunningly attractive with long blonde hair and a short, figure-hugging dress that would have made a monk doubt his vows of celibacy. Fairweather was smiling as the girl spoke. After a few minutes of conversation, the girl nodded and then walked away from him, returning a few minutes later with her coat and handbag. As the last of his guests departed, Fairweather strolled out of the back of the marquee arm in arm with the blonde. The assassin returned to his car. He didn't need to follow Fairweather. He knew where he lived and he could now make the assumption that Fairweather would have company for the night, whether or not he went for supper first.

CHAPTER 13

Fairweather looked at the girl sat opposite him. She was truly stunning. Her blue eyes were accentuated by large sapphire earrings and an even larger sapphire necklace that nestled in her ample cleavage. She was, at least in Fairweather's mind, very desirable and he'd therefore chosen this restaurant deliberately to impress her. Expensive, discrete and only five minutes' walk from his house, both the food and the service were exquisite. Over the last few years he had become something of a regular, so they agreed that he should order for both of them. Whilst they waited for the food to arrive, he set about charming his attractive companion. 'So, Camilla, tell me more about your latest exhibition.'

The blonde girl smiled. She'd known Fairweather for about six months and, while she hadn't seen a great deal of him, she'd grown to like him. She'd first met him when the gallery that exhibited her work had contacted her to ask whether she would be prepared to paint two large paintings to adorn the offices of Bubble.com. She had agreed, not just because Fairweather had offered to pay her extremely well but because she liked the idea of being associated with such a modern, cutting edge company. Lots of people visiting the company headquarters and seeing her two striking works had to be good for business. 'The exhibition is in the Mall Galleries on Pall Mall,' she said. 'And you'll like the pictures because they're all nudes.'

'Male or female?' asked Fairweather.

'Both,' answered Camilla. 'I took my nieces to the Victoria and Albert Museum a few months ago and was struck by the beauty of the statutes on display in the main hall. It set me to thinking that so much has changed over the last six hundred years or so but our bodies have remained basically the same. What was beautiful then is still beautiful now. When you look at Michelangelo's sculpture of David, which was commissioned over five hundred years ago, you see a perfectly proportioned and beautiful man who wouldn't be out of place today on the cover of *GQ* magazine. The same is true of Raphael's Three Graces. People thought them beautiful then and still think it now. So I've developed the theme a little and painted naked figures through the ages. I've tried to contemporise the figures by painting them in surroundings that indicate the age they are from and I've also given them attributes that were thought particularly attractive in the period they represent. So my girl from the nineties is slim and waif-like, like a young Kate Moss, whilst my woman from the eighteen hundreds has a fuller, more shapely figure.'

Fairweather was genuinely interested in what Camilla was saying. He liked her work. The two paintings she had done for him were huge, bright canvasses that drew comment from almost everybody who came to his offices. Fairweather also saw Camilla as a personal challenge. He admired her intellect and her enthusiasm but he was truly captivated by her body. He was determined to get her into bed. This was one reason he was taking such an interest in what she was saying now. 'That sounds fascinating,' he said. 'If I meet you at the galleries on Monday, will you give me a personal tour and explain which of the paintings are for sale?'

Camilla agreed. The prospect of a sale was a definite incentive, though, in truth, she also found Fairweather attractive. He was good looking and well dressed but his confidence was what she most admired. She'd noticed it again at the polo. He seemed to have a magnetic personality, dominating the people around him to become the centre of attention in an unforced and natural way.

It was late when they finished their meal. Fairweather ordered coffees and brandies for both of them and, putting his hand over hers, suggested she come back to his house to give him an artist's view of a painting he had recently bought. She knew it was a ruse but she was excited at the prospect of spending the night with him. And if this meant he bought a few more of her paintings when he visited the gallery on Monday, then that was no bad thing.

At midnight the assassin started to climb up the scaffolding at the back of Fairweather's house. Wearing gloves, black jeans, a black t-shirt and black hoodie, he also had a black balaclava in his pocket and the tools he would need to force entry into the house in a small pack on his back. He climbed easily. It was quiet and he was confident that he hadn't been seen. When he reached the top of the scaffolding, he moved carefully across the tiled roofs until he was above Fairweather's house. He started to move the slates aside. It was easily done. Though the house was old, it had been re-roofed within the last ten years and there was therefore little danger of the slates crumbling in his hands. He removed four slates and sawed quickly through the thin wooden slats to which the slates had been attached. He put the loose pieces of wood in his pack and then cut through the felt that formed the waterproof barrier underneath the slates. Within twenty minutes of starting the climb, he was lowering himself slowly into the roof space of Fairweather's house. Once inside, he switched on his head torch and found the trapdoor into the house. He now had two options. He could either wait in the relative safety of the roof space for Fairweather to return or he could lower himself into the house now and hide in one of the rooms. There were advantages and disadvantages to both options. On balance, he decided that the risk of being heard opening the trapdoor and getting into the house once Fairweather had returned outweighed the possibility of him setting off an alarm by lowering himself to the upper floor of the house before Fairweather came home. He tied a piece of thin rope to the bottom rung of the folding ladder attached to the trapdoor and used this to slowly lower the door open. When it was fully lowered, he climbed down through the hole, hanging from the frame before dropping the few feet to the corridor beneath. Taking a telescopic hook from his backpack, he extended it and used it to push the trapdoor closed behind him.

He moved down the corridor, careful not to touch any of the doors in case they were alarmed. He continued down two flights of stairs until he found what was obviously the master bedroom. Having had a quick look around, he then found a guest room and hid in the large walk-in wardrobe that led off the room. Closing the door, he opened his backpack and took out a pistol and silencer. He screwed the silencer into place, checked the magazine and sat down to wait. The silencer would do little to muffle the sound of a shot going off indoors but it made the pistol look more menacing and, if all went to plan, this was all that was going to be required.

Two hours later Fairweather opened the main door, allowing Camilla to enter the house first. 'Go on in', he said, 'I just need to switch the alarm off and I'll be with you.' He opened a sliding panel hidden behind a picture on the wall of the inner hall. He entered the code and the flashing red light turned green.

'Welcome to my humble abode,' said Fairweather, rejoining Camilla and ushering her up the opulent staircase to a sitting room on the first floor. The room was richly appointed with antique furniture and comfortable sofas. The walls were adorned with a mix of contemporary and traditional works of art. Camilla was impressed, recognising an early Hockney, two Lichensteins and what looked to be an original Dali. She accepted the glass of champagne that Fairweather offered her.

'Cheers,' said Fairweather, clinking his glass against hers. 'Now let me show you this painting.' He disappeared off to another room and reappeared carrying a heavily framed picture. 'I've just bought it,' he said, turning it round so she could see it. Camilla gasped then leaned in to study it more closely. It was a beautifully done painting of a horse. An original Stubbs. It wasn't as magnificent as Stubb's famous painting of the prancing Whistlejacket but it was a close second.

'I remember the sale being covered in the press,' said Camilla. 'The buyer was anonymous. We assumed it was a Russian or Chinese billionaire!'

Fairweather smiled. 'No, I bought it but I wanted to keep it quiet. Notwithstanding the two paintings of yours that I bought for the office, I buy art for me to appreciate, not others. And I like to keep my acquisitions reasonably quiet so I don't attract the wrong sort of attention.'

Camilla nodded in understanding. As surprising as it might seem, art theft was on the increase. Camilla's hand closed over Fairweather's on the gilded frame. 'You have an excellent eye for beautiful things,' she said.

'Thank you,' said Fairweather. He avoided the obvious response but leaned forward and kissed her gently on the lips. She responded, putting her arm round his neck and pulling him towards her, returning his kiss with a passion that surprised and delighted him. He stood up and, taking her by the hand, led her upstairs to his bedroom.

The assassin could hear the sound of muffled voices downstairs. He was in no rush having long ago learnt that patience was indeed a virtue, particularly when you were waiting for the right moment to kill someone. He had a plan but knew that he would have to improvise. One of the first things he had learned in the military was that things never worked out as you intended. The benefit of detailed planning was not the plan itself but the myriad possibilities that were considered during the planning process. Done thoroughly, this meant that you were ready for whatever happened when the plan started to fall apart. He could hear footsteps on the stairs and then the sound of the master bedroom door opening. Fairweather listened harder, straining his ear against the wall. He could hear quiet, intimate laughter and then the sound of clothes being removed. He had seen the blonde through his binoculars. Stunningly attractive, he envied Fairweather. 'Not a bad way to spend your last night,' he thought to himself.

An hour later, the sounds had stopped. He assumed that passion now spent, the lovers were sleeping soundly. But he took no chances and waited another hour before starting to prepare himself. Placing his silenced pistol down the back of his trousers and opening his backpack, he removed a bottle of chloroform and a pad of cotton wool. He placed these in his hoodie pocket, slipped on his balaclava and walked slowly out of the guestroom towards the master bedroom, stepping lightly on the outsides of his feet to minimise the sound of his movements. The bedroom door was open. Though the lights were off, there was enough light from the hall for him to see that both Fairweather and the blonde were fast asleep. Fairweather was lying on his back. He had pulled the white duvet up to his chest, leaving the blonde barely covered. She was lying on her side facing away from Fairweather. She was truly beautiful. The assassin stood for a few minutes, listening to their regular breathing. He took out the chloroform and cotton wool, opened the bottle and soaked the pad. He then moved quietly over to the blonde and held the pad over her mouth and nose for a few minutes. She stirred briefly but then her breathing slowed and her body relaxed. She was in a very deep sleep. Chloroform might be an 'old fashioned' drug but it still worked and its use was hard to detect afterwards. Satisfied that the blonde was now out for the count for at least the next hour, he replaced the chloroform and pad in his pocket and moved round to Fairweather's side of the bed.

He took out the pistol and slowly shook Fairweather awake. 'Mr Fairweather,' he said, 'I need to talk to you urgently.'

Fairweather's eyes opened slowly. He blinked several times then, when he saw the gun and the balaclava clad face, his eyes widened in fear. 'Who the fuck are you?' he shouted.

'Be quiet Mr Fairweather or I will kill you,' said the assassin in a quiet and measured voice. 'Get up, put your dressing gown on and come downstairs with me,' the assassin ordered. Fairweather complied, stumbling out of bed and scrabbling for the gown on the back of the bedroom door. The assassin directed Fairweather down the stairs and into the sitting room.

Although the lights were off, the assassin could see the Stubbs leaning against a sofa. 'A beautiful painting, Mr Fairweather, it must have cost you a great deal.'

'What do you want?' asked Fairweather. 'I've got money upstairs.'

'I don't want your money Mr Fairweather, I want to talk to you,' replied the assassin.

Fairweather was starting to regain his composure. He reasoned that if the intruder was wearing a balaclava to hide his face, then he wasn't intending to kill him.

'Open the windows,' ordered the assassin, waving his gun at the left of the two identical French windows. 'Wider. Now step onto the balcony and stretch your arms above your head towards the building across the square. Then come and sit down here.' Fairweather did as he was told, assuming that he was sending a signal of some sort to the intruder's accomplice. Fairweather sat down and watched as the intruder took out a glass phial and laid a line of what Fairweather assumed was cocaine on the glass topped table. 'It's just coke, it won't hurt you, take it,' ordered the assassin.

Fairweather looked at the intruder. 'Fuck off. Why should I?' he asked.

'Because it will make you more receptive to what I'm going to talk to you about and because I've got the gun and I'm telling you to,' said the assassin. Though his voice was quiet, there was no mistaking the menace that it contained.

Fairweather was no stranger to drugs. He dipped a finger into the powder and put it on his tongue. Satisfied, he took a small silver tube out of a cigarette box on the table and took a long snort.

'Again,' ordered the assassin. Fairweather complied and sat back on the sofa as the drug started to bite. The assassin watched Fairweather visibly relax. 'I need you to signal my partner again to prove that you are OK before I tell you why I'm here.' Fairweather stood and walked slowly over to the open window. He stepped onto the small balcony again and raised his arms as before. As he did so, the assassin came up behind him and, bending down, wrapped his arms round Fairweather's thighs. He straightened up with a grunt and lifted Fairweather off the ground, tipping him over the balcony rail. It happened so quickly that Fairweather barely uttered a sound before landing on the pointed railings below.

The assassin resisted the temptation to step out onto the balcony to check his handiwork. He didn't think that any of the square's many CCTV cameras were aimed directly at the window but he didn't want to take any unnecessary chances. He listened hard for a few minutes until he was satisfied that Fairweather wasn't making any noise and was therefore most probably dead. He took a last look at the Stubbs and then retraced his steps, stopping briefly at the bedroom door to check that the girl was still asleep. The covers had slipped off the bed and the girl lay naked, her breathing deep and regular. Her body was firm and tanned and, as his eyes tracked down from her head, the assassin noticed a small tattoo of a bird on her left buttock. Dark blue and with a long beak, it looked like a kingfisher. Conscious that he needed to keep moving, he smiled at the girl's sleeping form and then made his way to the loft hatch. Using the telescopic hook, he opened the catch, lowered the trapdoor and then pulled himself up into the loft. Moving quickly, he closed the trapdoor behind him and climbed up into the rafters until he found the hole he had made in the felt. He climbed through this and out onto the roof. It was quiet and dark. He opened his pack and removed a roll of tape, a tube of glue and the lengths of wood he'd cut to gain access to the attic. It took him five minutes to repair the damage he'd done. He knew that it wouldn't survive forensic scrutiny but he hoped that it wouldn't come to that. If all went well, the police would see this as a tragic accident. Any CCTV footage would show Fairweather opening the windows, presumably to get some fresh air, and then stepping out onto the balcony. It would then show him reappearing a few minutes later and, slightly unsteadily, stretching before appearing to lose his balance against the low railings and falling to his death. An autopsy on his body would show high levels of alcohol and the presence of cocaine which would explain his unsteadiness and loss of balance. The assassin knew it wasn't his most elegant work but it should suffice. The narrative was believable and this, in the assassin's experience, was the most important thing. The slates back in place, he re-traced his route across the roof to the scaffolding and slid quietly down to the pavement below. Within a few minutes, he was heading away from the Square, walking along Jermyn Street and into Piccadilly. It was surprisingly busy. An hour later, he was back in his hotel room, showering before packing his suitcase for an early start the next day.

CHAPTER 14

Highworth always got up early and caught the headlines on the kitchen TV while he waited for his coffee to brew. But this morning, he was only half listening to the news. Although it was Sunday, he had to go into the office for a potentially difficult meeting and he was thinking through how best to approach it. His mind also kept re-playing the events of last night. After the polo, he and Caroline had gone for supper at a newly opened restaurant in the centre of Farnham. A short walk from their house, it was an ideal end to the day. For some reason which he hadn't yet worked out, Caroline had been unusually flirty throughout dinner and, once they got home, she had wasted no time in undressing both of them. He was reliving the moment she'd removed his boxer shorts when the mention of Fairweather's name suddenly caught his attention. He turned up the volume as a reporter, standing in front of a large and elegant townhouse, started to explain what she thought had happened.

'We understand that in the early hours of this morning, Peter Fairweather, the CEO of Bubble.com, fell from a first floor window onto the railings below. The police are investigating what happened but we understand that Mr Fairweather died of the injuries he sustained in the fall. There appear to be no witnesses but the police are examining CCTV footage as well as interviewing a friend of Mr Fairweather's who appears to have been in the house at the time that Mr Fairweather fell to his death.'

Highworth smiled – the game was on. The on-the-scene reporter handed back to the newsroom where the business editor took up the story. He gave a brief summary of Fairweather's business career and, in particular, the spectacular rise of Bubble.com. He finished his report by questioning whether Fairweather's death would jeopardise the much anticipated roll out of Mymate, Bubble.com's new social networking application. Given the widely held view that it was Fairweather's personal energy and determination that were the driving force behind Mymate, the reporter suggested that the company might now have problems and that it would be interesting to see how the markets responded on Monday when the London Stock Exchange opened for business.

Highworth sat down and took a long drink of his coffee. All thoughts of last night's adventures with Caroline, as well as of the meeting in a few hours' time, were gone. Instead, he was thinking through what more he needed to do to exploit Fairweather's death. His planning to date had been meticulous but he nevertheless forced himself to go through a mental checklist to ensure he hadn't missed anything. Satisfied that, at least for the moment, there was nothing more he could do, he poured himself another cup of coffee and went upstairs to shower and change.

'Did you see the news darling?' his wife asked him as he entered the bedroom.

'Yes, tragic isn't it. We only saw him yesterday.'

'Yes', she replied, following her husband into the bathroom. 'It's a great shame,' she said. 'He promised me yesterday that he would consider joining the trustees of the art charity I'm setting up. I suppose now I'll have to find some other rich art lover to replace him and there don't seem to be too many of those around at the moment, at least not ones that I would want to work with on the board!'

Highworth smiled. A capable administrator and remarkably successful fundraiser, his wife ran the charities she was involved in with a steely determination. She liked to get her own way and she would only agree to people joining the board of trustees of 'her' charities if she knew that they wouldn't oppose her. Highworth knew that this is what would make it difficult. 'I'll see whether I can think of anyone,' he said. 'I've got a few ideas but I'll get the team to check out their finances before we discuss them. No point asking them to join only to find out they're not as rich as we thought they were!'

His wife came over and kissed him on the lips. 'Thank you darling,' she said, 'that would be really kind.'

Highworth showered and changed into a dark, single-breasted suit, blue cotton shirt and red spotted tie. Although it was the weekend, he liked to wear a suit whenever he went into the office. He was far more comfortable discussing business when he felt he looked the part. Moreover, he knew that his large frame intimidated people more when he was impeccably dressed in what he called his 'city armour' and this, he felt, gave him more of an edge. As he came downstairs, he looked through the hall widow and could see his car and driver outside. 'Bye darling,' he called to Caroline as he opened the front door and walked towards his car.

'Good morning Sir,' said his driver, Simon, as he opened the rear door of the Bentley limousine.

'Morning Simon,' replied Highworth as he climbed into the car. Simon had been with him for five years. Richards had suggested him. He was discrete, an excellent driver and had a quiet menace about him that kept people away. Highworth trusted him completely. Simon turned the radio to Radio 4 for the morning news and pulled out into the traffic. Fairweather's death was attracting significant coverage but there were no new facts. Highworth was intrigued who the friend staying over at Fairweather's might have been. 'One of the girls from the polo,' he thought to himself. He knew there would be no link between the death and him but he was surprised that the assassin had left what could turn out to be a loose end. He listened again to the news. More city experts – some of whom he knew – were giving their views on whether the death would have an impact on Mymate's rollout. The consensus view was that it would. The experts were all agreed that it was Fairweather's charisma and energy that made the company so successful and, as there were no obvious contenders to replace him as CEO, there would inevitably be an impact. Highworth felt the excitement in his stomach. Although he was already incredibly wealthy – the *Times'* Rich List had last year estimated his personal fortune at just less than eight hundred million pounds – the prospect of the huge killing he was about to make still excited him.

Simon stopped the car at the barrier that controlled entry into the Canary Warf area. 'Morning,' he said to the security guard, showing the guard his pass.

The guard looked at the pass and then in the rear of the car. 'Thank you, have a good day,' he said as he raised the barrier.

Simon drew up outside the high rise building that housed the office and got out to open Highworth's door.

'I'll be done by twelve,' said Highworth as he stepped out of the car and headed for the entrance. Simon nodded his acknowledgement and got back into the car. This would give him enough time to fill up with fuel and get some breakfast. He drove off to find a garage as Highworth stepped into the lift and pressed the button for the top floor. Visitors were always surprised how many people were in the building on a Sunday morning but, as Highworth had explained on several occasions, as the markets opened around the world on Monday, he didn't want to have to wait until his team had processed the weekend's happenings before deciding whether to adjust his investments. He expected his head of research to deliver a briefing and short supporting paper at eight o'clock every Monday morning summarising the weekend's key events and assessing the likely impact that these would have on his investments. He could then move quickly, taking new positions before the wider markets reacted to the world's events over the previous forty eight hours. If this meant that his team had to work shifts over the weekend, then so be it – he paid them well enough for their trouble.

Highworth went into his office and switched on the TV. Fairweather's death was all over the news. The police had given one statement already and, whilst this hadn't been televised, the reporter had attended it and suggested that the police were treating this as a tragic accident. 'Good,' thought Highworth though, in retrospect, even if the police thought there was something suspicious about the death, Bubble.com's share price would still drop like a stone, particularly given how much the media were linking the company's success to Fairweather's personal leadership. He reviewed his position. When the market closed on Friday, the shares were selling at 545 pence each. He didn't currently own any of the shares but he had undertaken to sell two million of them at 450 pence per share in just less than two months' time. He intended to start investing very heavily in the shares over the next week or so to honour his commitment. He expected the share price to drop to between 280–300 pence per share within the next week. To make the biggest possible killing, he would need to work out when the shares had reached their lowest point. The company would be quick to try and reassure its investors that Mymate remained on track and, eventually, market confidence would start to be restored and the share price would begin to rise. The company would try and do this as quickly as possible and well before Mymate was expected to be rolled out at the end of the year.

Highworth went through his initial sums again. If he got the shares for 300 pence, then he would make a quick three million on the short sell. If he were able to buy another five million shares for 300 pence then, when Mymate was rolled out at the end of the year and the share price soared to 900 pence, as his researchers suggested it should, he would make a further thirty million. In all likelihood, the shares would then plateau for a while whilst the market waited to see how Mymate was received. If it caught on quickly, then the price would begin to rise again. His researchers suggested it could go as high as 1800 pence per share within a year of its launch which, if it did, would see his profits rise to seventy-five million pounds plus the three million from the short sell. Not a bad return, he reflected, for the one hundred thousand it had cost him to rid the world of Mr Peter Fairweather!

CHAPTER 15

Isobel and Lucy got out of the taxi and looked around them. It was just before ten o'clock and the streets were full of life as people went about their daily business. Women in brightly coloured saris were bartering animatedly with street stall owners, trying to get the cheapest price for the chillies and herbs that gave their cooking its unique flavours. The men were more reserved. The majority of older men wore traditional Nepalese attire: a smart jacket with trousers that were baggy on the hips but tight around the calves. Younger men in their late teens and twenties were wearing jeans and t-shirts. Nearly all the men, whatever their age, were wearing hats. Lucy particularly liked the 'topis' worn by the older men with their traditional clothes. These came in a variety of colours but all had a similar shape, not unlike a Stetson but without the rim. Worn at a jaunty angle, they gave their wearers additional stature.

'Can I help you?' asked a middle aged man, noticing that Lucy and Isobel seemed unsure of where they were going. Lucy smiled and showed the man the address Harry had given them.

'The building you are after is down that street,' said the man, pointing the direction with his chin. 'If you walk down that street you will see a small Buddhist temple on your left. The building you want is opposite.'

'Thank you,' said Isobel, 'we're very grateful.'

The man smiled. 'You're welcome,' he replied.

Lucy and Isobel were always surprised at how polite the vast majority of Nepalese people were. It was one of the qualities she admired about them and one of the reasons she continued to enjoy travelling in Nepal. They set off down the road as indicated by the man and, within a few minutes, found Harry's address. It was an old and substantial four storey building that looked as if it had been important at some time in its past. The impressively large wooden door was studded with metal bolts, reminding Lucy of the main gate to Durham Castle, now home to one of the university's colleges. Like the Durham gate, it had a smaller Judas gate set within it. Lucy looked up at the building as she crossed the road towards the entrance. The windows were covered by intricately carved wooden screens. These provided privacy for the occupants whilst still allowing a breeze to cool the interior. The delicious smell of curry being prepared for lunch wafted out from the lower windows, reminding the girls that they hadn't yet had breakfast.

'You ring,' said Lucy pointing to the four buttons set in a panel on the wall next to the gate.

'OK,' replied Isobel, pressing the intercom buzzer.

Harry's voice answered almost immediately. 'Hi, come on in,' he said as he released the catch remotely.

The girls were surprised at the interior of the building. The main door opened into a vaulted archway that led to a small courtyard. In the centre of the courtyard was a fountain. Small trees and shrubs grew in the large and ornate pots that were arranged around it. Tables and chairs were grouped amongst the pots, providing quiet areas for people to talk, read or just enjoy the surroundings. The sound of water splashing gently in the fountain and the scents from the bushes created a calming atmosphere, providing a marked contrast to the noise and frantic activity outside.

'Hello,' said Harry, appearing from between two large plants. He was dressed in jeans, t-shirt and espadrilles and looked as if he had just got out of the shower. 'You made it,' he said with a smile.

'This is amazing,' said Isobel. 'I really wouldn't have expected to find this little oasis inside a block of flats.'

Harry smiled again. 'The building belongs to a friend. It's been in his family for generations. It was originally built as a family home for one of the Rana ruling elite in the eighteen hundreds. My friend turned it into flats about ten years ago. He lives in one of them and rents the other three to disreputable characters like me.' Lucy and Isobel both smiled at his self deprecating manner. 'Follow me and I'll show you where I live,' he said as he set off across the courtyard to an ornate stairwell in one of the corners.

'I'm afraid there's no lift,' he said as he started up the stairs. He stopped on the third floor and walked along the open corridor that overlooked the courtyard. Above their heads, large fans turned slowly to keep the air moving. Lucy had seen similar buildings in Morocco. She liked the style. It was light and airy, with the courtyard adding to the building's serenity.

She noticed a fine net draped over the courtyard from the roofs of the top floor. 'What's that for?' she asked Harry.

'It keeps the birds out, particularly the pigeons which, in the summer, are a nightmare!' he replied. 'Come in,' he said, opening another large and ornately carved wooden door. The girls followed him into his flat. Again, they were surprised.

'I like your rugs,' said Isobel, admiring the many rugs that covered the highly polished wooden floor.

'They're from all over,' said Harry. 'The ones the Nepalese make are excellent but my favourite is the large one in front of the fire. I got that on my last tour in Afghanistan. It was a gift from a friend I worked with.' The two girls followed his gaze. A comfortable looking sofa and two chairs were arranged around the rug, facing the fire. An avid reader, Lucy noticed the many bookshelves that lined the walls and went to investigate. Harry looked to have very wide interests. She expected the books about development and security but was surprised to find a whole shelf of books about artists and their work. The ones on gardening and yoga were equally unexpected.

'I'll give you a tour if you like,' said Harry, surprised that Lucy appeared to be taking such a close interest in his books. 'This is the sitting room and through here is the kitchen.' He led the girls into a large, modern and well equipped kitchen.

'Wow,' said Isobel. 'Not what I would have expected from a bachelor boy!'

Harry smiled sheepishly. 'I like to cook,' he said simply. The kitchen was well organised with plenty of worktops and a central island. Racks of herbs and the specialist nature of some of the utensils suggested that Harry's claim had substance. A double door led from the kitchen into his study. The walls were lined with bookshelves, but only to waist height. The wall space above the bookshelves was hung with paintings and, on one wall, several collections of framed photographs.

Isobel noticed two large oil paintings either side of the fireplace. She went closer to inspect them. They were both nudes, one of a man and one of a woman. The bodies, which were painted from the rear, were superb anatomical studies and seemed to be stepping into the dark canvases. The muscles and sinews of their bodies appeared to have real life in them. 'These are amazing,' said Isobel. 'Where did you get them?' she asked, noticing the small kingfishers painted in the bottom corners of the pictures.

'A friend of mine did them,' he replied. 'She's called Camilla Holt. She's based in London and becoming rather well known now. Did you spot the kingfishers in the corners?' he asked Isobel. 'She puts one in every painting instead of a signature but they're normally much harder to spot.'

'Like Cuneo,' suggested Isobel. 'He always painted a mouse in his pictures. The problem is that once you know where they are, you're always drawn to them and not to the painting itself.'

Harry laughed. Cuneo's military paintings were famous and he'd spent many an idle hour looking for mice when visiting different regiments and admiring the pictures in their officers' messes. Lucy went over to the photographs. Many were clearly taken in Africa, some in the mountains of Nepal and others in Afghanistan. They were mainly of people, close ups of faces, each full of character. The photography was very good indeed and wouldn't have looked out of place in *National Geographic*.

'Did you take these?' asked Lucy.

'Yes,' replied Harry. 'I'm a keen photographer as well as a keen cook!' Lucy wasn't sure whether Harry was being deliberately succinct in his answers but she wished he'd add a bit more detail. She was intrigued by him. He seemed to have a depth that she didn't expect in an ex-soldier. People were like onions, she often thought. Getting to know them was like peeling away the layers. It took time but it was invariably worth the effort, even if you eventually decided you didn't like what you'd uncovered. She'd tried explaining this to Isobel who, whilst she listened sympathetically, didn't agree. Isobel was a pragmatist and saw the world in black and white terms. She made snap judgements about people based on her first impressions and she seldom changed her mind. Lucy's other bit of wisdom that Isobel frequently disagreed with was that life was about the journey and not about arriving at the destination. Lucy couldn't remember where she'd read this but the older she got, the more it struck her as true. Whereas Lucy enjoyed the things that happened to her as she worked towards her goals, Isobel wanted to move on as quickly as possible, impatiently ticking off each milestone before moving on to the next.

Harry gave them a few minutes and then led them out of the study and up a broad wooden staircase to the next floor. 'Bedrooms and a bathroom,' he announced, before leading them to a wooden door that opened onto a small terrace. It looked out over the city's rooftops. The girls could feel the heat of the morning sun as they stepped onto the terrace.

'What a great view,' said Isobel.

'If you look over there,' said Harry, using his thumb to point like the Nepalese, 'you can see your hotel. And over there,' he said, again pointing with his thumb, 'is Durbar Square.' There were a couple of slightly battered but comfortable looking rattan chairs on the terrace as well as a hammock in one corner. Large pots containing leafy plants and a few dwarf fruit trees gave the terrace a Mediterranean feel. 'It's nice to sit up here with a beer and watch the sun go down,' said Harry.

'How often are you here?' asked Lucy.

'It depends,' replied Harry. 'If I'm working on a contract, then I may go five or six months without coming back. But if I'm between jobs, like now, then I'll stay for a few months.' Harry led the girls back to the kitchen and poured them all a coffee. 'Tell me about the expedition,' said Harry.

Isobel explained the plan in outline. 'We're going to travel to Pokhara within the next few days to meet up with the guides. We're then going to trek into the Annapurna Basin and establish a base camp. The plan then is to spend two weeks climbing the peaks.'

Harry wasn't sure whether he should be impressed or deeply concerned. Though the trek from Pokhara into the Annapurna basin was a tourist favourite, the Annapurna peaks were technically and physically demanding and only ever attempted by experienced and accomplished mountaineers. His concern was evident when he looked at the girls. 'I've done a bit of scrambling in the basin,' he said, 'and the peaks are quite a challenge you know, particularly at this time of year.'

Lucy smiled at him. 'Really?' she asked, through slightly gritted teeth.

'Yes,' said Harry. Isobel started laughing.

'What's so funny?' asked Harry.

'Nothing, I'm just touched by your concern for our welfare,' replied Isobel. Isobel continued to smile to herself as Harry led them out of the house to start his tour of the city. What Harry didn't know was that both Lucy and Isobel had climbed on the Annapurna Massif before, reaching the top of four of the six peaks until atrocious weather, and specifically the avalanche risk, forced them off the mountains. The reason they were back in Nepal on this expedition was to climb the peaks they'd missed the last time, particularly Annapurna 1 which, at over eight thousand metres, was one of the highest and most physically demanding mountains in the world. Both highly competent and experienced mountaineers, they were confident they would be able to achieve their ambition, provided the weather didn't close in again.

CHAPTER 16

Highworth stood up and looked out of his window. The view of the city was spectacular. As well as the iconic buildings that now dominated the city's skyline, he could see up the River Thames as far as the Houses of Parliament. He was admiring the view when there was a firm knock on his door. 'Come in,' he called, knowing who it would be. The man that entered the room was older than Highworth but looked equally as distinguished. One of the country's richest men, Sir Richard Knowles had a reputation as a shrewd and extremely capable businessman. He'd made the bulk of his money buying companies that were in difficulty, closing them down and then selling off their assets. His enemies – and there were many – said his approach was similar to that of Gordon Gecko, the asset stripper played by Michael Douglas in the film *Wall Street*.

'Thank you for meeting me at such short notice Charles,' said Knowles.

'It's always a pleasure Richard,' replied Highworth. He wasn't sure why Knowles wanted to see him but he was on his guard. They'd known each other for over twenty years. They had clashed a few times over the years but, whilst they weren't friends, they had a healthy respect for each other's talents.

'What is so serious Richard that we needed to meet on a Sunday morning?' asked Highworth, sitting in one of two leather armchairs that were arranged around a coffee table.

Knowles sat down in the other chair and looked Highworth squarely in the eye. 'Last year,' he began, 'I started taking an interest in Tokifora. I had my people dig into the company and, after several months' of research, it was clear to me that the company was going to fail, not immediately but certainly within the next twelve months or so. It was carrying far too much debt and its bankers were getting twitchy about whether they would be able to get their money back. Its product line was lacklustre. The computer processors it manufactured were being outperformed by its competitors and its research and development programme was in disorder and in no shape to deliver anything that would revolutionise the market and restore the company's fortunes. Or so I thought.' Knowles paused to take a sip of water.

'Do keep going Richard,' said Highworth. Highworth thought he knew where this was going but he was confident that he could handle whatever Knowles threw at him.

Knowles continued. 'When I thought the company was going to fail, I developed a plan to buy a significant proportion of the company's shares in order that I could mount a takeover bid.'

'Which would no doubt have been hostile given your reputation,' interjected Highworth.

'Quite,' replied Knowles. 'I made certain promises to people to raise the money I thought I would need. As you would expect, these included selling off some of Tokifora's assets at very competitive rates to some of my investors. The problem is that, against all expectation, the company's fortunes started to improve. In an incredibly short period of time it developed a revolutionary chip that, quite literally, has blown away the competition. The share price has soared beyond anything anyone could have predicted. Anyone, that is, except you Charles.'

Highworth fixed Knowles with a hard stare. 'Richard, you know as well as I do that my job is to spot the under-developed potential that others have missed and then invest the resources necessary to unlock it. You've said yourself that what Tokifora lacked was a credible R&D organisation. Well that's not quite true. One of their development teams had the germ of a brilliant idea but it required other experts to join the team to bring it to life. So that's what I did. I provided the money and the organisational structures necessary to bring the team together and the rest, as they say, is history.'

'I know what you did Charles,' said Knowles. 'I'd looked at this possibility when I did my initial research but, at the time, there was no way that the required experts could be persuaded to relocate to Japan and work with Tokifora to unlock the design's potential. They were all making huge amounts of money in their existing jobs and wouldn't move.'

The two men stared at each other. 'So what are you saying Richard?' asked Highworth.

Knowles continued. 'When the share price started to head North, I had my people try and work out what we had missed. How had we got it so completely wrong in terms of the company's prospects? We were about to invest millions of pounds based on an analysis that was clearly deeply flawed and, as you can imagine, this concerned me. They came back with a single word: coercion. It seems the brilliant engineers who joined the team, leaving their well paid jobs and, in some cases their families, did so because they were threatened. I understand that the two who didn't agree met with unfortunate and very fatal accidents within a week of each other. This surprised and interested me. I went back through some of your other 'amazing' investment successes over the last few years and, guess what, the pattern was the same. People were very reluctant to talk about it but, from what little they did say, we were able to piece together enough to realise that some of your most spectacular successes were the product of malignant actions taken, I very much suspect, by you or those working for you. Key people have behaved in certain ways because they were told that their families would be killed if they didn't. On at least four occasions, innocent people appear to have been killed to enable particular outcomes to be achieved, all of which benefited you hugely. I can't prove any of this yet, but I will.'

Knowles stopped and took another drink of his water. Though his voice was even and his hand steady, he looked slightly unnerved, almost as if it had only just dawned on him that he was confronting a killer about his sins, possibly leaving the killer no way out but to dispose of him as well.

Highworth smiled, 'that's a great conspiracy theory Richard. I particularly like the bit about my "malignant actions". It makes me sound very sinister. Now if you've finished telling me stories, I need to get back to the family for Sunday lunch.' Highworth stood up.

'Is that all you have to say?' asked Knowles, also standing up.

'Yes,' replied Highworth. 'I have no idea what you are talking about. You're losing it Richard. The fact that you got Tokifora so badly wrong is nothing to do with my comic book evil genius but the fact that you are getting old and losing your touch. Time to retire. You live near Wentworth, why not start playing golf and let those who still understand how the market works get on with the serious business of making money.' Highworth opened the office door. Knowles stared hard at him for a minute before storming out through the door and into the waiting elevator.

'I'm not going to let this go Highworth,' Knowles shouted as the elevator door closed.

Highworth went back to the window that he was standing at when Knowles had first entered his office. He closed his eyes and took several deep breathes. He'd long ago learned not to let his emotions get the better of him but this was potentially rather serious. He thought that Knowles would struggle to find any hard evidence linking him to the actions that he'd described but he was still concerned. If Knowles could make the connection, so could others. He closed his eyes again, thinking through what he needed to do to strengthen his position. 'Every problem has a solution,' he said to himself, 'the trick is to make sure you find it quickly enough.' He took out his mobile and dialled Richards' number.

The phone was answered almost immediately with a terse 'yes?' Highworth recognised the voice. 'We need to meet tonight. Usual place, usual time.'

'Got it,' replied Richards, severing the connection.

CHAPTER 17

Harry decided to finish his tour of Kathmandu with a late lunch in the Sheraton hotel. It wasn't the most ethnic of destinations but the bar on the top floor had a marvellous panoramic view of the city and Harry was keen to point out some of the sites that they hadn't managed to visit. Though the bar was busy, they found a window table from where they could see the airport and watch the planes landing and taking off. They ordered club sandwiches and soft drinks and continued chatting.

'Thank you for a really interesting tour,' said Lucy, 'it was fascinating.'

Harry smiled at her. He had enjoyed their company. They were funny, intelligent and deeply interested in everything he had shown them, asking lots of questions. He would be sad to see them go, particularly Lucy. 'What day did you say you were going to Pokhara?' he asked, trying to sound upbeat and positive.

'Probably tomorrow or maybe Monday,' answered Isobel. 'The trekking company that's supporting us is going to confirm tonight. The forecast's good for the next two weeks but after that it starts to get a bit dodgy. We need to get a bit of a move on if we're to crack both peaks before the weather breaks.'

'What will you do then?' asked Harry.

'Probably spend a few days in Pokhara recovering and then head back here for Dashain,' answered Lucy. Lucy was keen to experience the Hindu festival at first hand. It celebrated the victory of the god Durga over the evil goddess Kali and was the most significant festival of the Hindu religious year. 'What about you?' she asked.

'Not sure,' replied Harry, 'I was going to travel out to Everest Base Camp for a week or so. There's an expedition having a crack at the summit in a week's time and a couple of old friends are the lead climbers. I thought I'd go and give them a bit of moral support. But I've also got to try and find another job so I'll probably spend the next few days surfing the internet and e-mailing contacts to see what's coming up.'

'Everest sounds great,' said Isobel.

The two girls had discussed Harry the previous evening. They both liked him but, because there were two of them and only one of him, they decided that, at least for the moment, they would not encourage him to travel with them. Lucy was a bit disappointed about this but she understood that the last thing they needed right now was to fall out over a man. It had happened once before when they were in their teens and at school. They had both fallen for the captain of the rugby team, Tom Allbright. In the end, he didn't go out with either of them but they'd argued fiercely for months over who should have first crack at him. Looking back it seemed a stupid thing to have fallen out over but, at the time, it was intensely serious. Ever since, they had worked hard not to put themselves in a similar position again.

Conscious that she would soon be leaving Kathmandu and emboldened by her discussion with Isobel the previous night, Lucy turned to Harry and asked him why he wasn't spending time with his partner. Isobel gave her a hard stare; Lucy was clearly fishing. 'I was engaged for a year or so but we broke up about six months ago,' said Harry.

'I'm sorry, I shouldn't have asked,' replied Lucy.

'No, it's fine,' said Harry. 'It was amicable. We just wanted different things. I wanted to get more involved in development, particularly in Africa, and she wanted to stay in London and make a name for herself. It was never really going to work.'

'Does anybody want coffee?' asked Isobel, trying to lighten the mood. Harry and Lucy both nodded.

'When you get back to Kathmandu after Annapurna, let's meet up and I'll show you the bits of Kathmandu that we didn't get to see,' suggested Harry.

'That would be great,' said Isobel, moving aside to let the waiter put their coffees on the table.

Lucy slowly stirred sugar into her coffee. She was deep in thought. She'd seen something in Harry that made her want to get to know him better. This rather surprised her as she'd had very little success with men over the last few years. Most of them irritated her after the first few dates and, as a result, their relationships never really took off. But Harry seemed different and, for the first time in her life, she wished that Isobel wasn't with her.

Harry was also looking wistful. Although he was keen to trek out to Everest and see his friends, he would have changed his plans at the drop of a hat had the girls invited him to keep them company on the journey to Annapurna.

They drank their coffees and caught the elevator down to the hotel foyer. 'Thanks so much Harry,' said Isobel, 'we'll come and find you when we're back in town.' Isobel kissed him quickly on both cheeks and then announced that she needed the loo. She turned away from Harry, winked at Lucy and set off to find the hotel's toilets.

'Thanks Harry,' said Lucy, looking him squarely in the eye. 'As soon as we're back, we'll take you out for dinner and bore you with our war stories. You'll wish you'd never met us,' she said as she leaned forward to kiss his cheek.

Harry seized his opportunity. Instead of her cheek, he kissed her full on the lips. Although surprised, she found herself returning his kiss until, seeing Isobel returning from the toilets, she reluctantly stepped back from Harry. 'Bye Harry,' she said looking deep into his eyes, 'it's been fun.'

Isobel re-joined them. 'Come on,' she said, 'we need to get on if we're going to be ready to travel tomorrow.' She grabbed Lucy's hand and led her outside to one of the waiting taxis.

As she climbed into the car, Lucy turned to look at Harry. 'Can we pick up where we left off when I'm back?' she asked, smiling sheepishly.

'Yes, please,' said an enthusiastic Harry.

As the taxi pulled away from the kerb, Lucy waved goodbye. Harry watched the taxi join the traffic. It was all happening far too quickly but he felt immensely happy. Whatever he'd said in the restaurant, he'd found breaking up with his previous girlfriend really tough. Over the last few months he'd started to wonder whether it had been a mistake but, even though he'd only known her for twenty-four hours, Lucy had made him realise that ending the previous relationship had been the right decision. Her good humoured energy and enthusiasm were exactly what he needed to put his ex behind him. All he had to do now was to make sure that he met up with her after her trip to Annapurna. 'Who knows,' he thought, 'perhaps I can persuade her to stay for a few more weeks without Isobel.' Smiling, he started walking back towards his flat. For the first time in months he had a spring in his step.

'Well lover girl,' said Isobel as soon as the taxi was a few hundred metres away from the hotel, 'did he kiss you?'

'What do you mean?' asked Lucy.

'You know exactly what I mean,' answered Isobel. 'You've been like a couple of love struck teenagers all day,' said Isobel. 'I was going to suggest you got a room after lunch. I didn't because I thought you might agree and I'd lose you for the next twenty-four hours.' Lucy laughed. Isobel was pleased for her friend but couldn't resist the temptation to tease her, albeit gently. Isobel had watched Lucy struggle with her last few relationships. Although she'd tried to cheer her friend up, she couldn't help feeling that Lucy was her own worst enemy. Tall, athletic, articulate and highly intelligent, she could also be stubborn and impatient. Whilst Isobel loved all these things about her friend, she felt that many men felt threatened by such a capable and robust female.

'I really like him Isobel,' said Lucy. 'He's obviously a tough man but there's a softer, more thoughtful side to him. There's also a bit of vulnerability. He tries to hide it but it's there.'

'When we get back, why don't I stay for a few days and then fly home early so you can have a bit of time with him on your own,' suggested Isobel.

'Thank you Isobel, that's really kind. I might just do that,' said Lucy, hugging her friend.

Later that afternoon, the trekking company phoned to confirm that their transport would collect them early the next morning for the journey to Pokhara. They were excited but they had a great deal to do before they could leave Kathmandu. All thoughts of Harry vanished as they rushed around Kathmandu's secondhand climbing shops buying the last minute essentials which, because of weight restrictions, they had been unable to bring with them. Eventually, they bought the last few items – a high altitude stove and two four season sleeping bags – and then headed back to the hotel for an early night.

The next morning, they got up early, finished their packing and went down to breakfast.

'Full breakfast please,' said Lucy to the waiter.

'Me too please,' added Isobel. Both girls were determined to fuel up for the journey west. Lucy knew that although the road from Kathmandu to Pokhara, known as the Prithvi Highway, was one of the best in Nepal, it would still be a long journey. The early start meant that they would be out of Kathmandu before the morning rush hour but, even if the roads were reasonably clear, it would take six or seven hours to reach Pokhara.

Pokhara was Lucy's favourite Nepalese town. Four hundred metres lower than Kathmandu, the climate was warm, even in winter, and the lakeside was a mecca for travellers. Over the years, she'd met all sorts of interesting people in the cafes and bars that lined the town side bank of the Phewa Tal, Pokhara's famous lake. What made it all the more impressive was that you could clearly see the Himalayas on the northern horizon. They dominated the skyline with the Annapurna Massif clearly visible from almost anywhere in the town.

The girls ate their breakfast, collected their bags and paid their bills before going outside to meet Rajev, the guide from the trekking agency. 'Namaste,' he said as they introduced themselves. He helped them with the bags and led the way to a Toyota Landcruiser parked just along from the hotel's main entrance.

As Rajev opened the rear door and started to load their kit, the driver jumped out and came round to the girls. 'Namaste,' he said, 'my name is Sanjay, let me help you.' He smiled at them and opened the passenger doors. Lucy was reassured by the car; it certainly looked the part. It had solid looking bull bars and a winch on the front bumper. A huge expedition roof rack ran the length of the passenger compartment and jutted out over the bonnet. Lucy noticed the four jerrycans and three spare tyres fastened to the roof rack. They looked to be in good condition, as did the fourth spare tyre on the back of the rear door. Inside, air conditioning kept the car cool. Bottles of cold water had been placed in the rear drinks holders.

The last time she had made this journey, Lucy had been travelling with her then boyfriend who had wanted to travel 'authentically'. To him, this meant catching one of the multicoloured buses used by the locals. She'd sat on the roof for part of the journey but, after one particularly hair raising encounter with a herd of water buffalos, she'd decided to find a seat inside the bus. This had been a mistake. She sat next to a young man who, whilst perfectly friendly, was clearly ill. Every time the bus stopped, he rushed out of the door and into the bushes. She'd felt sorry for him at the time but, within twenty four hours, she'd had a chronic stomach bug that meant she had been unable to leave her hotel room or, more precisely, the toilet in her hotel bathroom for three days. Compared to the bus, the Landcruiser was a definite luxury.

Isobel, who had only been to Nepal once and that was when they last climbed in the Annapurna range, was apprehensive about the journey. Lying on her hotel bed last night she'd opened her *Lonely Plane Guide* and read aloud that 'you are thirty times more likely to die in a road accident in Nepal than in any developed country.' But Sanjay drove particularly well and both Lucy and Isobel soon began to relax into the journey. Rajev pointed out places of interest as they drove. He was articulate and knew the route well. He explained that he had been at school in Kathmandu but that his family came from a village north of Pokhara. He had therefore done this journey at the start and end of every term for nearly ten years.

Lucy was interested in why he had been sent to boarding school. Rajev looked pensive and then answered her. 'You've got to remember that we had a civil war in Nepal for almost ten years and life in the villages got increasingly hard as the war progressed. The Maoists used to take food and money from people to survive. This wasn't so bad but, as I got older, there was an expectation that I would join the local Maoist group. I suppose this would have been quite exciting but my parents wanted me to finish my education and not risk getting killed fighting government troops.'

'It must have been expensive to board?' asked Isobel.

'Yes,' replied Rajev, 'but I'm part of a big family and we all look after each other. One of my uncles works in Hong Kong as a construction engineer and he sent back enough money every month to cover my schooling.'

Lucy nodded in understanding. From her various trips she'd noted that strong extended families were a feature of Nepalese life. Everybody helps everybody else. Those lucky enough to be earning decent wages have a moral responsibility to share their wealth with less fortunate family members. Lucy had studied this phenomenon in other cultures. It seemed that the greater the levels of poverty and deprivation, the closer families tended to be. It was a survival mechanism.

The journey to Pokhara was interesting but uneventful. They stopped occasionally to stretch their legs, use the toilet or admire a particular view but on the first of these 'view stops', Lucy was irritated to find that her phone camera wouldn't work. In all the excitement of the previous evening, she'd forgotten to charge the battery. Isobel, who took the opportunity to accuse Lucy of being disorganised, therefore took the photographs.

As night fell, they drove into the suburbs of Pokhara and towards their hotel. The Lakeside was full of early evening life. The many stalls and bars along the banks of the Phewa Tal were doing a brisk trade. Teenagers on their gap years rubbed shoulders with trekkers, climbers and ageing hippies. It was a fun atmosphere and Lucy couldn't wait to get out and be a part of it. Rajev dropped them at their hotel and said that he would meet them the following morning to go through the detail of the planned ascents.

Lucy and Isobel checked in and were shown to their room. It wasn't quite as nice as the hotel in Kathmandu but it was clean and tidy. It would do for a few nights before they started trekking into the Annapurna Basin.

Lucy plugged her phone in to charge and headed for the bathroom. 'Can I shower first?' she asked Isobel.

'Sure' replied Isobel, falling onto the bed and closing her eyes. 'I'll have a little kip whilst you make yourself beautiful. I expect it'll take you a while!'

Lucy's phone started to beep as life returned to the battery. Isobel got up and looked at the screen. It said that Lucy had eight missed calls and four texts. Isobel knocked on the bathroom door and opened it a few inches. 'Someone's keen to get in touch,' she said, 'you've got loads of missed calls and texts.'

'Thanks,' shouted Lucy from the shower, 'I'll be out in a minute.'

Isobel closed the door and resumed her position on her bed. When Lucy came out of the bathroom five minutes later, Isobel was fast asleep. Lucy sat on her bed and picked up her phone, smiling as she looked at the screen. She assumed that the messages and missed calls were from Harry but, as she read the texts, her smile faded. They were from a family friend and they were all the same: 'Need to speak to you urgently, love Kate.' Lucy was starting to worry. Kate was an old and very close friend of her father's. The last time she'd seen her was when she was visiting her father about six months ago. She looked at her watch. Seven pm in Nepal was half past midnight in the UK. She found Kate's number in the contacts on her phone and pressed 'call', hoping that Kate would still be awake.

The phone rang for a few minutes before Kate's familiar voice answered. 'Hello?' she said.

Lucy could sense the stress in her voice. 'Hi Kate, it's Lucy,' she said.

'Oh Lucy, I've been trying to contact you all day. I am afraid I've got some dreadful news.' Kate was clearly in tears and was struggling to speak. 'Your father has been badly hurt. He's in hospital here in Edinburgh but it's not looking good. You need to come home, quickly.'

Lucy was shocked. Her father was the toughest person she'd ever known. Nothing ever happened to him, he didn't even get colds. 'What happened?' she managed to ask.

'I'm not really sure,' replied Kate. 'I got a phone call from the police this morning to say that your Dad had been stabbed and that they needed to contact his next of kin as quickly as possible. They'd found my number on his phone because he'd phoned me yesterday to tell me he couldn't meet me last night. We were going to have a drink together but he cancelled because he had to meet someone urgently. I've been at the hospital all day but he's been unconscious.'

Kate's words were tumbling out. She was clearly struggling to hold herself together. She'd been a friend of her father's for years and her obvious distress suggested that she cared deeply for him. Lucy suspected that they were more than just good friends. Ever discrete, her father had never confirmed it but Lucy suspected that he and Kate had been lovers for a long time.

They continued talking for a few minutes before Lucy said, 'Right, I'll get back as soon as I can. I'm in the middle of nowhere in Nepal.

I'll try and catch a flight back tomorrow.' Kate said that she would go back to the hospital first thing in the morning and that she'd phone Lucy if there were any changes in her father's condition. She'd also tell the police that Lucy was on her way. They had no idea who had stabbed her father and they were keen to talk to anyone who might be able to help them. Lucy thought about this. Given she hardly ever saw her father and that she'd been in Nepal for the last few days, she doubted she would be much help.

Lucy was crying as she woke Isobel. 'I've got to go home,' she said, 'my Dad's been badly hurt and they don't think he's going to make it.'

'Oh Luce, I'm so sorry,' said Isobel, holding her friend tight as Lucy explained what Kate had told her. 'Right, I'm coming with you,' said Isobel, 'you phone the hospital and I'll sort out the travel.'

Lucy did she was told. Eventually she got through to a nurse who was on the team looking after her father. 'He's been very badly injured,' said the nurse. 'He's fit and strong but he's lost a lot of blood and there's a fair amount of internal damage. The surgeons operated on him this morning but we're not out of the woods by a long way. He still hasn't regained consciousness and my strong advice is that you try and get here as soon as you can.'

Sobbing, Lucy thanked the nurse and said that she'd phone again later. Isobel had sprung into action whilst Lucy had been talking to the hospital, speaking first to the trekking company, then to an internal airline and then to Air India. She'd managed to book two seats on a flight from Pokhara to Kathmandu early the next morning but it proved more difficult to get a flight from Kathmandu to Heathrow. The only seats available were in Club Class for a flight leaving in the evening. Isobel disliked paying the extra money but, in this case, needs must.

CHAPTER 18

Highworth was sitting in front of a roaring fire, looking at the flames but lost in thought. He'd had supper with Caroline and then retired to his study, pouring himself a generous four fingers of whisky before collapsing into his favourite armchair. He particularly liked this room – indeed, it was one of the main reasons he'd bought the house all those years ago. It had a high ceiling, large ornate fireplace and spectacular views over the garden, though at this time of night all he could see in the windows was the flickering reflection of the fire. He'd furnished the room with care, allowing Caroline very little input into its decoration. It was masculine but elegant. Two old leather armchairs and a sofa were arranged in front of the fire which had an ornate and heavily gilded mirror over it. A club fender with a cracked leather top kept logs from falling out of the fire and onto the rug in front of the sofa. A large antique partners' desk with a green leather top was angled in one corner of the room. In the opposite corner was an old and highly polished round wooden dining table, a gift from Caroline for his fortieth birthday. It held an assortment of pictures of friends and family in various silver frames. The room could have come straight out of the property section of *Country Life*. Highworth was deep in thought. As was his custom when under pressure, he was thinking through the last few days' events, going over and over the detail in his mind until he was sure that he hadn't missed anything.

After his discussion with Knowles, he'd phoned Richards and arranged to meet him that afternoon before texting his wife, telling her not to expect him home until late. She hadn't complained. She knew that he didn't like working at weekends and she'd therefore realised that whatever was keeping him in the office must have been serious. Highworth had then phoned his head of research and told him to start digging into Sir Richard Knowles' recent investments as a matter of urgency. He'd explained that he was particularly interested in any losses that Knowles might have suffered as a consequence of Highworth's own investment strategies.

The head of research had listened intently. He wasn't particularly happy that his boss had phoned him at home on a Sunday but Knowles was one of the city's so-called 'big beasts' and he had been intrigued. Why was Highworth suddenly so interested in him? It was well known that the two didn't get on but, at least up until now, they had tolerated each other. What had changed? Once Highworth had hung up, the researcher had started work. He'd phoned round his team, allocating tasks, and had then logged into the work IT system from his home office. He could do a fair amount by accessing the work system remotely but the really sensitive information was kept on the secure computers at work and would have to wait until Monday morning.

Richards had been his usual reserved self when they'd met. He'd listened intently as Highworth had recounted his meeting with Knowles.

'So what are you concerned about?' Richards had asked. 'We've been very careful. Knowles' heavies might have persuaded one or two people to talk to them but there's a world of difference between that and getting them to make a formal statement to the police. None of them would be stupid enough to do that.'

'How safe is your assassin?' Highworth had asked. 'The TV reports of Fairweather's death said something about a girl helping police with their enquiries. Is she a lose end?'

'He's very safe,' Richards had replied. 'If he left her alive it was because she didn't know anything. I suspect that if he'd killed her as well it would have been difficult to make it look like an accident and that was what you wanted.'

Highworth had taken his time replying. 'My concern is that

the only thing linking you and me to our most recent activities is the assassin. Knowles is going to play hardball. He's lost a lot of money on Tokifora and he's going to work at this 24/7 until he has something he can use against me. If he has solid evidence, which I agree is unlikely, my guess is that he'll go to the police. If he doesn't, he'll take what he has and get a tame journalist to leak it into the press as 'unconfirmed rumours'. Either way, if he can make any of this stick, I've got problems.'

'What exactly are you saying?' Richards had asked.

'I'm saying that I want rid of the assassin,' Highworth had replied. 'Knowles is a Grade A bastard and I've made him look a fool. He won't forgive that and he's going to do everything in his considerable power to try and take me down. If we get rid of the assassin, we get rid of the one solid link between us and the less acceptable activities we've been carrying out.'

Richards had smiled thinly. 'I take it that when you say 'less acceptable activities,' you mean the people we've killed?'

'Yes,' Highworth had replied. 'I agree with you that none of the people we've bullied would be stupid enough to go on record against us so I am not worried about accusations of coercion. But if Knowles' people can somehow link our activities to the assassin and if they can get him to talk, maybe as some sort of plea bargain, then I think things might start to come seriously unstuck.'

Richards had considered this for several minutes before replying. He was an unemotional man but, whilst he had no reservations about the morality of killing the assassin, he was concerned about the time it would take him to find a replacement that he could trust. Highworth wasn't his only client and there were one or two jobs that other clients had suggested might need to be completed within the next six months or so. As Richards had explained to Highworth on several previous occasions, finding someone who is prepared to kill for a few thousand pounds is relatively straightforward but finding someone as skilled and reliable as the assassin is remarkably difficult.

Richards eventually replied. 'OK. If you are sure it needs to be done, then I'll do it.'

'It needs to be soon,' Highworth had said. 'Before Knowles' team start to dig anything else up.'

'No problem,' Richards had replied. 'If he's in the country, the problem will be resolved within the next forty-eight hours.'

They had then discussed the price, agreeing a figure of two hundred and fifty thousand pounds. Highworth had expected the figure to be higher. Richards would be doing the job himself and this would expose him to a fair degree of personal risk. Highworth had therefore been happy to agree the figure without too much discussion.

Highworth took a long drink of his whisky and went through his conversation with Richards one more time to see whether he could spot any lose ends. He was still bothered about the girl that the police said had been at Fairweather's house when he was killed. This was one reason he wanted the assassin dead. If the girl had seen something and she was somehow able to lead the police to the assassin, then the whole thing could start to unravel. Satisfied that, at least for the moment, there was nothing more he could do, he got up, drained his whisky, switched off the lights and headed upstairs to the bedroom to find his wife. He hoped she was still awake. He needed something to take his mind off his meeting with Knowles and his wife would know exactly how to do this. He smiled at the prospect, undoing his tie as he climbed the stairs.

CHAPTER 19

Harry woke up early. He'd opened his bedroom window the previous evening because of the heat and he could hear someone in the street below shouting directions to the driver of a lorry who was clearly having trouble reversing. He couldn't quite hear what they were saying but they were clearly getting increasingly agitated. A loud bang a few minutes later explained why. He'd always liked early mornings. When he was at school in Shrewsbury, he'd had to get up at six o'clock to go rowing before breakfast. Whilst his friends would complain about the early start, he enjoyed the walk down to the boathouse, listening to the sounds of the city starting to come alive. He remembered the sounds as if it were yesterday: toilets flushing, kettles boiling and dogs barking as they were put out to relieve themselves. He smiled at the memory, swinging his legs out of bed and padding naked to the bathroom.

He looked in the mirror. Though he hadn't shaved for a few days, he thought that he looked better than he had done in a while. The bags under his eyes were starting to go and the dry patches on his skin were disappearing. His last contract in Somalia had taken its toll, both mentally and physically, but he suspected that the reason he was starting to look so much better was that he was beginning to get over his ex. The thought of her prompted him to turn his hips so he could see his left buttock in the mirror. The face of a silver fish stared back at him. He smiled again. They'd managed to get two last minute tickets to a Chilli Peppers concert at Wembley. It had been an amazing experience, made all the more memorable as it was the band's last gig on a world tour that had lasted more than a year. They were high on its success and had played with a passion and precision that even Camilla, not their greatest fan, had found remarkable. Still humming the songs they'd heard, they headed into London to meet up with friends. Six hours of hard drinking later, he and Camilla had dared each other to get a tattoo. It had seemed like a good idea at the time, a way of proving their enduring love for each other. She went for a brilliant blue kingfisher, the signature symbol she was starting to use on her paintings, and then persuaded him to have a fish. He was sure there was some symbolism in the choice but it escaped him at the time and, unable to think of anything better, he agreed. He looked at the fish. He'd grown to like it and, though his relationship with Camilla was fast becoming ancient history, he thought he'd probably keep it. Camilla had certainly liked it; ever since he'd had it done, she'd called him 'fish' as a sort of intimate nickname.

He relieved himself then padded back into the bedroom, pulling on running shorts and an old airborne forces t-shirt. He laced up his trainers and checked the e-mail on his laptop. Still nothing from Lucy. He'd hoped to hear from her last night. She'd suggested she would send him a note when she'd had the chance to discuss the schedule with the trekking agency and, in particular, the guide who would be leading them into the mountains. He wished he'd given her his phone number rather than his e-mail address but he knew that the phone network was patchy at best and e-mail was by far the most reliable way of getting messages to each other. His concern was that he knew she'd be leaving Pokhara early this morning and if she didn't get the opportunity to send a message before she started up into the hills, she wouldn't get another chance until she returned from the climb and was back in the town. He was surprised how badly he wanted to hear from her. 'Maybe there'll be something by the time I get back,' he said to himself as he left the house and started to jog out towards the airport.

CHAPTER 20

Lucy and Isobel's flight to Kathmandu was delayed by three hours. By the time it eventually took off, both girls were seriously worried about making their connecting flight. An hour or so later, they landed in Kathmandu and, after a frantic dash through the airport, were able to check in their bags and board the flight to Heathrow. As the plane's doors closed, Lucy settled back in her Club Class seat, accepted a glass of champagne and thought of Harry. She turned to Isobel with a worried expression. 'I should have sent him an e-mail before we left. He thinks I'm going to be back in Pokhara in a week or so but that's not going to happen.'

'Not your fault Luce,' said Isobel. 'Why don't you send him one when we're back in UK. He'll understand.'

'I don't suppose I've got much choice now,' said Lucy. 'It's typical isn't it,' she went on. 'I meet the first man for years that I think I might really like and something dreadful happens to stop me spending time with him. Why does this always happen to me?'

Isobel laughed. It was the first time that her friend had talked about something other than her father since last night. 'Don't worry,' she said, reaching over to squeeze her friend's hand. 'If it's meant to be, he'll still be there in a few weeks' time when your father's out of hospital and starting to recover.'

Lucy sipped the champagne and wondered how her father was doing. She'd tried phoning Kate before they left Pokhara but without success. She'd left a few messages, hoping that Kate would pick them up and phone her back before she boarded the plane but the phone had stayed silent. Thinking about it now, Lucy realised that she hadn't really known her father when she was very young. He always seemed to be away, either on courses or, as he called it, on operations. The sudden death of her mother when she was sixteen had been the catalyst that brought them together. Lucy had loved her mother with a passion. They had been extremely close and Lucy had been devastated when she'd been killed by an out of control car that mounted the pavement and crushed her against a wall. The driver, an eighteen-year-old boy who'd already lost his license for driving whilst drunk, had run away from the scene of the accident but had been stupid enough to boast about it whilst drinking with friends in his local pub. Someone had overheard the conversation and had phoned the police. The boy was arrested, tried and eventually sentenced to five years in gaol. With good behaviour, he was out in three. It always struck Lucy as so unfair that her mother had lost her life but her killer had only had to spend three years behind bars. Her father held the same view. Perversely, it was their shared anger and sense of frustration that had brought them closer together.

Following her mother's death, her father had made a real effort, whenever he could, to travel to her school in York and to watch her play hockey or tennis for the school teams. After a match, if she wasn't going home with him for the weekend, he would take her to Betty's for afternoon tea. She loved Betty's. Right in the centre of York, it was comfortably old fashioned. There were always lots of grannies treating their grandchildren to cakes and buns and she loved the atmosphere. She particularly liked the multi-layered cake stands that they used. She could picture them now: small sandwiches on the bottom level, delicate slices of cake on the next and lots of colourful buns on the top plate. She used to eat two things from every level whilst her father told her what he had been doing over the previous week. She felt very close to him at those times. When she finished the sixth form and got a place at university, he had been truly delighted, telling her that her mother would have been incredibly proud of her. Neither he nor her mother had been to university. They had both left school at sixteen. Her mother had gone to work in her father's shoe shop whilst he had joined the Army as a boy soldier.

She'd seen quite a lot of him over the last few years. He lived in Edinburgh and Durham was only a few hours away on the train. Although he was abroad a lot, they normally managed to spend a weekend together every six weeks or so. He would meet her train at Edinburgh Waverley station and then, arm in arm, they would walk to his flat on George Street, chatting about what they had been up to. She really looked forward to these weekends. They would go out for supper, watch a movie or just sit in a bar and catch up. Edinburgh was a great place to spend an idle weekend and her father, although reserved by nature, had a dry sense of humour that made her laugh.

She noticed that he'd been much more relaxed since he'd left the Army and that he seemed to be earning a fair amount of money. She'd asked him what exactly he did on a number of occasions but all he would say was that he was doing freelance security work for some old Army friends. Kate, who occasionally joined them for supper or for a drink, was unable to shed any further light when, in a quiet moment without her father, Lucy had asked her what she thought he did. In all honesty, Lucy didn't really mind what job her father did. She was just pleased that he seemed to be happy. She liked his new flat and was delighted, though very surprised, when he told her that he'd found a new hobby. As far as she could remember, he'd never had a hobby in his life. An active man, she expected him to tell her that he'd taken up mountaineering or extreme skiing and she was therefore truly shocked when he explained that he'd started collecting oil paintings by old Scottish artists!

'Excuse me madam,' said a stewardess as she leaned over Lucy to pull the table out from the arm of her chair. 'Would you like the fish or the chicken for your main course?'

'The fish please,' replied Lucy. She was so lost in thought that she hadn't noticed the stewardess serving the people around her. She looked across the aisle at Isobel who was tucking into the chicken as though she hadn't eaten for a week. 'Hungry?' asked Lucy.

'Famished,' replied Isobel. 'I just watched a movie about a rat who was actually a chef and it reminded me that we haven't eaten since yesterday lunchtime!'

Lucy smiled at her friend. She was right. Lucy hadn't felt like eating anything the previous night and because of the early morning start they'd missed breakfast at the hotel. When they got to the airport, all they'd found was a coffee bar. Even when the flight was delayed, they'd been unable to get anything else for breakfast other than more coffee.

Lucy ate her meal, which was good, and closed her eyes. Within a few minutes she was fast asleep.

CHAPTER 21

Sir Richard Knowles got out of the taxi and walked up the steps of his club. He'd been a member of the Army and Navy, or the RAG as its members called it, for nearly thirty years and he was well known by the staff.

'Good morning Sir Richard,' said the porter. He'd seen Knowles arrive from his office at the front of the club and was holding the main door open for him.

'Morning Simpson,' replied Knowles. 'Do you know whether my guest has arrived yet?'

'Not yet Sir. I've been on for most of the morning and nobody's asked for you yet,' replied Simpson.

'Please could you direct him to the library when he does?' asked Knowles.

'Of course Sir,' replied Simpson. He liked Knowles. He was always friendly with the staff and, according to Simpson's friend in accounts, always donated generously to the staff Christmas Fund. This was important to Simpson. Like most clubs, the Army and Navy didn't allow tipping so the Christmas Fund was the staff's chance to earn a little extra for their hard work.

Knowles hung his coat in the cloakroom and then went upstairs to the library to read the papers until his guest arrived. He liked this club. Its exterior was a bit drab but the interior was impressive. The Club had an extensive collection of old paintings which it displayed in the public rooms. Oddly for an old soldier, Knowles' favourites were the ones of famous sea battles. He also liked some of the portraits, particularly the ones of Wellington. He wasn't a military historian but there was much about the man that he admired, particularly his gritty determination and robust integrity. His favourite uncle had taken him to Spain when he was seventeen and introduced him to Wellington's Peninsula Campaign. The uncle was an expert on the subject and they'd spent a leisurely two weeks visiting museums, castles and battlefields. The uncle also had a gift for bringing history to life and Knowles, who wasn't at all academic, was enthralled, particularly by the intimate details of Wellington's life. It was no surprise when, in his exams the following year, the young Knowles gained an A in History.

Knowles belonged to two other clubs in London but he preferred the Army and Navy for lunch because he rarely bumped into any of his city colleagues there. If they left the office at lunchtime at all, they tended to use the restaurants and clubs nearer to where they worked. His father, who had also been a member, had suggested he join the Club when he was first commissioned into the Rifles, one of the British Army's most illustrious infantry regiments. Although he'd only served for three years, he'd enjoyed his time in the Army. His father had encouraged his interest, believing it would be character building. Knowles agreed that it had been but it had also been tremendous fun. A talented sportsman, he'd spent three months a year skiing for his Regiment. Though the majority of the competitions were in Bavaria, their training usually took place in the French Alps. This was particularly enjoyable because the chalet they always rented was in Avoriaz, one of France's most popular ski resorts. The town came alive during the ski season with wealthy families, students and ski addicts from across Europe making the most of the town's bars, restaurants and nightclubs. Most importantly from his perspective, at least at the time, there seemed to be an endless supply of girls in their early twenties, all keen to spend their time with dashing young officers who could ski like professionals.

He'd first met his lunch guest at one of the bars in Avoriaz. At the time, James Briggs had been a student at Oxford University and he, along with the rest of the university ski team, were in Avoriaz training for the annual inter-university ski competition. One evening, the two were drinking with their respective friends in one of Avoriaz's more expensive bars when a particularly attractive girl walked in. She scanned the room as though looking for someone but, failing to find them, went and sat on her own at the far end of the bar. Both Knowles and Briggs were captivated. Tall and blonde, she wore a short jacket and the tightest pair of red jeans that either had ever seen. She eased onto a stool, wriggling her bottom into a comfortable position, and ordered a beer, chatting to the barman as he served her. Knowles assumed that she was waiting to meet someone but when, after ten minutes, she was still alone, he decided that he had to seize such an excellent opportunity and go and talk to her. Briggs had the same idea but, because he was sitting slightly nearer, Knowles got there first, climbing onto the stool next to the blonde and trying to catch the barman's attention. The bar was busy but it almost seemed as if the barman was deliberately ignoring him. Knowles sensed the girl watching him out of the corner of her eye. 'Andreas,' she called to the barman. 'When you've finished chatting up the girl in the red t-shirt, please could you serve this man before he dies of thirst.' The barman nodded.

The girl's English had the trace of an accent. 'Thank you,' Knowles said, turning to her. 'I was beginning to wonder if he didn't like me.'

'No problem,' the blonde girl replied. 'He fancies the girl in the t-shirt. As you're not a girl, he's in no rush to serve you!' She looked at him as she spoke. She had deep blue eyes and a light dusting of freckles over the bridge of her nose.

'I'm Richard Knowles,' Knowles said, taking the opportunity to introduce himself with his most winning smile. 'Can I get you a drink as a thank you?' he asked.

'Thank you but no,' the girl replied. 'I'm waiting for a friend and I've already had one beer. If I have any more before she arrives, I won't make much sense!'

The barman eventually came over and Knowles ordered a couple of beers. As he paid, he noticed a tall man about his own age lean against the bar on the other side of the blonde. The man held a fifty Euro note in his hand to catch the barman's attention. It worked. As soon as the barman had served Knowles, he went straight over to the tall man to take his order. Knowles couldn't help overhearing the tall man. He spoke in fluent French but switched to English when one of his friends came over to change his order. The tall man then turned to the blonde. 'You look thirsty. It's my birthday and I'm buying drinks for thirsty blondes. May I buy you a drink?'

'No, thank you,' the blonde replied. 'That's very kind but I already have a beer and this gentleman has also just offered to buy me one.' She nodded her head in Knowles' direction as she spoke.

Knowles was impressed when the tall man switched to German to continue his conversation with the girl. Knowles didn't understand what he was saying but the tall man soon had the girl laughing, although Knowles was disconcerted that she kept looking in his direction as she laughed.

The tall man paid for his drinks and carried the tray over to his friends at the far side of the bar.

'Your friend was very funny,' the girl said as the tall man walked away. 'I'm sorry that you didn't win your bet.'

'Bet?' Knowles queried. 'What bet?'

'He said that you had bet him twenty Euros that you could leave the bar with me within an hour,' she explained.

Knowles started to laugh, recognising that the tall man clearly saw him as competition for the blonde girl's attention and was trying to spike his chances. He'd done similar things to his friends in the past, although he'd never had the courage to do it to a stranger. 'Ah well,' he said. 'Now you know my evil plans, perhaps we can just chat until your friend arrives?'

The girl liked his disarming honesty and agreed. Knowles made the most of the opportunity. 'My friend is celebrating and is a little bit drunk. His wife's just had their first child. It came two weeks early so he's flying back tomorrow. But tonight, he's just proud to be a Dad.'

The girl's brow furrowed. 'Oh, how fantastic. He must be delighted,' she said.

As the tall man walked back towards them with an empty tray, the blonde noticed her friend waving at her from the door. 'I must go,' she said to the two men. 'Congratulations,' she said to the tall man, sliding off the bar stool. 'I bet you're delighted.' With that, she squeezed between the two of them and headed off towards her friend.

The two men watched her go and then looked at each other. 'What did she mean?' the tall man asked quizzically.

'Well,' Knowles said, 'once you'd kindly explained our bet to her, I felt obliged to explain that your wife had just given birth and that you were out celebrating.'

The tall man looked at Knowles incredulously. 'You said what?' he asked.

'I explained that you had had reservations about going skiing but that, as the baby wasn't due for another few weeks, your wife had insisted that you go. I also explained that this was your last night out with the boys before you flew home to see your wife and baby son. She was delighted for you!' Knowles smiled as he said the last bit.

To his surprise the tall man started to laugh. 'Touché,' he said. 'That serves me right I suppose.' He held out his hand for Knowles to shake. 'I'm Jim Briggs,' he said.

'Richard Knowles,' Knowles replied, shaking the proffered hand. 'Let me buy you a drink.'

That had been twenty-five years ago and the two had been the firmest of friends ever since. Knowles had left the Army and gone to work in the City whilst Briggs had finished his degree in modern languages and joined the police force. Many of his friends thought it an unlikely career for such a talented individual but Briggs was adamant that it was what he wanted. In the intervening years, he'd progressed from PC Jim Briggs of the Metropolitan Police to Sir James Briggs, head of the City of London Police. He'd been in the post for two years and was generally thought to be doing an extremely good job. His no-nonsense approach and absolute refusal to crony up to politicians and senior bankers made him unpopular with some but the media applauded his efforts. They had nicknamed him 'Straight Jim', suggesting that he was one of the few people in the country prepared to take on the big corporations if and when they started to sail too close to the legal wind. As the Commissioner of the City of London Police, he was responsible for all aspects of policing within the Square Mile. As well as departments that covered anti-terrorism and more routine police duties, his National Fraud Intelligence Bureau focused on economic crime and, in particular, the activities of the financial institutions within the City.

Briggs entered the club and asked for Sir James Knowles. Simpson took his coat and led him up two flights of stairs to the library where Knowles was waiting.

'Jim, thank you for coming,' said Knowles, getting out of his chair. 'Thank you Simpson,' he said to the doorman.

'Good to see you Richard,' said Briggs. 'It's been a few months.'

Knowles led the way out of the library and towards the dining room. As they walked, they asked each other about their respective families, catching up on domestic news until they were shown to a secluded table in the corner of the dining room.

'Do sit down Jim and I'll explain why, other than for your delightful company, I asked you to meet me.' Knowles indicated a chair and, moving round the table so that his back was against the wall, he sat down. The waiter gave them each a menu and poured iced water into their glasses.

'How much do you know about Charles Highworth?' asked Knowles, placing his menu on the table.

'Not a huge amount,' replied Briggs. 'He seems to be extremely successful. He's not come across our radar as someone we need to watch. I've met him a few times. He's always been pleasant enough. Why?' asked Briggs.

'What I'm about to tell you is off the record, at least for the moment,' said Knowles. 'I'm telling you because you're a friend and I need your advice.'

Briggs looked at his friend quizzically. In all the years he'd known him, Knowles had never once asked him for advice. He was intrigued.

'I've known Highworth for about twenty years,' began Knowles. 'I first came across him or, more correctly, International Valiant, when I was trying to buy a company called Demon Toys. The company manufactured dolls, mainly action figures based on film characters. It was a long established company and the shares were owned by family members. In its day it had been very successful but it had been making a loss for three or four years and the family were keen to sell. I wanted it because one of its factories sat on about five acres of land which I knew would become extremely valuable within a few years. The company didn't know this at the time and I'm not going to tell you how I knew; suffice to say that my plan was to buy the company, close it down and sell off the land. Everything was going as planned until, out of the blue, the company landed a contract to make all the action figures associated with the summer's highest grossing movie. You might remember the film. It was called *Only the Brave* and it exceeded everyone's expectations, it even picked up an Oscar or two. The action figures were a huge success. Needless to say, as soon as they'd landed the contract, the head of the family, a thoroughly decent old boy, decided he didn't want to sell after all.'

'What happened to the land?' asked Briggs.

'They kept it for a few years and then apparently sold it off for a significant sum,' answered Knowles.

'So how does Highworth fit into all this?' asked Briggs.

Knowles took a deep breath and then continued. 'About five years ago, I bumped into the head of the family quite by chance at a rugby tournament in York. We were sponsoring one of the teams and we decided it would be fun to watch a few of the games. The old boy bought me a beer. He said that he'd always felt bad having changed his mind about selling the company at the eleventh hour. I said that

I understood and that there were no hard feelings. I mentioned that it was a stroke of luck that they'd got the contract for the *Only the Brave* toys and that none of us could have predicted that. There was no luck in it, he said. I asked him what he meant. He was a bit cagey at first but, over a few more pints, he explained that an organisation called "International Valiant" had made them an offer they couldn't refuse. The deal was that if the family agreed to sell forty-nine percent of their shares, then International Valiant would ensure that they got the contract for the *Only the Brave* toys. The old boy was quite happy with the deal. They lost control of part of the company but they got a good price for the shares and the family remained the major shareholder. Moreover, the company got a new lease of life. He wouldn't tell me exactly how much he'd sold the shares for but he did tell me that International Valiant had sold them on several years later for a very substantial profit.'

'OK,' said Briggs, 'you were unlucky but I can't see anything dodgy so far.'

'No,' replied Knowles, 'but I was intrigued by the story and I decided to dig into it. You've got to remember that there was a fifteen year gap between the deal and the old boy telling me about it in York. It was hard to track anyone from the film company down but eventually we found a chap who remembered the incident well. He'd been the head of contracts at the time and he remembered the CEO forcing him to sign the contract with Demon Toys. He queried it because he reckoned that he could get a better deal with a different company but the CEO was adamant. It turns out that the CEO was an old friend and, after a couple of heated discussions, he admitted that he and his wife had been physically threatened. Apparently, he'd been told that if Demon Toys didn't get the contract, then something unpleasant would happen to his wife and children. It seems that the threats were very convincing.'

'Interesting,' said Briggs. 'I don't suppose you know who put the pressure on them?'

'No,' replied Knowles. 'The CEO died before I started digging around. The chap in contracts told me everything he knew – which wasn't much – but it set me thinking. The only beneficiary of this, other than the company itself, was International Valiant. I don't have the exact figures but I suspect they made several million out of the deal because by the time they sold their shares, the company had become the UK's major manufacturer of film-related toys. It had expanded significantly and was, by all accounts, flourishing. It still is as a matter of fact.'

Knowles paused. He took a long sip of his water and then signalled to one of the hovering waiters that they were ready to order. The waiter recommended the Beef Wellington which both men were happy to try. Knowles ordered a bottle of the Club Claret and then continued with his story.

'The story about Demon Toys made me think. I got my team to dig into International Valiant's deals over the last few years. I've invested a fair amount of money with them myself and we were therefore able to piece together a reasonable picture of their activity. There were some striking successes which nobody, and I mean nobody, would have predicted. We selected six of these and started digging deeper. Four of the six successes were remarkable. International Valiant seemed to know exactly when an event would occur that would cause seismic changes to share prices. On each occasion, they were doing exactly the opposite of what the rest of the market was doing and, as a result, they made hundreds of millions.' Knowles paused to allow the waiter to serve the wine.

'Go on,' prompted Briggs.

'I hired a discrete and very expensive firm of private investigators to add another level of detail to our research. I've used them before a number of times. They are very thorough and I trust them. They interviewed people in the six companies we'd selected and the story was the same: threats, a few physical assaults to reinforce the point, a handful of accidental deaths and a couple of supposedly random murders. Again, people were reluctant to talk but from what the investigators managed to unearth, it's clear that somebody has been engineering events to get the outcome they wanted.' Knowles stopped whilst the waiter served their food.

'This is quite a story Richard,' said Briggs. 'How sure of your facts are you?'

'Very,' said Knowles. 'The same thing happened again a few weeks ago with a company called Tokifora.' Knowles went on to explain his interest in the company and his discussion with Highworth.

'You realise that if what you are saying is true, you've put yourself in a lot of danger by confronting Highworth,' said Briggs.

'Yes,' said Knowles. 'That's why I wanted to see you urgently and why I'm explaining all of this. I've also had the team put everything we've discovered in a report. It's on this,' he said, taking a memory stick out of his pocket and waving it at Briggs. 'All the transactions we've been able to identify as well as the details of the interviews carried out by the private investigators are in the report. Where we can, we've also included newspaper cuttings about any deaths, accidental or otherwise, that we think are connected. It's quite a package,' said Knowles, handing it over to Briggs.

Briggs looked at it and then put it in his own pocket. He trusted Knowles but he was intrigued by his motivation. 'Why are you doing this Richard?' he asked.

'I might be a ruthless bastard Jim, but I've never broken the law. Highworth has cost me a small fortune over the years. I can live with that but he was one step ahead of me so many times that I was starting to lose faith in my ability to read the market. It was almost a relief when we worked out that he's not playing by the same rules as the rest of us. He needs to be stopped Richard, sooner rather than later.'

'I agree,' said Briggs. 'What do you suggest?'

'I've thought long and hard about this over the last few months. My initial thoughts were that I should leak it to the press but he's got so much to lose that he'll deny it to buy time and then do whatever it takes to silence the critics. He'll also try and destroy any evidence or anything that can link him to any of this. I've no doubt that he won't think twice about killing a few more people if it helps protect him and I'm therefore convinced that the only way to stop him is through the courts. I realise that this will take time and that you'll need to verify everything I've said but it's the only way.'

'I agree,' said Briggs. 'I'll look at the stuff you've given me tonight. If it stacks up, I'll get the team started on it first thing tomorrow. If we can make this stick, it's going to have very significant repercussions. I've no doubt that lots of very powerful people have money invested in International Valiant. They probably know nothing about any of this but they've made a great deal of money with Highworth at the helm and we're going to come under a lot of pressure not to prosecute him once word gets out.'

'Thank you Richard. By the way,' said Knowles, 'the password for the file is "Belinda".'

Briggs laughed. It was the name of the blonde girl they'd fought over in Avoriaz all those years ago!

CHAPTER 22

Isobel and Lucy fastened their seatbelts as the plane began its descent towards Edinburgh Airport. Looking through the windows Lucy could see the city lights far below her. Straining, she could just make out the black ribbon that marked the river as it led from the sea and up the Firth of Forth to the north of the city. Rain streaked the windows. 'What a surprise!' she thought to herself. It's always raining in Edinburgh. Not normal rain like everywhere else but big fat drops that soaked you to the skin in no time at all. Despite this, she loved the city. Both the Old and the New Town had their attractions. On balance, she preferred the New Town for shopping and the Old Town for a night out. Both were dominated by the Castle, a stunning building that seemed to grow out of the volcanic plug on which it was built. She'd been to a few parties there when she was younger. A friend of hers had been engaged to a young Army officer from one of the Scottish Regiments that had their Headquarters in the Castle. The parties had been great fun though, if she were honest, she'd never really mastered the highland dancing that seemed to be obligatory at most formal evening functions held north of the border with England.

The plane landed and within a few minutes they were invited to unfasten their seatbelts and leave the plane. 'Are you OK?' asked Isobel, clearly concerned for her friend.

'Yes, I'm fine,' replied Lucy with a weary smile.

They collected their bags and took a taxi to the city hospital. She tried phoning Kate on the way to tell her that they had arrived but there was no answer. She left a few messages on the answerphone and sent her a text telling her that they would be at the hospital in twenty minutes. Her phone beeped a few minutes later. It was a text from Kate telling her that she'd meet them outside the main entrance. Lucy assumed that Kate must be in the hospital and unable to talk on the phone. 'That's a good sign,' she thought to herself.

The taxi approached the main entrance of the hospital and Lucy could see Kate standing outside, having a cigarette. 'Here's fine,' Lucy said to the taxi driver as he pulled up outside the main door. Isobel paid the driver whilst Lucy got out and went to Kate.

'I'm so sorry Lucy,' said Kate, bursting into tears. 'I'm afraid he died about four hours ago. He never really regained consciousness except for one brief moment when I was telling him that you were on your way. I spoke to him for hours but this was the only time that he gave any sign of having heard me. I'm so, so sorry.' She pulled Lucy to her and held her tight, her tears falling on Lucy's shoulders.

Lucy was numb with shock. She couldn't believe that her indestructible Dad, the man who had been the one constant source of strength throughout her life, was dead. 'Surely there's been some sort of mistake?' she thought to herself. 'It can't be true.' She started to sob uncontrollably. Isobel caught her as she slipped from Kate's grasp and started to fall to her knees on the pavement. 'Why my Dad?' she shouted. 'Why is it my Mum and my Dad that have to die?' Isobel helped her to her feet and hugged her tightly. She led her to a bench opposite the entrance and sat her down.

'It's all right, Lucy, let it all out,' said Isobel, gently stroking Lucy's hair off her forehead.

'But it's not all fucking right is it?' shouted Lucy. 'My Dad's dead.'

Isobel was lost for words. She'd never seen her friend so upset and she wasn't sure what to do other than to hold her and to try and comfort her. Slowly, Lucy's cries subsided. Eventually, she stood up and took several deep breaths. She was trying hard to get a grip of herself. 'Can I see him?' she asked Kate.

'Yes, I should think so,' replied Kate. 'I told the doctors that you'd be here very shortly. They said they wouldn't move him until you'd had a chance to see him and to talk to them. Are you sure you want to do this?'

'Yes, I must,' she replied. 'I need to see him one last time. I need to say goodbye.' She still didn't believe it. She needed to see for herself that this wasn't some sort of cruel mistake.

Kate led Lucy into the hospital. They took the lift to the second floor in silence. Kate was sobbing quietly into her handkerchief. Lucy stood in silence. She suspected she was in shock. He'd always seemed so indestructible that she'd never really thought about what life would be like without him. All through her life, he had been there; big, strong, capable and always hugely supportive. She'd loved him so much. All of a sudden she felt very alone indeed. The tears started to well up in her eyes again and she reached for Kate's hand. 'You loved him didn't you Kate?'

'Yes, yes I did,' replied Kate. 'I've loved him for years.' She would have continued but the lift arrived at the second floor and the door opened. Kate led them down the corridor.

Lucy's heart was beating fast. She could feel the anger welling up inside her. She was angry that someone had taken her father from her and that he had died before she had had the chance to say goodbye. This wasn't how it was supposed to be.

They went into a single room off the main corridor. It smelt of antiseptic. This surprised Lucy. She'd never experienced death at first hand before but she'd expected the room to smell musty and old. Her father lay on a single bed behind a curtain screen. She pulled the curtain aside and looked at his face. His eyes were closed and he looked peaceful, as though in a deep and satisfying sleep. There were no marks or bruises. A young doctor came in and pulled the curtain the rest of the way back. He turned to look at Lucy, compassion clear in his eyes. 'Are you his daughter?' he asked.

'Yes,' replied Lucy without taking her eyes off her father. 'Yes, I am.'

'I'm so sorry,' he said. 'We did everything we could but the knife penetrated deep into his body. There was a lot of internal damage. We were amazed that he hung on for so long. He must have been a tough man.'

'Yes, he was. He was very tough. Do you know what happened?' she asked the doctor.

'Not really,' he replied, 'but I'll tell you what I know. An ambulance brought him in yesterday. He'd been stabbed and then left for dead down a back alley. Somehow, he'd crawled to the main road before passing out. A couple of students found him and called 999. The ambulance brought him here and we operated as soon as we could but there was too much damage. It looks like whoever did it knew exactly what they were doing but I'm not sure the police see it that way.'

'What do you mean?' asked Lucy.

'I spoke to the police after we'd operated and told them pretty much what I've just told you. They didn't seem that interested. We get lots of stabbings at weekends, not as many as in Glasgow but a fair few. They seemed to think it was just one of those things, an argument that ended in a fight or a mugging.' The doctor paused. 'The police were here this afternoon. They left when they realised that your father wasn't going to regain consciousness.'

'Thank you,' said Lucy, turning to face the doctor. 'Thank you for trying to save him, he would have appreciated that.' Lucy stared at the doctor. He was in his early thirties. He looked familiar but Lucy couldn't place him.

Isobel came into the room and stood next to Lucy. She squeezed her hand. 'I'm so sorry,' she said. 'I was hoping we were going to get here and find that it had all been a dreadful mistake.'

'Me too,' said Lucy. 'But there's no mistake. My Dad's dead and there's nothing I can do about it.' There was a long silence before Lucy asked if she could have a few minutes alone with her father.

Kate, Isobel and the doctor left the room. Lucy found her father's hand. She loved him so much and now he was gone. The tears welled up in her eyes. She took a deep breath, more to control the anger that she could feel simmering inside her than to stop the tears. 'I'll find whoever did this Dad,' she said to his body. 'And when I do, they'll wish they'd never been born.' She leaned over and kissed him on the forehead. Then she went and found the doctor in the corridor. She could grieve later; she had a lot to do.

CHAPTER 23

Harry answered the phone on its third ring. He'd just got back from his run and he wanted to grab a shower before going out to meet friends for lunch. The only reason he'd answered the phone was because he thought it might be Lucy. He was a bit concerned. He hadn't heard anything from her since they'd kissed in the hotel foyer before she left for Pokhara. He hoped that she was all right and that she hadn't had a sudden change of heart. 'Hello?' he said into the phone, remembering too late that Lucy didn't have his phone number.

'Fish? Is that you?' Harry recognised the voice of his ex-girlfriend.

'Yes, are you all right Camilla, you sound odd?' asked Harry.

'No, no I'm not all right. I need you Harry,' said a clearly strained Camilla.

'What's happened?' asked Harry. As he waited for her to answer, he looked at the two nude paintings either side of the fireplace that Lucy and Isobel had admired. Camilla had done them. They were of Camilla and Harry. He was drawn to the one of Camilla. She'd got her own bottom just right, thought Harry. He smiled to himself as he remembered the fun they'd had taking the photographs on which the paintings were based. Camilla had made him walk around the room naked whilst she, also naked, took photographs of his back view. They'd changed roles three or four times until Camilla was eventually satisfied that she had enough reasonable photographs to work from. They'd both found the exercise surprisingly exciting and it had therefore taken longer than it should have done because they'd stopped to make love twice, the first time at Harry's insistence and the second at Camilla's. The urgency in Camilla's voice put an end to Harry's wistful reminisces.

'Fish, something awful has happened and I don't know who else to phone. The police are ignoring me and I'm sure I'm being followed. I'm scared Harry, please help me,' pleaded Camilla.

Harry was concerned. Camilla was not easily frightened. They'd parted on good terms but she was stubborn and proud and he knew that she wouldn't have contacted him unless something had really spooked her.

'Take your time and tell me what's happened,' said Harry, pouring himself a coffee and settling down into an armchair. His friends would have to wait. He liked Camilla and he was determined to be there for her. He knew that whatever her faults, she would have done the same for him, even though they were no longer lovers.

Camilla took a deep breath and started to talk. She explained about Fairweather and being in his flat the night he died. She remembered going to bed with him but she fell asleep after they'd made love and the next thing she knew, someone was waking her up to tell her that her lover was dead. She'd originally accepted the police's view that it was an accident but she was starting to have reservations. For the last few days, she'd had the strongest feeling that she was being followed. She also felt that someone had been in her flat. She couldn't put her finger on why – everything was in its place and just as she'd left it – but it just felt as if her space had been violated.

Harry listened intently. He found himself getting angry when Camilla said that she'd spent the night with Fairweather. He realised he had no right to. They were no longer a couple and she was free to do whatever she wanted. But still, the image of her sleeping with someone else hurt. Perhaps he wasn't over her yet he thought to himself. Camilla continued talking for about twenty minutes, explaining how she'd met Fairweather and how she had ended up with him that night. She was clearly upset but she held it together long enough to finish her story.

'Why do you think you're being followed?' he asked when she'd finished.

'I just do,' she said. 'I feel as if someone is watching me all the time. I keep turning round suddenly to see if I can see them. I haven't yet but I just get this creepy feeling. It's scary and the police aren't interested at all. They're very clear in their own minds that Fairweather had a dreadful accident. They think I'm suffering from shock and that my nerves are getting the better of me. If I'm honest, I get the feeling they think I was partly responsible. They keep asking me about the drugs but in all the time I knew him, I never saw him take any. We certainly didn't do any on the night he died. He might have got up and had a snort when I was asleep but you know how I feel about drugs. If I'd thought that Fairweather was a regular user, I wouldn't have been interested in him, no matter how many of my paintings he'd bought.'

Harry didn't doubt her sincerity. One of her best friends had died of a drugs overdose in her late teens and she was violently opposed to them. 'OK,' said Harry. 'What do you want me to do?' he asked.

'I don't know,' replied Camilla. 'I just needed someone to talk to. If you were here in London, I'd ask you to stay with me for a few days but I realise that you can't. Just talk to me for a while, tell me what you're doing.'

Harry told her what he'd been up to. He didn't mention Lucy, not because he was worried about her reaction but because he wasn't sure exactly what was happening. Lucy didn't have his phone number but she said she would e-mail him when she got to Pokhara and had a better idea of when she might be returning to Kathmandu. He hadn't received an e-mail yet and he was due to begin his journey to Everest Base Camp in a few days' time. Although his phone could receive e-mails, he knew that once he was up in the hills he would lose mobile coverage and that there would be no chance of any messages reaching him until he headed back towards Kathmandu. Camilla was clearly frightened and part of him felt that he should go and help her. Although they'd only been engaged for twelve months, they'd actually been together for four years. It was a long time and they were still close friends, even though they were no longer lovers. But if he went to London to help her, he'd miss any chance of spending time with Lucy when she returned from Pokhara. He needed time to think things through. Should he try and contact Lucy through the trekking company and explain what had happened? But if he said he was flying off to see an old girlfriend, she might think that he was still in love with her. How many prospective new girlfriends would be happy to see their new man disappear off to spend time with an ex? Not many, he supposed.

He and Camilla talked for another hour. She was calming down and when Harry suggested she go and stay with friends for a few days, she agreed. Her best friend, also an artist, lived on Dartmoor in an old farmhouse that she was renovating. It would be just what she needed. A change of scenery and lots of fresh air. Harry promised to phone her the next day before she went to see how she was doing.

Camilla felt better after she'd spoken to Harry. He was always so reassuring. She'd loved that about him. Resourceful and calm, few things ever phased him. She'd been sorry when they'd split up but they'd both agreed that it was for the best. He desperately wanted to do development work in Africa and she was determined to stay in London and consolidate her position as an emerging new artist. And although she'd found the first few months hard, she was making it work. Or rather, she was until this happened. She phoned up her friend and arranged to travel down to Dartmoor the next afternoon. She'd have to tell the police but she was sure that they would have no objections provided they knew where she was. She was excited about getting out of town and spending some time in the hills. She loved Dartmoor. She'd spent her holidays there as a child and she knew the eastern moors well. Her friend's farmhouse was in the village of North Bovey. It was small, had a great pub and was sufficiently far off the tourist track that you could walk for hours without bumping into anybody else. She couldn't wait.

Harry lay in the bath thinking about what to do. He desperately wanted to see Lucy again. He kept replaying their kiss over and over in his mind. He'd only known her for a few days but there was already something between them. He didn't know what it was. He just knew that he wanted to be with her. She was funny, bright and interested in him. This was a new experience. Camilla had many good points but asking him what he felt about things wasn't one of them. She was usually so wrapped up in what she was doing that she rarely asked his view of anything. It wasn't that she was self-obsessed, it was just that she was so focused on her painting that all they ever seemed to talk about was how to further her career. Lucy, on the other hand, had asked his views on all sorts of things, not just the historical buildings they'd visited on the tour of Kathmandu. After half an hour of thinking things through, he felt he had the solution, at least for now. He would see how Camilla was when he phoned in the morning. If she was feeling a bit better and was still intending to go and stay with her friend, then he would stay in Nepal and, after the Everest trip, would try and spend some time with Lucy. But if Camilla was still struggling when he phoned, then he would fly to the UK to be with her. He'd have to take his chances with Lucy. If she was half the girl he thought she was, he felt sure she'd understand. Satisfied that he had a plan, he got out of the bath, dried himself and padded into the bedroom to get dressed. Ten minutes later, he left the house and headed into town. He was running a bit late but provided he didn't get stuck behind one of Kathmandu's seemingly endless festival parades, he reckoned that he would just about make it in time for lunch.

CHAPTER 24

Lucy, Isobel and Kate left the hospital and took a taxi to George Street. Kate had suggested they stay with her but Lucy wanted to go back to her father's flat. Although she was rarely there, her father had insisted on turning one of the rooms into 'her' bedroom. One wall was covered in framed photographs of her in various school sports teams. Another had pictures of a young Lucy with her mother and father. The shelves were full of old school books and the paperbacks she'd read as a teenager. Her possessions made the room familiar and homely, even though she'd never spent any of her childhood there. She felt safe in the flat, the main reason she'd wanted to go back there rather than to Kate's.

The taxi stopped outside the block of flats. Lucy paid and started to walk towards the main entrance. Kate had been there many times before but, wanting to be discrete, she let Lucy lead the way. Lucy opened the main door and climbed the stairs to her father's flat. She took out her key and opened the door, switching on the lights as they entered the hall. It was immaculate. Like many soldiers used to keeping their kit together, her father was a neat and tidy man but, even so, it looked as though the house had been cleaned earlier that day. The flat smelt of air freshener and the rugs were neatly aligned on the highly polished wooden floors.

'Your Dad was a very tidy person,' said Isobel as she entered the living room.

'Yes,' replied Lucy. 'But he wasn't here that often and I suspect that helped. He had a cleaner who came in a couple of times a week to keep the place ticking over when he was away. Come in to the sitting room while I think about what I need to do next.'

Kate went and sat next to Lucy on the sofa and reached for

her hand. 'You don't need to do anything immediately. I can help you with the funeral arrangements if you'd like and I know which solicitors your father used. It might be best to see them in the next few days as your father went to talk to them earlier this week. Your father was a meticulous man and I've no doubt he will have left them clear instructions on what to do if anything happened to him. I know it sounds macabre and I'm still not sure exactly what he did to make his money but he seemed to think there was a fair amount of risk involved.'

'Thank you Kate,' said Lucy, genuinely relieved that Kate was willing to help her. 'I'm really grateful for your help. You knew Dad well and he would have wanted you to be involved.'

'Thank you,' said Kate. They sat in silence for several minutes. 'It's late Lucy and neither you nor Isobel have eaten anything since you landed. Do you want me to see if there's anything in the kitchen?' asked Kate.

Isobel, who had a very healthy appetite, looked at Lucy expectantly. 'No thanks,' said Lucy. 'We'll make a cup of tea and then go to bed. Can I ring you tomorrow when I've had a chance to think things through and get some sleep?'

'Of course,' replied Kate, standing up. 'I'll leave you to it.' Lucy and Isobel stood up to kiss her goodbye. 'See you tomorrow but if you need anything during the night, just phone,' said Kate as she left the room.

The girls heard the front door close behind Kate. 'Tea?' asked Isobel.

'Yes please,' replied Lucy. 'I can't believe he's gone. The flat looks just the same as it always did. I keep expecting him to come through the door and tell me that it's all been a horrible mistake.'

Isobel didn't really know what to say. She hadn't lost anybody close to her but she could see the pain that her friend was in. She went over and sat next to Lucy, putting her arm around her and pulling her close. Lucy started to cry, sobbing into Isobel's shoulder.

'Why him Isobel? Why did it have to be my Dad that gets killed by some drunken yob in a bloody pub? Why couldn't it have been somebody else?'

'I don't know Luce,' said Isobel, starting to cry herself. 'I just don't know.'

'I want to find who did this and if the police won't help me, then I'll do it myself,' said Lucy. Isobel didn't doubt that she meant it.

Isobel got up and went to the kitchen. She was surprised at how well stocked it was. She put the kettle on and found the tea bags. Five minutes later, she carried a tray of tea and biscuits into the sitting room.

Lucy was looking at the paintings on the wall. Some of them were new to her, as was the one propped on an easel near the fireplace. 'This is very new,' she thought to herself, noticing the wooden container that it must have come in on the floor. Lucy didn't know much about art but the latest acquisition – if that's what it was – must have cost a fair bit judging by its obvious quality. The container had a Sotherby's sticker on it and Lucy made a mental note to contact them in the next few weeks to discuss her father's paintings. She had absolutely no idea as to their value but he had built up an extensive collection over the years and she knew that he would want her to look after it. Or if not look after it, at least understand its value before deciding what to do with it.

'What did your Dad do, Lucy?' asked Isobel.

'I'm not really sure,' replied Lucy. 'He was always a bit cagey when the subject came up. He used to say that he was in security but exactly what this meant, I don't really know. The only thing I know is that it seemed to pay OK as he was forever going to auctions and galleries and buying new paintings. It's one of the reasons he liked living in Edinburgh. I'll show you tomorrow if you like but Dundas Street has got some great little galleries and art shops on it.'

'That'd be great,' said Isobel, handing Lucy a cup of tea. 'Drink this and then let's think about going to bed. I'm knackered and we could both do with a good night's sleep.'

'OK. Will you stay with me for a few days Isobel?' asked Lucy. 'Kate's great but I don't know her well and I could do with the support.'

'Of course,' replied Isobel. 'I'll stay for as long as you want me to. I've got nothing better to do anyway. I was going to spend a week or so with my family after Nepal but that can wait.'

'Thank you,' said Lucy, clearly relieved that she wouldn't be on her own, at least for a week or so. Lucy stood up. 'Let's go and sort out the beds.' She led the way down the hall and into the guest room. The bed was already made and there were clean towels on the end of the bed. 'The bathroom's through there,' she said to Isobel, pointing at a door at the foot of the bed.

'This is really nice,' said Isobel, opening the door to the en-suite bathroom and peering inside. 'He really did have good taste your old man! I shall be very comfortable here.'

Lucy smiled. One of the things she liked about Isobel was her straightforward way of looking at things. Though she was academically brilliant, she had a very practical approach to everyday life. Very little worried her and she seemed able to impose an iron discipline on her emotions that Lucy envied.

'Why don't you send an e-mail to Harry telling him what's happened before you go to bed?' suggested Isobel as she started to undress.

'What a good idea,' replied Lucy. 'I think I'll do that now. Good night Isobel and thank you for being here with me.'

'No problem Luce,' replied Isobel. 'It's what friends are for. See you tomorrow. Wake me if you need me during the night.'

'Night Isobel. I'm just in here,' said Lucy, pointing to the room opposite Isobel's. 'See you tomorrow.'

Isobel got into bed. She stared at the ceiling, thinking through the day's events. She was worried about her friend. The brutality and apparent randomness of her father's death would have come as such a nasty shock that she suspected Lucy would be numb for a while yet. She'd have to watch her carefully over the next few weeks and try and find some way of helping her cope. She knew nothing about psychology but she was in no doubt that having both parents die so suddenly and so violently would inevitably have some sort of longer term impact. She heard the toilet flush. She strained her ears for sounds of her friend and heard Lucy sobbing quietly as she walked down the corridor and into her own bedroom.

CHAPTER 25

Sir James Briggs sat in an old leather armchair next to the fire in his study. His dog was asleep at his feet. Although she was getting on a bit, she still had plenty of life left in her. He'd got her from Battersea Dogs' Home when she was still a puppy. Long legged for a Staffordshire bull terrier, she had the breed's characteristic flat head, powerful shoulders and narrow hips. Indeed, she could look quite menacing when she was agitated, something that always amused him given she had been christened 'Princess' by the carers at the dogs' home and he'd never quite got round to changing her name. He ruffled the dog's neck and poured himself another glass of whisky. He had nearly finished reading the report that Knowles had given him. He'd had his PA print out the content of the memory stick and then secure it in her safe. He didn't want any of his team looking at it just yet. Briggs was amazed at the depth of the analysis. It was outstanding work and he made a mental note to ask Knowles for the name of the firm of investigators he'd used. Briggs was in no doubt that if everything in the report could be corroborated, then there was a cast iron case that linked Highworth to a whole string of prosecutable offences. If they could bring this to court, then a conviction would be almost inevitable, even with the brightest of defence lawyers and the most inept of juries. Highworth would be looking at a very long time in gaol – indeed, it would be highly likely that, even if he lived to a ripe old age, he would die there. Briggs smiled to himself and then looked down at his dog. 'Well Princess, what do we do now?'

CHAPTER 26

Camilla's train arrived at Newton Abbot in the early evening. It was just starting to get dark as she got off and started to walk towards the exit. She could see her friend, Ellie, waiting for her near the ticket office. There were lots of people at the station and it took Ellie a few minutes to spot her friend. When she did, her face lit up and she started to wave. Camilla waved back excitedly, struggling to feed her ticket into the automatic barrier.

'Hello darling,' said Ellie, wrapping her arms around Camilla in the tightest of hugs. 'It's so great to see you. You look fantastic.'

'You always say that. I look like shit and you know it,' replied Camilla laughing. She was pleased to see Ellie. They had been great friends since art school. They'd shared a flat together in London for a few years after they had graduated and until Ellie, tired of city living, had returned to Dartmoor where she'd grown up. It was a brave move for an aspiring artist but she'd applied for a job as an art teacher at one of the private schools in Exeter and, to her surprise and despite the stiff competition, she'd got it.

'How's it going?' asked Camilla, linking her arm through Ellie's as they walked towards Ellie's old Land Rover.

'Really well,' replied Ellie. 'I'm selling more of my work, which is clearly good, the house is taking shape and my love life has improved significantly since I last saw you.'

'Go on,' encouraged Camilla. Ellie kept her sexuality reasonably quiet. She didn't deny it but she didn't advertise it either. She wasn't ashamed of being gay – indeed, she was proud of it – but she knew from personal experience that, however open minded they might claim to be, some teachers, particularly in girls' schools, could be extremely old fashioned in their views. Camilla understood this but suspected that her low profile hadn't helped her friend find a suitable partner.

'She's called Sarah and she's an English teacher at a school near Ashburton. We're taking it slowly but I think this time it might be serious. She moved in with me about a year ago and, so far, it's working out really well.' Ellie paused for breath. 'You'll like her. She's bright, fun and deeply spiritual. In fact, you'd probably describe her as a bit of a hippy. As you can imagine, we fit right in in Ashburton!'

Camilla laughed. She knew Ashburton well. One of the so called 'gateways to the moor', it was a picturesque little town. It nestled in the foot of a valley that led onto the moor and up towards Hay Tor, probably Dartmoor's most famous landmark. Climbing to the top of the Tor was something of a ritual for Camilla whenever she came to Dartmoor and she was determined that this visit would be no different, regardless of the circumstances.

Ellie took Camilla's bag and, opening the boot of her Land Rover, put it behind the back seat. It was an old long wheelbase Defender model, similar to the ones that the British Army used to use. She'd bought it when she first moved back to Dartmoor and, though it was expensive to run, it came into its own in winter. The girls climbed in and Ellie started the engine, flicked on the lights and, leaving the station car park, pulled onto the main road towards Ashburton. Neither Ellie nor Camilla saw the rental car pull out of the car park behind them and follow them as they headed out of Newton Abbot.

'So how long before the house is finished?' asked Camilla.

'Probably the rest of my life at this rate,' answered Ellie. 'Everything seems to cost more than I expected and this has slowed progress but you'll notice a difference. Two of the bedrooms are finished and they fitted the Aga in the kitchen a couple of months ago. They've also just installed the wood burner in the sitting room so we have heat at last!'

'I admire you Ellie,' said Camilla with genuine respect. 'You've set your sights on something and you're determined to get there.'

'Yes but I'd get there a bit quicker if more people bought a few more of my paintings,' said Ellie humorously. 'But there's a new gallery opened up in Bovey Tracy and they've agreed to exhibit some of my work next month. If it sells, then there's the real possibility of a regular contract. I've also persuaded the landlord at the Ring O'Bells in North Bovey to put some of my paintings in the bar. That's working out quite well. The village has changed over the years and a lot of the houses have been bought by the London set as second homes. I'm not sure whether that's a good thing or not for the community but it's good for me as they seem to like having paintings of Dartmoor in their London homes. I suppose they're a talking point.'

Camilla looked through the window as they passed through Ashburton and started to climb onto the moor. It was pitch black outside and starting to rain. She was glad that she was here with Ellie. Her friend's warmth and obvious pleasure at seeing her had restored her spirits.

'So tell me what happened, Camilla, with Peter Fairweather. I didn't press you on the phone because I could tell that you were mega stressed but, now that you're here, it would be nice to know what's going on.' Ellie looked across at her friend. 'You don't have to if you don't want to. We can just not talk about it if it's easier you know.'

'No,' said Camilla, 'I've imposed myself on you and I owe you an explanation.' Camilla then proceeded to tell Ellie everything that had happened to her.

'Wow, Camilla,' said Ellie. 'That's quite a story. Do you think he was murdered?'

Camilla didn't answer immediately. 'I didn't at first but odd things have been happening over the last few days and I'm beginning to wonder. What scares me is that if he was murdered, then whoever did it must have been in the house and must have seen me. I was asleep and I didn't see or hear anything but they might not know that. That's one reason why I haven't been too pushy with the police.

If there is anything dodgy going on, then the last thing I want is for the police to start agitating and for them to announce that they're investigating what now appear to be the suspicious circumstances surrounding Fairweather's death. I can't think of a surer way of getting me killed.'

'When you put it like that, I can see what you mean,' said Ellie. 'We're nearly there. You'll see the village lights when we go round the next bend and down towards the river.'

Camilla could make out lights on the hillside ahead as they rounded the bend. Ellie was a capable driver and knew the roads well but she slowed to walking pace as they crossed the stone bridge over the river below the village.

'It's really beautiful here isn't it,' said Camilla.

'Yes, that's why I refuse to leave. This is my "forever place",' said Ellie as they entered the village.

They drove up the hill and past the village green. The pub looked to be busy. They could make out figures in the bar and one or two dogs fastened up outside the main door.

'I'll take you for a drink later if you like. But first you need to eat,' said Ellie as she pulled up in front of her house.

Ellie jumped out of the car and grabbed Camilla's bag from the back. 'Come on,' she said, 'I want you to meet Sarah.'

Camilla was nervous about meeting Ellie's partner. Ellie knew her friend well enough to recognise her apprehension. 'Don't worry, she won't bite,' she said, grabbing Camilla's hand and dragging her towards the front door.

The door opened before they reached it. 'Come on in,' said a blonde girl holding the door open for them. 'I'm Sarah. Welcome to our home.'

'Hi,' said Camilla, introducing herself. 'I've heard a lot about you.'

'I bet,' replied Sarah, smiling and welcoming the returning Ellie with a kiss. 'All good I hope. What will you drink? We have wine, beer or, if you prefer, we can even run to spirits.'

Camilla gratefully accepted a glass of red wine and looked around the room. She also tried to look at Sarah without being too obvious. Camilla guessed that she was about her own age, late twenties or early thirties. Strikingly pretty in a wholesome, Scandinavian sort of way, she wore her blonde hair pulled back into a tight ponytail. Her round tortoise shell glasses gave her an academic look that seemed slightly at odds with the outsize lumberjack shirt and tight faded Levis that she wore.

'What an amazing transformation,' said Camilla. 'The house looks great.' Though she didn't say it, she also thought that Sarah looked great.

'Thank you,' said Ellie. 'There's still a lot to do but it's getting there.'

The kitchen was huge and extended nearly the whole length of the barn. The working area was at one end and focused around the very large reconditioned Aga that Ellie had mentioned in the car. In the middle of the room was an old refectory dining table with bench seats either side. At the far end, an old sofa and two armchairs were arranged around a cast iron wood burner. Camilla noticed a small brown and white Jack Russell dozing in a basket, clearly enjoying the heat of the wood burner. Bookshelves ran the entire length of the walls. Most were full to capacity but one or two of the shelves had been cleared of books and held an odd assortment of quirky ornaments. Rugs covered the stone floor in the seating area and under the dining table. The room was warm and cosy. It had the natural shabby chic look that many of her London friends desperately tried to recreate in their town houses, normally without success.

'You must be knackered, come and sit down,' said Ellie, opening the door of the wood burner and adding another log to the fire. 'More wine?' she asked.

'Yes please,' said Camilla, sitting on the sofa. 'This is really cosy. It was almost a shell when I last saw it and you were living in a sleeping bag upstairs. You've done a great job; it's like something out of *Country Living* magazine! And so many books, they add real character.'

'Most of those are Sarah's,' said Ellie. 'There's another room full upstairs. If we ever get round to it, we plan to put them in shelves on the landing. Either that or we'll turn one of the bedrooms into a study and put them in there.'

'It's one of the problems with being an English teacher, I can't bear to throw books away which means I need more and more space every year,' said Sarah, joining the conversation. She was cooking on the Aga and had to keep turning round to see the other two. Whatever she was making smelt great, thought Camilla as she started to realise how hungry she was.

'It's not being an English teacher that's the problem, it's working in a secondhand bookshop. Sarah gets first refusal on any books that the shop doesn't want. Needless to say, she never turns any down!' explained Ellie.

Sarah laughed. 'That's fair,' she said, turning and smiling at Ellie. 'But it's amazing what you end up reading just because someone gives you the book for nothing.'

'Such as?' asked Camilla, enjoying the gentle conversation and beginning to relax for the first time in days.

'Well,' said Sarah, 'take last week as an example. We did a house clearance following the death of an old philosophy professor from Plymouth Uni. He had zillions of books, many of which the bookshop already had. Lots of them were also very niche and not worth a huge amount so we were allowed to choose ten each to keep. I chose two books by Michel Foucault. I'd never really read any of his work before but now I'm an avid fan. It was hard going at first because he uses a vocabulary that I wasn't familiar with but it really makes you think about the nature of relationships and the power plays that exist in society.' She stopped as she noticed Ellie doing theatrical yawns. 'I'm sorry, Ellie keeps telling me that I'm becoming very boring about it.'

'You are,' said Ellie getting up. 'But Camilla is more intellectual than I am so don't let me stop you. Come on Boot, time to pee.' The dog's ears pricked up and, seeing Ellie moving towards the door, he jumped out of his basket and ran towards her.

Ellie opened the outside door. Boot shot out and then turned, barking at Ellie to follow him. Sarah and Camilla continued chatting about Foucault. The discussion about philosophers reminded Camilla of a film she'd recently seen on You Tube called 'What if money was no object?'.

'It's brilliant,' she said, 'all about living your dreams. It's by a chap called Alan Watts. I'd never heard of him before but he's got an amazing voice and what he says makes a huge amount of sense. I'll see if I can find it tomorrow and show it to you,' said Camilla. 'It's the sort of thing you could show to your pupils to make them think about what they want to do in life.' She was starting to like Sarah. When Ellie first mentioned her, she was worried that Sarah might be taking advantage of her good natured friend. But the more she talked to her, the more she realised that Sarah was one of the good guys and that she and Ellie were an ideal match. 'How did you two meet?' asked Camilla.

'In the bookshop,' said Sarah. 'I was working on a Saturday morning. Ellie came in, browsed for about half an hour in a suspiciously odd way and then very nervously asked me if we had a copy of *Carol* by Patricia Highsmith. We did as it happens so I showed her where it was. I was feeling a bit mischievous so when she paid, I asked her why she wanted it. She went bright red and stuttered something about it being for a friend.'

'What's significant about *Carol*?' asked Camilla.

'Well, Patricia Highsmith was bisexual and though she is most famous for her stories about Ripley, particularly since Matt Damon and Jude Law starred in the film adaptation, she also explored the theme of lesbian love in *Carol*. Actually, it was originally called 'The Price of Salt' and was published under the pseudonym of Claire

Morgan. It's a bit like E M Forster and Maurice, although Forster was dead before any of his less "wholesome" stories were published.' She signed the parenthesis around wholesome with her fingers. 'When she'd paid for the book, I told her that if she wanted to read anything else along similar lines, I'd lend her my own copies to save her buying them,' continued Sarah. 'As soon as I'd said that, Ellie visibly relaxed. We met for coffee a couple of times over the next few weeks and the rest, as they say, is history! We're very similar in so many ways that, if I think about it deeply, particularly after a few glasses of wine, I can't help but think that we were destined to be together. It just took us a while to find each other and it happened in a book shop in Ashburton of all places!'

'This is getting far too deep,' said Ellie who had heard the last couple of words as she struggled through the door with a basket full of logs. 'Can we eat yet or do we have to keep drinking wine?' asked Ellie. The dog ran between Ellie's legs and headed for the warmth of his basket.

'No, we can eat. Come and sit down and I'll serve it up,' said Sarah.

Camilla and Ellie sat down at the table as Sarah started to serve supper. It was boule bas served with crusty homemade bread and salad. Camilla tasted it. It was outstanding. 'God this is good,' she said.

'Thank you,' said Sarah. 'I'm glad you like it.'

'It's a Sarah speciality,' explained Ellie. 'It takes a bit of making but Sarah wanted to make an effort as she's never met you before and she was keen to make a good first impression.'

'Thanks for that Ellie,' said Sarah. 'You're not supposed to say things like that, at least not whilst I'm within earshot.'

'No, but it's true and I'm really grateful to you for being so thoughtful,' said Ellie.

'So am I,' said Camilla. 'To Sarah,' she said, raising her glass. Sarah and Ellie copied her and their glasses clinked together.

They continued talking until the early hours of the morning, finishing off another two bottles of wine and a large slab of Brie. Camilla couldn't remember when she'd enjoyed an evening quite so much. They were so different to the likes of Peter Fairweather and the people that she normally met up in London. They were much more grounded and not remotely interested in talking about money and the things they had recently bought. She found their company refreshing and stimulating. But she was dead on her feet and needed to sleep.

'I've got to go to bed,' said Camilla standing up unsteadily. 'I'm knackered. I've had a great evening, thank you very much for supper Sarah, it was brilliant.'

Sarah smiled. 'No problem. It was lovely to meet you at last having heard so much about you.'

'Come on, I'll show you to your room,' said Ellie, getting up. Camilla followed her out of the kitchen and up the stairs to the first floor. 'You're in here,' said Ellie, opening the door to one of the bedrooms and switching the light on. 'There's a small en suite bathroom through the door over there,' she said, pointing to the far wall. 'I've put fresh towels in there. Will this be OK?' she asked.

'It's lovely Ellie, thank you, this'll be great. And no wonder you're so happy with Sarah, she's fantastic,' said Camilla.

'Thank you,' replied Ellie, 'she obviously likes you. She was worried you'd disapprove of us. I said you were my oldest friend and that you'd be happy if I was happy.'

'You were right. I'm very happy indeed that you have found a soul mate at last. I just wish I could be so lucky,' said Camilla. 'Nite Ellie and thanks again for everything,' said Camilla, pecking Ellie on the cheek. 'See you tomorrow.'

Having said goodnight to Camilla, Ellie went downstairs. Sarah was tidying up. 'She's very nice,' said Sarah. 'I can see why you two are so close.'

'Thank you for making an effort Sarah,' said Ellie, 'I'm really grateful. It matters to me what Camilla thinks and I know she thought you were great. Come on, let's go to bed, we can finish off tomorrow.'

'OK,' said Sarah. 'I'll just check the fire. Nite nite Boot,' she said, ruffling the top of the dog's head as she secured the catch to the wood burner's door. But Boot wasn't interested. His ears pricked up and he started to bark. He was clearly agitated. He jumped out of his basket and ran to the main door. 'Come on boy,' said Sarah, 'there's nothing out there except the odd fox. Back to bed.'

'What's the matter with Boot?' asked Ellie from upstairs.

'Not sure,' Sarah replied, 'I think he's heard something outside, probably a fox. I'll leave him to it. He'll calm down eventually.' She switched off the lights and went upstairs, leaving Boot sitting by the door, ears straining for any more unexpected sounds.

CHAPTER 27

Richards could hear the dog bark as he moved towards Ellie's Land Rover. He wore a dark balaclava, gloves and black clothes. The day sack on his back and the webbing belt around his waist were also black, designed not to be seen at night. He had a pistol holstered on one leg and a knife on the other. He looked the part but he was out of practise and he cursed himself for not seeing the twig in his path. It broke as he stepped on it and he realised that it was this that had alerted the dog. He stood perfectly still and concentrated on slowing his breathing. If they let the dog out, it would be a matter of seconds before it found him and he'd then have two choices. Either try and make a run for it, hoping that whoever had let the dog out wouldn't see him, or kill the dog and then, as quickly as possible, incapacitate whoever was with the dog before they had the chance to raise the alarm. Neither option was ideal. He'd rather get rid of the girl on ground of his choosing and at a time of his making. Accepting that he might not have that luxury, he moved his hand down to the wicked looking knife that was sheathed in the holster on his thigh. He withdrew it and lowered himself into a crouch, holding the black bladed knife out in front of him.

As he waited to see what would happen, he thought about the discussion he'd had with Highworth the previous night. Highworth had clearly been spooked by his discussion with Knowles and he was now trying to close off as many loose ends as possible. He couldn't understand why the assassin had let the girl live when he'd killed Fairweather. He was convinced that this was a loose end and he'd told Richards to get rid of her. 'Try and make it look like an accident if you can. But if you can't, you can't,' he'd said. 'I just want her dead and out of the way.'

Richards had tried to reason with Highworth, pointing out that if there was any chance of her compromising Fairweather's murder, then the assassin would have killed her without a moment's hesitation. He'd also pointed out that, so far at least, the police seemed to accept that Highworth's death had been a tragic accident. If the girl were also to die, it might raise their suspicions. But Highworth wasn't to be persuaded. 'Just kill her,' Highworth had said. 'It's one less thing to worry about. Let's not forget that if I go down, you'll be coming with me.'

'OK. I'll take care of it,' Richards had said, smiling thinly. He wasn't worried about Highworth's threat. As soon as it looked as though Highworth was going to talk, Richards would find a quick and effective way of silencing him. He had absolutely no intention of letting Highworth implicate him in any of this. He knew that he could get to Highworth and, if necessary, his family wherever the police tried to hide them. But, for the moment at least, it made sense to play along with him. 'Who knows,' Richards thought to himself, 'this might all wash over and we could be back in business within a month or so.' It was worth the risk. Although he had other customers, Highworth was the most reliable and he paid extremely well.

Richards started to relax the moment he saw the downstairs light go off. The dog stopped barking and, within a few minutes, the upstairs lights went off as well. It was obvious that the people inside were going to bed. 'Good,' thought Richards, taking a small black box out of his pack and placing it under the rear bumper of the Land Rover. It was a magnetic tracking device. Richards knew that he would now have little difficulty following the Land Rover. This was a relief as the journey to the farmhouse had been difficult. Once they'd got up onto the moor, there was very little traffic and he'd had to kill his headlights for most of the journey to avoid raising the girl's suspicions that she was being followed. Having seen where they'd stopped, he'd driven past the house and parked up an old farm track about a mile away. He'd then changed into his black combats and walked back, taking a cross country route in order to avoid houses and roads. He'd managed to find a bit of high ground about two hundred metres from the house from which he was able to watch what was happening inside. He had night vision goggles in his pack but the girls had left the curtains wide open and, armed with binoculars and a powerful zoom lens on his camera, he'd been able to watch the evening unfold, taking photographs of the three girls' faces whenever the opportunity arose. He'd sent them through to one of his colleagues to see whether they could identify them from the police records that they had access to. He didn't expect a match but it was always worth checking. It was surprising how many people were recorded in government files. All it took to access them was someone who needed a bit more money than they were being paid by the state.

Satisfied that the house was now quiet for the night and confident that he could track the Land Rover if and when it moved, he retraced his steps back to his car. Once there, he quickly changed into the walking clothes he'd worn on the way from the station and reversed the car onto the road. It was quiet as he turned the car round and headed into Mortonhampstead. It was a small moorland town and he knew that at this time of night people would be curious if he tried to book into one of the few hotels or bed and breakfasts. He therefore decided to push on to Exeter, confident that he would be able to find a travellers' hotel either in the city or near the airport. They'd be used to people coming and going at odd hours and he was keen to remain as forgettable and anonymous as possible.

As he drove off the moor, he thought about the assassin. He was genuinely sad that he'd had to kill him. They'd met at short notice in a pub in Edinburgh on the pretext of a new mission. Once they'd discussed the details of the supposed target, Richards had said his farewells and left the pub. He'd deliberately chosen a quiet pub in an even quieter road. He'd hidden in the shadows outside the main door and, as the assassin followed him out a few minutes later, he'd gone up behind him, put an arm around his neck and stuck the knife into his back. He had been aiming to go between the ribs and into the heart but the assassin, perhaps sensing that something was wrong, had started to turn just as Richards grabbed him and started to push the knife into him. As a result, the knife had missed the heart and entered the gut. Knowing that he'd inflicted enough damage to kill the assassin, Richards lowered his target slowly to the ground before leaving the scene. He'd then gone to the assassin's flat and searched it meticulously. It had taken him most of the night but he was confident that there was nothing hidden that could lead anyone to him. He'd left the flat immaculate, reasoning that if he had ransacked it, the police would be unlikely to accept that the assassin had just been mugged and would start looking for a deeper motive.

CHAPTER 28

Lucy woke early and padded from her bedroom into the kitchen. She made a pot of fresh coffee and turned the TV on. The presenter was describing a train crash in Madrid, suggesting that it might have been the work of terrorists and that there were similarities between it and a train crash in Holland the previous month. 'It's all doom and gloom,' thought Lucy, pouring a second cup of coffee to take to Isobel. 'A single incident like a train crash or a mugging ruins so many peoples' lives so quickly. It's not just the dead,' she thought, 'it's the families left behind that have to pick up the pieces.' She could feel tears welling up in her eyes as she thought of her father. 'Whoever you are and wherever you are, I'll get you you bastard,' she said to herself, thinking of her father's mugger. She picked up the coffee she'd made for Isobel and walked down the hall towards Isobel's room.

'Hi,' said Isobel, coming out of her room and nearly knocking the cup of coffee out of Lucy's hand. 'Got to pee,' she said as she rushed into the bathroom. She left the door open so that she could continue chatting to her friend. 'How did you sleep?' she asked, noting how red her friend's eyes were.

'OK actually,' replied Lucy. 'I think the shock and the journey from Nepal have taken it out of me. I only got up because I want to start trying to work out what happened to Dad.'

'I don't blame you, where do you want to start?' asked Isobel, flushing the toilet and washing her hands. She was worried about her friend but had decided that the best way to help her was to try and be as up-beat as possible. If Lucy wanted to focus her anger on trying to find her Dad's killer then that was fine by her. She didn't for a minute think that Lucy would be any more successful than the police but, if it helped, she was happy to humour her and support her as best she could.

'I think we should go to the solicitors first. I want to know why Dad went to see them earlier in the week. Perhaps he told them something.'

'Good plan. Is that for me?' asked Isobel, looking at the coffee in Lucy's hand.

'Yes, I thought you'd like some.'

'Thank you Luce,' said Isobel. 'You're a star, you know that don't you?'

'Yes, so you tell me!' replied Lucy. Isobel was a nightmare until she'd had her first coffee of the day and Lucy was prepared to do whatever it took to make the day as easy as possible.

'As soon as it's nine, I'll phone the solicitors and see if we can get an appointment for this morning,' said Lucy. 'Come and have some breakfast. There's some bread and cereals but not much else I'm afraid.'

Isobel followed her friend into the kitchen, plonking herself down on a chair in front of the TV whilst Lucy put a few slices of bread in the toaster. After breakfast, the girls showered and changed. Lucy phoned the solicitors and got through to a charming and very understanding man who agreed to see them mid morning. She then phoned Kate and arranged to ring her again after they'd seen the solicitor. The last thing she did before leaving the house was to send an e-mail to Harry explaining what had happened. She explained why she'd left Nepal so quickly – it seemed like months ago, not a few days – and asked him for his phone number so she could phone him in a few days once she'd sorted out the funeral and worked out what to do next. She hadn't forgotten about Harry. She was still keen to see him again but, for the moment, he would have to wait.

They arrived at the address the solicitor had given them a few hours later. It was in the Old Town, just off the Royal Mile, in a beautiful old Victorian red brick building. The brass plaque on the wall next to the main door confirmed that they were at the offices of McLeod, McLeod and McKnight.

'Very smart,' said Isobel, admiring the highly polished brass door fittings. 'The more I see of your Dad's world, the more I realise what a stylish man he was. What happened to you? Perhaps the style gene skipped a generation.'

'Ho ho,' replied Lucy. 'Sometimes I forget just how unfunny you are.' Isobel smiled to herself. She decided to try and be as normal as possible and was pleased that her friend was getting at least some of her old bounce back.

Lucy went up the steps to the door and pushed it open. It led into a hallway which served as a reception.

'Miss Masters?' asked a middle aged lady from behind an old mahogany desk. Lucy nodded. The lady stood up and walked round the desk towards Lucy and Isobel. 'My name is Sheila Jones, I'm Mr McLeod's secretary. If you take a seat, I'll tell him you're here.' She pointed at an old chesterfield sofa in an alcove. 'Please help yourself to the coffee and tea on the table.'

'Thank you,' replied Lucy, walking over towards the table and pouring two coffees. She handed one to Isobel and sat on the sofa next to her friend. Five minutes later, a smartly dressed man in his mid to late fifties came over to them.

'Miss Masters?' he asked. Lucy nodded.

'I'm Murdo McLeod,' said the man. 'I was your father's solicitor. I'm so sorry to hear about his tragic death, please accept my sincere condolences.' He shook Lucy's hand before turning to face Isobel.

'Thank you,' said Lucy, introducing Isobel and asking that she be allowed to remain with her throughout their discussion. McLeod agreed. Isobel noticed his voice. It was deep and measured, with a soft Scottish lilt. He reminded Isobel of her father. Well groomed, his shoes were highly polished and the trousers of his three piece tweed suit had razor sharp creases down their fronts.

'Please come into my office,' McLeod said, leading the way past the reception desk and towards the back of the building. The girls followed, noticing the smell of wood polish and the large framed pictures of austere looking lawyers in robes and wigs on the walls.

McLeod's office was big and well furnished. A partner's desk with a green leather top stood in one corner. An informal seating area was arranged beneath a bow window with a sofa and two easy chairs positioned around a coffee table. 'Please sit down,' said McLeod, indicating the sofa with his outstretched hand.

Once they were all seated, McLeod picked up a leather folder from the table. 'Tell me, Miss Masters, how much did you know about your father's affairs?' he asked.

'Not much I'm afraid, he wasn't very forthcoming about his personal affairs, even with me,' replied Lucy.

'No, I suspect he wasn't.' McLeod paused, taking a sip of water before he continued. 'I was an Army lawyer before I became a family solicitor and I served with your father a number of times over the years. I suppose I've known him a long time, about twenty years actually, and I reckon I knew him as well as any man. Anyway,' said McLeod, 'he recently added some additional details to his will and earlier this week he gave me a sealed envelope to give to you should anything happen to him.'

'Why do you think he did that?' asked Lucy.

'I've been thinking about that myself in view of what's happened,' replied McLeod. 'He said he was just tidying up some loose ends because he was going away for a while but, to be honest, he seemed a little distracted. I asked him if everything was OK but, as you suggested, he kept his affairs very much to himself. He said he was fine, just doing a bit of what the Army calls "personal admin". I'll give you the letter in a minute but let's start with the will.'

'OK,' said Lucy.

'It'll have to go through "confirmation", rather like probate in England, before we can release anything but I can give you an outline of what's in it now. I probably shouldn't but I know how much you meant to your father and, given the circumstances, I'm sure it's what he would have wanted. You are the major beneficiary. As there aren't any other siblings, I presume you're happy if I give you a quick summary of what's in the will?' he asked, looking over the top of his glasses.

'Yes, thank you,' replied Lucy. 'Anything that can shed some light on what happened to him would be helpful.'

'You don't think it was a straightforward mugging?' McLeod enquired carefully.

'No, I don't,' said Lucy. 'It's too much of a coincidence. He sorts his affairs out and a few days later he's killed. Also, my father may have been as tough as old boots and an obstinate old bugger but he was very careful to avoid trouble. He would walk away from it whenever he could and I just can't accept that he would get himself into a position where a mugger could get the better of him. And the other thing is that the doctor at the hospital said that it looked like it was done by someone who knew what they were doing. He didn't say it exactly but he gave the impression that the injuries weren't those you'd expect to see from a casual mugging. There may be nothing in it but I need to check it out, even if I end up wasting my time.'

'OK Miss Masters, I think I understand. Let's start at the beginning.' McLeod paused, taking another sip of water and opening the folder. 'Your father was a wealthy man,' said McLeod, looking Lucy in the eye. 'Far wealthier than you would expect a retired Army officer to be, particularly one on a modest Major's pension. The banks will have to confirm the exact state of his accounts but he was worth more than three million pounds, at least he was last year when we re-wrote his will. His art collection alone is worth about seven hundred thousand pounds, probably more if you include the pictures on loan to some of the galleries in town. In addition to his George Street flat – on which there is no mortgage – he also had a few offshore accounts. I presume the details of those are in the sealed envelope

I mentioned. As I suspect the taxman doesn't know anything about these, it's probably best that you keep the details to yourself. I only know they might exist because he asked my advice a few years ago, as a friend rather than as a solicitor, and I assume he acted on it.'

'Goodness me,' said Lucy, not sure what else to say. She was completely shocked. Her father had always been very careful with his money. He'd never discussed his financial affairs with her but she had assumed that the flat was rented and that he was doing a bit of security on the side to supplement his pension. He gave no indication of having a great deal of money. Notwithstanding the packaging from Sotherby's that she'd found at the flat, she'd always assumed that the paintings he collected had been bought at local antique shops. 'I'd never have guessed. Other than his paintings, which I didn't realise were so valuable, he didn't live the high life.'

'No,' said McLeod. He stared at Lucy for a few minutes, lost in thought as if weighing up whether or not to explain something to her. He took a brown envelope out of the folder and held it in his hand. 'Miss Masters, although your father didn't share the detail with me, I have an idea of what might be in this letter. He gave me strict instructions that you were to read it here, make whatever notes you wanted, and then you were to destroy it in my presence before you left these offices. I will hold you to that. But I will also try and add whatever detail you want after you've read it. But be warned, your father was an unusual man and I have a very strong suspicion that the letter will shock you.' He paused and took another sip of water.

'Go on,' prompted Lucy.

'Your father was a sniper in the Army you know. I presume you know what that means?' he asked, his voice low and serious.

'Yes,' replied Lucy in an equally low voice, not sure where this was going. 'I think it means he killed people.'

'It does. And he was very good indeed at his job, probably the best of his generation. I came across him in Bosnia when I was the legal advisor in the headquarters. Most of my job involved interpreting the rules of engagement that our forces operated under. Essentially, I had to work out when and how our troops could engage the enemy. What I mean by that is that it was my responsibility to tell our troops when they could and couldn't open fire. It was very tightly controlled as you can imagine. Abiding by the rules was of huge importance in order to maintain the legitimacy of the NATO mission. I came across your father again in Iraq and again in the early stages of Afghanistan, just before I left the Army. What he did whilst in the Army was entirely legal and was fully supported by his chain of command. Indeed, and as I'm sure you're aware, he got an MBE for his services in Afghanistan. But I have a suspicion that when he left the Army, he continued doing what he did so well, only this time for money rather than for the government. I'm only telling you this because I don't want you to be shocked by whatever you read in the letter. And of course I might be wrong.'

'I'm not sure I understand what you mean Mr McLeod,' said Lucy in a faltering voice. She reached for Isobel's hand, squeezing it tight until Isobel protested.

'There's no easy way of explaining this Miss Parker,' replied McLeod, 'but I'm pretty sure that when he retired your father became what the old westerns used to call "a hired gun".'

'I knew he did security but are you saying that he became a mercenary? I know that some of his friends from the Paras did that.'

'No, I don't think you'd call him a mercenary. I'm sorry to use the movies to explain what I mean but, in today's cinema vernacular, I suspect he'd be called a hitman or an assassin.'

'An assassin!' exclaimed Lucy, visibly shocked. Isobel screeched as Lucy squeezed her hand even tighter.

'Sorry,' said Lucy, letting go of her friend. 'You think my father was some sort of hitman?'

'Yes, that's about the size of it,' replied McLeod, handing Lucy the letter. 'I'll leave you to read this and then, once you're done, I'll try and answer any questions you might have.'

'Thank you,' said Lucy, her hands shaking as she started to open the letter.

'You might want this,' said McLeod, handing Isobel a legal pad and a couple of pencils. He then left the office, closing the door quietly behind him.

'Fuck me Luce,' said Isobel. 'This isn't quite what I expected.'

'Nor me,' said Lucy, taking several thick pieces of paper out of the envelope and unfolding them slowly. She started to read as Isobel poured them both a glass of water from the jug on the table. Isobel watched her friend's face for her reaction but Lucy remained unemotional.

After ten minutes, Lucy put the letter down. Though she was dying to know what the letter said, Isobel waited for her friend to speak.

'McLeod was right,' said Lucy, her voice full of emotion. 'It's all here. The names of the people he's killed, the amount he was paid for each job and the numbers of the bank accounts in which he's deposited all the money, along with the passwords and codes necessary to get it released. I can't believe it. I can't believe my Dad would do such a thing.'

'I'm sure he had his reasons,' said Isobel. 'He was a good bloke, not some thug.'

'He asks me not to judge him but to accept his word that the people he killed were bad people who deserved to die. People who were beyond the law; people, he says in the letter, like the boy who killed my mother.'

'There you go,' said Isobel, struggling to think what else to say. Isobel remembered Lucy telling her that the boy who had driven the car into her mother had been killed in some sort of tragic accident shortly after he'd been released from prison. Isobel couldn't remember all the facts but she remembered that he'd apparently fallen to his death from the Firth of Forth Bridge after a dare went wrong. She didn't want to ask whether Lucy's father had admitted to killing him in the letter.

Lucy took a deep breath and continued. 'He says he was concerned that something might happen to him. He had a bad feeling, he says. His regular contact was apparently a man called Richards. The chap had asked to meet him but something in Richards's voice had alerted him. He says he couldn't put his finger on it but his sixth sense was tingling and, as it had saved his life so many times in the past, he was taking precautions. He says that if I'm reading this letter, then he's dead and that if his death was violent, it was probably caused by Richards. Oh Isobel, what am I going to do? He says that Richards is extremely dangerous and that we shouldn't go looking for him. The only reason he says he's explaining all this is that he thinks there's a slight chance that Richards might come after me because he might think that I know all about what he's been up to. He wants me to take the money, which he says is about three and a half million pounds in his UK bank accounts plus quite a lot more in offshore ones, and go and hide out abroad for a few years until things calm down. He says I can trust McLeod one hundred percent but that on no account should I go to the police.' Lucy stared at her friend, her eyes welling up.

'I suppose that makes sense,' replied Isobel. 'If he's spent the last ten years trotting round the globe killing people, I don't suppose the police would be very sympathetic.' She saw her friend wince as she spoke. 'I'm sorry Lucy. That was insensitive of me.'

'That's all right. I know what you mean about the police,' said Lucy.

'Don't worry Luce, we'll sort it out.' Isobel tried to sound reassuring but she had no idea what to do. Indeed, she was already starting to feel scared that someone might have followed them to the solicitors. 'First things first Luce, let's do what your Dad wanted and write the details of the offshore bank accounts down. At least then you'll have the money to leave the country if it starts getting hairy.'

Lucy forced herself to calm down, taking deep breaths until her heartbeat returned to normal and she stopped crying. 'You're right

Isobel, I need to get a grip of myself for my Dad's sake. I'll read the numbers out, you write them down. My hands are still so shaky that I don't think I could write straight at the moment.'

Five minutes later they'd copied down all the information they needed from the letter. Isobel went to get McLeod. He returned, looking sombre. 'Everything OK?' he asked.

'Yes, I think so,' replied Lucy. 'You were right about how he made his money. Thank you for warning me. It's quite a shock.'

'Yes, I imagine it is. Are there any questions you want me to try and answer?' asked McLeod.

'Thank you but no, not at the moment. I need to think about what's in the letter but, if I may, could I come and see you again in a few days time if I need to?' asked Lucy.

'Yes, of course you may,' replied McLeod. 'As soon as the police and the sheriff's office have confirmed the cause of your father's death, we should be able to get on with implementing his last wishes. It shouldn't take more than a week or so as his will was all correct and in order. Again, I probably shouldn't tell you this yet but he left about half a million to a Miss Catherine Newton. I don't know whether you know her?'

'Kate? Yes, I do. She was a close friend of my father's. I think she was his girlfriend, though it sounds odd describing a fifty-year-old as a girlfriend.'

'You can give her an idea of what's in the will but, as I said, it won't be confirmed until after confirmation. We'll then invite you and her for the formal reading of the will. In the meantime, if you need an advance or anything to help cover the costs of your father's funeral, do let me know as we can certainly arrange something.'

'Thank you,' said Lucy standing up. 'What do you want me to do with the letter?' she asked.

He handed her a lighter. 'If you would be good enough to hold it over the bin near the desk and set fire to it, I'd be very grateful. If your father had wanted me to see it, he'd have shown it to me.'

Lucy did as she was asked, dropping the last few charred bits of the letter into the bin and watching as they curled up and turned to ash. She then gave McLeod her mobile phone number and, shaking his hand as she left the office, she went out into the street with Isobel.

'What now?' asked Isobel.

'A drink. I need a drink. It's not every day you find out that your Dad was a hitman and that he's left you several millions in order that you can escape from some psychopathic murderer who's probably, even as we speak, trying to work out how to kill us.'

Isobel laughed in spite of the circumstances, grateful for the release. The tough old Lucy that she knew of old was returning.

CHAPTER 29

Camilla woke up to the sound of Radio Four's *Today* programme. It was a bit distant but she could make out Sarah Montague, the presenter, giving some senior intelligence analyst a hard time about the west's inability to predict terrorist atrocities. Her door was open and the sound was coming from downstairs. She looked at the alarm clock on the bedside table and noticed the cup of tea. She hadn't heard anyone come into the room but the tea was hot and had obviously only been there for a few minutes. She sat up in bed and took a long drink. Hot and sweet, exactly as she liked it.

Sarah appeared in the doorway. She was dressed in her jeans and looked as though she'd been up for hours.

'Good morning, how did you sleep?' she asked.

'Well, thank you,' replied Camilla. 'Thank you for the tea.'

'You're welcome,' said Sarah. 'There's no rush but I've made you a bacon sandwich if you'd like one. I can bring it up here if you want.'

'Thank you,' replied Camilla, 'I'll come downstairs. Just give me a minute.'

Sarah smiled and went downstairs. Camilla could hear her talking to the dog as she went past its basket. It barked excitedly as Sarah opened the outside door, letting the dog into the garden. Camilla got out of bed and put her dressing gown on over her t-shirt and pull ups. There was a mirror on the wall and she caught a quick glimpse of her face. Much better than last night, she thought to herself, the bags under her eyes were going and her skin looked less puffy. She went in to the bathroom, used the toilet and then splashed water on her face. 'That's better,' she thought to herself. She picked up her cup of tea and went downstairs. Sarah was just putting a bacon sandwich on the kitchen table.

'There you go,' said Sarah. 'There's more if you want it. I'm afraid you're stuck with me for a few hours. Ellie's gone into Morton to get the papers and to talk to some bloke about a trailer he's selling. She'll be back for lunch. We thought we'd go to the pub. I don't know when you were last here but the food's good and it'll get us out of the house.'

'Sounds great,' replied Camilla. 'I could do with a bit of fresh air. Thank you for the sandwich,' she said, taking a mouthful. It was good. The bacon was thick and the bread tasted as though it was home made. They chatted amicably whilst Camilla ate her sandwich and drank her tea. Sarah was a real gem, thought Camilla. 'I'm not keeping you from work am I?' asked Camilla.

'Not at all,' replied Sarah. 'One of the benefits of being a teacher is the holidays. We broke up for half term last Friday and Ellie and I have both got two weeks off. So you're not keeping us from anything at all, except watching day time TV and arguing about whose turn it is to walk the dog.'

Camilla laughed. 'You're not going away?' she asked.

'No,' replied Sarah. 'We've got workmen coming in next week to plaster the third bedroom and start work on the old stable block. We're turning it into a studio for Ellie. Her work's starting to sell and we're running out of space for all her stuff. She's been painting in the kitchen but it's not ideal. Boot keeps chewing tubes of paint and he peed on one of Ellie's canvasses last week so we've borrowed some more money and decided to get on with the studio. I'll show you if you like when you're dressed, it's really exciting.' Her enthusiasm was infectious and Camilla couldn't help thinking how lucky she and Ellie were to have found each other.

'OK,' she said. 'Thanks for breakfast. I'll go and get dressed.' With that, she put her dishes in the sink and went upstairs. Ellie and Sarah were so welcoming and such easygoing company that her worries were starting to fade. She felt a thousand times more secure than she had in London. It had been a good idea of Harry's to spend a few days with Ellie on Dartmoor. She decided that she'd phone him in the evening to put his mind at ease.

Camilla dressed quickly and then went downstairs. Sarah was waiting by the door with Boot. Together, they went outside and walked to the old stable block that they were converting into a studio. Sarah explained the plan. It was ambitious, thought Camilla, but it would be worth the effort. If Ellie's paintings were starting to sell as well as Sarah had suggested, then the sooner she had a decent studio, the better. Buyers are very quick to find a 'new' artist if they can't get what they want, when they want it. Or that was her experience at least.

CHAPTER 30

Harry got back from town and went into his study to check his e-mail. He'd hoped to hear from Lucy the previous day but although he'd received lots of e-mails about potential jobs, there were none from her. He was due to leave for Everest the following morning and he was starting to get a bit concerned. He didn't really want to begin his trek until he knew when he had to be back otherwise he risked missing Lucy completely. He switched on his laptop and went into the kitchen to make a cup of coffee whilst the computer booted up. He was a coffee aficionado. He took a handful of beans and put them in the hopper at the top of the electric grinder. He loved the smell that the beans gave off as the grinder did its work. He scooped the ground coffee into the metal filter and attached it to the Gaggia. Camilla had bought it for him as a birthday present. It had been expensive but it made superb coffee and it was well worth the money. Hissing and wheezing, it forced boiling water through the compacted coffee grinds to produce a slow stream of steaming brown liquid. Eventually it stopped and he added a spoonful of brown sugar, picked up the cup and headed back to his office, sipping the coffee as he went.

He sat at his desk and clicked on to his e-mail. There was a fair bit of rubbish but he spotted the e-mail from Lucy almost straight away. He opened it and read it quickly. It explained that she had had to leave Nepal urgently because of what had happened to her father and that he had died before she'd managed to get to the hospital. It was short and to the point but it also said that she wanted to see him again. Once things calmed down, she said that she'd try and get back to Nepal before he started his next assignment, whenever that might be.

Harry sat back in his chair and took a long drink of his coffee. 'Bugger me,' he said aloud, opening one of the desk drawers and fumbling for the pack of cigarettes and the lighter that he knew were there. He found the packet of Camels, took one of the cigarettes out and lit it. He inhaled deeply. He'd tried to give up but sometimes, particularly when he was under real pressure or deeply disappointed, it helped him relax. 'Of all the bad luck,' he thought to himself, 'poor Lucy.' He started to type a response, telling her that he was sorry for her loss and that he would miss her but that he would be in Kathmandu for several months yet if she wanted to come back out when things were calmer. He re-read his draft several times before he sent it. Whilst he was disappointed, he wanted to remain up-beat for Lucy's sake, though, if he were honest with himself, he actually wanted to fly to the UK immediately, take Lucy in his arms and tell her that everything would be all right. But he suspected that it was too early in their relationship for this. He didn't want to frighten her off. He thought about this for several minutes. In every relationship, he thought, someone has to make the first move towards real commitment even though, in doing it, they risked rejection. He'd thought he would be happy to make the first move, perhaps when Lucy was back in Kathmandu, but he wasn't so sure now. Dejected, he went to the bathroom to run a bath. He hoped that Lucy would reply quickly and that her reply would give him an idea of when he might see her again.

CHAPTER 31

Sir James Briggs had spent a difficult twenty-four hours. He'd slept badly and had got up early to put Princess out for a pee and to re-read the file that Knowles had given him. There was no doubt in his mind that the evidence was compelling. There was also no doubt that there was a real opportunity here. He reached for the phone and searched for a number that he had never had cause to use before. It was answered almost immediately.

'It's Jim Briggs, from the City of London Police. We need to meet as a matter of some urgency.'

He agreed a time and place that evening and hung up.

CHAPTER 32

Lunch at the Ring O'Bells had been excellent. Camilla and Ellie had had the steak sandwich whilst Sarah had tried the Caesar Salad. They'd shared a bottle of very decent Pinot Grigio and were now digging into sticky toffee pudding. Camilla was struck by how many people had come over and said hello to the girls. 'Is it always so friendly?' asked Camilla.

'Most of the time,' replied Sarah. 'It's sometimes a bit less so at the weekends, particularly in the summer when it's full of tourists or the weekend crowd from London.'

'They like us because we live here all year round,' added Ellie. 'We pop in about twice a week and that seems to be enough to convince the regulars that we're serious about being part of the community, that and the fact that Sarah has started playing the piano for the local amateur dramatics group. That's made us, or rather Sarah, very popular recently.'

Camilla laughed. 'Really?' she enquired.

'Really,' said Ellie. 'It started one evening in here actually. I'd popped in to get a few packets of crisps and I overheard the chap who runs the 'am dram' group bemoaning the fact that his regular pianist, an elderly lady called Margo, had decided to leave the village to be near her grandchildren in Topsham. It's not far from Exeter but it's too far from here for her to drive up every week.'

'What happened next?' asked Camilla, enjoying the story.

Sarah took over the narrative. 'Ever the helpful villager, your friend Ellie kindly suggested that she had a friend, me of course, who might be interested in helping out until they found a more permanent solution.'

'You could have said no,' said Ellie, laughing almost uncontrollably.

'Yes, but it would have been difficult as you well know given the 'am dram' group leader is a local publisher who also happens to be chairman of the governors at my school.'

Ellie was crying with laughter. She hadn't really meant to drop her friend in it. She realised that she should have discussed it with Sarah before she volunteered her services but, to her great credit, Sarah had taken it all in her stride and had duly paraded at the village hall for her first rehearsal. To her surprise, she'd enjoyed it hugely. The group was an interesting mixture of professionals, housewives, students, schoolchildren and workers from the local farms. They were very friendly and actually quite good. They were doing Gilbert and Sullivan's *Pirates of Penzance*. As well as being one of Sarah's favourite comic operas, she knew the music well as she'd been in a production whilst at university.

'It's actually really good fun,' said Sarah. 'As Ellie said, it's also been a really useful way to get to know the community. I suppose we were a bit worried when we started living together that people might disapprove of us. But if they do, they keep it to themselves.'

'That's true,' added Ellie. 'But I suspect it also helps that we're discrete. We don't sit here mooning over each other, for example.'

Camilla laughed. Having found Sarah, Ellie seemed much more at ease with her sexuality. She'd never been embarrassed about the fact that she was gay but she'd never advertised it either, preferring not to talk about it. It was good to see her being much more open.

After lunch, they went back to the house for coffee. There were no real plans for the afternoon but Ellie and Camilla were keen to clear rubbish from the stable block before the workmen started the following day. Ellie said that Camilla could borrow the Land Rover if she wanted to go and walk up Hay Tor. 'Take Boot,' she suggested. 'It'll do him the world of good to get some fresh air and you might enjoy the company.' The dog's ears pricked up at the mention of his name and his tail started to wag as Ellie threw his lead at Camilla.

'Thanks Ellie, what a good idea.' She went upstairs to change into jeans and walking boots. She'd also brought her old Barbour and a woolly hat with her as she'd been caught out on the moor before and she had no intention of being wet and cold, even though the weather looked like it might hold. Ellie gave her the Land Rover's keys as she came downstairs. 'I won't be long,' she said to Ellie. 'I just want to walk to the top and look at the view. I might take a few pictures if the weather holds but I'm doing nudes at the moment, not landscapes, so don't worry!'

Ellie smiled. Their painting styles were so different that they had never really been in competition with each other, even when they were at college together. 'But what if I starting doing nudes?' asked Ellie.

'You won't,' replied Camilla. 'You did one at college if you remember and it ended up looking like the elephant man. Just remind me what the teacher said to you?'

'Fuck off Camilla,' replied Ellie, throwing a tea towel at her. 'He was half blind and didn't know his arse from his elbow.' In truth, Ellie had been experimenting with pop art and had tried to complete the picture using only dots of paint, like Roy Lichenstein had done in his famous picture of a pilot pulling the triggers of his machine guns. It wasn't a success and her teacher, a traditionalist who despised modern art, had been extremely critical, calling her a 'talentless idiot.' That her talent was so obvious in everything else she did seemed to escape him.

Camilla and Boot got into the Land Rover and started down the hill towards the old stone bridge that led up towards the moor. It was drizzling slightly, enough to need the wipers every few minutes to clear the windscreen. The road was narrow and she had to keep pulling in to let traffic coming in the opposite direction get past her. She was content. She loved the moors with a passion. It was such a contrast to London and her normal life that the two places might have been on different planets. It also reminded her of her parents. Both now dead, she'd spent many happy weeks with them on Dartmoor during the school holidays, paddling in the rivers and walking over the hills. The road climbed its way onto the top of the moors and she pulled in to admire the view. To her left was Hound Tor, a loose collection of rocks and boulders on top of a small hill that provided an ideal proving ground for young climbers. There were usually one or two groups from local youth clubs or outdoor schools putting up ropes and practising their techniques before venturing onto the more challenging peaks. In the distance she could see Hay Tor. It was an unusual peak and from some angles looked like a giant version of the sort of ramp that water skiers would use to do jumps. A gentle slope led up from the car park to a sheer face which dropped about a hundred feet to the ground below. The face was a climbers' paradise. Its smoothness made it technically difficult but the easy approach on the reverse side meant that putting a rope on the top and then lowering it down the face was a straightforward business. She could see one or two pairs of climbers from the road. Their bright clothing stood out against the dark grey of the rock face. She'd tried climbing in her teens on a summer adventure camp when she was at school but she didn't really like it. She preferred walking to dangling on the end of a rope several hundred feet up a mountain.

The roads were still reasonably quiet as she turned into the Hay Tor car park. There were twenty or so other cars, most of which were parked near the information kiosk and toilets at the bottom end. She was a bit worried about Boot getting run over if he got loose so she drove to the far corner, away from the kiosk. She ruffled the dog's head as the Land Rover came to a stop. 'This could be the beginning of a beautiful relationship,' she said to the dog. 'But you've got to behave yourself if you want to do this again.' She attached the lead to his collar and then got out of the car. As she walked round to open the passenger door to let Boot out, she saw another car pull into the car park and head towards the kiosk. Camilla put on her Barbour jacket, pulled her woolly hat down over her ears and opened the door to let the dog out of the car. It jumped down onto the grass and started to yap excitedly, wagging its tail and running round Camilla's legs. It took her a few minutes to untangle herself from the lead but once she started walking towards the hill, it started to calm down. The rain was getting heavier and a wind had started to blow across the hill. The weather was starting to close in and there were far more people coming down the hill than going up. She inhaled deeply, enjoying the feel of the rain on her face and the freshness of the air. She felt alive and glad to be out in the elements.

When she was halfway up, she turned round to admire the view. She could see the Land Rover in the car park below her but not much more. The weather was closing in and she realised that she'd have to hurry to get to the top if she wanted to be able to see anything when she got there. There was a single walker about two hundred feet away from her, also going up the hill. She couldn't see his features as he had his hood up and his head down to keep the rain off his face. 'At least I'm not the only idiot going up rather than down in this weather,' she thought to herself, nodding to a couple who walked past her on their way down to the car park. She started back up the hill. Boot continued to strain on the lead. He was clearly enjoying being outside and in a new place with lots of interesting smells. His head was lowered and moved from side to side as he sniffed the grass. She increased her pace, stepping out to get to the top as quickly as possible. Eventually, the grassy slope ended and the rock began. The first part was a gentle scramble but she wanted to get right to the top and this involved using some old steps that had been cut into the rock years ago. She'd read somewhere that this had been done in the nineteenth century by a local stonemason called Alan Yabsley. She remembered the surname because it was so unusual. A metal handrail had also been added to allow the less energetic to enjoy the spectacular views that the summit provided, at least on a clear day. The handrail was long gone and the worn steps were now wet and slippery. But her boots had non-slip vibram soles and, provided she was careful, she was able to continue climbing up. She needed to use her hands occasionally to steady herself and, reasoning that it would be safer for both her and Boot if she let him off the lead, she stopped in the lee of a large boulder to unfasten him. As she turned round to unclip the lead, she noticed that the person she'd seen before was now at the foot of the rock and just about to start ascending the steps. She was pleased that she wasn't alone as the weather was deteriorating and it was beginning to feel increasingly desolate up on the peak. She knew that the Dartmoor weather was deceptively dangerous and that it could change in an instant. She'd read the *Hound of the Baskervilles* on her first visit and not quite believed Conan-Doyle's description of the thick mist which he'd observed could blanket the moor within a matter of minutes. Her scepticism had been dispelled on a subsequent visit when she'd found herself isolated from a group of friends having gone off to find a bit of privacy for an emergency pee.

'Not far now,' she said to Boot, patting him on the rump as she unclipped his lead.

Freed at last, Boot shot off ahead, leaving Camilla to climb up after him. Eventually, she arrived at the top. There was a large flat slab of rock on which three or four people could stand. At one end was a large boulder which was wedged in place by five or six smaller ones. Through the drizzle, Camilla could see that a short length of climbing rope had been looped round the boulder. Another rope, which disappeared over the cliff edge, was attached to the loop by a metal karabiner. Camilla edged as close as she dared to the cliff edge to see if she could see the climbers. If she leaned over, she could just see the top of a helmet about twenty feet or so below her. She heard Boot barking but as she started to turn to see what he was barking at, she felt a tremendous push in the small of her back. She screamed as she started to fall over the edge of the cliff. Everything seemed to slow down. One minute she was on the rock slab and the next she was falling. Her body continued to turn as it fell over the edge and she saw the man who had pushed her. It was the same man who had followed her up the hill. He had his hood up but she could see his features clearly. He had brown eyes and unremarkable features. He just looked like an ordinary middle aged man. His eyes held hers. They were the hardest eyes she had ever seen. No compassion at all. And then she was gone, falling through the air with her arms flailing.

CHAPTER 33

Ellie was in the kitchen cooking supper when the phone rang. It was getting dark and she assumed it was Camilla phoning to tell her when she'd be home. She picked up the phone. A male voice asked her to confirm her name and then said that he was from the police. There had been an accident on Hay Tor involving somebody who might have been driving her Land Rover. Ellie's heart almost stopped. 'Yes,' she said, 'I lent it to a friend. Is she all right?' Ellie asked.

'She's in Exeter hospital and she's unconscious but I understand she's stable,' replied the policeman.

'What happened?' asked Ellie, sitting down at the kitchen table and reaching for a pen and paper.

'It seems she might have lost her footing. She was apparently at the top of the Tor when she slipped and fell over the edge. The weather won't have helped. The rain's been getting heavier all afternoon and, what with the wind, the top will have been treacherous. Luckily for her, there were some climbers on the face checking that the rock was stable for a climbing course they're running at the weekend. She fell on one of them, which slowed her fall, but the chap couldn't hold her and she fell the rest of the way to the ground. If the ground hadn't been so wet from all the rain we've had, I suspect it would have been much worse.'

'So she's alive?' asked Ellie.

'Yes, but she has a broken leg, a dislocated shoulder and, as I said earlier, she's unconscious. We got her name from the credit cards in her wallet but we're trying to chase up her next of kin. You don't have an address or a phone number for them do you?'

'No I don't. Her parents are both dead. I think she has a brother but they don't see each other and I certainly don't have his details. I think I might be the closest thing she has to a next of kin, certainly in this country. She's staying with me at the moment. How did you get my number?'

'From the Vehicle Licensing Agency,' replied the policeman. 'We checked the registration of the Land Rover against their database and it gave us your details.'

Ellie asked a few more questions to confirm which hospital Camilla was in and which ward she was on. Just as she was about to put the phone down, she remembered why Camilla had come down to Dartmoor in the first place.

'One more thing Constable,' she said, 'it may be nothing but my friend came to stay with me because she thought she was being followed. Whilst she was staying with a friend of hers in London, he had a tragic accident and died. Ever since then she's felt as though someone has been watching her. If what she's saying is true – and I've no reason to doubt her – then this might not have been an accident. Someone might have pushed her.'

The policeman listened. Ellie could tell by his lack of response that he wasn't convinced. No doubt he felt that she was just another idiot tourist. It happened every year. Ill-equipped people getting themselves into trouble because they failed to appreciate just how quickly the weather on Dartmoor can change.

'I can tell by your silence that you don't believe me but please at least think about it. My friend knew Hay Tor well. She's been up it hundreds of times and in all weathers. I don't think she'd have just fallen off. Were there any witnesses?' asked Ellie.

'No,' replied the policeman. 'The climbers were about halfway down the face and didn't see anything until your friend quite literally landed in their laps. Nobody saw anything from the car park because the visibility was so bad. Except for the climbers, it seems that your friend was the only person on the Tor.'

'But please check with the London police about her being followed. I'm sure they knew,' pleaded Ellie.

The policeman said that he would. He also said that they'd found a dog that appeared to be with Camilla and that they had collected the Land Rover from the car park as the keys had been in her pockets when she fell. They offered to drop both off at Ellie's house to save her collecting them.

Ellie thanked them and went to find Sarah. She had an uneasy feeling about this and she wanted Sarah to give her a lift to the hospital. The sooner she was with Camilla, the happier she'd be. She also thought that she'd track Harry down and ask his advice. She knew that he and Camilla were no longer together but Harry was tough, capable and no doubt still cared for Camilla. If anyone could help her work out what to do, she knew it would be Harry.

CHAPTER 34

Sir James Briggs went down the steps and into the bar. It was doing a brisk trade. People were queuing to get served and most of the tables were full. He looked around him. He hadn't been here before but it looked familiar. He never really understood why pub chains decorated all their premises the same. He supposed it made economic sense but it meant that once you'd seen one of their pubs, you'd seen them all. He saw Highworth at the far end of the room. He was sitting in an alcove, reading a paper and sipping a glass of red wine. He looked out of place. They'd agreed to meet where nobody would recognise them but, ever the policeman, Briggs couldn't help but notice that they were ten or fifteen years older than the majority of the clientele and that, dressed in a suit, Highworth definitely stood out. Judging by the accents he could hear around him, Briggs reckoned that the pub was almost entirely full of Australians and New Zealanders. And, judging by the size of them, most of them, including the women, played rugby.

He eventually fought his way to the bar and ordered a pint of lager. Two minutes later, he made his way over to Highworth.

'Charles,' he said, sliding into the seat opposite Highworth. 'Thank you for meeting me. I have something that may be of interest to you.'

Highworth looked at Briggs. He knew him by reputation and had met him a couple of times at city functions but they weren't friends. He also didn't trust him. He was known as 'Straight Jim' and Highworth wouldn't be surprised if he was wearing a wire to record the conversation.

'What do you want?' asked Highworth, getting straight to the point.

'A friend of mine has given me a file which links you pretty firmly to a fair number of very serious crimes. I believe there is enough there to put you away for a very long time. But I'm a reasonable man, close to retirement, and I think we might be able to do a deal.'

'What sort of deal?' asked Highworth, eying Briggs closely.

Briggs handed a thin file across the table. 'Have a look at that first,' he said. 'It'll give you an idea of the sort of thing I'm talking about.'

Highworth opened the file and took out three or four sheets of closely typed paper. He started to read. 'Where did you get these?' he asked when he'd finished. He tried not to show it but he was unnerved. The notes gave a very succinct summary of his involvement in Demon Toys. More worryingly, it also summarised 'accidents' that had happened to some of the Tokifora staff and linked these to some of Highworth's investment activities. There was nothing concrete. Taken in isolation, both of the short case summaries, if that's what they were, could be dismissed as suspicious but not damning. But taken together, they were highly suspicious and amounted to pretty convincing circumstantial evidence.

'There are lots more of those,' said Briggs, confirming Highworth's worst fears. 'About thirty in fact spanning nearly twenty years. They tell a compelling story.'

'What exactly do you want?' asked Highworth.

'Ten million pounds,' answered Briggs. 'I suspect I could ask for a lot more but I'm neither greedy nor stupid. Ten million is enough for me to 'lose' the files and kill off any further investigation.'

'Why are you doing this?' asked Highworth, still suspicious.

'I'll give you the short version,' replied Briggs. 'I'm due to retire next year. I've been passed over for the Met and my pension, though generous by government standards, is paltry compared to what you city boys get. Put simply, I want to enjoy my retirement and I can't do that on what Her Majesty is going to pay me. This is a one-off opportunity. It's now or never.'

'Well that's honest at least,' said Highworth. 'I need to think about it.'

'I'll give you forty-eight hours and then I set the wheels in motion. You'll end up in gaol for a very long time if this comes to light. And just in case you get any funny ideas about lining me up with an unfortunate accident, I've left instructions in my office to release the papers in my safe should anything unexpected happen to me.'

'What if you have a heart attack?' asked Highworth, almost humorously.

'You'd better pray that I don't,' replied Briggs, sinking the remainder of his pint and standing up.

'Damn,' said Highworth, watching Briggs walk away 'Damn, damn, damn.' He realised that he was being out manoeuvred and he didn't like it. He also recognised that he couldn't kill his way out of this. He suspected that Knowles was behind it but the more he thought about it, the more he realised that he had no real choice. He finished his wine and went outside. His car pulled up next to him. 'Home,' he said to his driver. Simon put the Bentley in gear and pulled away from the kerb. Within a few minutes the big car was accelerating through the early evening traffic. Highworth sat in the back in silence. He had a headache and his clarity of thought had, at least for the moment, deserted him. He closed his eyes and tried to sleep but his mind was racing. Somehow he needed to find a way out of this. He started to examine all the options.

'There's a way out of this,' he said to himself, 'I just need to find it.'

CHAPTER 35

Harry was on the roof terrace when he heard the phone ring. He ran downstairs to his study and answered it just as the answerphone was starting to kick in. It was Ellie. He'd spent a lot of time with her when he and Camilla had been together so he knew her well. He was shocked at her description of what had happened to Camilla and he agreed that this was no coincidence.

'I'll get the next flight out,' he said to Ellie. 'She phoned me a few days ago. She was obviously scared and I suggested she go and stay with you. To be honest, I thought she was in shock. I thought a few days on Dartmoor with you would calm her down but it looks like she was right to be concerned.'

'I went to see her this evening,' said Ellie. 'She's still unconscious and badly bruised. Her leg's broken but it's not too bad. A clean fracture which the doc says should mend OK. I know she'll be happier once you're here as the police aren't taking this seriously at all. They think she just slipped and fell. If it hadn't been for the climbers, she'd be dead. What worries me now is that if someone did try and kill her, once they know she's alive they might try again. I've left Sarah with her but if someone is determined to get her, I'm not sure what Sarah and I will be able to do about it.'

'Just make sure that she's not alone. Talk to the police again and if they haven't done so already, insist that they speak to the London police. They'll see the connection eventually,' said Harry, though he was far from confident that the two different police forces would put two and two together. Harry had worked with the police when he was in the Army and he remembered only too well how difficult it could be to get different police authorities to work together. It didn't seem to be a problem for the most high profile crimes as

Scotland Yard would invariably take the lead, but Harry suspected that Camilla's accident was a long way from being high profile.

Once he'd spoken to Ellie, Harry spoke to the airline and managed to get a flight to Heathrow that evening. He then booked a taxi to take him to the airport and spent the hour before it arrived packing his bags. There was just enough time to send an e-mail to Lucy before the taxi arrived. He wasn't sure exactly what he'd be able to do when he got to London but he knew that he couldn't just sit here in Nepal whilst the two women in his life who meant anything to him were struggling thousands of miles away. As he rushed around packing his bags, he smiled as he thought of what one of his old bosses used to say to him when he was in the Army. 'Don't confuse activity with progress, Harry. Sometimes, the best decision is to decide not to do anything at all.' Harry didn't doubt that this was sometimes true. But in this case, he knew he had to do something.

The flight from Nepal was uneventful. He slept most of the way, arriving at Heathrow in the early hours of the morning. He collected his bags and went to the Hertz desk to hire a car. Whilst he waited in the queue he used his phone to check his e-mail. Lucy had replied. She was sorry to hear about Camilla but was delighted that he was coming to UK. She included her mobile number in the e-mail and asked him to phone her when he landed. Harry's mood immediately lifted. He'd hoped that Lucy would be keen to see him and it appeared that she was. He was still smiling when the girl behind the Hertz desk asked him what sort of car he wanted. Knowing that he would be heading straight down to Dartmoor and that, according to Ellie, the weather would be unlikely to improve over the next few weeks, Harry asked for a Land Rover. The girl was apologetic and explained that the nearest thing they had left was a new Range Rover. Though the daily rate was more than he wanted to spend, Harry agreed. It had been a long time since he'd driven a really decent car and he was looking forward to the drive down to Dartmoor and then, if Lucy agreed, up to Edinburgh. He caught the courtesy bus and headed out of the terminal and towards the rental car parks. The Range Rover was waiting for him at the Hertz car park. It was black with tinted windows and a cream leather interior. He doubted whether it had ever seen a muddy field or a wet dog in its short life. 'Soon change that,' thought Harry as he thanked the Hertz representative for showing him the car's controls and closed the driver's door. Within a few minutes, he was heading away from Heathrow and towards the M25, the orbital motorway that circles London. It was still early and the roads were reasonably clear. Provided he got out of London before the rush hour started, he reckoned it would take him about four or five hours to get to Ellie's house. His plan was to stop after a few hours to phone Lucy, get some breakfast and confirm his arrival time with Ellie.

CHAPTER 36

Lucy and Isobel were up early. After they'd seen the solicitor the previous day, they'd gone into town, ending up at a piano bar called Fingers until the early hours of the morning. It was hidden away in a basement on one of the side streets that led up to George Street. She always seemed to end up at Fingers after a night out in Edinburgh. The live music was invariably good and it had a particularly late licence. It also seemed to attract an eclectic and interesting group of people; lots of older students, artists and media types as well as high earners from the financial institutions. There had been a blues band playing; an exceptionally versatile female singer and guitarist supported by a pianist and alto saxophone. They'd played a fair amount of Nina Simone – which had suited Lucy's mood – as well as some of the less familiar songs by Muddy Waters. The girls finished the evening doing Tequila Slammers with a couple of post grads from Edinburgh University.

'What's the plan?' asked Isobel, wandering into the sitting room in pull-ups and t-shirt.

'Well Harry's flying in to UK this morning which is the best news I've had for a few days,' replied Lucy.

'So am I going to be with Lucy the love-sick puppy or Lucy the tough minded go-getter this morning?' asked a mischievous Isobel, smiling at her friend as she gratefully accepted the coffee that Lucy had again made her.

'A bit of both,' replied Lucy. 'I want to try and track down the man that Dad met the night he was stabbed. I'm not quite sure how to do this but Dad said in his letter that he was an ex-Army type and that he thought he was based in London. Now that Harry's here, he might know how we go about tracking down an old soldier called Richards.'

'Luce, your Dad was very clear. He said you were to leave the country for a few months and that on no account were you to try and track Richards down.'

'I know,' replied Lucy. 'But think about it Isobel. I can't just go and hide. Where would I go? How long would I go for? And all the time I'm hiding, I'd be asking myself what happens if he finds me? I think the best thing to do is to try and find him and then somehow lead the police to him. I don't think I'm safe until he's out of the way.'

Isobel was pleased that the feisty redhead she knew and loved was back with her but she had her doubts about the wisdom of the two of them trying to track down the man who had most probably killed Lucy's dad.

'OK. I agree you have to do something but promise me we won't do anything too dodgy until Harry's with us. He must have some old Army friends he can call on to help us.'

'Agreed,' said Lucy. 'I want to start by finding out about the money in the offshore accounts. The more money we have access to, the easier I suspect it will be to track this chap Richards down. Murdo McLeod said he'd contact the friend of his who arranged Dad's offshore accounts for him. He said he'd try and get me an appointment this morning at eleven thirty. I've got the address and the chap's name. He's called Timothy Warton. McLeod said we could trust him but he suggested we should keep what we now know of Dad's activities to ourselves. It's all a bit dodgy this isn't it? No wonder my Dad liked to get up in the hills to clear his head.'

Lucy went to her room to get her mobile and phone Kate. She realised that she hadn't spoken to her since they'd been together at the hospital. She'd decided she was going to keep the details of how her father earned his money to herself at this stage but she wanted to tell Kate what the solicitor had said about the money he'd left her. She also wanted to pick Kate's brains about funeral arrangements. Unless the police changed their minds about the circumstances, it was likely that the body would be released within the next few days and she wanted to get the funeral over and done with as soon as possible. 'No point delaying the inevitable,' she thought to herself.

Kate was shocked that Lucy's father had left her half a million pounds. She'd have been even more shocked, thought Lucy, if she'd known just how much he had managed to amass during his clearly very profitable second career as an assassin. But, as she had decided she would, she kept this to herself. Lucy thought that Kate was trustworthy but the less people that knew what her father did, the better.

Having spoken to Kate, Lucy showered, dressed and confirmed the arrangement to meet Murdo McLeod's financial friend later that morning. She couldn't help thinking about her father but she felt better knowing that she was now doing something to try and bring his killer to justice. 'You knew I'd do this, Dad,' she said to herself, looking towards the ceiling as she spoke. 'I'm assuming you're up there and not down below, though given what you've been doing for the last few years that might not be a safe assumption,' she said under her breath.

'Come on then,' she said to her friend.

'Where are we going?' asked Isobel, absentmindedly scanning the TV channels in the hope of finding something interesting to watch.

'First stop is the police. I want to see whether they've made any progress. Then we're going to see the dodgy banker bloke that McLeod recommended. I've checked with McLeod's office and the meeting with Warton is still on for eleven thirty. Then I'm going to buy you lunch in a particular pub I want to visit.'

'OK,' said Isobel, picking up her Barbour jacket as she followed Lucy out of the door. Although she was deeply sad about the circumstances, Isobel had to admit that she was rather enjoying this. It was certainly more interesting than trying to find a job, though she recognised that she would have to give her future employment her full attention in a few weeks. That or face being unemployed.

The taxi dropped them outside the police station and, after several minutes of discussion, the desk sergeant eventually showed them to an empty office and told them to wait until he had found the detective dealing with her father's murder. She was surprised how similar the office was to the ones they always showed in detective programmes on TV. A plain table with two chairs arranged either side. The walls were empty except for a couple of health and safety signs. One helpfully explained the correct procedure for lifting large boxes and the other told them where the nearest fire exits were and which part of the car park they should assemble in should the building have to be evacuated. Eventually, the door opened and a tall man in a light grey suit entered the office.

'Hi, my name's Detective Constable Jake Douglas. I'm leading the investigation into your father's murder,' he said, pulling out a chair and sitting down opposite the two girls. Isobel reckoned that he was in his late twenties and about six foot three. Handsome in a rugged sort of way, his nose had obviously been broken in the past and he had a few scars above his eyebrows. She noticed the size of his hands and the way that the sleeves of his suit jacket were stretched tight over his upper arms. 'A rugby player,' she thought to herself, smiling at him in her most engaging way.

'Hello,' said Lucy. 'My name's Lucy Masters and this is my friend Isobel Johnson. Can you tell us whether you've made any progress? '

'Hi,' said Isobel, extending her hand for him to shake. He took her hand and shook it. His grip was firm but she noticed that he was careful not to squeeze her hand too hard. Isobel also noticed that he didn't wear a wedding ring but that he had a small signet ring on the little finger of his left hand.

'I'm so sorry about your father,' began the detective. 'I'm also sorry that I'm not able to add too much to what I think you already know. It seems your Dad was attacked outside of a pub and that his wallet was taken. Nobody saw anything and there was no CCTV covering that part of the street. There have been a couple of similar incidents in the last few months but, to be honest, we don't know whether there's any connection or not. We've put feelers out to see if our informants can tell us anything and we've pulled a few of the most obvious suspects in for questioning but I am afraid that at the moment we have no real idea who attacked your father.'

'Detective, my Dad was a very tough man. He was a Para and had been for about thirty years. He knew how to look after himself and I can't believe that he'd have allowed someone to mug him. It just doesn't add up,' said Lucy. 'There's got to be more to it. I know you won't believe me but I think someone deliberately killed him. I know his wallet was stolen but you see that in the movies all the time. They do it to make it look like a mugging.'

'OK, Miss Masters,' said the detective slowly. 'But do you know of any reason why anyone would want to kill him? Was he in debt? Had he been seeing someone he shouldn't have been?' The Detective looked Lucy in the eye as he questioned her. 'I'm not saying you're wrong but we need a motive. His wallet was missing and sadly that might have been motive enough for someone. Is there anything else you can think of that might explain why someone would want him dead?'

Lucy paused before replying. 'No, I don't think so, I just can't believe that he would be stupid enough to get himself mugged.'

'Regrettably it happens all the time,' said the Detective. 'Someone goes into a pub and orders a pint. They get their wallet out to pay and someone stood next to them gets a great opportunity to see how much cash they're carrying. We all do it without thinking about it. Did your father usually carry a fair amount of money?'

'I don't think so,' replied Lucy. 'He was a careful man. He grew up in one of the roughest council estates in Glasgow and spent years in the Army working in some of the world's most dangerous places. He was just too streetwise to make such a silly mistake. And the doctor at the hospital said it looked like he'd been stabbed by someone who knew what they were doing.'

'Miss Masters, last year there were ninety-seven murders in

Scotland. Of these, just over sixty percent of the victims were killed with a knife or other sharp instrument, compared with less than forty percent in England and Wales. Lots of youths carry knives here and most of them know how to use them. It's part of the culture I'm afraid. The doctor that spoke to you would know this if he'd been here for a while so I suspect he's probably new to Scotland. I am really sorry about this but you have my word that we'll keep looking for whoever did this. It'll be no consolation but there are only seventy-seven unsolved murders on file in Scotland even if we go back as far as 1866. We'll get the bastard that did this but it'll take time.'

'Thank you,' said Lucy. 'I just wanted to make sure that you were taking this seriously and not just brushing it off as one of those things that happens in a capital city.'

'You have my word,' said the Detective. 'But if you think of anything at all that might help us, please let me know.' He gave Lucy a card with his name and contact details on it. 'Phone me anytime. My direct number is on the back, as is my mobile. And if we get any leads, we'll let you know straight away.' He stood up and shook hands with both Lucy and Isobel.

'Do you play rugby?' asked Isobel, letting go of his hand.

'Yes,' replied the Detective. 'I play for Heriots. Why?'

'Just wondered,' replied Isobel. 'You look like a rugby player.'

The Detective smiled at her. 'You should come and watch a game sometime. We play every Saturday at the Stadium in Goldenacre. It's up from the Botanical Gardens, you can't miss it.'

'I might just do that,' replied Isobel, still smiling.

The Detective led them out of the building, said farewell and went back inside.

'Tart,' accused Lucy once the door had closed behind him. 'We're here to talk about my father's death and you start flirting with the copper leading the investigation. You're unbelievable!'

'I'm sorry,' said Isobel, genuinely contrite. 'I know I shouldn't have but I just wanted to hear him say something. His voice was great!'

'I'll admit he was rather nice in a strong sort of caveman way,' replied Lucy. 'He's definitely an improvement on your usual sort.'

Isobel laughed. 'He was nice wasn't he? Why didn't you tell him a bit more about your Dad?'

'Not yet,' replied Lucy. 'I agree we might have to but I want to see if we can do a bit ourselves first. I'm still not sure how the police are going to react when they learn what Dad did to earn his money, even if the people he killed weren't very nice. But if we do decide we need to tell the police more, then I promise that we'll talk to that chap first. And you can phone him and make the appointment,' added Lucy, prodding her friend in the ribs.

The Detective went back to his desk. The meeting wasn't quite what he had expected. He wasn't making much progress with the murder and, if he were honest with himself, he wasn't optimistic that things would get any better. The facts and figures he'd given the girls were true but this appeared to be a straightforward mugging in the sense that someone had simply killed the man to get his money. It might not have started like that. If the man was as tough as the daughter suggested, then the Detective could see that he might have tried to have a go at the mugger. The mugger might have threatened him and asked him to hand his wallet over and the father might have tried to resist, causing the mugger to stab him even though that hadn't been his original intent. But there was also something about the girls that didn't seem quite right. It was almost as if they were keeping something from him. He made a mental note to contact them in a few days time to see whether they had had any thoughts on why someone might have wanted Lucy's father dead. It was a long shot but they were nice girls, particularly the shorter one, and he would be quite happy to spend an hour or so talking to them again, even if it didn't take the case any further forward. He couldn't be sure but he felt as though the shorter of the girls had been flirting with him. Perhaps she would turn up at one of his rugby matches.

Lucy and Isobel took another taxi into the Old Town. They passed Waverley Station as they headed across the city towards the Royal Mile. It always surprised Lucy just how busy railway stations were, whatever the time of day. They crossed the Royal Mile and then headed down towards Grassmarket, stopping in the main square. She liked this part of Edinburgh. The narrow cobbled streets and tall buildings had, she suspected, changed little over the last few hundred years. She paid the taxi driver and started walking towards Victoria Street. She had been here many times before. It was a steep climb up towards the Castle but the street had a real charm. The tall buildings housed offices and flats on the upper floors but at ground level there were lots of smaller restaurants and a few excellent pubs. Isobel followed, surprised at the seemingly endless procession of tourists walking down from the Castle towards their waiting coaches.

'Do you ever shop here?' Isobel asked Lucy.

'Sometimes. There's some really cool shops but they tend to be expensive,' answered Lucy, stopping opposite a beautifully preserved Georgian building. 'I think this is the address McLeod gave us.' She took a piece of paper out of her pocket and checked the address she'd written down in McLeod's office with the brass number on the sturdy looking black door in front of her. 'Yup, this is it,' she said, pressing a discretely hidden intercom button on the door frame. It was answered almost immediately.

'Good morning, can I help you?' asked a well modulated female voice.

'Yes please. My name's Lucy Masters. I believe I have an appointment with Mr Warton,' answered Lucy.

'Please come in. Mr Warton will come down and meet you,' replied the voice.

Lucy heard the sound of the lock being released and pushed the door open. Isobel followed her inside. 'Wow,' said Isobel when she saw the inside of the building. She'd expected something similar to Murdo McLeod's offices but this was completely different. The building's façade might have been Georgian but the interior had been completely gutted and re-built along very modern lines. At its heart was a central glass atrium. Looking up, Isobel could see that each of the six floors above her opened onto the central atrium which, at ground level, was filled with exotic looking plants. The roof of the atrium was also made of glass, allowing the late morning sun, which was almost directly overhead, to flood the building with light. It reminded Lucy of Harry's flat in Kathmandu, except that there was far more glass. Lucy turned as she heard the quiet whoosh of a door opening behind her. A man stepped out of a glass-sided lift and came towards them.

'Miss Masters?' he enquired. Lucy nodded. 'My name is Timothy Warton,' he said, extending his hand towards Lucy. 'I'm terribly sorry to hear about your father. A tragic business.'

'Thank you and thank you for seeing us,' replied Lucy, shaking his hand. She introduced Isobel and then explained why she'd come to see him. Warton listened politely and then suggested they follow him up to his office. He led the way towards the lift. He could see the girls looking around the inside of the building.

'We had the renovations done a few years ago,' said Warton as the lift doors closed. 'It's much better than the pokey old offices we used to have.'

'Yes,' replied Lucy, 'it's quite remarkable.'

The lift stopped on the sixth floor and opened onto a corridor that ran between the central atrium and the glass walls of the offices that lined the four sides of the building. There was an air of quiet efficiency. Lucy noticed that people were going about their business in a calm and unhurried manner. There were no raised voices and even the phones seemed to ring in a subdued way. Warton led them to a large corner office, stopping in front of the glass door to enter a code into a keypad.

'What exactly does your company do Mr Warton?' asked Lucy.

'We provide financial advice,' answered Warton. 'We specialise in providing a range of discrete financial services to people with particular needs. I'll explain more in a moment.'

The office door clicked and Warton pushed it open, stepping aside to let the girls enter. He followed them in. 'Please do sit down,' he said, pointing at a glass conference table at the far end of the room. The table looked as though it had been set up for the meeting. It had four black leather chairs arranged round it, two on each side. A pencil and pad had been laid out on the table in front of each of the chairs. A jug of iced water and four glasses stood on a silver tray in the centre of the table.

Lucy and Isobel sat down on the far side of the table. Lucy looked round the office as Warton closed the door. It was very different to Murdo McLeod's. Whereas McLeod's office had been comfortably old fashioned, this was ultra modern. What little furniture there was seemed to be made entirely of leather, glass or black metal. At the other end of the room to the table was a glass desk with another expensive looking leather chair behind it. The only things on the desk were a slim laptop, a phone and a black leather folder. Lucy noticed that the two pictures on the wall were modern watercolours of the Castle, one looking South from the Firth of Forth and one looking up from Grassmarket. There were no personal items in the office, nothing to indicate the sort of man that Warton might be. The only hint of colour came from a beautifully woven rug that filled the space between the desk and the conference table.

Warton went over to his desk and picked up the folder. He opened it as he walked back towards the table and started to read as he sat down opposite the two girls. Lucy watched him as he read. He looked about forty-five. Of average height, his light grey suit fitted his slim figure perfectly. His dark brown hair was swept back from his forehead. Though slightly greying at the temples, it was thick and immaculately cut. He was, she thought, quite handsome in a sort of TV anchor man way. She wondered what her father had made of him. He didn't have much time for city types. 'They're all clones,' he used to say. 'Eton, Oxford, City. The thick ones join the Guards or go in the Navy.' She smiled as she thought of her father. She was starting to realise just how important he had been to her, even though she hadn't seen much of him.

'Miss Masters?' said Warton gently, conscious that Lucy was lost in thought.

'Sorry,' said Lucy, 'I was miles away.'

'That's OK,' said Warton. 'I was just saying that I saw your father about two years ago. I wouldn't normally go into the details of what we discussed but Murdo McLeod phoned me last night and asked me to be straight with you. I am not entirely comfortable with this but, given the circumstances and as a personal favour to Murdo, I'll do what he asked. If you don't understand anything I say, please do stop me and I'll try and clarify. Do you understand?'

'Yes, thank you,' replied Lucy.

'Your father came to see me for advice on where he could deposit several million pounds without too many questions being asked. He wanted to be able to access the money from anywhere in the world, at any time of day and at very short notice. He also wanted to be able to shield it from the UK tax authorities if he chose to.'

'Is that legal?' asked Lucy.

'Having the accounts is, yes,' replied Warton. 'As a UK resident, it would have been illegal for him not to pay tax on any interest he earned but simply having money in an offshore account is perfectly legal. If you are resident in the US, then you have to declare any amount over ten thousand dollars that you have off shore but we are more civilised here in the UK. Provided you pay the tax you owe, you can have as many offshore accounts as you like.'

'OK,' said Lucy, 'please continue.'

'We opened numbered accounts for him in three separate banks, one in the Cayman Islands, one in Gibraltar and one in Switzerland. We advised him to spread his money across a number of banks because, in some respects at least, putting your money in an offshore account can be riskier than putting it in your high street bank. For example, the compensation you receive if an offshore bank collapses is very often a great deal less than what you would receive if your money was in a UK bank and it went bust. It therefore made sense to try and mitigate the risk by investing in different banks and in different geographic locations. He wanted the accounts to be as anonymous as possible so we suggested numbered rather than named accounts. Again, this is entirely legal but the difficulty with this setup is that now that he's passed away you will struggle to get access to the money without the account numbers and the passwords that protect them.'

'I think I have those,' said Lucy. 'Murdo McLeod gave me a letter from my father which had the details of three offshore bank accounts in it. The details included the names of the banks, the account numbers and the passwords. I've got them with me.'

'Good,' replied Warton, 'we can go through those in a minute. As I said, there's nothing illegal about having the accounts but there is an expectation that he would declare any interest he earned and pay any tax that was due. There's also an assumption that he earned the money legally and that he paid tax on it when it was given to him. Now that he is unfortunately deceased, the money should be included in his estate and should be taken into account in calculating any inheritance tax due. Strictly speaking, you shouldn't access the accounts until his estate has been settled.'

'OK,' said Lucy. 'I think I understand.'

'But there is a problem,' continued Warton. 'Your father wanted the accounts as a sort of financial parachute. Quite a few of our customers do this. The money is only ever used if things go badly wrong for them here in the UK. I have no idea how your father made his money. It's none of my business but I suspect he didn't pay any tax on it when it was earned. I also suspect that he didn't declare any interest. Because of this, you may have to answer some pretty awkward questions if the money were to be included in his estate. It's clearly up to you but you might wish to consider whether you should keep the existence of this money to yourself.'

'Won't the banks tell the UK authorities?' asked Lucy.

'No. The accounts are numbered and not in your father's name. Even if the banks knew that your father had died, there is nothing to link him to the money in the accounts as we set them up in a particularly complicated way to obfuscate ownership. In terms of tax, the banks take the view that it is a personal responsibility. Their job is to keep the money safe and pay whatever interest is earned straight back into the accounts. They leave it to the customer to determine how much tax is due, both when the money is earned and on any interest that they pay, and then to pay it to whichever government should receive it. Normally, but not always, it's the government of the country in which the customer is a resident. If you think about it, this approach makes sense. Each of the banks will have money from thousands of different customers living in lots of different countries. Each country has a different tax regime and therefore each customer's circumstances will be unique.'

'But what does this mean for me?' asked Lucy. 'Can I access the money or not?'

'Yes. You have the account numbers and you have the passwords. In the globalised era in which we live, that and access to the internet is all you need to transfer the money pretty much wherever you want. But I would suggest that you need to be careful. If you transfer large sums into your UK bank accounts, then there is a danger that you will attract unwanted attention. The UK banks have a responsibility to report any large and unusual movements of capital. It's all part of the government's drive to reduce money laundering. I think you have a number of options open to you.'

'OK, I'm still with you,' said Lucy.

'One option is for you to declare the money in the accounts and ask that it be included in your father's estate. Eventually, you might get some of it back. The problem with this is that we know he probably didn't pay any tax on it and Her Majesty's Customs and Revenue will be able to check this by going back through your father's tax returns. We could try and say that he paid tax in a different country or that it was exempt from tax but we will need to prove this. If we can't, then things will start to get complicated and they will want to deduct income tax before they even begin to think about inheritance tax, and that's if they accept that it was earned legally which they might not. The other option is to keep the accounts to yourself. There are some circumstances in which this might be legal but I suspect they don't apply in this case. You therefore need to understand that, as a UK resident, you might be breaking the law if you were to do this. But you might consider the risk to be worth it, particularly if you were planning to live abroad.'

'What would you do?' asked Lucy.

Warton smiled. 'It depends. The problem you have is that if you wish to keep the money secret from the UK authorities, then you need to avoid it going through your UK bank. The best way to do this is to use a debit card that links directly to the offshore accounts. Perhaps surprisingly, most offshore banks now do this. They are, in many ways, becoming increasingly like their high street cousins. This would mean that you could spend the money as and when you liked without it ever going through your UK bank. Clearly, if you took out a large sum of money to buy a particularly smart house in Edinburgh and if this appeared to be beyond your means, then there is a chance that someone might start asking questions. So you would need to be careful. But your father also had a fair amount of legal wealth. I know for a fact that he paid tax on all the money that went into his UK accounts and I recall, certainly two years ago, that his savings amounted to several million.'

Lucy thought for a moment. 'OK. So after I've paid inheritance tax on my father's legal estate, I will be several million pounds better off and this will be legally mine.'

'Yes,' replied Warton.

'If I 'fess up about the money in the offshore accounts, the authorities are going to start asking all sorts of questions about how my Dad earned the money and what tax he might or might not have paid. If they think he earned the money illegally, they will most probably keep it.'

'Yes, you should be OK though because you didn't know about the money until he died.'

'But if I keep quiet about the money, I can use it, perhaps when I'm abroad, and the UK authorities might not find out about it.'

'Exactly,' said Warton. 'You need to remember that trillions of pounds move through the global financial systems every day. It's very hard to spot a few millions or hundreds of thousands being moved around illegally unless you are specifically targeting an individual and tracking his activities. You're only talking about a few thousand so, provided you're careful, you should be absolutely fine.'

'Really?' asked Lucy.

'Yes. To give you an example, do you remember Charles Taylor, the old Liberian leader?'

'Yes,' replied Lucy. She'd done some research on him for her dissertation.

'Well when he was tried a few years ago, it was estimated that he had over three hundred million dollars stashed away in various banks. Very little of it has been found so far and the chances are that it will remain hidden even though some of the best forensic accountants in the world are now trying to track it down.'

Warton got up from the table and went over to his desk to fetch the laptop. 'If you let me have the account numbers and the passwords, I'll show you how to access the money and we can see how much your Dad built up since we opened the accounts for him.'

Lucy and Isobel watched as he switched the computer on and then, over the course of the next hour, logged into each of the three accounts. It was no more complicated than using the online facility that most high street banks now provided. Warton also requested a debit card in Lucy's name to be sent from one of the banks to his office. He explained that doing this provided a link between her and the account and that she should therefore only keep a modest amount in it, transferring money in from the other accounts as and when required. There was still a risk associated with doing this but he felt that it was the most pragmatic way of giving her access to the money. 'Just be careful with the card and keep the balance in that account reasonably low. The card should be here in a few days. If you leave me your number, I'll phone you when it arrives so you can come and collect it or I can send it to you,' he said to Lucy.

Lucy and Isobel left Warton's office about thirty minutes later. They'd both asked more questions, particularly when Warton confirmed that her father had managed to build up a total of five and a half million pounds in the three accounts.

'You're even richer than you were yesterday,' said Isobel, squeezing her friend's shoulder as they walked back towards Grassmarket. 'One minute you were a struggling student, buying secondhand climbing gear in a dodgy shop in Kathmandu, the next you're planning which executive jet to buy!'

'Yes. But I'd still rather have Dad here,' replied Lucy, wistfully. 'I miss him and what saddens me most is there was obviously a side of him that I knew absolutely nothing about. I thought he just did the odd security job for a few friends. If I'm honest, before all this I thought he must have had quite a sad sort of life. He had Kate and his ex-army mates but I didn't realise he was actually jetting round the world as some sort of high end hit man, knocking people off for hundreds of thousands of pounds and then stashing the money away in offshore accounts. It's all a bit unbelievable, like something out of a movie. I keep expecting someone to tell me that there's been a mistake.'

'I see what you mean,' said Isobel. 'It's a bit like that film with Arnold Schwarzenegger and Jamie-Lee Curtis. She thinks she's married to Mr Boring. She wants a bit more excitement in her life so she starts to have a fling with some secondhand car salesman who pretends to be a secret agent. Only it turns out that Mr Boring is actually the real spy.'

'*True Lies*,' said Lucy, 'that's the name of the film.'

'Yes, well it's a bit like that isn't it?'

'I suppose so,' said Lucy reflectively. 'Come on and I'll buy you lunch with some of my ill gotten gains. I want to go to the pub that Dad had his last drink in. That nice rugby playing policeman mentioned its name when we saw him. It's not far from here, only you won't remember because you were too busy flirting with him rather than paying attention to what he was saying.'

'That's not fair,' said Isobel, looking hurt. 'OK, it is fair but he was extremely nice. I even like his name,"Jake". It's sort of manly. I might even go watch him play rugby this Saturday if we're still here. I prefer him to Mr Warton. I thought he was a bit too smooth. I'm not sure I'd trust him.'

'I know what you mean,' said Lucy. 'But he's got as much to lose as we have if he admits any of this to anybody.'

'How do you mean?' asked Isobel.

'Well, for one thing, I've got this,' said Lucy, bringing out a small tape recorder from her pocket. 'I bought it last year when I broke my arm. I dictated one or two chapters of my dissertation into it and got one of the university secretaries to type it up for me. It worked really well.'

'You clever thing,' said Isobel, genuinely impressed. 'I didn't see you turn it on.'

'No, I switched it on when we went up in the lift. I didn't tell you because I thought you might find it difficult to be natural. I'm sorry.'

'That's OK,' said Isobel. She smiled at her friend. 'I wouldn't have trusted me either. I'd have probably said something and given the game away.'

Lucy linked her arm through her friend's and steered her down the hill towards Holyrood House Palace. The pub her father had been attacked outside was down one of the side streets midway between the Castle and the Palace. Her phone buzzed in her pocket. She took it out. It was a text from Harry. He was in UK and heading down to Dartmoor to see Camilla. He would phone early afternoon to catch up. She smiled as he had ended his text with a few crosses.

'Anything important?' asked Isobel, noticing her friend's smile.

'It's Harry. He's landed at Heathrow and he's on his way to see his friend in hospital. He'll phone later this afternoon when he's seen her.'

'Is he going to come and see us?' asked Isobel.

'Doesn't say. I hope so but I'll ask him when he phones.' She sent him a quick reply. 'Come on, Isobel,' she barked, increasing the pace in an attempt to avoid any further discussion about Harry. So much had happened in the week or so since she'd kissed him goodbye that she hadn't really had time to think about what might happen next. If she was honest with herself, she wasn't really sure what she felt about him. She knew she wanted to see him again soon, but whether as a friend or as a lover she didn't really know.

CHAPTER 37

Harry's phone lit up as Lucy's reply arrived. He'd just pulled off the Devon Expressway and was heading into Ashburton. He'd agreed with Ellie that he would stop at her house and that they would then go to the hospital together to see Camilla. That way he would have the chance to chat things through with Ellie and try and work out what to do next before he saw Camilla. He headed into the centre of Ashburton and found a parking space in the main car park. He hadn't been to the town for years. The last time was to visit a girlfriend whose father had owned an antique shop on the high street. The shop specialised in fireplaces and, over the course of a very enjoyable weekend, much of it spent in a pub with the girlfriend and her father, he'd learned more about fireplaces than he suspected he would ever need to know. He looked at Lucy's reply. 'Glad you're safely here. Looking forward to seeing you. Speak later. Lucy. XX.' Harry was relieved. It was short and sharp but definitely positive. He wondered whether she'd put the kisses after the text because he had or whether she would have done this even if he hadn't. 'Why do I do this to myself?' he said aloud. 'I should just be happy that she's OK and that she's replied.'

Harry got out of the car and walked into the centre of the town. He had been driving for about five hours and he needed to stretch his legs and get something to eat. He'd forgotten how lovely Ashburton was. Nestled at the foot of the moors, it looked reasonably prosperous. He noticed there were even more antique shops than when he'd first come here but there were also more delicatessens and a few new cafes. A few of the outdoor equipment shops that he remembered were still there, including one which had a mannequin dressed as a climber half way up the outside wall. It made him smile. He was all for local businesses and he made a mental note to buy any outdoor clothing he needed from the shop.

He found a cafe and ordered a bacon sandwich and a coffee. It was next to a large secondhand bookshop which appeared to be doing a brisk trade. He found a table in the window and watched the world go by as he waited for his food to arrive. The people outside were a mix of walkers, locals doing their shopping and one or two obviously foreign tourists.

'Bacon roll and a coffee?' asked a girl in a waitress' outfit.

'Yes, thank you,' said Harry, looking up. The girl who served him looked about sixteen. 'Probably a holiday job,' thought Harry. He ate the sandwich and drank the coffee. Both were excellent and he ordered another coffee 'to go' for the journey up onto the moor.

Harry left the cafe and returned to his car. He checked his phone again. No messages. He sent a quick text to Ellie telling her that he would be with her within the hour and drove the car out of the car park, turning left towards Hay Tor. Ten minutes later, he rounded a bend and saw Hay Tor in front of him. It was impressive. The mist had cleared and he could clearly make out people on the top. He pulled onto the verge to see if he could see where Camilla must have fallen. She was lucky to be alive. The rock face was sheer for about a hundred feet. He could see climbers dotted across it. The odds of Camilla falling onto a climber who just happened to be secured to a rope whilst he checked the looseness of the rock were thousands to one against. She was very lucky. If the weather had been clear, Harry suspected that whoever had tried to kill her would have been able to see that he had failed. In a way, the mist saved her life. Without it the killer might well have noticed the climbers on his walk to the top.

Harry pulled back onto the road and drove towards Ellie's house. It took him thirty minutes to reach the valley below North Bovey. He had enjoyed the journey. The landscape was truly beautiful. Though the hills were windswept and desolate, the valleys were wooded, with streams cascading down the hillsides. There were very few houses.

He'd noticed one or two but there weren't many and they were miles apart. One particular house had caught his attention when he'd had to pull in to let a car going in the opposite direction get past him. It was called 'Moor Crest'. In its heyday it must have been a truly wonderful family home. He wondered what it must have been like to grow up in the middle of Dartmoor. 'Not easy,' he thought to himself. 'Fine if you're older but much harder for a teenager.' He kept going until he arrived in North Bovey and saw the pub. Ellie had given him directions from there to her house and he had little difficulty finding the track that led up to the old barn. He parked next to an old Land Rover, killed the engine and got out. The door of the old barn opened and he recognised Ellie.

'Hello stranger!' she said as she hugged him. 'Didn't think I'd be seeing you again.'

'No, I don't suppose I expected to see you again quite so soon either.' Harry smiled. He'd always liked Ellie. She could be dogmatic and argumentative but they'd always found common ground. He also admired her. He knew that coming out had been hard for her and that, even now, her parents disapproved.

'How's Camilla doing?' asked Harry.

'She's alive,' replied Ellie, leading him into the house. 'But she's badly hurt and it's going to take a while for her to recover fully. She regained consciousness about an hour or so ago. Sarah spoke to her briefly but she's very tired. The police aren't really interested in talking to her, "as and when" apparently. They still think she fell off the top. In fact, if I'm honest, I think they think she was a bit of an idiot to be up there in the first place given how bad the weather was. They haven't said it but I wouldn't be surprised if secretly they think she was trying to kill herself.'

'Really?' replied Harry. 'They just don't want the hassle of having to investigate a murder.' He put on a comic Devonshire accent: 'This is Devon. Murders don't happen down here. Bad for the tourist business.'

Ellie smiled. 'That's probably exactly what it is. But Sarah's with her now so I'm happy that she's in good hands.'

'Is Sarah the nurse?' asked Harry.

'No,' replied Ellie sheepishly, 'she's my partner.'

'Really? That's great. I can't wait to meet her,' said Harry, trying not to embarrass Ellie.

'Yes. But be nice to her Harry or I'll get mad with you. We've only being living together for about a year and Camilla's the first of my old friends that she's met. I don't want you to frighten her away with any of your army banter.'

Harry laughed. He had no intention of frightening her at all. In fact, he was deeply grateful to her for helping to look after Camilla. He was also intrigued to see what sort of girl Ellie had found. He looked around the kitchen to see if there were any photographs of the two of them together but he couldn't see any.

'I'm sorry you and Camilla broke up,' said Ellie, handing Harry a cup of coffee.

'It was tough but I suspect it was for the best,' replied Harry. 'We both wanted such different things that our relationship was starting to come apart. We tried, but her paintings were starting to sell and she was beginning to earn some real money at last. The last thing she wanted to do was to go to Africa with me.'

'I understand. I don't suppose I'll ever have that problem,' said Ellie laughing.

'Nonsense,' replied Harry, 'Camilla told me that your work is becoming very popular down here.'

'True but it takes so long. I'm still having to teach to supplement the income but I'm optimistic that I'll get there eventually. Drink up and we'll go to the hospital and see Camilla. I'll drive, you must be knackered.'

'Thank you,' said Harry, following her out of the door.

It took about an hour to reach the hospital in Ellie's Land Rover. They chatted throughout the journey, catching up on each other's news and trying to make some sense of what had happened to Camilla.

'We both know Camilla,' said Ellie. 'She's tough and determined but I've never seen her so scared before. I think there's a lot more to this than meets the eye and I wouldn't be at all surprised if there really was someone trying to kill her.'

'But why?' asked Harry.

'The only thing I can think of,' replied Ellie, 'is that somebody thinks she knows something about the death of that Peter Fairweather chap. It must have been awful for her to wake up and find the man she'd spent the night with had died whilst she was asleep.'

They arrived at the hospital. It was clearly busy and it took them a while to find somewhere to park. Eventually, they made it into the hospital, taking the lift to intensive care.

'If she's starting to recover, why's she still in intensive care?' asked Harry.

'They're still worried about possible damage to the brain,' replied Ellie. 'She had a hell of a fall and she has only just started to regain consciousness. They'll keep her where she is until they're absolutely sure she's OK. As soon as we can though, I'd like to get her home.'

The lift doors opened and they could see the door to intensive care. Ellie rang a buzzer. A nurse answered and, once they'd confirmed who they were, she let them in. Harry noticed how quiet it was. There were lots of nurses and doctors but very few patients. He could see Camilla at the far end of the ward. She had three or four tubes going into her and she was connected to a bank of machines. A TV screen displayed her heart rate, blood pressure and a few other vital signs that Harry didn't recognise. Camilla looked to be asleep. As they approached, a very attractive blonde girl of about Harry's own age came out from behind a screen and smiled.

'Hi,' she said, 'I'm Sarah.'

'Hello,' said Harry, shaking her hand. He was genuinely taken aback. He wasn't sure what he'd expected but he hadn't expected this. She was truly beautiful. She kissed Ellie on both cheeks and then started to tell them how Camilla had been doing.

'She was conscious for about thirty minutes. She wasn't very lucid but the doctor explained that it might just be the effect of the painkillers she's on. They've put her shoulder back in and set the leg.'

Harry looked at Camilla. She was in a hospital gown and the pot on her leg was clearly visible. She looked pale and very frail. He desperately wanted to hold her and take care of her. He moved round the side of the bed so he could hold her hand.

'Camilla, it's me, Harry,' he put his head close to her ear and spoke softly. Her eyes flickered but nothing more. He turned to the girls. 'Why don't you two go and get a cup of coffee and I'll stay with her for a while.'

'OK,' said Sarah, 'but remember, she's very tired and probably in a lot of pain. You see that control in her left hand?' Harry nodded. 'It's got a button on it that releases morphine. If she wakes up and is in pain, get her to press it a few times. It takes a few minutes to take effect so make sure she doesn't get carried away. The nurse looking after her is called Rachel. She's the one with the short, dark hair over there.' Sarah pointed towards a central isle.

Harry could see the nurse that Sarah was taking about. 'I see her,' he said.

'They have a copy of the vital signs screen over there so if anything happens, they'll come over. There's one nurse for every two patients so don't worry about calling Rachel over if you get worried about anything.'

'OK, thank you,' said Harry, pulling up a chair and sitting close to the bed so he could hold Camilla's hand. He kept talking to her quietly, hoping that she would at least hear his voice, even if she couldn't understand what he was saying. He started telling her what he'd been doing in Nepal. After about fifteen minutes, Camilla opened her eyes. Harry watched them struggle to focus. He stood up so she could see him.

'Hello,' he said to her. Her eyes widened as she recognised him. She tried speaking but only managed a croak. Rachel came over.

'Hello,' she said to Camilla. 'Do you want some water?' Camilla nodded her head slowly. Rachel held a small glass of water to her lips. 'Slowly,' she ordered. 'There's no rush, plenty more where that came from.'

The water seemed to give Camilla life. She smiled slowly. 'Hello Fish, you took your time getting here.'

Harry could feel the relief flooding over him. 'Thank God,' he said to himself. He smiled at her and squeezed her hand. 'You certainly know how to scare the shit of me don't you? How do you feel?' he asked her.

'Not too good. I woke up a few hours ago, or at least I think it was a few hours ago, and Sarah explained what had happened. She told me I was very lucky to be alive. I don't feel very lucky! I've got a hell of a headache, my shoulder's killing me and I don't think I'll be walking for a while.'

'It'll take time but you're out of the woods. As soon as the doctors are happy that you're starting to mend, we'll get you home to Ellie's. Can you remember what happened?' asked Harry.

'A bit. I remember being on the top of Hay Tor and then someone pushed me. I didn't slip. I was close to the edge but not that close. Boot started barking and I was turning round to see if he was OK. And then I felt a huge push in the small of my back and I was falling. But I saw him Harry. I saw the bloke who pushed me. He had the deadest eyes I've ever seen. He had a hoody on but I'll never forget his face. I'd definitely recognise him if I saw him again.'

Harry's pulse started to quicken. 'Really? We need to tell the police. I wonder why he tried to kill you?' he asked.

'I don't know. I can only assume that it's got something to do with Peter Fairweather's death. Either that or someone bought one of my paintings, decided they didn't like it and thought they'd get their own back on me when I refused to give them their money back!'

Harry smiled at Camilla's attempt at humour. It wasn't very funny but it was a good sign. She was returning to normal.

'Do you think you could describe your attacker to the police?' asked Harry.

'I can do better than that, I can draw him. I'm an artist, Fish, remember?'

'Oh yes. I certainly remember that.' He thought of the paintings in his flat in Kathmandu. 'Nobody's ever painted me naked so beautifully! A definite work of art!'

Camilla started to laugh. It hurt her but she couldn't help it. It had taken her hours to paint the nude of Harry, mainly because he kept suggesting changes to make him look even more athletic than he already was. She'd refused to embellish the painting on the grounds of, as she put it, 'artistic integrity'. But he'd been happy with the finished product.

'OK,' said Harry. 'If I get you a pencil and paper, do you want to have a go?'

'Yes please. It's my left shoulder that I hurt so I can try.'

Rachel looked at Harry. 'She must take it very slowly. There's no rush and we don't want to overtire her at this stage.'

'I understand. But maybe she can just draw for ten minutes or so. The sooner we have an idea of who we are looking for, the better,' said Harry. Camilla squeezed his hand.

'I'm so tired Fish, I'm glad you're here but I think I'm going to have a short nap. I'll see you when I wake up.'

'Have a snooze and I'll go and get the pencil and pad,' said Harry, relieved that she was able to talk and that she was lucid. He could see Sarah and Ellie walking towards him. He went to meet them and suggested they chat outside in the waiting room. They found an empty corner and Harry explained what Camilla had said. He was clearly excited.

'I suspect the next thing we should do is to talk to the police. I'm surprised they haven't kept someone here to keep an eye on her,' said Harry.

'Why would they?' asked Ellie. 'They are convinced it was either an accident or an attempted suicide. I wouldn't be surprised if they think Camilla's making it up so she doesn't look an idiot.'

Sarah handed Harry a card. 'When we first arrived, the police gave us this. It's got the name of the officer who we spoke to written on it.'

Harry read the card. 'Thanks, I'll go and give them a buzz and see what they say.' There were signs in the waiting room asking people not to use mobile phones in the intensive care area so Harry stood up and went into the corridor. He returned ten minutes later. 'I'm amazed,' he said to Ellie and Sarah. 'They said they would send someone round this afternoon to talk to Camilla but only after I forced them to take her seriously. They're clearly not interested. I suppose it's easier for them if it's just an accident and not an attempted murder. Less paperwork I suspect!'

'I hate to say this,' said Ellie, 'but I told you so. We'll go and sit with Camilla. Why don't you go and grab a coffee and then we'll sort out some sort of roster. I think one of us needs to be with her all the time. If someone did try to kill her, then we can't afford to leave her on her own.'

'Thank you,' said Harry. The girls got up and walked down the corridor towards the intensive care ward. Harry watched them go. They were chatting to each other as they walked and Harry couldn't help thinking what a good match they were. He also couldn't help noticing how great Sarah looked in her jeans, particularly from the back. 'Lucky old Ellie,' he thought to himself with a smile.

Harry took the lift down to the main entrance. He went outside and found a quiet corner of the building, away from the comings and goings of the main entrance. Though the sun shone, it was cold. 'Winter's definitely on its way,' he thought to himself as he took out a cigarette and lit it. He inhaled deeply, enjoying his first cigarette of the day. He had two phone calls to make, one to Lucy and one to a couple of friends whose help he reckoned he was going to need, particularly when Camilla came out of hospital. He started with Lucy. He got straight through to her. She sounded pleased to hear him. He explained where he was and what had happened. He also told her how irritated he was that the police seemed to be taking no real interest in what had happened to Camilla.

'I know the feeling,' said Lucy. 'I am convinced that my Dad's murder was more than just a random mugging but the police don't seem to agree. I've just had lunch in the pub near where he was killed. They don't remember anything. I got the feeling that even if they did, they wouldn't tell me anything. It's that sort of pub. Everyone stopped talking when Isobel and I walked in. We were the only women in the place. They reluctantly served us some lunch but it was crap. It's not the sort of place my Dad would have gone to through choice.'

Harry listened as Lucy talked. She sounded frustrated at the lack of progress and angry at the police for not taking her concerns seriously.

'What are you going to do next?' asked Harry.

'I'm not sure,' said Lucy. 'My father's funeral is going to take place tomorrow. It'll be a small affair, probably just me, Isobel, Kate and a few of his old buddies up here in Scotland. That's fine because his old Regiment has been in touch offering to help organise a memorial service for him at the end of the month. Apparently, word of his death spread fairly quickly on his old Para Regimental net and there are quite a number of people who would like to commemorate his life with some sort of Regimental service. It would probably be too much to ask them all to come up to Edinburgh so I've agreed to either Aldershot or Colchester. They're going to get back to me with a few suggested dates.'

'That's great,' said Harry, encouragingly.

'It is. If I'm honest, I'm incredibly touched that they want to hold a service for him. I didn't realise he was so well regarded. But there is some other stuff that I need to discuss with you. I think I need your help to try and track somebody down.'

'OK,' said Harry. 'That sounds interesting. Do you want to tell me now?'

'No, I think we need to discuss this face to face. As soon as we've buried Dad, I'll fly down South. If you're going to stay on Dartmoor for a week or so, then I'll try and catch a flight to Exeter and perhaps we can meet there.'

'Good plan,' said Harry. He was excited at the prospect of seeing Lucy again. In a way, seeing Camilla had been helpful. He realised that, whilst he was still very fond of her, he didn't love her anymore. Lucy had shown him there was definitely life after Camilla and he could feel himself moving on.

Having spoken to Lucy, Harry lit another cigarette and made a call to an old friend from his army days. He briefly explained the situation and the friend agreed to help him. Satisfied that his plan, such as it was, was beginning to fall into place, he finished his cigarette and went back inside. He found Ellie and Sarah sitting by Camilla's bed. Camilla was awake and talking quietly to them whilst she tried to sketch her attacker. Harry looked over her shoulder at the pad. He never ceased to be amazed at how good an artist Camilla was. The face staring back at him looked real. The attacker had worn a hoody and this meant that she didn't know whether he had long or short hair, or even if he was bald. But even without knowing this, there was no doubt that the picture was easily good enough to identify someone from. It was, Harry felt, so much better than the usual sketches the police seemed to rely on when trying to track someone down. They all seemed to look the same, regardless of the race, age or build of the individual.

'That's amazing,' said Harry, genuinely impressed.

'Well, I admit that it's a reasonable sketch. But whether it actually looks like the man who tried to kill me is another matter,' replied Camilla. 'I think it does but I only saw him for a few seconds. His eyes made the biggest impression. I looked straight into them as I started to fall. They were really scary, utterly devoid of any emotion.

They were the dead eyes that you read about in books but don't believe actually exist.'

Harry pulled over another chair and sat down on the other side of the bed to Ellie and Sarah. 'So,' he said, 'what's the plan?'

'We've just spoken to the doctor,' said Ellie. 'Provided there are no complications over the next twenty-four hours, Camilla should be OK to come home tomorrow after lunch. They're going to do a scan this afternoon just to check that there's no swelling around the brain. That's the big concern apparently. Camilla's shoulder and leg will hurt but they'll get better over the next few weeks. Any swelling on the brain, though, could require surgery.'

'Shouldn't they have checked for this before?' asked Harry.

'They did,' replied Ellie. 'But they want to run a final check before letting her go.'

Harry took hold of Camilla's hand and squeezed it. 'Soon be back in my tender loving care. Bet you can't wait!'

Camilla smiled. 'Anything would be better than this. They're very kind but I can't wait to get out, even if it means having to put up with you bossing me around. Will you be able to take me back to London?'

'Not so fast Camilla,' said Ellie. 'I'm not letting you go until I'm sure you're OK. I'd rather you were here with us than back in London on your own, at least until we know you're safe from whoever tried to kill you. I know Harry would try and look after you on his own but it will be easier with the three of us.'

Camilla looked visibly relieved. She didn't want to impose on Ellie and Sarah but, even with Harry by her side, she was scared of going back to her flat in London. Harry, Sarah and Ellie worked out a roster to ensure that there was at least one of them with Camilla at all times. They agreed to do shifts of eight hours each. That way, everyone would get a sixteen hour break between their shifts, enough time to sleep, eat and generally sort themselves out. Ellie suggested that she should take the first shift so that Harry could go back to the barn with Sarah and settle in. He looked done in after the flight and the long drive down from London. Now that he'd seen Camilla and reassured himself that she was OK there was no reason for him to stay at the hospital.

'Thank you,' said Harry, standing up to peck Camilla on the cheek. 'Hang in there babe,' he said to her, squeezing her hand again. 'You'll soon be up and at 'em.' He picked the sketch pad up and looked at the drawing. It really was quite exceptional. He turned to Ellie. 'When the police come this afternoon, can you make sure they take a copy of this with them? It might help persuade them that it wasn't just an accident?'

Ellie nodded. 'I'll try but I don't hold out much hope. Take care you two and we'll see you later.'

Harry and Sarah said goodbye and then left the ward. It was raining hard as they walked from the hospital's main entrance to the car park. Fifteen minutes later they were heading out of Exeter and up onto the moor. Even in the rain, it looked stunning. 'I can see why you like it down here,' he said to Sarah, trying to break the ice with her.

'I love it,' she replied. 'There's a sense of community down here that I haven't experienced before,' she said. 'Almost as if people come together because the environment can be so challenging.'

'Where did you live before?' asked Harry.

'I was in London. I worked in public relations for an oil company. It paid well but it was extremely hard work, particularly over the last year or so.'

'Why?' asked Harry, genuinely interested.

'Well, we'd been accused of not looking after the environment as well as we might have done, particularly in the Niger Delta. There was a court case pending and it was attracting a lot of media attention. The PR department was heavily involved and I was working extremely long hours. I didn't mind this but the narrative we developed to explain what we were doing was full of half truths. We could have done a great deal more to help the locals but it would have cost millions and, quite simply, the company wasn't prepared to sacrifice any more of its profits than it had to. It was then that I decided I needed to get out and do something I believed in. Also, I hated having to commute on the tube, particularly late at night.'

'So you made a lifestyle change and came down here?'

'Yes,' replied Sarah. 'I've got a degree in English and I applied to Exeter Uni to do a teaching diploma.'

'Why here?' asked Harry.

'The Uni's got a great reputation and there are some really good schools down here for work. In a way, it's the best of all worlds. You have all the benefits of a vibrant and multi-cultural university city within a few miles of some of the most beautiful countryside in the UK. There are not many places like that, particularly ones that are also near the coast.'

'Is the coast important?' asked Harry, intrigued.

'It is for me,' replied Sarah, 'I'm a bit of a surf freak in the summer and Barnstable's not far away which is fantastic. It used to take me most of the weekend to get there when I lived in London.'

Harry was also a keen surfer. He'd been to Barnstable a few times and he also knew the Cornish surf beaches well. They spent the rest of the journey back to the barn comparing notes on which beaches were the best at what times of year. By the time they got back, they knew enough about each other to know that they would become friends.

'I know you're knackered,' said Sarah as they pulled up at the barn, 'but do you fancy a pint, my treat?'

'I never say no to a woman who offers to buy me a drink,' said Harry. 'Lead on.'

The two of them walked to the Ring O' Bells, chatting amicably as they went. Sarah liked Harry. He was interested in what she said and he clearly had no difficulty with her and Ellie being a couple. 'I'll cook you something to eat after we've had a drink or two,' said

Sarah, opening the door of the pub and leading Harry to the bar. They ordered a couple of pints and found a quiet table near the fire so they could continue talking without being overheard. Sarah asked Harry about his past and what he felt the future held. He told her about Lucy and that he was really looking forward to seeing her. 'Why don't you bring her here,' suggested Sarah. 'She can stay with us, at least until you know what you're going to do next.'

'Thank you,' said Harry. 'That's extremely kind of you. I'll suggest it to her when I speak to her tonight. I think you'll like her.'

They continued chatting for an hour or so until Sarah suggested they go and get some food. Harry was starting to fall asleep and she realised he needed to rest. He'd been on the go for the best part of twenty-four hours and he looked utterly shattered.

CHAPTER 38

Highworth was still angry that he had been out manoeuvred by Briggs. He'd spent the best part of the night trying to work out how to turn the situation to his advantage. He accepted that he couldn't just kill Briggs. Even if Briggs hadn't actually copied the file containing the evidence against him and left instructions for it to be opened in the event of anything happening to him, the death of a senior policeman would be likely to attract considerable attention whether it looked like an accident or not. Highworth went through the other options open to him one last time and decided that, at least for the moment, the most pragmatic way forward was for him to agree to Briggs' terms and pay him the ten million he'd asked for. He realised that this could be the thin end of a wedge and that Briggs could keep coming back to him for more but he reckoned he could avoid that by getting some sort of proof of Briggs' involvement. He would discuss it with Richards but they might be able to film the money being handed over or, if Briggs insisted on the money being transferred electronically, get some sort of recording of the two discussing the transfer. At least then he'd have an insurance policy against Briggs blackmailing him for more money in the future. Losing the money didn't bother him. Ten million was chickenfeed given how much he would make out of Fairweather's death. It was the feeling of vulnerability that really irritated him. He didn't like someone like Briggs, or Knowles for that matter, having power over him. He thought about Knowles. He was in no doubt that Knowles was behind this. He suspected that Knowles had gone to see Briggs, alerting him to his suspicions about Highworth, and that Briggs, close to retirement and seeing a one-off opportunity to make some real money, had decided to take matters into his own hands. Once he'd paid Briggs off he would have to deal with Knowles once and for all. 'Another issue to discuss with Richards,' he thought to himself.

Satisfied that he'd considered all the options open to him and identified the 'least worst', he sent a text to the mobile number Briggs had given him confirming that he would pay. He looked at his watch. Only a few hours of the forty-eight that Briggs had given him to make a decision remained. 'Good,' thought Highworth, 'I hope he sweated waiting for my reply.' Highworth went into the kitchen. Caroline was cooking supper. He went up behind her and wrapped his arms round her, kissing her gently on the back of the neck.

'You're very affectionate this afternoon, what's happened?' asked his wife.

'Nothing really,' replied Highworth. 'I just reminded myself how lucky I am to have you.'

Caroline turned round to face him. She looked into his eyes. He was not really an emotional man and something must have prompted this. She kissed him on the lips and put her arms round his neck, pulling him towards her. Highworth responded. She broke the kiss and looked into his eyes again. 'We've got a few hours before supper will be ready,' she said, taking hold of his hand and leading him out of the kitchen and towards the stairs. 'Why don't we go and have a bath. You need to relax.'

Highworth didn't complain. He'd found a solution to his immediate problem. Moreover, when he'd checked Bubble.com's shares an hour or so ago, he was delighted to note that they were continuing their journey south. Their price had been 545 pence at the time of Fairweather's death but they were now selling for 350 pence due, no doubt, to the amount of television coverage that Fairweather's death continued to attract. The business correspondents were doing a fine job of stressing that it was Fairweather's personal energy that had made Bubble.com so successful. Without him, they suggested, the company's future looked bleak. Notwithstanding the company's valiant efforts to reassure the public that it remained on track to deliver Mymate, Highworth was convinced that the television coverage would lead to the price dropping even further. 'Once it reaches 300 pence, I'll start buying,' he thought to himself. He had to honour the short sell he'd agreed to but he also wanted to buy as many shares as he could before it became apparent that, even without Fairweather, the company would actually deliver Mymate on time as it was suggesting. Once it hit the market, Highworth was confident that it would be a game changer in terms of social networking. This would cause the share price to rocket upwards and he would make the killing he so desperately wanted.

Briggs and Knowles were proving to be an irritating distraction but Highworth's confidence was beginning to return. He knew that he might well have to change the way he operated after this but he was beginning to think that he might just get away with it: Richards had dealt with the girl, or so Highworth thought; Briggs was going to 'lose' the evidence he'd got, albeit at a cost of ten million; and Knowles, well Knowles might well have to have a nasty accident if Briggs was unable to neuter the threat he posed. Highworth started to smile as they reached the bedroom.

He pulled Caroline close and kissed her hard. Her hand went to his waist and started to undo his belt. He could feel himself responding to her touch as her hand worked its way inside his boxer shorts. 'Life's not so bad after all,' he said to himself as he started to undo the zip at the back of Caroline's dress. She felt its tight fit begin to loosen as his hand travelled slowly down her spine, unfastening the zip. When he reached her bottom, she stepped back and, staring deep into his eyes, shrugged out of the dress. It fell to the floor at her feet. She took his hand and put it between her thighs. Delighted that she wasn't wearing any underwear, he undressed quickly and pulled Caroline down onto the bed. Within minutes, they were making love with a passion that surprised them both.

CHAPTER 39

Sir James Briggs was out walking his dog on Clapham Common when his phone beeped. He looked at the screen. It was the text from Highworth agreeing to pay the ten million he'd asked for. 'Excellent,' he thought to himself. Briggs had considered his next move in considerable detail. He would ask Highworth to wire the money to a numbered offshore account that he had opened years ago. The account had been set up as part of an investigation into money laundering. He had been a relatively junior detective at the time, based in the market city of Salisbury in Wiltshire. The case was his first real exposure to the world of global finance and he'd set up the account to try and prove how easy it was for someone to transfer money from the UK to an anonymous account in an offshore bank. It had been an interesting exercise. His painstaking work eventually led to the conviction of a particularly unpleasant drug dealer but it also ignited the interest in financial crime which had eventually led him to his current appointment.

At the beginning of the investigation, Briggs had assumed that the numbered accounts advertised by some banks, particularly those in Switzerland and Lichtenstein, were still anonymous. He had therefore been surprised to learn that, since the nineties, the law had required banks operating in even the most discrete of countries to know the identities of their account holders. Though banks offering numbered accounts made every effort to keep their customers' identities secret, they can be forced to reveal the name of a particular account holder if presented with a court order. There are, however, other ways of obfuscating ownership. Briggs' research identified that opening an account in the name of an offshore company is one of the most common ways of achieving further anonymity. This company could be registered in the name of another offshore company which, in turn, could be registered in the name of another one. At the time, it had reminded Briggs of the Russian dolls that one of his aunties used to collect. He had been fascinated by them as a child. Opening the largest doll revealed an identical but smaller one which, when opened, revealed another identical but even smaller doll. A persistent team of detectives might be able to track ownership of a particular account down to what the banks call the 'beneficiary owner' but this would take a huge amount of time and would require the sort of leverage that only governments could wield. Moreover, it is quite conceivable that, having followed the financial trail to its end, the 'beneficiary owner' listed on the parent company's documentation could turn out to be a fictitious character set up using a false identity.

Though he admired the complexity of nested offshore companies, Briggs had taken a much more straightforward approach when he opened the offshore account as part of his investigation. He had simply asked a junior colleague on the team to open it as a numbered account using his own name as the 'beneficiary owner'. Fortunately for Briggs, the colleague had subsequently died of natural causes and the account, which never contained anything more than the few hundred pounds necessary to open it, had been forgotten about. Briggs should have closed it at the end of the investigation but, fascinated by his introduction to white collar crime, he had left it open in case he ever needed it for further research. Somewhere in the bank's computer system the account would be annotated as belonging to a Mr S R Mason but Briggs knew that it would be unlikely to attract any unwarranted attention. It was seldom used and the annual bank charges were paid automatically from the balance in the account.

The account wasn't the most secure place to put ten million pounds but it would have to do, thought Briggs. Even if someone wished to try, it would be almost impossible for them to link the account to him. The bank, one of the Cayman Island's most discrete, would make it as difficult as possible for anyone, including a national government, to find out anything about the account, including where the ten million had come from. Checking his watch, Briggs realised that it was unlikely that Highworth would still be in his office. He decided that he would phone him the following morning on his way to work to arrange their next meeting. 'No point in making it easy for anyone to follow what I'm doing,' he thought to himself as he walked past the phone box he intended to phone Briggs from the following morning.

Ten minutes later, he was back in his flat. It was part of a large Victorian house. Although it was comfortable, it was, felt Briggs, far too small for a man of his stature. He started to whistle as he thought of the beach house he intended to buy in Belize with some of the money that Highworth was about to give him. He liked Belize. It was still developing as a tourist destination but some of the Cayes, particularly Ambergris Caye, were sufficiently westernised that he knew he would be comfortable. In fact, he thought, it would be perfect for someone like him who wanted to keep a low profile and spend their retirement fishing and painting. He made a mental note to find out about the feasibility of taking Princess with him. He'd formed a real affection for his dog and he had no intention of leaving her behind.

CHAPTER 40

Harry woke up early. He realised that his body was still on Kathmandu time. He tried going back to sleep but it was no good, he was restless. He got out of bed and pulled shorts, t-shirt and trainers out of his suitcase. He dressed quickly and went downstairs. Sarah had left a note. Harry read it quickly. 'Gone to hospital to relieve Ellie. Make yourself at home. See you later. Sarah.' He wasn't sure what time he was expected to replace her at Camilla's side but he reckoned he had time to jog a few miles before he needed to go. As he laced up his trainers, Boot started to bark. Harry thought the dog wanted to go out with him but a few minutes later he heard the sound of a car pulling up outside the house. 'Clever boy,' said Harry, ruffling the dog's head. Harry opened the door just as Ellie was getting out of her Land Rover.

'You're up early,' she said, smiling as she saw Harry.

'Couldn't sleep,' he replied. 'I thought I'd go for a jog to get the blood flowing.'

'Good plan,' said Ellie. 'Do you want some company?' she asked. 'If you give me a minute to change, Boot and I'll come with you.'

Harry didn't really want to run with Ellie. He wanted to push himself, working up a sweat to rid himself of the stiffness he always felt after a long flight. He suspected he wouldn't do this if Ellie came with him but, before he could reply, she'd dashed inside to get changed. Harry looked at Boot. His legs looked so short that Harry doubted he'd be any better than he believed Ellie would be. 'Oh well,' he thought to himself, 'maybe I can go out again later.'

Ellie reappeared five minutes later. Harry was surprised. She looked the part in Lycra running tights and a fluorescent Ron Hill top. She told Boot to get his lead as she pulled out an old pair of trainers from a basket near the door. 'Thanks for waiting,' she said to Harry, patting Boot as he brought the lead to her in his mouth. 'I'll give you a quick tour of this part of the moor. It's beautiful at this time of the morning. We should see a bit of wildlife.' She opened the door and stepped outside.

Harry followed her out. There was a light drizzle and the sun was not yet fully up. Boot was clearly excited and started jumping up and down. 'Come on the Boot,' said Ellie, jogging off down the lane with his lead. Harry caught up with her and they ran side by side down the track and into the village. A few minutes later, Ellie slowed down and opened a gate to let Boot into a long sloping field. He scampered off towards a stream at the bottom of the valley. 'He knows where he's going,' said Harry, impressed that Ellie's breathing seemed quite normal despite running.

'Yes. He should do, he does this most mornings,' replied Ellie, closing the gate after letting Harry through. 'Sarah and I run most days. If we can, we go out with Boot before work but sometimes we can't and he doesn't get to go out until the evening.'

Ellie started down the hill. She was an economical runner, with a long stride and an easy gait. As he watched her out of the corner of his eye, Harry started to have doubts about his initial assessment of her running ability. Camilla wouldn't run to save her life and he'd wrongly assumed that her friends would have a similar view of exercise. His doubts turned into concerns as they started up the other side of the valley. Ellie showed no signs of slowing down. More worryingly, she seemed able to maintain a coherent conversation as she ran, pointing out local landmarks and fleeting glimpses of animals as they followed the track up the hill. Ellie slowed down when they reached the top of the hill. 'Long or short?' She asked Harry.

'Long,' he replied, wondering if he would regret this show of soldierly bravado.

'I thought you'd say that,' said Ellie smiling. 'I'll take you down the next valley towards Hound Tor. You'll see it on the horizon. There's a killer hill up to the car park and then we'll swing back, following the road. It'll take us about an hour if you're up for it.'

'OK,' said Harry. 'Let's go.'

Ellie set off at an easy pace. They followed an old track that ran along the far side of the valley before heading down through a wooded area towards the stream. Boot was clearly enjoying himself, running well ahead of them and then diving off the track and into the undergrowth when he heard or saw something of particular interest. After about fifteen minutes, the track reached the stream. They crossed over using stepping stones that looked as though they had been there for hundreds of years. The track continued along the side of the stream, climbing slowly up towards the head of the valley. Ellie's pace never faltered. She maintained a steady rhythm, jumping the odd fallen branch with ease. Harry realised that she was extremely fit and suspected that, if she chose, she could increase her speed without too much difficulty. They turned a corner and, as the trees cleared, Harry could see the track leading up to the car park. It was impressively steep. 'The next bit's a bugger,' said Ellie, turning to look at Harry. 'We normally race up this bit and stop at the car park at the top. Sarah calls it 'butt hill' because she thinks it's good for her bottom. I'm not so sure about that but it certainly gets you breathing hard,' said Ellie with a laugh. 'Ready?' asked Ellie.

'OK,' said Harry, suspecting he would regret this. He kept his thoughts on the hill's effects on Sarah's bottom to himself, though he secretly agreed that the hill deserved its name. Ellie started up towards the car park, increasing her pace until she was breathing hard. Harry struggled to keep up with her but he was determined that he wouldn't fall behind. They ran side by side, both straining to maintain what even a professional athlete would call a 'good pace'. After five or six minutes of real effort, they reached the car park. Boot was waiting for them, his tail wagging with excitement.

'He always beats us,' said Ellie, ruffling Boot's head. 'He may be small but he's incredibly fit. He won the dog race at Widdecombe

Summer Fair last year so he thinks he's a bit of an expert.'

'You have a dog race here?' asked Harry.

'Yes. It's just a bit of fun really.' She started to laugh as she remembered last year's race. 'Loads of dogs line up and sprint about forty metres to a finish line. Half of them leave the track and go and find their owners. It's absolute chaos. But some of the dogs, like Boot, are highly disciplined professionals who don't like the idea of coming second at all!'

'It's a very different life down here isn't it?' said Harry thoughtfully, thinking of the life he'd shared with Camilla in London.

'It is and it's as near to perfection as I suspect I'll ever get,' replied Ellie. 'If you've got your breath back, we can jog slowly home. And I mean jog. I let you push me on the outward leg but let's agree just to enjoy the scenery on the way back.'

'OK,' replied Harry, pleased that Ellie had found the run hard. His thoughts started to wander as they followed the road home. He'd never really thought about it before but he could see himself settling down somewhere like Dartmoor. He'd always assumed that he would crave the exotic excitement that places like Kathmandu seemed to offer. But with the right partner he could see the attraction of a house deep in the British countryside with friends like Ellie and Sarah popping in for dinner. 'A dog would be nice, something a bit bigger than Boot,' he thought to himself. He realised that for the first time in his life he was starting to think about putting down roots. He'd never really done this before because he wanted to be able to travel and work wherever he chose. Dogs, houses, cars and other possessions seemed to him to anchor you to a particular place. They made it difficult to be impulsive and meant that you couldn't just leave whenever you chose. 'Maybe that's not a bad thing,' he said to himself. He wondered whether Lucy liked dogs. He vowed to ask her when they next spoke.

Eventually, they arrived back at Ellie's house. Though they'd tried to keep the pace to an easy jog, the last mile or so had been quite fast and they were both breathing hard.

'Whenever you run with someone else, you always end up going faster than you'd really like,' said Ellie, opening the front door and leading the way into the house. 'But thank you for letting me come with you, I appreciate it.'

'I should thank you,' said Harry. 'It's beautiful here. I can see why you've settled down in this part of the world. I wouldn't have seen as much of it if you hadn't given me the guided tour.'

'If we get showered and changed, I'll drive you to the hospital. We need to give Sarah a break and she and I need to do a few things in Exeter.'

'Are you sure?' asked Harry, 'I'm happy to drive.'

'No, that's fine,' said Ellie. 'But before we go, could you give me a hand to bring some logs up from the cellar? We like to keep the burner going throughout the day at this time of year and the cellar is the best place to dry them out before we add them to the pile next to the stove.'

'OK. Where's the cellar?' asked Harry. He was intrigued as he couldn't see an obvious door that looked like it would go downstairs.'

'It's here,' said Ellie, pulling back one of the rugs. Harry could see a large trapdoor set neatly set into the floorboards. It looked like something off a ship. It had a sunken brass handle set at one end and two large brass hinges at the other. Ellie opened the hinged handle and pulled the trapdoor open. It was heavy but it had two weights acting as a counter balance and Ellie was therefore able to open it without too much effort. A wide wooden staircase led down into the dark. Ellie pressed a switch at the top of the steps and the lights in the cellar burst into life. 'Follow me,' said Ellie, going down into the cellar. Harry followed. It was huge, running the full length of the house. The walls were made of brick but had been painted brilliant white. Harry noticed that the girls had set up a very basic gym at the far end of the room. A heavy duty treadmill and a weights bench were set up on two sides of a large square gym mat. A punch bag hung from a beam in the centre and Harry could see gloves, head guards and pads on a shelf behind the treadmill.

'Very impressive,' he said. 'Do you use it much?'

'Only in winter. If we can't face running in the driving rain first thing in the morning, we come down here. It's all right for the moment but, if we ever have enough money, we're going to put a proper staircase in and turn it into a cinema room, games room and proper gym. It's got no central heating at the moment so it's too cold to use for watching TV, although it's alright in the summer. We had some great parties here in July and August!'

Ellie showed him the pile of wood that she and Sarah had stacked against one of the walls. 'If you could grab as many of those logs as you can and take them upstairs, that would be great.'

Harry did as he was asked. They did two trips each, stacking the logs in the fireplace either side of the stove. 'By the time we get back from the hospital, they'll be perfect,' said Ellie, rubbing her hands to get rid of cobwebs. 'I'm going to have a shower,' she said. 'If we meet down here in about thirty minutes, we'll have time for a coffee before we go.'

'OK,' said Harry, following her upstairs to the bedrooms.

He closed his bedroom door and sat on the bed to check his phone. There was a message from Lucy: 'Funeral went well. Managed to get early flight to Exeter. Arriving tomorrow morning at 0700hrs. Will hire car. Can you send directions? XXX'. He smiled, something he found himself doing a lot when he thought of Lucy, and sent a text back telling her that he'd meet her at the airport. He then undressed and showered, changing quickly into jeans, t-shirt and fleece. Fifteen minutes later, he was downstairs making the coffee. He was looking forward to seeing Lucy again. He was also intrigued to know what it was that she'd found out but didn't want to tell him on the phone when they'd spoken the previous day. Ellie and Sarah had both already suggested that Lucy stay with them at the farmhouse, at least for a few days until they knew what they were going to do next.

Ellie joined him ten minutes later. She was wearing a slim fitting dress with an expensive looking cardigan over the top. He handed her a cup of coffee. 'You look very nice,' he said, passing her the milk.

'I'm taking Sarah for lunch. My treat. I had a bet with her about the Tors. I lost. I said there were only about a hundred. She said there were far more and showed me a website that listed over four hundred named Tors. Even allowing for some of them being known by three or four different names, I had to agree that there were more than a hundred. So I owe her lunch and, as we're in Exeter anyway, we thought we'd go today.'

They continued chatting as they drank their coffee. Ten minutes later, they left the house, climbed into Ellie's Land Rover and set off for the hospital. Neither of them saw the man in walking clothes and flat hat watching them through the window from a table inside the pub. But then he wasn't remarkable in any way, just a middle aged walker enjoying a morning coffee with a local newspaper. Nothing could be more normal in the middle of Dartmoor.

CHAPTER 41

Richards watched them go. Things weren't exactly going to plan. He'd assumed that the girl's fall from the top of Hay Tor would have killed her. Concerned that someone might have seen him follow the girl up the mountain, he'd made a swift departure from the scene of the accident and hadn't gone round to check the body at the foot of the face. The only reason he now knew that she hadn't been killed was because, once he'd returned to London, he'd monitored the local internet news to see how the 'accident' was being reported. Eventually, he'd spotted a short article explaining how a falling walker had been miraculously saved by some climbers on Hay Tor. The article was thin on detail but it did explain that she had been taken to Exeter Hospital and that although she was still unconscious she was expected to make a full recovery. Richards was clearly irritated that the girl hadn't died but he was also relieved that the article had given no suggestion that it had been anything other than an unfortunate accident. Once she regained consciousness, however, Richards realised that she might well be able describe what happened to the police. He saw no reason why they wouldn't believe her story and he suspected that she would be able to describe him reasonably accurately having seen his face before she fell. They might well be able to use her description to find and arrest him, but he knew he'd left no evidence at the scene and she would therefore need to testify in person for him to be convicted. Because of this, he realised that he had little option but to kill her. He'd considered trying to get at her in the hospital but, following a quick visit the previous evening, he realised that it would be difficult. The presence of her friends and the security of the Intensive Care Unit, as well as the CCTV cameras that were positioned at key points near the entrances, would make trying anything at the hospital an extremely risky proposition. He'd therefore decided that the best thing to do was to wait until she was discharged. She might go home to London but he suspected that she would go back to her friends' house and stay on Dartmoor for a week or so to recover. The way he saw it, if she'd felt safe in London, she would have stayed there in the first place rather than travel down to Devon.

He wasn't yet sure how he'd get to the girl once she was back at the house but his experience told him to be patient. He'd decided to watch the house and its occupants in order to try and identify any patterns that he could exploit. He realised that things would change if and when the girl returned but he'd long ago learned that time spent in reconnaissance was seldom wasted. 'Things would change,' he'd said to himself. 'But the post will still arrive at the same time and the dustbins will still be emptied according to a schedule. Walkers will still go through the village and village life will go on.' All he needed to do was to spot a weakness in the pattern of life that he could exploit. 'I'll give it a few days,' he said to himself. 'If I can't see a way, then I may have to do something more obvious.' He didn't doubt that he could kill the girl whenever he wanted but, at this stage at least, the aim was still to make it look like an accident of some sort.

Richards' only other concern was the recent arrival of the big man in the Range Rover. He'd seen him out running earlier that morning with one of the girls and he suspected that he was an ex-soldier. Lean and fit, there was a hardness about him that Richards knew well. It came from years spent in austere environments fighting for survival and it gave people a confidence in their own physical abilities that was apparent in the way they moved. Richards had taken photographs of the man and e-mailed them to one of his contacts to see whether they could identify him. 'The large scar on his face should help,' he'd told his contact. 'My instincts tell me that he's an old soldier but he might not be British Army. If you draw a blank with your Ministry of Defence friends, try ex-French Foreign Legion and ex-US Special Forces.'

CHAPTER 42

Highworth's morning was proving more productive than he had dared hope. The short update that his team had put together on Bubble.com's recent performance was reassuring. It listed some of the larger institutional investors who were now beginning to sell their shares and suggested that this would encourage others to do likewise, causing the price to drop as predicted. Satisfied, Highworth closed the file and leaned back in his chair, smiling as he remembered last night. He wasn't sure why but Caroline had been even more passionate and adventurous than usual. He must remember to get her some flowers or something. It wasn't her birthday or even an anniversary but she was so good at taking his mind off things that he felt he needed to thank her. He was also sure that such a display of affection would end in another night of passion and he reckoned he had the stamina for at least one more of those before the weekend. The phone on his desk rang quietly. 'Yes,' he said, putting it on speaker.

'It's Sir James Briggs,' said his PA. 'Shall I put him through?'

Highworth sat upright. 'Yes,' he replied, his good humour evaporating.

'I'm glad I've caught you Charles,' said Briggs, sounding far too cheerful. 'I'm going to give you the details of the bank account I want you to transfer the money into. The transfer is to be completed by six this evening. Once I've confirmed that the money is safely in the account, I'll destroy the files I have on you. I'll also fix Knowles. Clear?'

'Yes,' replied Highworth. 'How are you going to ensure that Knowles doesn't find someone else to tell his story to?'

'You don't need to worry about that,' replied Briggs. 'You have my word that within the next few days he will cease to be a problem. I know one or two things about him that he will not want to become public. That's all you need to know. 1800 hours, remember. Any later and I start the formal inquiry into your activities. And just so you know, if it were to go ahead tomorrow it would kick off with a discrete little leak to the FT. Nothing substantive just the usual "unofficial police sources have confirmed that they are about to launch an investigation into the dealings of etc etc etc." You know the sort of thing. I'll rant and rave about leaks but the story will be out there.' Briggs gave Highworth the details of the account and told him to read them back.

Once he was content that Highworth had them, Briggs hung up and stepped out of the phone box, whistling as he walked towards the underground station. If it all went according to plan, he would be a great deal richer before he went to bed that evening. He was looking forward to going to Belize. He had already booked two weeks holiday and this would give him plenty of time to get the ball rolling in terms of buying a house and transferring what few assets he had, including his beloved dog, Princess. He'd thought of taking the money and just staying out there but, on balance, he'd decided that he needed to come back and carry on as normal until his retirement early next year. 'No point drawing attention to myself just yet,' he'd thought to himself. 'It's not in Highworth's interests to do anything stupid and nobody else knows about our little deal.'

The only thing he needed to do now was to keep Knowles quiet. He'd told Highworth that he already had this in hand but, although he'd given it a great deal of thought, he hadn't yet come up with a pragmatic way of doing it. Knowles would expect to see an investigation beginning as soon as Briggs had had the chance to go through the file. Briggs had decided that he would tell Knowles that the investigation had started but that it would take them several months of painstaking and very discrete research to construct a case that would stack up in court. This was believable and would buy Briggs enough time to come up with a more permanent way of getting Knowles to back off. He'd already tasked one of his more talented detectives to dig through Knowles' life and see whether there was anything that could be used against him. He suspected that the financial side would be well above board but he had heard a rumour or two that Knowles had had a couple of mistresses over the years and that he was also partial to the odd call girl. He'd told the detective that he suspected Knowles was being blackmailed but also that he was clearly concerned about the repercussions of talking to the police. He was therefore being uncooperative and wouldn't confirm whether or not someone was putting pressure on him. The detective had accepted the story. He'd done similar investigations in the past and there was no reason for him to doubt the well respected intentions of his boss, particularly as he knew that Briggs and Knowles went back a long way.

When he had briefed the detective, Briggs had mentioned the rumoured mistresses. He'd told the detective to take a close look at Briggs' personal life as well as his professional one. 'He's hiding something,' Briggs had said to the detective, 'but I don't yet know what. I think he's being blackmailed into doing something that will upset the markets. This makes it our concern, particularly as he won't cooperate.'

'Why don't you just arrest him?' the detective had asked.

'For what?' Briggs had asked. 'All we have at the moment is suspicion and a few stray rumours about his personal life. We have nothing on his business dealings that we can charge him with. If we pull him in now for questioning, his blackmailers will suspect that something's wrong and will most likely disappear off the radar. I want to find out what it is that they have on Knowles before we do anything and then I want to turn the tables on them. If we simply scare them off, they'll try again with someone else. I want to catch them. But this must remain between us for the moment. I don't want anyone else involved just yet.' As he said this, he put his hand on the detective's shoulder and gave him his most sincere look. 'I trust you more than anyone else on the team to keep this quiet. But don't worry, I'll make sure you get the credit when we catch the bad guys.'

The detective had smiled. Briggs had a reputation for sharing the credit amongst his team and for rewarding those who delivered the goods. The detective trusted him implicitly to keep his word and was flattered that Briggs had selected him for the job. 'I won't let you down, Sir,' he'd said to Briggs.

Briggs stopped before going down the steps into the underground. Thinking through his conversation with Highworth, he realised that it might be useful to have a little more detail about Knowles' personal life in case Highworth started to doubt the story that Briggs had given him. He reached for his phone and dialled the detective's number.

'It's Briggs,' he said when the detective answered. 'How's it going?'

'OK,' replied the detective. 'You were right about the mistress. He's seen a woman a couple of times whilst his wife has been away visiting friends. She's about twenty years younger than him, probably in her mid thirties, and extremely attractive. Well dressed, tanned and very up market. Way out of my league I suspect!'

Briggs laughed. 'It's not his daughter is it?' he asked, knowing that Knowles had two daughters, one of whom lived in London.

'Not unless he's taken to kissing his daughter passionately on the lips when he meets her and patting her bottom. They've had lunch together on both occasions and then gone back to a flat in Clapham. He's normally left after a few hours and gone back to work. I'll do some more digging whilst you're away but he's very careful. When they've met, they've eaten at very discrete little restaurants where he would be unlikely to meet anyone from the City. I'll produce a written report for you for when you get back from your holiday in Belize.'

'Thank you,' said Briggs. He congratulated the detective on what he'd managed to uncover so far. It was good work. He'd only been on the case a few days and already he was starting to make progress. Briggs didn't doubt that there'd be more. He'd made the blackmail story up to convince the detective that Knowles was worth looking into but the rumours about a mistress and the call girls were true. He'd heard them a few times over the years but he also knew that Knowles had become a very powerful man over the last decade or so and, in his experience, the more powerful people became, the more they started to believe that rules and social conventions didn't apply to them. This was something of a hobby horse of his. He'd written a few articles about it for the odd academic journal and he'd recently started to lecture on it. At least once a week, a newspaper would carry a story about a politician, senior policeman, army general, bishop or CEO of a multinational whose fall from grace could be attributed to forgetting that the law also applied to them, not just the 'little people' who worked for them.

'It's more than greed,' he'd recently suggested at a seminar he'd been invited to speak at. 'They believe that because they are so successful, they can have what they want. Their behaviour has few checks and balances within their own organisations. The people around them are usually junior to them and, if they are aware of what's going on, they don't comment because they are fearful of their own careers. This is one of the reasons that executive boards have non executive directors. In an ideal world, the non execs are there to question board decisions, prevent "group think" and ensure that chief executives and other board members do the right thing for the company and not for themselves. I say in an ideal world because the reality is that most non execs don't really do this. They enjoy the kudos and financial rewards of being on the board and they tend not to rock the boat too much for fear of being replaced. Moreover, whilst I wouldn't say there's a conspiracy here, the people at the top of the commercial and public worlds often know each other. They went to the same universities, they have the same friends, their kids go to the same schools and they attend the same parties. If you want to establish a second career as a non executive director, it's not a good idea to get a reputation as a difficult person who makes life hard for the chief executive, at least not if you want him to recommend you to one of his buddies at the head of another company or public body.'

The irony of his position wasn't lost on Briggs. He was about to make a great deal of money by doing something entirely illegal. 'But the difference', he rationalised, 'is that I know what I'm doing is wrong. I'm doing it simply because I want the money, not because I believe it's my right'. He put his phone back in his pocket and started down the steps into the underground. Within minutes, he was on the Circle Line and heading for his office.

CHAPTER 43

Ellie and Harry arrived at the hospital just as lunch was being served on the ward. Camilla was propped up in bed, waiting for her food to arrive. She looked much better. Her colour had returned and Sarah explained that she and Camilla had spent the morning doing crosswords and watching TV.

'She's back in the land of the living,' said Sarah, getting up and packing her things away.

'How do you feel?' asked Harry, sitting on Camilla's bed and taking her hand.

'Much better, thank you,' she replied. 'My head still hurts and it's hard to move with this sling on my arm and my leg in a pot but, overall, I think I'm on the mend.'

'I spoke to the doctor on the way in,' said Harry. 'He thinks you should be able to go home tomorrow. They're going to keep you here today and tonight. They were thinking of transferring you to another ward but things are quiet and they're still a little bit worried about your head.'

'That's good,' said Camilla. 'I like it here. The nursing staff are great.'

'We'll see you later,' said Sarah. 'We're off for lunch. It's Ellie's treat and I'm going to pick the most expensive dish on the menu.' She laughed as she saw the look on Ellie's face.

Ellie recovered quickly. 'That's fine,' she said, 'McDonalds isn't very expensive, even if you have a double burger and a huge coke!'

'I'm not going to bloody McDonalds,' said Sarah. 'We're going somewhere nice.' She grabbed Ellie's hand and started dragging her out of the room.

'See you later,' called Ellie over her shoulder. 'We'll be back in a few hours.'

Harry watched them go.

'They're such a good couple,' said Camilla. 'I've known Ellie for years and I've never seen her so happy. She looks great and Sarah is really nice.'

'They're a good match,' agreed Harry. 'I suppose that's all everyone wants isn't it, someone to share their life with?'

Camilla looked at him quizzically. 'Goodness me Fish, do you feel OK?'

'Ho, ho,' said Harry, realising that Camilla was teasing him. 'I just mean that when you're eventually ready to settle down, it must be really nice if you find someone who loves you to do it with.'

'Yes, I suppose that's the general aim. But we're too young to start thinking like that. Too much to do before we're going to be ready to step onto life's hard shoulder and let the world pass us by.'

'Maybe,' said Harry. 'But what happens when you meet someone you really like and you know that if you don't commit to them, they're going to leave you. You feel too young to settle down but you know that, if you let them go, you might never meet anyone like that again. Do you think you'd spend the rest of your life regretting not committing to them when you had the chance?'

'I assume you're not talking about us Harry? I take it you've either met someone or, as you start to enter middle age, you're worrying about whether you're going to spend the rest of your life alone, a sad old bastard who can climb mountains and ski but who goes home to an empty house every night to feed his cat.'

'Firstly, I'm not middle aged and, secondly, I don't like cats. And yes, I might have met someone. Well, I think I might have but I'm not really sure what she really thinks of me.'

'Go on,' said Camilla, prompting him for more. 'I promise I won't tell anyone.'

Harry thought about it. He'd been with Camilla for years and he knew that they'd always be close friends. They'd split up because they wanted different things and that wouldn't change in a hurry.

There was no chance of them getting back together again. There was no acrimony between them and she seemed genuinely interested.

Harry waited until the nurse had served Camilla's lunch and then, whilst she ate, he told her about how he'd met Lucy in Nepal and everything that had happened since. He was honest with her about his feelings. In truth, he valued her views on whether the relationship might work. She asked the odd question between mouthfuls.

'I can't wait to meet her,' said Camilla as Harry finished his story. 'She sounds great.'

'I think she is,' said Harry. 'But I hardly know her. I just know that I want to be with her. I can't stop thinking about her. Anyway, you'll meet her tomorrow when they let you out. She's flying down from Scotland in the morning and the girls have said she can stay at the house whilst we work out what we're going to do next.'

'I'll tell you what, I'll give you my considered view when I've seen you together for a few days,' said Camilla, enjoying her new-found role as Harry's relationship advisor. 'The only advice I'd offer you now is that you should only regret the things you do, not the things you don't do.'

'I don't mean this unkindly Camilla,' said Harry, 'but that's very profound for you.'

'Fuck off Fish,' replied Camilla, laughing. 'What I mean is that if you are in doubt, you should go for it. It's better to regret having made the mistake of doing something than to spend the rest of your life wondering what might have happened if you'd had the courage to go for it.'

Harry laughed. They continued chatting amicably for the next few hours, reminiscing about the things they used to do together and the people they knew. Camilla had stayed in touch with most of them, even the ones who had originally been Harry's friends rather than hers. Most were doing well, working hard to establish themselves in their careers. Harry felt his phone vibrate. He took it out of his pocket. It was a text. He read it: 'Should be with you before midnight.

Got the stuff. See you then. H and G.'

'Anything interesting?' asked Camilla.

'No, just some friends who said they'd help me out. You'll meet them later when you're back at the house.'

Harry didn't want to alarm Camilla by explaining that the friends had agreed to help him protect her until he'd somehow managed to find whoever had tried to kill her on Hay Tor. He'd asked them to meet him at the house, arriving after dark so as not to draw unnecessary attention to themselves in the tiny village.

One of the nurses came in and suggested that Camilla needed to sleep. 'You can stay,' she said to Harry, 'but she needs to rest. I'll get you a cup of tea and I've got today's paper if you want to read something.'

Harry thanked the nurse. She returned with the tea and dimmed the lights in the room. The curtains were closed and Harry soon found himself struggling to stay awake. His body was still adjusting to UK time and the run that morning had added to his tiredness. He finished his tea, put the cup on the table next to the bed and closed his eyes. Within minutes, he was fast asleep.

CHAPTER 44

Lucy had spent the morning with Isobel, going through her father's belongings. The funeral had been the previous day. About ten people had been present. They'd held a short service and then cremated the body at the city crematorium. Kate had been extremely tearful. Afterwards, she'd admitted that she and Lucy's father had been lovers for years and that she had looked forward to spending the rest of her life with him. She wasn't sure that they would ever have got married but she told the girls that they had been planning to buy a small cottage on the Isle of Skye together. 'It would have been our retreat from the world,' she'd told Lucy after the funeral. At one point Kate had leaned across the small table they were sitting at and, taking tight hold of both of Lucy's hands, had looked her straight in the eye. 'He was very proud of you, Lucy, you know that don't you. He might have been a man of few words but he always kept me up to speed with what you were doing and he always said it with such wonder in his voice, almost as if he couldn't believe that he was your father.'

'What will you do now?' Lucy had asked, fighting back the tears and wanting to change the subject.

'I don't know,' Kate had replied. 'I might still go and buy that cottage on Skye. It won't be the same without him but I suspect that's why he left me the money. He knew I didn't need it for everyday life. I've got a good pension and a fair amount invested in various funds. He knew that.'

'That sounds good, did you have anywhere in particular in mind?' Lucy had asked.

'Near the Cuillins,' Kate had replied. 'Your father and I spent a fair amount of time walking along the ridge. We'd stay in the Sligachan

Hotel and then spend the day scrambling over the mountains.'

'It's beautiful up there,' Lucy had agreed. She knew the hills well. She'd been on several university expeditions to the Cuillins and she had some amazing photographs of herself stood on an outcrop called the Cioch. It meant 'breast' in Gaellic and it jutted out from the face of one of the mountains. It was spectacular and had been used as a location in a number of films. 'Can I come and stay when you get the cottage?' Lucy had asked.

'Of course, you'll always be welcome. I want us to stay in touch. I just wish your father was with us to enjoy it.'

All things considered, Lucy thought that it had been a good service and that her father would have approved. He didn't like fuss. 'Just get on with it,' she could imagine him telling her.

She sat on the floor in the sitting room, going through the contents of her father's drawers one by one. There wasn't much in them. He was remarkably tidy. She'd found a load of files in a cupboard in his bedroom. They contained copies of his most recent bills. Gas, electricity, a few bank and credit card statements. There was nothing unusual or suspicious about any of them.

Isobel had gone off to get changed. She was going out for a drink with Jake, the policeman they'd met at the station. He'd turned up at the funeral in a dark suit, white shirt, black tie and highly polished shoes. He'd made an effort and Lucy appreciated that. He'd told Lucy that they were working hard on the case but that they weren't making much progress. 'Nobody seems to have seen or heard anything at all,' he'd said.

'That's not good,' Lucy had replied.

'No, it's not,' Jake had admitted, 'but it's also a bit odd. Normally, if there's a mugging or a murder, someone hears something and, because we know who to talk to, we start to hear rumours. We haven't heard anything at all and this makes me think that whoever did it was from out of town. Not one of our regular offenders.'

'What will you do?' Lucy had asked.

'We'll keep talking to people but we've also asked the police in other areas to keep an ear out for anything that might be connected.'

Lucy was pleased that Isobel was going out. She wanted a bit of time on her own but she was also happy that Isobel had met someone who seemed to be decent, honest and reasonably normal. Isobel's previous boyfriends had had little in common with each other except for their oddness, or so it seemed to Lucy. Lucy could hear Isobel coming out of the bathroom. A few minutes later she could hear the hair dryer being switched on. Lucy kept going through her father's things. 'He was an assassin,' she said to herself. 'He must have hidden his assassin stuff somewhere.' She had no idea what an assassin would need by way of tools of the trade but, so far, she had found nothing unusual at all.

'Lucy, I need your help,' called Isobel. Lucy stood up and went to find Isobel in the bedroom.

'I've lost an earring,' said Isobel, 'and I can't find it anywhere.' Isobel was wearing her tightest and shortest dress. Lucy had to admit she looked stunning. It was black and beautifully cut, showing off her curves to excellent effect. 'It's down there somewhere, only this damn dress is so tight I can't bend down and look.'

Lucy laughed, dropping onto all fours and starting to look between the gaps in the bedroom's highly polished wooden floor. After five minutes of detailed searching, she thought she could see it. It had fallen down between two floorboards. She tried to reach it with her little finger but couldn't. 'I need a screwdriver or a knife to get it out,' she said, getting up and going to the kitchen.

'You star,' said Isobel. The earrings had been a gift from her mother and she would have been sad to have lost one.

Lucy returned with a kitchen knife. She sat on the floor and slipped the blade into the crack. The more she tried, the more the earring seemed to slip deeper into the gap. Lucy changed tactics and tried to lift one of the floorboards. To her surprise, it came up relatively easily. She lifted two or three others up. The earring seemed to have slipped into the insulation that filled the gaps under the floorboards. She pulled this up as well.

'Bugger me,' she said, uncovering what looked like a metal trap door. 'What have we here?'

'What it is?' said Isobel, lifting her dress up over her hips so she could crouch on the floor next to Lucy.

'It looks like some kind of floor safe,' said Isobel, removing more floorboards and insulation.

A few minutes later both girls were kneeling down, looking at a small metal door with a keypad on it. Lucy pressed a few of the number pads. A small screen above the keypad displayed an error message.

'Try his birthday,' suggested Isobel.

Lucy converted her father's birthday to a six digit number and entered it. The error message appeared again. She tried her mother's birthday, his old Army service number and his phone number. More error messages.

'Try your birthday,' suggested Isobel.

Lucy entered the day, month and year of her birth. The door clicked and opened a few millimetres. Lucy put her fingers under the edge and started to open it, apprehensive at what she might find.

Isobel helped her lift the door. They were both silent as they stared at the contents. The safe was lined with black foam rubber, like a camera case. Only instead of cameras and lenses, it contained an evil looking rifle, a large telescopic sight, a few pistols, several sharp looking knives and a collection of passports. There were also a few wads of what looked to be fifty pound notes held together with elastic bands.

'Wow,' said Lucy. 'So this is where he hid his assassin stuff. There must be a couple of hundred thousand pounds there.'

'I suspect this is the emergency stuff,' said Isobel. 'I don't suppose he used this stuff routinely. The money and passports would be all he'd need to get out of the country in a hurry. And he could protect himself with the guns and knives if he needed to.'

Isobel looked at her watch. It was nearly six. 'I'd better get a move on,' she said. 'I agreed to meet Jake at seven at Tiger Lilly's but I'll stay if you want me to.'

'No. You go. A change of scenery will do you good. You'll have fun but perhaps it would be better not to tell Jake about all this, at least not yet.'

'No. I suspect you're right. He'd only jump to conclusions that would be unhelpful at this stage,' replied Isobel.

'If you want to stay here for a few days, that's fine you know,' said Lucy. 'I'm happy to fly down to Exeter on my own. Harry's going to meet me so I won't be lonely.'

'Are you sure?' asked Isobel. They'd discussed it briefly that afternoon. Jake had sent Isobel a text inviting her to go with him to Murrayfield to watch Scotland play Wales at rugby. Lucy could tell that Isobel really wanted to go but the game was at the weekend, a few days after they were supposed to be flying down to meet Harry.

'You go. I promise I'll be fine,' said Lucy. 'You can stay here as long as you like. If you get bored or if I need you, you can always fly down and meet me in Devon.'

'OK,' said Isobel. 'Thank you.'

'No problem. But try not to wake me up when you come back in. The taxi's coming at five so I suppose I'll need to be up about four.'

'I'll be as quiet as a mouse,' said Isobel, screwing up her nose and making squeaking noises whilst she put the finishing touches to her make-up.

Lucy laughed. 'You do scrub up well you know,' said Lucy, looking her friend up and down. 'You look great.'

'Thank you. All compliments gratefully received,' said Isobel, kissing Lucy on the cheek before grabbing her coat and heading off down the hall.

Lucy heard the front door slam behind Isobel. She sat on the floor and looked at the contents of the safe. She wondered whether her father would ever have told her about his secret life had he lived. 'Probably not,' she thought to herself. She still wasn't sure what she felt about it. Her father had become a very rich man by killing other people. Sure, some of them no doubt deserved to die but was it right that her father had been the one to kill them? What would her mother have thought if she'd been alive? 'Not very much,' thought Lucy. Lucy remembered her mother as a placid and loving woman. She didn't think of her very often but, when she did, she was overcome by a sense of life's unfairness. 'Why my Mum?' she used to shout at the sky when she was young. She'd discussed it with Isobel when they were at school together. Isobel's view hadn't changed in all the time she'd known her. She had no faith and her view was that life was basically what you made of it. Crap things happened every day. There was no reason for any of it, it just happened. The only thing you could do was try to make the best of it.

Lucy's phone buzzed, rousing her from her thoughts. It was a text from Harry. 'Looking forward to seeing you. Will be there at 7. Safe journey. Xxx.' Lucy smiled. It would be good to see him again. The thought lifted her spirits.

'Coming alone. Miss you too. See you then. Xx.' Lucy sent the text and stood up. 'Get a grip girl,' she said aloud, mimicking her father's voice. She put her suitcase on the bed and started to pack. She took some of the money from the floor safe before closing the door and putting the floorboards back in place. 'Unless you knew it was there, you'd never find it,' she thought to herself. Whatever she felt about the morality of what he'd done, he was her father and she was determined that she would bring his killer to justice. She had a name from the letter McLeod had given her and she knew he was ex-Army. She felt sure that Harry would know how to start tracking him down. 'And then,' she thought, 'those weapons might just come in handy because if the police won't nail him, I will.'

Chapter 45

Ellie had volunteered for the night shift at the hospital. It was getting close to midnight and Harry and Sarah were sat around the kitchen table, chatting about the day's events when they heard a car pull up outside the house. Boot started to bark.

'It's OK boy,' said Harry, reaching over to ruffle his head. 'It's just some friends.' Harry went over to the door and opened it. It was pitch dark outside and he could just make out the shape of a four wheel drive parked next to his Range Rover. He went out, closing the door behind him. As his eyes adjusted to the dark, he could see two figures getting bags out of the back of the car. He walked over towards them.

'Thanks for coming boys,' he said as he approached them. 'I really appreciate it.'

'No problem,' said one of the men. 'Always glad to help out.'

Harry shook both their hands and grabbed one of the bags. It was heavy. 'Follow me inside,' he said, 'and I'll give you a beer.' Harry led the way towards the front door. The men followed him.

When they were inside, Harry introduced them to Sarah. 'This is Hemraj and this is Ganesh,' he said, 'two of my oldest and most trusted friends.' Sarah came over to them and shook their hands.

Can I offer you two a beer?' she asked. They nodded, smiling at her. Sarah wasn't quite sure what to make of them. They were both short but one of them, Hemraj, had the shoulders of a professional wrestler. As he took his jacket off, she couldn't help notice the size of his arms. They were huge. Ganesh was slimmer and seemed to smile more.

'Do sit down,' said Sarah as she handed them each a beer, slightly nervously.

'Thank you,' replied Ganesh. Hemraj smiled and nodded his thanks.

'The boys were with me in the Army,' said Harry. 'They're Gurkhas. They left a few years ago.'

'What do you do now?' asked Sarah.

'We work in security,' answered Ganesh. 'We've just come back from the Middle East.'

'What sort of security do you specialise in?' asked Sarah, fascinated despite herself. She'd never met anyone quite like the two men who now sat in front of her.

'At the moment, we're doing anti-piracy on ships going through the Straits of Hormuz,' answered Ganesh.

'Is it dangerous?' asked Sarah.

'For the pirates it is,' said Ganesh, 'but not really for us. We're very well armed and the ships we're on are very big. Plus the area is now patrolled by the Navy so we don't see too many pirates anymore. It's very different to what it was like a few years ago.'

Sarah had never met a Gurkha before and she wanted to ask more questions. But she held her tongue. 'There would be plenty of time,' she thought. She busied herself tidying up the kitchen whilst Harry talked with them. She could see them out of the corner of her eye. There was an easy familiarity amongst the three of them. They clearly knew each other very well. Harry had switched to what she took to be their native language. He was obviously fluent. She noticed the two men looked very different. Their skin was the same light brown but whereas Ganesh was fine featured and slim, Hemraj was heavily built with high cheek bones and a broad forehead. Harry later explained to her that Ganesh came from the western plains near Nepal's border with India. Hemraj, on the other hand, came from the mountains near Everest. 'He's from the same stock as the Monguls,' explained Harry. 'His family have been sherpas for generations but he left the hills to join the Army. He's immensely strong, rather quiet and probably the hardest man I've ever met,' said Harry. 'He was blown up in Afghanistan a few times so he's also a bit deaf,' added Harry. 'Ganesh, on the other hand, is probably the best tracker the Army's ever had and certainly one of its best snipers. I suspect this won't mean much to you but he can hit a matchbox size target from over a kilometre away. The reason he isn't unduly worried about pirates is that they rarely get close enough to whatever ship he's on to pose a threat. Once they've been positively identified, Ganesh makes sure they get the message that it really isn't worth their while to try and take the ship. He's very good at his job by all accounts.'

Sarah thought about what Harry had told her. She'd never met anyone who made their living working with guns and she wasn't quite sure how she felt about it. She also didn't really know whether Harry was telling her that Ganesh made his living shooting people, albeit bad people who were intent on doing evil things, or whether he merely fired warning shots at boats used by the pirates to dissuade them from attacking. Looking at them, she could believe that the two Gurkhas were dangerous people. Despite their smiles and impeccable manners, there was something deep within them that she felt she could see in their eyes. It made her shiver. She was extremely glad they were on her side.

Sarah left the boys to it and went to bed. Harry sat with them and they talked through what they would do when Camilla came home. 'The key thing,' Harry said, 'is that you stay out of sight. Somebody obviously thinks she knows something that makes her a threat and the sooner she's out of the way, the happier they'll be. So from the moment she gets home, I am assuming that person will be watching us, looking for an opportunity to kill her. What I hope gives us an edge is that they will be expecting three girls and me. On the assumption that they didn't see you arrive, we should have a slight advantage.'

The Gurkhas asked a few questions and made further suggestions. Harry listened to their advice. They had a natural eye for the ground and were seeing the problem from a fresh perspective. They agreed that they should move into the cellar in order to avoid anyone seeing them. Harry said that he would go and hide their car in one of the old stables whilst they took their bags down into the cellar and started to get their equipment ready. Harry showed them the cellar door and then went out with Boot to park their car.

When Harry came back in, he went down to the cellar and found that the Gurkhas had set up two camp beds. They had unpacked their bags and laid out their equipment on two large waterproof sheets which were on the floor between the beds. Harry was surprised at how much stuff they had brought. 'God knows where you got all this,' said Harry, 'but I am impressed!'

'Like old times,' said Hemraj, passing Harry a pair of the latest night vision goggles. 'These NVGs are amazing,' said Hemraj. 'It's as clear as daylight with these on. And the range is a real improvement on the old things that you'll remember. We use them on the ships. There's a lot less light pollution at sea so the stuff that we were using in the Army just wouldn't cut it. Not enough ambient light.'

Harry handed them back to Hemraj. 'New rifle Ganesh?' asked Harry.

'Yes, very new,' said Ganesh, picking up a beautifully made sniper rifle. 'It's an Accuracy International AX338. I got it a few months ago. It fires the same ammunition as the old army sniper rifle but it's more accurate. Still bolt action and still quite heavy but it's an improvement on the old model, or at least I think it is!' Ganesh knew a great deal about sniper rifles. He had been a member of the British Army's Shooting Team for several seasons and had won the coveted Queen's Medal at Bisley on three separate occasions. The medal is given to the highest scoring shot at the Army's annual shooting competition. One of the benefits of winning is that the rest of the team carry you on a chair to the clubhouse where you join the great and the good for lunch. The lunch can be a bit of an ordeal but winning the medal is the ultimate prize for a professional shot. For Ganesh to have won it three times was a remarkable achievement.

Harry looked at the rest of the equipment. He recognised trip flares, three Glock pistols, a couple of shotguns, another set of NVGs and three powerful looking torches. 'One of the pistols is for you,' said Hemraj. He reached down and picked up one of the Glocks, checking that it was empty before handing it to Harry. 'They're nice,' said Hemraj. 'Again, another improvement on the old Brownings that we used to have.'

Harry held the pistol in a firing position with his arms outstretched. It felt very comfortable. 'How many rounds does it hold?' he asked.

'Seventeen,' replied Hemraj. 'But they are 9mm so, provided you hit the target, you shouldn't need too many. There are some holsters in the black bag under the bed if you want to get one out.'

Harry did as he was told, opening the bag and retrieving one of the holsters. They were designed to conceal the weapon but also allow easy access. Worn under a jacket, nobody would notice the pistol tucked under the arm. Hemraj passed Harry a small box of ammunition. 'There's more if you need it but this should suffice for now,' said Hemraj. The three of them spent the next hour checking the equipment, loading the weapons, replacing the batteries in the torches and NVGs.

Ganesh started to change out of his jeans and fleece and into black combats.

'Going somewhere?' asked Harry.

'I want to have a look round before we call it a day,' Ganesh replied. 'I need to get a feel for the ground before anyone starts trying to get to the girl. If you're happy, I'll take a bit of a walk for an a hour or so.'

'Fine,' said Harry. 'I'll draw you a quick sketch of the ground around the house if you like.'

'That'd be helpful but I also got these off Google Earth before we came down here.' Ganesh reached into a slim briefcase and pulled took out a handful of images that he'd printed off that afternoon. They were extremely clear and showed the house and its immediate surroundings. Harry noticed that Ganesh had marked particular areas with a pen. They made an approximate circle around the house.

'The ringed bits are where I would watch the house from if I wanted to take a shot at someone staying here. I need to check them because, as you know, what looks like a great place in a photograph can be a really bad place on the ground. I'll go and check them out. I've also got a few of these that I want to put in position.'

Ganesh held up what looked like a small web-cam. 'These are really good,' he said. 'I'll try and cover the main approaches to the house. That way, if someone tries to get close, we should see them.'

'Are they cameras?' asked Harry.

'Yes, watch,' said Ganesh. He walked over to the far end of the cellar and placed one of the cameras on the weights bench. He fiddled with it for a few minutes then came back to where Harry and Hemraj were sitting. Hemraj had a laptop open on the bed. He turned it to face Harry. The screen showed the three of them crowded over the laptop. Harry waved and the image on the screen waved back. It was very clear.

'They've got a range of about 200 metres and the batteries will last for a few days,' said Ganesh. 'They're not very good in low light conditions but we should be able to get around that by keeping the lights on outside the house. I've also brought some trip flares but I'm not sure they'll add anything.'

Ganesh finished getting changed and then took a small black rucksack out of one of the bags. He packed the cameras in it, took the aerial photographs off the bed and checked that his torch worked. 'Don't wait up,' he said. 'I shouldn't be more than a few hours. If I see anything interesting, I'll call you,' he said to Hemraj, holding up one of the small Motorola walkie-talkies that they used on the ships. Hemraj nodded.

Harry went upstairs with Ganesh. He turned the outside lights off and opened the front door. Ganesh smiled at Harry before disappearing into the night. 'He certainly looked the part,' thought

Harry. Dressed from head to toe in black and with a balaclava pulled down over his face, Harry doubted very much that he would be seen.

Harry went back down to the cellar to find Hemraj.

'Bhiralo goyo?' asked Hemraj.

'Yes,' replied Harry laughing. 'Bhiralo' had been Ganesh's nickname when he had been the lead scout in the Battalion's Reconnaissance Platoon. Nepali for 'cat', it was an apt sobriquet given the feline and sinuous way that Ganesh seemed to move when stalking somebody. He'd spent years refining his technique as the chief instructor of the British Army's Jungle Warfare School in Brunei. Working with the local Eban tribesmen that the Army employed to teach jungle craft, he'd established a reputation for being able to track anyone over any terrain, a skill he'd transferred to Afghanistan with remarkable success.

Hemraj had noticed the weights at the far end of the room and wandered over to look at them. 'Do you think the girls would mind if I used the weights for an hour or so?' he asked Harry. 'I need to stay awake until Ganesh gets back so I might as well use the time productively.'

'I'm sure they wouldn't mind,' replied Harry. 'I've got to leave for the airport to collect Lucy in a few hours so, if you're happy, I'm going to go and get a few hours sleep.'

'Crack on,' replied Hemraj, removing his shirt and putting on a pair of fingerless weightlifting gloves. Harry watched him for a few minutes as he went over to the gym area and started adding additional weights to the bars. He looked incredibly strong. 'If anything,' thought Harry, 'he's got even bigger since he left the Army.' An accomplished martial artist, Hemraj had black belts in both Judo and Tae Kwon Do. He was built for the former but preferred the latter having spent several years as the Army's heavyweight Tae Kwon Do champion. Watching him now, Harry understood why the Commanding Officer had always selected Hemraj as his personal bodyguard whenever they were deployed on operations. Not only was he impressively built, but his dark and impassive eyes sent a very clear 'don't fuck with me' message to anyone who looked into them. Hemraj reminded Harry of a young Mike Tyson. But whereas Tyson had seemed to struggle to control the rage burning inside him, Hemraj had absolute control of his emotions.

Harry left Hemraj in the cellar and went up to his bedroom. He sent another quick text to Lucy wishing her a safe journey, undressed and collapsed into bed. He was asleep within minutes.

CHAPTER 46

Richards was in London having driven up early that evening. After he'd finished his morning coffee at the Ring O'Bells, he'd spent a few hours walking in the hills around the village. He had chosen his route carefully to ensure that he could see the house at all times but it had been extremely quiet. Once the blond man and the girl had left, presumably for the hospital, there had been no noticeable activity. After his walk, he'd taken the opportunity to fit a tracking device to the Range Rover and then, satisfied that there was little to be gained by watching an empty house, he'd headed for London. He wanted to see the contact who was trying to identify the blond man for him and he also needed to pick up some additional equipment, which included a sniper rifle, that he now felt he might need. But, though both of these were important, the main reason that he'd decided to return to London was a text he'd received from his girlfriend. Her husband had been called away at short notice to attend an urgent diplomatic meeting over in Dublin. This meant that she was free for the night and, seeing an unexpected opportunity, she'd sent Richards a text suggesting that she should come and spend it with him. He'd agreed readily.

When he arrived in London, he'd gone straight to the contact's house. The contact had quickly summarised what he had discovered: 'His name is Harry Parker. He's ex-British Army. Gurkha. First rate linguist. Did three tours in Afghan, one with a special unit of some sort. He left the Army about three years ago. Now lives in Nepal and works in development as a freelance contractor. He's been shot a few times and got that nasty scar in Somalia earlier this year.' The contact had given Richards a thin file. It contained photographs of Parker and a brief resume of everything he'd uncovered. Richards had scanned the notes, asked a few questions and then, eager to get away, had said that he would call if he had any further questions. So far he hadn't phoned.

He'd got back to his flat just before the girl arrived. They'd had fun. They hadn't seen each other for a week or so and their enthusiasm lasted for several hours. She was now asleep in his bed and he was lying in the bath thinking through what his next move should be. His contact had described Parker as a 'capable bloke'. He'd also said that Parker was sought after by the development agencies, particularly when they needed something done quickly in an environment that was likely to be hostile. From the notes in the file it was obvious that Parker had few reservations about killing his fellow man. He'd been responsible for several deaths in Afghanistan whilst serving in the Army as well as in Somalia whilst working for a development agency. 'Not one to under-estimate,' Richards said to himself. The more he thought about Parker, the more he realised that making the artist's death look like an accident might be asking too much. 'As long as she dies and as long as her death doesn't lead the police to me or to Highworth, maybe it doesn't need to look like an accident after all,' he thought to himself as the germ of an idea started to take root. 'Yes, it might work,' he said to himself, smiling as he noticed the girl standing naked in the doorway.

'Room for one more?' she asked, holding up two glasses of champagne.

'Of course,' he replied, admiring the firmness of her body as she walked slowly towards him. She handed him one of the glasses as he sat up to make room for her.

'To diplomatic conferences in Dublin,' she said, raising her glass to his as she stepped into the bath. 'May they hold many more!'

CHAPTER 47

Harry's alarm went off at five thirty am. He showered, dressed and went downstairs to make coffee. Boot was snoring gently in his basket and Harry tiptoed around him to avoid waking him up. He put the kettle on and went down into the cellar whilst it boiled. Both the Gurkhas were asleep. Their kit was neatly laid out. Harry noticed that both had weapons within easy reach of their beds and assumed that they also had pistols under the covers with them. He was grateful to both of them for helping him out. He'd sent the sketch that Camilla had drawn to some ex-Army friends in London but, so far, he had heard nothing. He had no idea whether the person trying to kill Camilla was a professional assassin or just some hired yob from London. Of the two, he was assuming the former, hence the need for the Gurkhas, at least until he could be sure.

He heard the kettle whistle and went back upstairs. Boot opened one eye as he heard Harry searching the cupboards to find the cafetiere. Eventually he found it. Reassured that all was well in the world, Boot closed his eye and went back to sleep. Harry made the coffee and poured it into a thermos mug to take with him in the car. He was looking forward to seeing Lucy. He left the house, got into the Range Rover and, as quietly as he could, drove down towards the main road. It was still dark and the village was quiet. The few street lights cast just enough light for Harry to see a fox pad across the village green. It disappeared down a track that ran along the side of the Ring O'Bells and down towards the stream that he had crossed with Ellie on their run.

Harry switched his headlights to main beam as he left the village and started to climb the hill towards the Moretonhampstead road. There was no other traffic and very little ambient light. His headlights illuminated a badger crossing the road ahead of him. He slowed until it reached the other side, disappearing into the undergrowth. Early morning was, he felt, a magical time of day. The world seemed to belong to animals, not people. As a soldier, he'd come to prefer operating at night. It was safer, particularly for movement. Though night vision goggles enabled their wearer to see in the dark, their field of view was restricted and, unless they were pointed directly at you, you were unlikely to be seen. An owl flew across the road in front of him. It looked as though it had a small rodent in its beak. 'Off to feed its young,' Harry said to himself.

Moretonhampstead was starting to wake up as he drove into it. A small and now thriving town, he'd read somewhere that there had been a settlement here since 700AD. He saw a few lights starting to appear in the windows of the houses lining the streets. He pulled up outside the newsagents and went inside to buy cigarettes. It had just opened. A man was sorting out the newly arrived newspapers, undoing the bundles that they had been delivered in and putting the papers on racks in the shop's entrance.

'Morning,' said the man cheerfully, 'seen any snow yet?'

Harry had listened to the weather forecast as he'd dressed. 'Not yet,' he replied, 'but I'm sure it's on its way!' The man smiled. Harry asked for a packet of Camel cigarettes. He realised that he had started smoking regularly again but, given the circumstances, he decided not to be too hard on himself. 'I'll stop when I get back to Nepal,' he thought to himself, paying the man before going back to his car. He lit a cigarette and inhaled deeply as the car left Moretonhampstead. The smoke caught at the back of his throat. It reminded him of early mornings in Afghanistan, sitting outside the operations room with a coffee and a cigarette, scanning intelligence reports as the sun started to rise above the mountains far on the horizon. There was more traffic on the roads as he joined the Devon Expressway for the run North to the airport. He switched on the radio and turned it to Radio 4. The *Today* programme was just starting. He listened as John Humphries – the main presenter – gave a lucid summary of a speech the Prime Minister had given the previous day. Under pressure from the opposition, the Prime Minister had been defending his Government's decision not to impose further regulation on the financial sector. Harry listened with half an ear. He was more concerned about how Lucy would react when she saw him. He realised now that this is what had created his sudden urge to smoke. He decided to play it cool and to let her set the pace. It felt slightly odd being nervous and he had to admit that he hadn't felt like this for years. Normally confident and self-assured, he felt like a sixth former about to collect the prettiest girl in the school for their first date!

Harry arrived at the airport just as Lucy's plane was coming in to land. He parked and went to wait in the arrivals hall. Ten minutes later, Lucy came through the double doors that screened the customs area from the waiting masses. He had to admit that she looked great. Skinny jeans, blue Converse All Stars, close fitting pink fleece and her trademark baseball hat. Her hair was pulled back and her pony tail poked out through the back of the hat. Her face lit up as she recognised him. Isobel was a great friend but Harry exuded such confidence and inner strength that she could feel the stresses and strains of the last few days starting to subside as she walked towards him. Even though she hardly knew him, she felt sure that if anybody could help her unravel her father's death, it would be Harry.

'Welcome to Devon,' said Harry, putting his arms around her. He wasn't sure what to do next, whether to peck her cheek or kiss her on the lips but the decision was made for him as Lucy's mouth closed over his.

'God, it's good to see you Harry,' she said, stepping back to look at him. 'We've had a hell of a time in Edinburgh and you won't believe what I've found out about my Dad.'

'I can't wait to hear about it,' replied Harry, surprised but delighted by Lucy's obvious pleasure at seeing him. He took her bag. 'Let's get in the car and I'll take you for breakfast in Ashburton so you can tell me all about it.'

Lucy linked her arm through his as he led the way to the Range Rover. Its lights flicked on as he pressed the remote control.

'Very nice,' said Lucy. 'Were you feeling particularly rich when you hired this?'

'No,' replied Harry, 'I wanted a four wheel drive for Dartmoor and this was pretty much all they had. But it is nice and a bit of luxury now and again is good for the soul. It reminds me of why I work!'

Harry put Lucy's bag in the boot and they climbed into the car. It was still warm from the journey to the airport. 'So,' said Harry, 'tell me all about what's been happening and what you've found out about your Dad.'

'Well,' said Lucy, 'it turns out there was a lot more to him than met the eye. Give me one of your cigarettes and I'll tell you more.'

Harry fished the packet of Camels out of his pocket and handed them and his lighter to Lucy. She lit one for each of them and then started to tell him what had happened since they last met. She went into as much detail as she could remember about her discussions with her father's solicitor and his financial advisor. She told him about the letter and her father's confession that he had spent the last few years killing people for money. When she finished, she was crying quietly, the tears rolling down her face.

Harry reached across and squeezed her hand. 'Christ, Lucy,' he said, 'I can see why you're upset. It's almost unbelievable. So your Dad was an upmarket hitman and not a part time security guard as you thought. Quite a shock I should think.'

'Yes, a real shock,' she replied, drying her eyes. 'But the oddest thing is that, in a way, I'm rather proud of him. It always seemed so sad to me to imagine him manning the door at some concert, turning away drunks with his ex-Army mates. But I am shocked at how much he managed to make. You'd never have guessed given the way he lived.'

'Really?' queried Harry, not wanting to appear too inquisitive.

'Really,' replied Lucy. 'His legal estate totals just over four and a half million pounds. There's three and a half million in UK bank accounts, about eight hundred thousand in paintings and a flat worth just over three hundred thousand. There's also five and a half million in the offshore accounts I mentioned. All in all, I think he was worth just short of ten million pounds. McLeod said he was planning to retire when he got to the ten million mark. It seems such a shame that he was killed having got within spitting distance of his magic retirement figure. I'd much rather he was here now working out how to spend it all, ideally with Kate.'

'It's such a shame but ten million's a lot of money to retire on. He could have retired much earlier. I wonder if he had a particular plan that required so much money,' said Harry.

'I've been wondering that as well,' replied Lucy. 'I know he'd intended to buy a cottage with Kate up in Skye and I suspect he was also planning to buy something abroad, somewhere he could use his offshore money without arousing suspicion but I've no idea where.'

'What will you do with it all?' asked Harry.

'I'm not sure yet. I'll have to pay death duties on the legal estate and that'll take a fair chunk of the money but it'll still leave me with a few million more than I had a month ago. As for the offshore accounts, I really don't know. I might buy something abroad and spend part of the year there.'

'There's no rush to decide,' said Harry. 'You can take as long as you like to work out what you want to do with your newfound wealth.'

'You're right. I suspect it'll take me a while to get used to not having to count every penny,' replied Lucy. 'I've been a post graduate student on a small research grant for so long that I won't feel comfortable going on a spending spree, particularly as I didn't earn the money.'

'What about the chap your Dad said might try and kill him?' asked Harry.

'It's funny,' said Lucy. 'My Dad was a very careful man and he was obviously worried that something might be wrong before he met the man he called Richards. Apparently, meetings with Richards were usually planned well in advance. I suppose they had to be given my Dad was away a lot. Dad's sixth sense was extremely well developed and the short notice nature of this last meeting clearly set it tingling, warning him that something was not right. The problem I've got is that if I take the name to the police, I'll pretty much have to admit that Dad was killing people and I'm not sure whether I want to do that. It's not about the money – which I suspect they would want to confiscate – but more about his reputation. It would eventually find its way into the papers and I really don't want that.'

'What else have you got on this Richards chap?' asked Harry.

'Dad said he was in the Army and definitely ex-Special Forces. According to Dad's letter, he'd had to leave under something of a cloud, though Dad didn't say what sort of cloud.'

'OK,' replied Harry, clearly intrigued. 'I might be able to help. I've still got some friends in the SF world. I'll ask them what they know about anyone called Richards who might have had to leave rather suddenly and we'll see what they come back with.'

A few minutes later, they arrived in Ashburton. It was still early but already the car park was filling up. Harry found a space near the bookshop that Sarah worked in. It looked as if it was just opening for the day. The door was open and several small trestle tables were in the process of being set up in front of the shop to display the older and less valuable books that the owner clearly hoped would draw customers inside. Lucy paused and looked through the window.

'I'd love to have a look round later this week if we have time,' she said to Harry. She noticed Harry's quizzical look. 'I'm an academic remember. I love books!'

'Of course. I'd almost forgotten. When do you find out about your PhD?'

'Next week. I phoned up the University yesterday and they confirmed that the results would be announced next Monday or

Tuesday. I'm not that worried but it would be good to know for sure that I don't have to re-write any of my thesis.'

'What subject did you do it on again?' asked Harry.

'The securitisation of development aid in Sub-Saharan Africa,' replied Lucy, pleased that Harry was interested.

'And what was your conclusion?' he asked. He was genuinely intrigued having worked on a number of development projects in that part of the world.

'That the rhetoric is there in terms of the high level strategies produced by Western governments but that, on the ground, it's business as usual. There's little evidence to suggest that the increased money being directed at conflict affected and fragile states is making any difference in terms of the west's security. The discourse is persuasive but nothing has changed in terms of what the NGOs are actually doing. It's all a bit depressing really. Western Governments are telling their people that they need to spend more money in developing countries and people support it because they think it will make them safer. But unless the NGOs change what they are doing and focus on building institutional capacity rather than on alleviating poverty, there's little prospect of any enduring improvement in the west's security.'

'You care about this don't you?' asked Harry.

'Yes, I do,' Lucy replied. 'I care about it because we spend billions on development aid but there seems to be no real mechanism for holding governments to account. The west is skint. In spite of this, Western governments remain virtually unchallenged in the way they spend their development aid.'

'Let's eat here,' said Harry, stopping outside one of Ashburton's many small cafes and restaurants. 'They do a mean fried breakfast and the coffee is superb.'

They went in and found a table in the window so they could watch the town waking up. 'This reminds me of Durham,' said Lucy. 'Isobel and I used to spend hours sitting in a coffee shop near Elvet

Bridge watching the world go by. It's one of my favourite pastimes.'

They each ordered full fried breakfasts. Harry went outside to phone his friend in the SF world whilst they waited for their food to arrive. He recognised that it was a bit of a long shot but he reasoned that if, as Lucy's father had suggested, Richards was ex-Army then someone should know where he was and how to contact him. Once he had a confirmed identity, he would be much better placed to work out how best to proceed. He was determined to do his best to help Lucy get to the bottom of her father's death and to hold whoever was responsible to account.

He went back in to the cafe and sat down just as breakfast was being served. It was the same girl who had served him earlier in the week. He smiled at her and then turned to Lucy, leaning across the table so that he would not be overheard. 'My friend will send me an e-mail when he's dug around a bit,' he said to Lucy. 'He recalls the name but can't remember the exact circumstances of Richards' departure.'

'Well that's progress,' said Lucy excitedly. She was reassured that with Harry's help she had a much better chance of finding out why her father had been killed and of tracking down whoever was responsible. The breakfast was excellent and they chatted amicably as they ate. After several more cups of coffee, they decided to continue on their way to Ellie's house.

'We'll go over the moor if you like,' suggested Harry. 'The weather's closing in a bit and we're expecting snow but the views should still be worth it.'

'I'd like that,' replied Lucy, taking his hand in hers as they walked back towards the car.

They followed the road up onto the Moor. It was overcast and raining slightly but the sun occasionally broke through the clouds and shone with a brilliance that lifted Harry's spirits. Harry stopped in the Hay Tor car park. 'Do you want to stretch your legs? The view from the top should be impressive, even in this weather.'

'Yes please,' replied Lucy, grabbing her coat as she got out of the car.

They crossed the road and set off up the hill.

'Can we look at the face first?' asked Lucy. Harry had explained about Camilla's fall and lucky escape. He led the way to the foot of the face. It looked small from the car park but, standing at its foot, it was easy to see why Camilla's attacker had thought she would die if she fell off the top. The rock face was sheer. Cracks in the rock ran up and down as well as along the length of the face but they were small and offered little by way of hand or footholds.

'It looks a hard climb,' suggested Harry.

'Yes,' replied Lucy. 'But not too bad if you follow the features. You can see where climbers have used chalk to help them grip,' she said, pointing out the tell tale smears of white chalk around some of the features. 'The hardest part is probably the first ten feet or so,' she said, going close to the face.

Harry watched as she reached up and grasped the edge of a very small ledge. 'If you can get your hands in that crack up there, where the overhang juts out,' she said, pointing with her chin, 'then I reckon you can nail this easily enough.' As she said this, she lifted her feet off the ground, brought her knees up to her chest and placed her feet high on the rock below her hands. The soles of her feet appeared to be stuck to the flat rock face as she launched herself upwards and slightly outwards towards the crack. Harry watched mesmerised. He'd done a great deal of climbing himself but even he was surprised at how fluid and controlled her movements were. Her right hand just made it into the crack, closing round a feature out of sight to Harry. She hung there by one arm, her feet now dangling in free space. She moved her other arm up and placed her hand in the crack to give her two reasonable handholds. She then pulled herself up using her arms, letting go with one hand to reach for a higher hold. She had to do this a few more times before she was able to find a reasonable foothold. She was now about fifteen feet above the ground. 'The rest's OK,' she said, turning to look at Harry. Harry wasn't quite sure what to say. In the space of a few minutes, Lucy had demonstrated to him beyond any doubt that she was an extremely capable climber. Harry thought about having a go himself but realised that he would be unlikely to succeed. The upper body strength required to do what Lucy had just done was significant and whilst he was clearly a great deal stronger than her, he was also a lot heavier. He suspected that he lacked the power to weight ratio that gave Lucy her advantage.

'That was very impressive,' he said to her with genuine admiration in his voice. 'I didn't realise you were so good.'

'Not that good,' replied Lucy modestly, 'but I love it. I spend every weekend I can climbing. If we have the time, it would be great to nail a few of the Tors whilst we're here.'

Harry agreed.

'The problem now is getting down,' she said, 'catch me if I slip.' She started to inch sideways, looking for a way down that avoided the overhang. Harry watched, keeping level with her in case she slipped. But she didn't and two minutes later, she jumped nimbly onto the grass beside him. She took Harry's hand again as he led them back to the path and on towards the top of the Tor. There were one or two other people going up the rough steps cut into the rock and they followed them up to the top.

'Great view,' said Lucy. 'There's some good belay points up here for a top rope on the face,' she said, 'some of them look well used.'

'Lots of schools use it during the week and it's packed at the weekend apparently,' said Harry. 'That's what saved Camilla. Two instructors were up here checking the face for loose stones. They had a beginners' class the next day.'

'Let's come during the week then,' said Lucy. 'I don't want to have to queue to climb. I just want to turn up and do it, preferably in the sun,' she said, smiling and looking up at the sky.

They stayed at the top for a few minutes taking in the view and then started the climb down towards the car. The rock was wet and slippery, particularly where it was well worn, and they found themselves on all fours at some points. Fifteen minutes later, they were back at the car park and ordering hot drinks from a refreshments van.

'Whoever pushed Camilla knew what he was doing,' said Lucy. 'You said it was raining hard on the day she fell and that the visibility was poor. I'll bet the rock was even more slippery. I don't think you set off to push someone off a cliff in bad conditions unless you have at least some idea of what you're doing. There's no point killing her and then getting stuck yourself.'

'I bet you're right,' said Harry, handing Lucy a cup of tea and a cigarette. 'I bet our man Richards turns out to be an experienced mountaineer as well as an ex-soldier.' They continued talking whilst they drank their tea and smoked their cigarettes.

The weather was starting to clear as they got back in the car and resumed their journey to Ellie's house. Both were lost in thought. Harry was thinking about a possible future with Lucy in it. He didn't want to appear too keen in case he frightened her off but the more he found out about her, the more he realised he liked her. She was very different to the women he'd been out with in the past. Though she was clearly sensitive and caring, she was also tough and determined, a combination that Harry found particularly attractive.

Lucy was thinking along similar lines. She knew that she'd showed off on the rock face but his comments about her climbing ability in Nepal had irritated her. Though she and Isobel had laughed about it at the time, his assumption that just because they were women they would be unable to handle the Annapurna routes had annoyed her. 'Easy girl,' she said to herself. 'You like him but take it easy and don't scare him off.' She was aware that many men found her a threat but she wasn't prepared to pretend to be needy and pathetic when she wasn't. She wanted an equal to share her life with, not someone to fight her battles on her behalf. She looked at him out of the corner of her eye. He was ruggedly handsome but, unlike most of the men she had been out with, he was also good fun, interesting and compassionate about wanting to make a difference.

'We're nearly there,' said Harry, breaking her train of thought. 'This is the village I mentioned. The pub's over there,' he said, pointing to the Ring O'Bells. 'And this is Ellie's house,' he added as he turned into the track leading up to the house. He stopped the Range Rover outside the main door. He could hear Boot barking inside as he turned the key in the lock. Lucy followed him inside, dropping her bag on the floor and kneeling down to ruffle Boots' head.

'What a gorgeous little dog,' she said, tickling his tummy as he rolled onto his back.

'He likes you,' said Harry. 'You wouldn't believe how fit he is for such a little chap. I went for a run with him yesterday and he was amazing.'

'That's because he's a Jack Russell,' said Lucy. 'We had one called Billy when I was growing up. They're incredible little dogs, tremendous endurance and really feisty. He looks very muscular. He must get a lot of exercise.'

'He does,' replied Harry. 'The girls take him out most days and they are no slouches when it comes to running. Ellie nearly killed me when we went out yesterday and she says Sarah's much fitter. I've made a mental note to myself not to jog with her.'

'I'll go with you if you like,' said Lucy. 'I haven't run for a few days and could do with a stretch. But don't go trying to prove how fit you are. I just want a jog.'

'OK,' said Harry. 'Let's go out tomorrow morning when we know what's happening to Camilla.'

'How is she?' asked Lucy.

'She's on the road to recovery. There's no brain damage and her breaks should mend in time. She'll be home this afternoon all being well. Ellie and Sarah have gone to collect her so she should be here in a few hours.'

'I'm a bit nervous about meeting her what with her being an old girlfriend,' said Lucy.

'There's no reason to be,' Harry replied. 'It's ancient history now. She only asked me to help her because she doesn't have any immediate family, at least not that she's still in touch with. We parted friends and we were together so long that I suppose phoning me seemed the natural thing to do.'

'I suspect you make her feel very safe,' said Lucy.

'Possibly, but she's far safer now these two are here,' replied Harry, smiling at the two Gurkhas as they came up the stairs from the cellar. Harry introduced them to Lucy. They shook her hand. Harry made a pot of tea and they all sat at the kitchen table.

'How was your walk last night?' Harry asked Ganesh.

'Very interesting,' he replied. 'It looks as if someone has been watching the house. There's a small gap in the tree line about two hundred metres up the hill. It's a good position. There's a clear view of the front door and there's virtually no chance of being seen.'

'How did you find it?' asked Lucy.

'It's an obvious place if you know what you're looking for. Clear line of sight to the house, no roads or tracks running nearby and enough overhead cover to keep the worst of the weather off. There were a few broken twigs and the grass had been flattened. Not much but enough.'

'How can you be sure that it's not just a couple of kids making out?' asked Lucy.

'Too little damage to the grass and no foot prints. Whoever's been there has made an effort to hide their tracks. It's been wet over the last few days and kids making out wouldn't have cared if they'd made a few footprints in the mud. But someone had gone to the trouble of raking over the muddy areas with a branch.'

'Could you shoot from there?' asked Harry.

'Yes,' replied Ganesh. 'It would be an easy shot but I've got it covered with one of the cameras so we should get some warning if someone goes back with that in mind. There's also a badger set nearby so we might get some interesting nocturnal viewing whilst we're waiting.'

'Did you see anything else?' asked Harry.

'Not really,' replied Ganesh. 'The house is actually quite well tucked away. There were a few other places that you could watch the house from but they're nearer to public footpaths and therefore not ideal if you don't want to be disturbed. I've got those and the main approach to the house covered so we should get some warning if someone tries to sneak up on us.'

'Good work,' said Harry. His phone buzzed. He took it out and looked at the screen. It was a text from his Army friend telling him to check his e-mail. He did as he was told. The attached document took several minutes to download but when it did, it was obvious to Lucy and the Gurkhas that he didn't like what he was reading.

'It's about your man Richards,' said Harry. 'My friend has found out quite a lot about him. It seems he left the SAS several years ago. He was forced to resign for sleeping with his Commanding Officer's wife and the wives of two of the Sergeant Majors. Apparently he was something of a ladies' man.'

'Go on,' encouraged Lucy.

'He's now some sort of freelance fixer for the rich and indiscrete. He's expensive and, according to my friend, not someone to cross in a hurry. A very dangerous man apparently. He's been implicated in several murders but there has never been enough evidence to pin anything on him. It seems he gets others to do the dirty work, only getting personally involved in the hands-on stuff when he's got no choice. The physical description says he's of average height, ordinary looking and that he's in his late forties now. My friend's got a photograph he's trying to send through.'

'This is starting to make sense,' said Lucy. 'It sounds like this is the right man and I'll bet my Dad was one of the people who helped him fix things.'

'The photograph's downloading now,' said Harry.

CHAPTER 48

Highworth had transferred the money into Briggs' account the previous night and was now watching the news whilst having a late breakfast. He'd got up early but had decided to work at home for the day. He had spent half an hour trying to get in touch with Richards, leaving several messages on his answerphone. He wasn't too worried. Richards had never let him down yet but he would be happier when he knew the girl was dead.

He took his coffee and went through to his study. He was still in the t-shirt and boxer shorts he'd slept in. He would shower and change after he'd checked the markets on his laptop. Bubble.com's share price had gone down but he was a little surprised that it hadn't dropped even further. He'd given orders to his team to start buying when the price reached 300 pence per share. They were now trading for 315. 'A few more days,' he thought to himself, 'and I will be well on the way to nailing this.' He realised that the company was working hard to try and persuade the City that, whilst Fairweather had been an important part of their success, they could still deliver Mymate without him. The City was not yet convinced and the price had therefore continued to drop but he would need to watch it carefully. Timing is everything and if the price started to increase because of growing confidence, then he might have to pay more than the 300 pence he had set as the target price. The trick was to know when the market was starting to turn. His problem was that once he started to buy large quantities of shares, his very action would trigger a rapid increase in their price. People watched International Valiant's dealings very closely. Its phenomenal success meant that people often copied its investment strategies in the hope of cashing in on something Highworth knew but they didn't. If he started buying an unusually large number of shares, others would no doubt sense a killing and start buying as well.

He sat back in his chair, put his feet on his desk and continued to scan the share prices. Tokifora's shares were continuing their downward trajectory. Nothing too unnerving but he was glad that he had disinvested in the company. He'd banked a very healthy profit from Tokifora but it was time to move on and he thought he had identified his next target after Bubble.com.

The company was called 'Kendo Oil' and it specialised in innovative fracking technology. He'd been following the UK fracking debate closely. It was an interesting process and consisted of forcing high pressure water into oil pockets located deep underground. It was expensive but recent increases in the price of oil were making it more attractive. The UK Government had suspended fracking following a number of minor earthquakes that were supposedly a consequence of trials carried out in Blackpool. Not surprisingly, the major opponents were the Greens but, sensing a populist bandwagon, a number of politicians from the main parties were also voicing their concerns. The most vociferous of these was a man called Simon Copley. He was a back bench Conservative MP from a particularly affluent area that was supposedly rich in deep oil reserves. Highworth had little doubt that his objections were based more on the concerns of his Eton cronies and the possibility that their large estates might be forcibly purchased than on any real concern for the environment. But he had recently learnt something about Copley that he suspected could be used to encourage him to be far less vociferous. It transpired that Copley, who was married with three teenage children, had been seeing several rent boys. There was nothing necessarily illegal about what he was doing and other politicians had weathered storms when similar proclivities had become public knowledge but Copley had made the importance of family values and Christian morals the cornerstones of his election campaign. Highworth therefore suspected that he would go to considerable lengths to keep his 'habit' quiet. If he could convince Copley and a few other MPs to change their minds and to major on what an opportunity fracking might present, then 'Kendo Oil' and its major shareholders would be well placed to benefit.

'Hello Darling, anything interesting?' asked his wife coming into his study and interrupting his reverie.

'Maybe,' he replied, taking the fresh cup of coffee that she offered him. 'How much do you know about fracking?' he asked her.

'Not much more than we did last night,' she replied mischievously, pushing his feet aside and perching on the edge of his desk. She was meeting some of the friends on her Art Committee for lunch and was dressed in an immaculately fitting Chanel twinset. Her blonde hair was cut into a fashionable bob and the light blue of her clothes accentuated her eyes.

Highworth laughed. His wife looked truly stunning. She had always been attractive but whereas many of her friends were starting to show their advancing years, she was ageing beautifully. Good genetics no doubt helped but she also kept herself fit and was careful not to over indulge at the many lunches and dinners they attended. 'With a wife like yours, who needs a mistress,' one of his closer friends often said to him. It was true, particularly as very few mistresses would be as sexually adventurous as his wife.

'I think I've found my next target,' he said to his wife. 'It's called Kendo Oil and it manufactures equipment for extracting oil by fracking. It's reasonably well known in the US where the technique is now commonplace but, as a UK company, it struggles to compete in the US marketplace. I think it would flourish over here if the Government gave the go ahead for fracking.'

'And will it?' asked his wife.

'It will shortly once I've sorted a few of its teething problems out.'

'Well, I'd love to stay and hear all about it,' she said, leaning forward to slide one of her hands slowly up his inner thigh. Her hand stopped just below his shorts. She looked at him, turned her head on one side and raised an eyebrow as if considering what to do next.

He stared back at her, his eyes imploring her to continue.

She smiled and slid her hand inside his shorts. She could feel him getting hard as she played with him. When he was fully erect, she extracted her hand and stood up, smoothing her skirt down over her hips. 'If I don't go now, I'll be late,' she said, leaning over to kiss the scar on his forehead.

'You little tart!' he said, lunging forward to grab her waist. Laughing, she neatly sidestepped his arm and started to walk towards the door.

'Plenty of time for that later darling,' she said over her shoulder. 'Bye bye for now!'

He watched her go. She was deliberately swinging her hips as she left the room. He sighed and tried Richards again. Still no response. 'Where the hell is he,' he said aloud. He wasn't concerned about Richards, he just hated not being able to speak to people when he wanted to. And he was just a little bit irritated that, not for the first time that week, his wife had fired him up only to leave him frustrated.

CHAPTER 49

Harry watched as a face materialised on his phone's screen, his eyes widening in surprise as he recognised the features. 'It's the man Camilla drew, the one who tried to push her off Hay Tor!'

'I don't know why but somehow that doesn't surprise me,' said Lucy. 'This whole thing is becoming so surreal that almost anything could happen and I wouldn't be shocked. Does your friend include an address where we might find Mr Richards?' asked Lucy.

'No,' replied Harry. 'His note said that he was working on it but that Richards keeps a very low profile and that his current whereabouts seem to be unknown.'

'I bet he's the man who's been watching the house,' said Ganesh. 'It would fit. Whoever was up in the wood line had been trained to cover his tracks. I've run courses for the SAS in Brunei. We teach them how to avoid being tracked by people like me.'

'Sounds like he should have paid more attention to his lessons,' said Harry.

'Possibly, but in fairness to him,' replied Ganesh, 'he wouldn't have expected someone like me to be tracking him here. As far as he's concerned, he's watching a house with a few girls and you in it. He might guess you were in the Army once but he doesn't think you know about him and he certainly wouldn't expect you to be out there in the woods looking for signs of covert surveillance. He's just ensuring that anyone who walks the dog there regularly doesn't spot anything unusual.'

'So we have an edge,' replied Harry. 'We know about him and where he's been watching us from but he doesn't know about us, or at least you two,' he said, looking at the Gurkhas. 'All we need to do now is keep it that way.'

'So what's the plan?' asked Lucy.

'Well,' said Harry. 'I think we get Camilla home and then wait for Richards to make his move. I don't think there's much more we can do unless my friend manages to get a current address for him. If he does, we can go and pay him a visit.'

'You're sure it's the same man?' asked Ganesh. 'It's all a bit of a coincidence isn't it?'

'Yes, I'm sure,' replied Harry. 'It's only a coincidence because we don't understand the connection. Once we've worked that out, I'm hoping that things will start to fall into place.'

'OK,' said Ganesh, clearly not convinced. 'And you're sure he'll try and get to Camilla?' asked Ganesh.

'I think so. He tried to kill her to protect something. Camilla doesn't know what but it must have something to do with Peter Fairweather's death. Camilla isn't dead so Richards, or whoever is employing him, must still be concerned. Perhaps they think that Camilla knows something that could link Fairweather's death to them.'

Lucy looked at Harry, the colour draining from her face. 'Did you say "Peter Fairweather"?'

'Yes,' replied Harry, 'why?'

'Fairweather was my father's last target. It was in the letter McLeod gave me. Dad killed him but he had to make it look like an accident. I have no idea why and I've no idea who my Dad was taking his orders from, other than Richards, but I think that must be the link. Fairweather's death must connect my Dad's murder to the attempt on Camilla's life. Richards might be able to explain the connection in more detail but I bet we'll need to nail the man who's pulling Richards' strings before we'll understand all this.'

'What about going to the police?' asked Ganesh.

'We tried that in Scotland. They still believe my Dad's death was the result of a mugging that went wrong. They don't buy the idea that someone specifically set out to kill him. Why would they? As far as they are concerned, my Dad was just a retired Army officer who did a bit of security work on the side. Why would anyone want to kill him?'

'That's the same with Camilla,' said Harry. 'I've tried to convince the police that someone pushed Camilla and I've even shown them the picture that she drew. They weren't interested. They either think it was an accident or, and I haven't told Camilla this yet, they think she tried to commit suicide. They didn't quite admit it but I sensed that they think Camilla's drawing is her way of trying to divert attention away from a failed suicide.'

'But if you tell them everything you now know, surely they're more likely to believe you,' suggested Ganesh.

'Possibly,' agreed Harry. 'But we'll have to tell them what Lucy's Dad did for a living and that'll make the headlines of every newspaper in the UK. Also, there's a good chance that the moment Richards is arrested, the man who's behind all this will disappear and we'll never get to the bottom of it. Richards is just the fixer. I want to know who's pulling the strings. Unless we nail him, Camilla will never be safe.'

The next hour was spent discussing what to do next. Eventually, they agreed that once Camilla was home, they would wait and see whether Richards made his move. If, after two or three days, nothing had happened then they agreed that they would go to the police with what they had. They also agreed they would not tell Camilla that whoever had tried to kill her before was probably watching the house. Having decided on a tentative plan, Harry suggested that they go for a walk and then have lunch at the Ring O'Bells. He'd thought about going to Moretonhampstead but heavy snow looked imminent and, although the Range Rover was a capable four wheel drive, he didn't have snow chains with him and he was reluctant to risk getting stuck given Camilla was expected home that afternoon. He asked the two Gurkhas if they wanted to join him and Lucy but they declined, preferring to remain hidden in the house and also sensing that he probably wanted to be on his own with her. He'd explained how he felt about her the previous night. They were pleased for him and wanted to give him the opportunity to spend time with her before things kicked off.

CHAPTER 50

Richards had enjoyed himself. His female friend had left earlier that morning in case her husband phoned home. He was now sorting out the equipment he felt he would need to finish the job. He had re-read the file on Harry Parker. It reaffirmed his original diagnosis. Not a man to under-estimate but he wasn't worried. He had the advantage of surprise. Whilst Parker would be playing happy house nurse to his female friend, Richards would be working out how to kill her, and him as well if necessary.

He had deliberately not answered his phone when Highworth had rung. He was obviously phoning from home as his name flashed up on Richards' mobile phone screen whenever it rang. Richards wasn't worried about Highworth but he didn't want to have to explain that the girl wasn't yet dead. He knew that Highworth would overreact and, frankly, he felt he could do without an angry and emotional outburst this early in the morning, especially as it had started so well. Moreover, he had things to do. He needed to get over to one of his lockups to retrieve his sniper rifle and the night sights he suspected he would need. He'd long ago abandoned any idea of keeping weapons at his flat. It was just asking for trouble. He kept absolutely nothing at home that could link him to his illegal activities. Extra money, passports, combat clothing, weapons and everything else he had collected over the years that enabled him to do his job were stored in several innocuous lockups across London. He looked at his watch. If he left within the hour, he could be back on Dartmoor by mid afternoon. He would also have time to change his hire car. Again, experience had taught him to change his cars as often as he could. People were more likely to remember a car if they had seen it more than once.

He showered, changed and left for his lock up. An hour later, he was heading out of London in a newly rented Hertz Subaru, fully equipped for what he suspected might lie ahead. The car was a pleasure to drive. He'd wanted something quick but he also wanted four wheel drive. The forecast had suggested that it might snow on higher ground within the next twenty-four hours or so. At over four hundred metres above sea level, Dartmoor was sufficiently high to get a regular dusting at this time of year and he didn't want to get stuck, particularly having carried out the kill.

The first part of his plan was reasonably straightforward. He intended to phone Exeter Hospital mid morning to confirm whether the girl had been released. If she had, he would book into a hotel and then, as darkness fell, he would head up onto the Moor. If she hadn't, then he would find a location near the hospital from which he could observe the main entrance. The second part of the plan kicked in when the girl was back at the house in North Bovey. It wasn't sophisticated but it should do the job. With luck, it might even look like a tragic accident.

CHAPTER 51

Camilla was released by the hospital mid afternoon. Her doctors were happy that she was recovering well and that there was nothing further to be gained by keeping her on the ward. They had given Ellie and Sarah strict instructions to bring her straight to Accident and Emergency if she started to show signs of dizziness. Other than that, they said that she now just needed time for her body to recover. The journey from the hospital was uneventful but, as they started to climb up towards Moretonhampstead, it started to snow. Ellie was secretly pleased. Every now and again Sarah would suggest they get rid of her old Land Rover and buy a newer saloon car but Ellie was adamant that they needed a four wheel drive. She knew they probably didn't, at least for most of the year, but whenever the weather deteriorated and driving on the Moor became difficult, she took the opportunity to remind Sarah of how lucky they were to have such a capable car. 'Lucky we've got the Landy,' she said to Sarah as they continued to climb towards Morton.

'Yes,' said Sarah. 'We're very lucky. As we are on the other two days of the year when we actually need four wheel drive.' She smiled as she said this. She knew that Ellie was emotionally attached to her battered old car. It symbolised the lifestyle choice she had made when she moved from London.

The snow was getting heavier. Ellie could see that it was beginning to settle on the road and she could feel the car slipping slightly on the corners. She changed down and put her headlights on. It was only mid afternoon but it was beginning to get dark. The roads had been gritted a week or so ago but because of the near constant rain, there was little salt left on the carriageway. Recognising the danger, the cars in front were beginning to slow down.

'This could be interesting,' said Ellie, braking to avoid a car coming in the opposite direction which looked to be slipping across the central white line. 'Another thirty minutes or so of this and some cars are really going to struggle, especially on the tops. Can you check the chains are in the back?' she asked Sarah.

Sarah checked. Ellie kept a large plastic box in the rear of the car which was filled with all sorts of off-road paraphernalia. It contained a tow rope, jump leads, a collapsible shovel and four snow chains, one for each wheel. They'd had to use them a few times last year. The chains made the world of difference, giving the car grip on even the most slippery of snow-covered roads. They also had a winch on the front of the car. They'd practised using it earlier in the year when it had just been fitted but, so far at least, they'd never had to use it in earnest. Sarah suspected that Ellie was hoping they would have to.

'This is looking bad,' said Camilla, peering through the windscreen. 'Do you think we'll make it?'

'The difficult bit is the road from Morton to North Bovey,' said Ellie. 'There are one or two steep bits that might be a bit of a challenge. But we can use the chains if necessary to give us some traction.'

They passed a number of cars going in the other direction but the few cars that were in front of them were stopping in Moretonhampstead. This made sense. As they entered the town, they could see that it had been snowing hard for several hours. It would be much worse up on the Moor and most of the vehicles they had been following wouldn't be able to cope with any more snow on the roads. They drove into the centre of town. It was eerily quiet. The shops were still open but there were few people about. Several inches of snow covered the main road. One or two vehicles had made tracks through the snow but these were fast being covered. They continued through the town, pulling into a small layby on the far side. 'Chains,' said Ellie looking at Sarah.

'Chains,' Sarah agreed with a smile.

They got out of the car. 'It's beautiful,' said Sarah, looking across the valley to their front. The fields were covered in snow. In the space of a few hours, the countryside had been transformed from damp and miserable to white and pristine. It was incredibly quiet. The snow continued to fall.

'It's like something out of a fairytale,' said Ellie. 'I love it when it's like this.'

'I know what you mean,' said Sarah. 'Everything looks clean and the world seems calmer.'

They got the snow chains out of the back and fitted them to all four tyres. Ellie recognised that this was probably over-kill but she daren't risk sliding off the road with Camilla still in plaster.

They got back in and Ellie inched back onto the carriageway. She could feel the difference immediately. The snow chains bit into the snow and gave her tremendous traction. She used the smaller of the two gear levers that older Land Rovers have to put the car in low ratio. This increased the torque and enabled her to decrease her speed but still keep the engine revving at a reasonable rate. The car made steady progress up and down the hills until they came to the outskirts of North Bovey. A car was slewed across the road with its front wheels in a ditch, though there didn't appear to be any damage to the bodywork. It had simply slid into the side of the road and the front wheels had mounted the slight verge and then lodged in the drainage ditch. The publisher from the local amateur dramatics group was standing next to it talking into his mobile phone. He waved at the girls when he saw their car approach. Sarah got out and went to talk to him.

'He's stuck,' she said to Ellie, coming back to the car. 'I said we'd try and tow him out.'

Ellie agreed that they should give it a try. Sarah could see that she was enjoying this. Ellie got the tow rope and attached it to the tow hook at the back of her friend's car. She turned the Land Rover round and fastened the other end of the rope to her own tow hook. She put the Land Rover into gear and slowly started to pull the stricken car out of the ditch. The Land Rover's wheels slipped slightly but the chains did their job and within a few minutes the car was free of the ditch. Sarah went over to talk to the man again. They agreed that the best plan would be for him to park his car at the side of the road and then allow the girls to give him a lift to his house which was near their own. Within a few minutes, they were on their way with the man in the back next to Camilla.

'I think the snow's here to stay for the week,' said the man as they drove slowly through the village. 'I suspect I'll be working from home for the next few days at least,' he said.

The girls agreed. It was quite exciting being cut off. Most people kept extra provisions at home for occasions like this and, provided nobody needed urgent access to medical facilities, it was no big deal. During term time, the children made the most of a few extra days off school with the added delight of snow on the hills, spending most of their time sledging in the valleys. They dropped the man opposite his house and then continued home. The house looked delightful as they turned off the main road and into the drive. It was like something off a Christmas card. Everything had a perfect covering of snow, even Harry's Range Rover. Wisps of smoke blew out of the chimney. The Gurkhas had obviously kept the fire going.

Boot was excited to see them as they opened the door and helped Camilla into the house.

'We're home,' called Ellie as she took her coat off and went to put the kettle on. Ganesh's head appeared from the cellar.

'Hello,' he said. 'We've tried to keep the fire going but I'm not sure how successful we've been.'

Ellie thanked them for making the effort. She was grateful for the warmth of the house as they settled Camilla on the sofa in front of the wood burner. 'Anything happening?' Ellie asked Ganesh.

'Not really,' he replied. 'I saw a few foxes earlier this morning but, so far, it's been quiet. Harry's back with his friend Lucy. They've gone for a walk and then for a late lunch at the Ring O'Bells. I suspect they have a lot to talk about,' said Ganesh with a mischievous smile. 'I'll go and get Hemraj,' disappearing back into the cellar.

Camilla had been watching them talk. Ellie realised that she hadn't introduced them and, as the Gurkhas re-appeared, she made the introductions. Hemraj shook hands and then went back into the cellar to monitor the cameras. 'If I don't,' he said, 'I can guarantee that something will happen and I'll miss it.' Ganesh stayed to chat to Camilla. He asked her about her injuries and then, conscious that it might upset her, he gently questioned her about the man who had pushed her off the cliff. He was trying to get a feel for the person he was up against. How big was he? How old? How did he move? Did he look to be armed? Was he right handed or left handed? Camilla tried her best but, although it all seemed to happen in slow motion, she had actually only seen him for a matter of seconds. Ganesh was nevertheless grateful for her answers. Though Harry was convinced that Camilla's assailant and Richards were one and the same, Ganesh wanted Camilla's personal take on her attacker before her recollection became 'tainted' by whatever they might learn about Richards. Ganesh knew that any snippet about a potential enemy could turn out to be the difference between life and death, no matter how trivial it might seem. And from what Camilla had just told him, the man he would soon be pitted against sounded very capable, whether or not it was Richards. He would certainly not make the mistake of underestimating him.

CHAPTER 52

Harry and Lucy had walked about a mile or so up onto the hills when the snow began to fall. They kept walking for a while but, as it started to get heavier, they found some trees to shelter under at the edge of a small wood.

'The snow reminds me of Nepal,' said Harry, lighting two cigarettes and passing one to Lucy.

'Yes,' she replied. 'If my father hadn't been killed, I would have just completed my last ascent in Annapurna and I'd be heading back to Kathmandu by now.'

'Would you have come and seen me?' asked Harry.

'Of course,' she replied, turning to face him. 'I'd agreed with Isobel that she'd travel back to UK and that I'd stay a while in Nepal so I could spend some time in Kathmandu with you.'

'Really?' asked Harry, pleased.

'Really,' replied Lucy, taking his hand in hers. 'You didn't finish showing me around. There were three or four places you mentioned that I was still keen to see.'

'OK,' replied Harry, not really sure whether she'd wanted to return to Kathmandu to spend time with him or to see the sights that he'd not had the time to show her.

'I also want to know more about you,' she said, as if reading his mind. 'Now that I've met some real life Gurkhas, I want to know why you really left the Army as they seem such good blokes.'

Harry looked at her. 'OK, well let's start getting to know each other better by having lunch. I'm starting to freeze and the lure of soup and a steak sandwich is becoming too much to resist.'

They started walking back down towards the village. The snow had already covered the tracks they'd made on their way up. They were both silent, lost in their own thoughts. Lucy felt herself being increasingly attracted to Harry. She recognised that she wasn't very good at reading his emotions. He was obviously pleased to see her but she wasn't sure whether this was because he felt a sense of duty towards her, a need to help her in her time of need, or because he genuinely found her attractive. His slight awkwardness with her made her think that he also didn't really understand how he felt about her himself. On the positive side, she felt that there was a depth to their relationship that belied the short time they'd actually known each other.

'I'm not sure whether a heavy snowfall like this is good or bad,' said Harry. 'If the roads get much worse, we could be cut off for days. If the chap we think is Richards tries anything, the police are going to be slow to react and we might have to deal with him ourselves.'

'I expect the Gurkhas will be a big help if things start to get sticky,' said Lucy.

'Yes,' replied Harry. 'They are very good indeed in a fight.'

They chatted about them as they walked. It was clear from the way he spoke that Harry had a deep affection for both of them. He'd known them a long time. He explained that they had been young nineteen year olds when he'd first met them. He'd just been commissioned from Sandhurst and they were the first two soldiers he met when he joined his first platoon.

'What was it like?' asked Lucy.

'A bit surreal,' said Harry. 'I was just a year or so older than them and I was their newly commissioned platoon commander. I had an old sergeant to guide me but it's quite a responsibility. Sandhurst tries to prepare you for your first command but it's quite daunting turning up after nine months training and suddenly being put in charge of thirty Gurkhas. Most Gurkhas serve the full twenty-two years so many of my platoon had already seen active service in Bosnia, Kosovo, Iraq and Afghanistan. They had a huge amount of combat experience and I had none. It gets a bit easier once you've done the language course and spent a bit of time with them but it's still hard and it takes a while to earn their respect.'

They continued chatting until they arrived at the pub. It was quiet and they found a table near the fire. They ordered their food and chatted as they watched the snow falling outside. The food was excellent. The waitress suggested that they make the most of it as she wasn't sure how long they would be able to stay open if the snow kept on. 'The road will be closed for a few days if it keeps on like this,' she said. 'We normally run out of beer first. The locals tend to use the pub more in the evenings when the village is cut off. Something to do with shared hardship I expect,' she said as she disappeared off towards the kitchen.

They finished their meal and, after large cups of strong black coffee, decided to go back to the house to see whether the girls had returned with Camilla. Lucy was subdued as they walked up the drive. She'd enjoyed talking to the Gurkhas and she was looking forward to meeting Sarah and Ellie but she was nervous about meeting Camilla. Harry obviously still cared for her, otherwise why would he have flown half way round the world to be at her side? Though she had no claim on Harry – they'd only met a week ago – she found herself seeing Camilla as competition for Harry's attentions. 'Get a grip girl,' she said to herself. 'Otherwise you'll make a fool of yourself.'

Harry sensed her apprehension. 'It'll be fine,' he said, squeezing her hand as they approached the front door.

CHAPTER 53

Richards had phoned the hospital on the journey down to Dartmoor, pretending to be a relative. They wouldn't give him much detail over the phone but they confirmed that she was being released that afternoon. He realised that she would be out before he got to Exeter but he wasn't concerned. He expected her friends to take her back to the house in North Bovey. Once she was there, he would have time to watch the house for a day or so before making his move. Whilst he wanted to finish it, he had as much time as he needed. 'Better to wait for success than rush to failure,' he said to himself as he drove.

He arrived in Exeter late that afternoon. The local radio station said that it had been snowing heavily up on Dartmoor but, being several hundred metres lower, Exeter had escaped with only light rain. The snow on the hills wasn't unexpected and Richards had come prepared. Over the years, he'd spent a fair bit of time in Norway taking part in Arctic warfare exercises. He was therefore no stranger to operating in snow. He found a travel lodge on the outskirts of the city and booked a room. It was modest but sufficient for his needs. He intended to sleep for a few hours, have some supper and then, as darkness fell, try and get as close to the house as he could. The place he'd watched it from before would be ideal, provided no farm animals had decided it would also be a good place to shelter from the snow.

CHAPTER 54

Sarah was sat on the sofa talking to Camilla when Harry and Lucy came in. Ellie was upstairs making up an extra bed in the room that Harry and Camilla had both slept in. The third bedroom was still a mess. They had started to strip the wooden floor and remove the many layers of wallpaper that had been put up over the years but they had a fair way to go.

'Put Camilla and Lucy in the spare room and I'll sleep downstairs with the boys,' Harry had said when they'd discussed sleeping arrangements the previous evening.

'Are you sure that's wise?' Ellie had asked. 'What if they don't like each other?'

'I'm sure they will,' Harry had replied. 'The worst that can happen is that Camilla bores Lucy to death by describing my many faults in intimate detail. But I don't think she will.'

Sarah stood up as Lucy and Harry came in. Harry did the introductions.

'I've heard a lot about you,' Sarah said to Lucy, shaking her hand. 'I'm really sorry about your Dad but we're delighted that you are able to stay for a few days.'

'Thank you,' replied Lucy. 'And thank you for letting me stay. I really appreciate it.'

Camilla got slowly to her feet. 'Hi,' she said, holding out her hand. 'I'm Camilla. I've also heard a lot about you and I'm really pleased to meet you.'

Lucy looked for any signs of hostility but there were none. Camilla was making an effort to be open and friendly. Lucy was grateful to her. She was also surprised. Camilla was about her own age and very attractive in an arty sort of way. Her injuries, particularly the bruising around her eyes, didn't help her appearance but there was no doubt that she was a good looking woman.

'How's the recovery going?' Lucy asked, trying to be friendly as well.

'Come and sit down and I'll tell you,' said Camilla, plonking herself back on the sofa and patting the seat next to her. Lucy sat down and the two fell into animated conversation.

Harry was relieved and grateful to Camilla for making this easy. He looked at Sarah who winked at him theatrically. 'Tea?' she asked.

Ellie came downstairs as Sarah was pouring the tea. She saw Lucy sitting next to Camilla and looked quizzically at Sarah. Sarah smiled and nodded. Reassured, Ellie went to introduce herself. Lucy stood up to shake hands. Ellie took the hand. 'I'm so sorry about your father,' she said. 'It must have been an awful shock.'

'It was,' said Lucy. 'I'm slowly coming to terms with it. Thank you for your concern.'

'Have the police made much progress?' asked Ellie.

'No,' replied Lucy. 'They think it was a mugging that went wrong. They've heard nothing from their touts and they're now pretty sure it wasn't a local that did it. They think it might have been someone from out of town and that they left in a hurry when it went wrong. I don't think they're very optimistic about catching them.'

'And what do you think?' asked Ellie.

'I think he was murdered by a man called Richards. Harry and I think it was the same man who tried to kill Camilla. The picture Camilla drew of her attacker is almost identical to a photograph of Richards that a friend of Harry's sent through this morning. I don't think there's much doubt that it's the same man but we've been struggling to work out what the connection is.'

Harry could see that Ellie, Sarah and Camilla were all surprised by the news. 'Why don't I fill you all in on developments over the last twenty-four hours,' offered Harry. 'That way, everyone will know what's happened and what we might expect over the next few days.'

Sarah and Ellie came and sat with Camilla and Lucy in front of the wood burner. Harry eased himself into one of the armchairs and started to explain everything that he'd found out. Lucy watched him as he spoke. His face was animated as he explained what his friend had uncovered about Richards. The girls asked the occasional question but Harry spoke well and Lucy could imagine him in uniform briefing his soldiers. She wished she'd known him then. He started to explain about Lucy's father. He was careful not to go into too much detail but Lucy interrupted him and told them pretty much everything she knew about her father. She didn't talk about the amount of money he'd managed to amass but, even without that, they were clearly shocked. 'Are you sure about this?' asked Sarah. 'It all sounds so unbelievable.'

'I know exactly what you mean,' said Lucy. 'It's not every day you find out that your Dad was an assassin but I am afraid it all seems to be true.'

Harry continued talking for another twenty minutes. He concluded by saying that, as Lucy had suggested, the thing they didn't yet understand was why Richards had apparently killed Lucy's Dad and why he had also tried to kill Camilla.

'So what happens now?' asked Camilla.

'Well,' Harry began hesitantly, looking at Camilla. 'We think that Richards might try again. I don't know why he wants to get you but he's clearly worried that you know something, perhaps to do with Fairweather's death. We know from the notes that Lucy's father left that he killed Fairweather on Richards' instructions. We also know that Richards is a high class fixer and that he was therefore most probably working on somebody's behalf. Lucy and I discussed it this afternoon and our view, which we accept might not be right, is that somebody thinks you know something that could link them to Fairweather's death. It looks like someone is clearing up after themselves. With Lucy's Dad out of the way, the only person who knows anything about the Fairweather death, other than Richards, is you.'

'But I don't know anything,' protested Camilla.

'We know that,' said Harry, emphasising the "we", 'but someone clearly thinks you do. And I suspect they won't rest until you are also out of the way.'

'Harry!' said Lucy in a shocked voice. 'You don't need to put it so bluntly.'

'I'm sorry Camilla,' said Harry. 'But there's no easy way of explaining this. I think you are in real danger. That's why I asked Ganesh and Hemraj to come and stay for a few days.'

'So you think he'll try and get me now I'm out of hospital,' asked Camilla.

'Yes,' replied Harry. 'But you're safe here. I think we have a bit of an advantage in that Richards doesn't know we suspect him. He thinks he has the initiative and that gives us a slight edge.'

'When do you think he'll try to get me?' asked Camilla.

'I don't really know,' answered Harry. 'But I think we need to work on the assumption that he's watching us and looking for an opportunity. He'll try and make it look like an accident but I suspect that might be difficult.'

Camilla had gone pale. Ellie took her hand and squeezed it. 'Don't worry,' she said. 'We're now all in this together and we won't let anything happen to you.' Camilla didn't look particularly reassured but she smiled anyway.

Harry went on to explain about the cameras that Ganesh had installed. 'The snow's a bit of a blessing,' he said. 'It'll make it harder for Richards. He won't try anything unless he can guarantee that he can get away and if the snow continues, that'll be difficult.'

They talked for the next few hours, trying to confirm the connection between Lucy's Dad's murder and Camilla's attack. Eventually, Sarah ordered them to sit at the table for supper. As she opened the oven, the smell of roast pork made Camilla realise just how hungry she was. The hospital's food had been OK but it was nothing like home cooking. Ellie poured them all a glass of wine. 'To us,' she said, raising her glass. The others copied her. Lucy joined in but couldn't help thinking that it was all rather surreal. Even as they sat there, it was highly likely that there was a man somewhere outside apparently intent on killing at least one of them. Surely they should be doing something other than having a roast meal and a glass of wine. 'But what more can we do?' she asked herself. 'The police aren't remotely interested and Harry and the Gurkhas appear to have the bases covered. I suppose it's just a question of time and letting things unfold.'

They ate slowly, enjoying the meal and the conversation. Prompted by Sarah and Ellie, Lucy explained what her dissertation was about and Camilla encouraged Harry to talk about his recent experiences in Somalia. They were all hungry and animated. Harry suspected this was at least partly because of the circumstances. He had seen it before on operations. Soldiers about to undertake potentially dangerous missions either go quiet and reflective or become louder than usual as their nerves start to get the better of them. He limited himself to one small glass of wine but was pleased to see that all the girls except Lucy were drinking a bit more. 'Might help them relax,' he thought. He caught Lucy watching him and smiled. She smiled back.

Just after midnight Ellie, Sarah and Camilla decided to go to bed. They all helped clear away and Harry made a pot of coffee which he took downstairs to Hemraj and Ganesh. Lucy came with him. They were doing shifts, watching images from the cameras on two laptops. 'More badgers,' said Hemraj as he accepted a mug of coffee from Harry. 'I've never seen so many badgers in my life.' He pointed to one of the laptops with his chin. The picture was surprisingly clear. Although it was gone midnight, the full moon and the white snowy background made it easy to spot the large badger as it waddled across the screen. A couple of seconds later, another smaller badger followed. Lucy stayed with them for another half hour or so and then announced that she was going up to bed. Hemraj suggested that Harry should get some sleep on the extra camp bed they'd set up.

Although he was reluctant at first, he was soon fast asleep. Hemraj remained on duty.

Hemraj shook Harry's arm. 'Wake up, there's something you need to see.'

Harry was wide awake in an instant. Ganesh was already fully dressed. Instead of black combats, he was wearing a white arctic smock and white combat trousers. 'What is it?' asked Harry.

'Someone's just moved into the hide,' said Ganesh. Harry looked at the screen. He could make out a human shape lying prone where the badgers had been. What looked to be a rifle was on the ground next to them.

'He moved slowly into position about ten minutes ago. He's good. No light and no unnecessary movement. He's definitely armed but I think he's using binoculars or some sort of thermal imager or NVGs at the moment,' continued Hemraj. Harry watched the screen. The camera was positioned behind the man and it was therefore difficult to see what was in his hands. He occasionally moved his feet in a bid to stay warm.

'What do you think?' asked Harry.

'I think we should give him an hour or so of complete boredom and then I'll go and say hello,' said Ganesh. He was fully dressed now. He had a pistol strapped to one thigh and was sliding a mean looking kukri into a scabbard on his waist belt. 'I think we need to try and bring him back here so we can ask him a few questions about his boss. But it's so quiet out there that getting close to him might be difficult. A small diversion here at the house would be helpful when I get really close to him.' They discussed this for several minutes, deciding what to do.

Ganesh was matter of fact as he prepared to leave the house but Harry was only too aware of the dangers. If the man outside was Richards, then he was a formidable opponent. Well armed and experienced, he might be taken by surprise but, once captured, they knew that he would be looking for every opportunity to escape or to kill his captors. Harry knew that Richards had been expensively trained for just this eventuality and he therefore realised that they would need to be extremely careful with him.

Ganesh clarified a few last details with Hemraj, pulled his white balaclava down over his face and then went upstairs. Richards could see the front of the house from where he was lying and Ganesh therefore slipped out of the back door. A hedgerow ran close to the back of the house and up the hill directly opposite Richards. Ganesh went through a small gate set into the hedge and then turned and followed it to the top of the hill. It was about seven foot high and there was little chance of Richards seeing Ganesh but he moved quietly, careful not to startle any nocturnal animals that might give his presence away. As he approached the top of the hill, he skirted sideways, dropping down into a small valley that would allow him to circle round behind Richards. He knew the ground well. He had been over the route several times during the day but he was still careful to stay in dead ground.

Hemraj and Harry continued to watch the image on the laptop. Richards remained still, giving no indication of having seen or heard anything untoward. Harry checked his watch. A few more minutes and Ganesh would be in position. Harry put his coat on and checked that he had the Range Rover's keys in his pocket. Hemraj looked at Harry and nodded. Harry went upstairs and turned the kitchen lights on. Hemraj saw Richards shift slightly as he brought his arms up to his face. 'He's got the binos in position,' called Hemraj. Harry switched on the external lights and opened the back door. He was slightly apprehensive but knew that Hemraj would alert him if Richards gave any sign of going for the rifle that still lay by his side. He walked over to the Range Rover, clicking the automatic lock on his key fob as he went. The car's indicator lights flicked on and off a few times. Harry opened the boot and started to take out a small case.

Hemraj watched the screen. Richards was clearly focused on what Harry was doing. As Hemraj continued to watch, a white shape appeared behind Richards. It was Ganesh. He saw Ganesh lean forward and gently move the rifle out of Richards' reach. He then prodded Richards in the back with his own rifle. He couldn't hear what Ganesh was saying but he saw Richards roll slowly over onto his back, away from his rifle with his arms outstretched. Richards then removed his own balaclava as Ganesh stepped back slightly. Hemraj knew that this was the most dangerous part of the operation. Richards would no doubt be carrying other weapons and would be looking for an opportunity to get to them before Ganesh had the chance to react. Hemraj watched as Ganesh threw a set of handcuffs on the ground next to Richards. Ganesh's rifle never wavered. It was pointed straight at Richards' chest as he sat up and started to put the handcuffs on. Richards was taking his time but, clearly urged on by Ganesh, he eventually held his arms up in front of his face with the handcuffs on. Neither man moved for several minutes. Eventually, Hemraj saw Harry appear on the screen. He was carrying one of the Glock pistols. He placed it on the ground next to Ganesh as he went towards Richards, careful not to place himself between Ganesh's rifle and the handcuffed man. He approached Richards from behind, reaching over to check the handcuffs before lifting him on to his feet and frisking him expertly. He removed a pistol that had been holstered on Richards' waist and a wicked looking knife that had been sheathed on his thigh. Hemraj continued to watch as Harry's hands patted Richards around the groin and then worked their way down to his boots. He removed another knife, sheathed down the inside of the boot, and a small pistol which had been fastened to his ankle. Hemraj didn't doubt that Richards would be carrying other weapons but, for the moment at least, he would be unable to get to them with his hands in handcuffs. After a few more minutes, the three men started to walk off the screen. 'So far, so good,' thought Hemraj. He was pleased but not really surprised. Richards had not expected to be ambushed, particularly by someone who obviously knew exactly what he was doing.

Ten minutes later Hemraj heard the men enter the house above him. He put on a similar balaclava to Ganesh and waited at the bottom of the stairs. Harry led the way down into the cellar. Hemraj grapped Richards by his outstretched arms and led him to the far end of the room in silence. He had put plastic sheeting on the floor and rigged up a curtain that could be pulled across, effectively turning the area where the gym had been into a secluded room. He stopped Richards in the centre of the plastic sheeting and took out a Stanley knife. Harry saw Richards flinch. Ganesh moved round to Hemraj's side with the rifle still aimed squarely at Richards' chest. Richards was left in no doubt that he would be shot if he tried anything. Hemraj quickly cut away all of Richards' clothing until he was left standing naked in the centre of the plastic sheet. Neither of the Gurkhas had said a word since Richards had entered the house. Hemraj then went to the side of the room and picked up an old wooden chair which he positioned behind Richards. Putting his large hands on Richards' shoulders, he pushed him down until he was sitting on the chair. Harry was in no doubt that Richards would have felt the power in Hemraj's arms as he did this. Harry then watched as Hemraj took a roll of industrial duct tape out of his trouser pockets and wrapped it round Richards' torso and the back of the chair. His arms were pinned in front of him, his hands covering his groin. He cut the tape and then did the same with his legs. There was little chance of him being able to wriggle free, even if Ganesh wasn't there to keep an eye on him.

Hemraj then moved round to face Richards. He spoke slowly and clearly.

'Mr Richards. If you do as I ask you, you will live. If you do not, I will kill you. Is that clear?'

Richards remained silent, staring at Hemraj impassively. Harry had to admit that it was an impressive performance. Hemraj was scary at the best of times. Hugely muscled and with the deadest eyes that Harry had ever seen, he was a fearsome figure but Richards seemed to be taking it all in his stride.

'I know who you are Mr Richards and I know that you have been well trained for circumstances such as this. Let me tell you what I want to know and then you can reconsider whether or not you wish to help me. If you do, I give you my word that I will let you live. If you do not, then my friends and I will no doubt be disposing of your body in the morning. You will not be the first man I have killed Mr Richards and I suspect you won't be the last.'

Harry had to admit that Hemraj's polite and even delivery was particularly terrifying. There was no anger and no emotion. He was simply telling it as it was. Again, Richards just continued to stare at him. Hemraj smiled, his teeth visible in the balaclava's mouth slit. He started to explain everything they knew about Richards, from his service in the Army and his forced resignation through to his involvement in tasking and then killing Lucy's father. He quickly summarised the abortive attempt on Camilla's life and concluded by describing how they had watched Richards move into position that night. Richards tried not to show it but he was clearly shaken that they knew so much.

'So what I want to know, Mr Richards, is who ordered you to kill the assassin and the artist girl. If you tell me that and it checks out, then we will release you. If not, then, as I said, you will die. I promise you, it will be painful. I will spare you the detail but, just to give you something to look forward to, I will start by removing your penis. Think about it,' said Hemraj, 'we will find out eventually anyway when whoever tasked you starts looking for you.'

Richards began to realise that he was not dealing with a bunch of amateurs. He was irritated with himself for being caught so easily. He had made the fatal mistake of underestimating his enemy. He had focused on the blond man and the girls. It didn't even occur to him that the blond man might have called for reinforcements. And it certainly didn't occur to him that he would be able to call on the services of two such capable operators. As he looked into his questioner's eyes, he realised that the man would have absolutely no hesitation in killing him. He could see death waiting there. Cold, devoid of emotion and utterly ruthless, he realised that this wasn't a bluff. His train of thought was broken by the man talking to him again.

'I will give you one hour to think about what I have said. I will then come back and give you a chance to talk. I will not torture you if you do not talk to me, I will simply kill you very painfully. Do not try and escape. My friend will be covering you with his rifle. He will shoot you if you try anything.'

Hemraj walked back to the other end of the room and then climbed the stairs to the kitchen followed by Harry. Ganesh remained downstairs with Richards. 'What do you think?' asked Harry quietly when they were seated at the kitchen table removing their balaclavas.

'I'm not sure,' said Hemraj. 'He's certainly very tough and very well trained. He'll be thinking about what he's got to lose. Hopefully, there won't be much loyalty between him and his boss. I suspect it'll depend on how seriously he takes my threat. If he believes that I'll kill him, then he'll talk. If he doesn't, then maybe he won't.'

'I think you were pretty convincing,' said Harry. 'I was scared and I'm on your side. You can have a look if you like, I've got it all on this.' He held out a small digital camera.

'No thanks,' replied Hemraj. 'I'll take your word for it.'

Harry made a pot of tea and they talked quietly about what their next move should be. After an hour, they replaced their balaclavas and went down back downstairs. Hemraj went to the far end of the room and stood in front of Richards. He took out his knife and placed it on the weights bench opposite Richards. He then removed one of the Glocks from a bag on the floor next to the bench and took a silencer out of his trouser pocket. Slowly and deliberately, he screwed the two together. He placed the weapon on the bench and picked up the knife. Richards watched. He'd had an hour to think things through. What he'd seen in his captor's eyes had unnerved him. He was in no doubt that the calmly spoken and powerfully built man who seemed to be leading the interrogation would kill him if he didn't cooperate. Were he still a soldier, he would have been preparing himself for the inevitable. Whatever his faults, there was no way he would have betrayed his regiment and his country just to save his own skin. But he wasn't a soldier anymore, he was a businessman. He had a commercial arrangement with Highworth and he was in no doubt that, were Highworth in his position, he would have little hesitation in telling his captors what they wanted to know. He decided to do the same. If they were stupid enough to let him go, then there would be plenty of time for him to get his own back. The important thing was to get through the next hour. He wouldn't volunteer information but he would answer their questions.

'I'll talk,' said Richards calmly as Hemraj walked towards him with the knife. 'The man's name is Charles Highworth. He runs an investment fund called 'International Valiant'. He's been manipulating share prices by killing off selected individuals. Not surprisingly, he's made a huge amount of money doing this.'

'Go on,' said Hemraj.

'Something scared him recently. I don't know what or who but he suddenly wanted to get rid of anything that might link him to the killings. That's why the assassin had to die. He wanted the girl dead because, for some reason, the assassin didn't kill her when he took out Fairweather. I don't know why he didn't but Highworth thought this was a mistake. He thought that the girl might somehow be able to lead people to him. I didn't see how and I tried to talk Highworth out of it but he wasn't to be persuaded. He was very spooked and he wanted the girl dead.

'Where does Highworth live?' asked Hemraj.

'I don't know,' replied Richards.

'And I don't believe you,' said Hemraj, taking a step towards him. 'You are a very careful man Mr Richards and I have no doubt that you know all about Mr Fairweather. It won't have escaped you that if he's trying to sever the connections between him and the many murders he's initiated, you are an obvious target. You will have your own insurance policy and this will have included finding out everything you can about Mr Highworth. I'll ask you one more time, what's his address?'

Richards said nothing but, as Hemraj's knife moved slowly towards his groin, he relented. He gave Hemraj Highworth's address in Farnham. 'Thank you Mr Richards. We will check out what you've said and, if what you have told me is true, we will let you go. This might take a while. I am now going to put a blindfold on you. Do not try anything.'

'I need to pee,' said Richards.

'So pee,' replied Hemraj. 'You will stay exactly where you are until we are happy that your story checks out. I will get you a glass of water but, if you need to use the toilet, you will have to do the best you can as you are, at least for the moment.'

Hemraj and Harry left Ganesh with Richards and went upstairs. Although it was still early, Lucy was in the kitchen making coffee. 'You've had fun,' she said when she saw Harry and Hemraj removing their balaclavas. 'Coffee?' she asked, placing two steaming mugs on the table. She wasn't concerned about the welfare of the man they had in the cellar. She realised that in all probability he had killed her father. In doing that he had, at least in her mind, forfeited whatever rights he might have had to fair treatment.

The three of them sat at the table as Harry explained what had happened. 'So what do we do now?' asked Lucy. 'We can't let him go until we've checked out his story. That might take several days and even then we're going to have to think about what exactly we do with him. If we let him go, there's nothing to stop him tracking us down and killing us at some time in the future. I don't want to spend the rest of my life looking over my shoulder.'

'No,' replied Harry. 'I get that but let's cross one bridge at a time. I suspect he's telling the truth about Highworth. He's got nothing to gain by lying to us. Highworth just used him to achieve outcomes in order to make lots of money. I know Richards killed your Dad but I suspect you want to know why Highworth wanted your Dad dead, why he got Richards to kill him?'

'You're right,' replied Lucy. 'I do want to know.' For the next hour or so, they discussed what their next move should be. Eventually, they reached a decision. Lucy went to wake the others whilst Harry and Hemraj continued developing the plan.

CHAPTER 55

Highworth was beginning to get agitated. He had left more messages on Richards' phone but there was still no response. Bubble. com's shares had dropped to 310 pence but still hadn't reached the magic 300 figure. He was beginning to wonder whether he shouldn't just buy them at 310. He knew this would push the price up but he would still make a killing, both on the short sell and over the longer term once Mymate was successfully fielded. He looked at his watch. It was still early but, unable to sleep, he decided to get up. His wife was fast asleep next to him and he was careful not to wake her as he climbed out of bed. He put on a dressing gown and went downstairs to make coffee and phone his driver, Simon.

'Where the hell is Richards,' he said to himself as he tried Richards' number again. Still no response. He left another angry message and hung up. He wanted closure on the girl from the Fairweather killing but he also wanted Richards to do some background work on Simon Copley, the MP opposing fracking. The sooner he could start to put pressure on Copley, the sooner he could set the Kendo Oil ball rolling. He wasn't impatient but once Bubble.com's shares hit 300 pence and his team starting buying, he would need something else to keep him occupied.

An hour later, Highworth was in the back of his car and heading into London through the early morning traffic. Simon remained silent. He recognised the mood his boss was in and he therefore concentrated on his driving. He knew only too well that at times like this any sudden braking would elicit a sharp rebuke from the back seat.

Simon dropped him off and Highworth marched into the foyer of his office building. He ignored the 'good mornings' of the receptionist and the security guards and took the waiting lift straight up to his office. Once at his desk, he phoned Briggs' office. His mood didn't improve when he was told that Commissioner Briggs was on holiday for two weeks. His tried Briggs' mobile. Another answerphone. He could see his PA arrive through the glass wall that separated his office from hers. The door was open. 'Coffee,' he shouted. 'Now.'

'Yes sir,' she responded, surprised and disappointed that he was in so early. Like his driver, she recognised his mood and her heart sank. He was foul to work for at the best of times. When he was like this, he was utterly unbearable. For the thousandth time that year, she thought about leaving the company, or at least him, but the money was exceptional. She bit her lip and made the coffee. She even smiled when she went into his office and put the cup on his desk. Highworth didn't respond. He was watching share prices on one of the TVs opposite his desk. The UK stock exchange hadn't opened yet but, across the world, other markets were trading and he was looking for trends and opportunities. He pressed the intercom and told his PA to send his head of research in to him the moment he arrived in the building. He wanted to get his team working on Kendo Oil.

CHAPTER 56

Harry, Lucy and Hemraj arrived in Farnham just before lunch. It had been a long drive but the only difficult bit had been getting off the Moor. Although it had stopped snowing in the early hours of the morning, the roads had still been covered when they'd left the house and they had had to use Ellie's snow chains for the first few miles. The roads had still been treacherous beyond Moretonhampstead but there had been far less snow and the Range Rover's traction control had meant that they were able to dispense with the chains.

Hemraj knew the Farnham area well. As a young Gurkha soldier he had joined his Battalion when it was based in Church Crookham, a small town located a few miles west of Farnham. The UK Gurkha Battalion had eventually relocated to Shorncliffe in Kent but, other than a new housing development where the old barracks had been, little else had changed. Hemraj had pointed out the Long Valley training area that lies between Farnham and Church Crookham and had explained that this was where he had done his airborne selection course. Densely wooded, it was criss-crossed by a network of forest tracks, all of which seemed to have remarkably steep hills somewhere along their length. Hemraj had grimaced as he had explained how his instructors used to make them sprint up and down the hills until they could hardly walk. 'They said it was character building,' said Hemraj. 'It wasn't. It just hurt!'

Lucy laughed. Hemraj was one of the quietest men she had ever met and his humorous comment surprised her.

They had put Highworth's address into the car's SatNav. It showed that they were now within two hundred metres of the house. There was little traffic and Harry was able to slow to walking pace without causing an obstruction. The new Range Rover didn't look out of place in what was obviously an exclusive residential area. They looked at the houses on either side of the road. They were large and extremely private with high walls and secure looking gates. Some had CCTV cameras mounted on discrete poles, others had signs that warned of guard dogs. As they drove past Highworth's house, Hemraj filmed the entrance on a small digital camera.

'Automatic gates, no CCTV that I can see, no signs of dogs, floodlights over the porch,' said Hemraj into the camera's microphone.

They had used Google Earth to give them an idea of the house's layout. It was set back from the road and surrounded by gardens. It might be difficult to get in but, once inside, there was little chance of being seen from the road. The rear garden backed onto a small wood which they had decided might be used as a covered approach. Harry started to smile as he looked at the house next to Highworth's. It was for sale. The sign gave the name of one of the country's most exclusive estate agents.

'Why don't you give them a ring and see if we can view the house?' he suggested to Lucy, pointing out the sign.

Lucy smiled as she dialled the number. 'What a good idea,' she said. 'We can stop and have a look through the gate. Nobody would think that was suspicious.' Harry pulled up on the kerb in front of the house. He got out with Hemraj whilst Lucy spoke to the estate agent.

'I've booked us in for two o'clock this afternoon. They've had a number of viewings but no offers so far. It's on the market for six million but the agent thinks they might be willing to drop to five five,' she said to Harry.

'A bargain,' said Harry. 'Does it have a pool?'

'It does,' replied Lucy laughing. 'And a tennis court with retractable lighting and its own changing room. It sounds very nice indeed.'

They could see the front of Highworth's house from the gate. It seemed very quiet. Earlier that morning they'd spent an hour or so searching the internet for facts about Highworth. A great deal had been written about his spectacular investments and his family's charitable activities. They now knew that he was married to a woman called 'Caroline' and that her father had been a well known banker. Perhaps not surprisingly, there was little else about his domestic life other than the fact that he didn't have children. They had phoned his office on the way to Farnham on the pretext of confirming whether he would be prepared to give an interview for a magazine later in the month. His secretary had listened politely and had then told them to put their request in writing. They had tried to get her to confirm whether he was in the office by suggesting she ask him there and then whether he would be prepared to give the interview but she had been the model of evasive discretion. 'If you drop him a note setting out why you wish to interview him, I will ensure that he considers your request,' she had said before putting the phone down.

'As we can't do anything more until two o'clock, why don't we have lunch?' suggested Hemraj. 'There's a really nice pub not too far from here that serves great food.'

They agreed and Hemraj directed them out of Farnham and along a succession of country lanes until they came to a place called Well. Harry saw the pub as they entered the village. It was a typical English country inn. The walls were covered in ivy and a vine grew over a wooden frame that enclosed the outdoor seating area next to the main entrance. They went into the bar. It was quiet and they were able to find a secluded table next to the fire. They ordered sandwiches and started to discuss what their next move should be. Harry knew that they needed to move fast. Richards was a dangerous man and there was a limit to how long they could keep him chained up in the cellar. Whilst he would prefer to observe Highworth for a few days before making a move, he knew that he didn't have the time. He would have to do his best and just accept the risk that came with his lack of reconnaissance. The woods at the back of the house were useful in terms of gaining access to Highworth's house. If the house that was for sale was empty, then it might also provide a way of approaching

Highworth's property without being seen from the road.

They ate their lunch and discussed the options. After an hour or so, they had the makings of a plan. It wasn't perfect but it would suffice. Harry went outside to have a cigarette and to phone Ganesh. He didn't doubt that Ganesh could keep Richards under control but surprise was essential to his plan and he wanted to check that there was no way that Richards could communicate with Highworth. 'Keep him secured,' said Harry when he got through. 'We can look at letting him stretch and go to the toilet after we've seen Highworth but, for the moment, I don't want to take any chances. If Richards were somehow to send a message to Highworth, it would make life very difficult for us.'

Ganesh understood. He was a little perplexed as to why Harry thought he would consider letting Richards go, even to the toilet. He knew what the man was capable of. He'd asked the girls not to go into the cellar and to avoid discussing anything that might jeopardise what Harry was doing in case Richards overheard them. He wasn't being unnecessarily cruel to Richards. He'd fed him breakfast and was ensuring that he drank sufficient water to remain hydrated but, beyond that, he'd no intention of being friendly. Richards had tried engaging him in conversation a few times but Ganesh had ignored him. They had both done the same training and Ganesh realised that Richards was trying to create a bond with him. Research suggested that captors were less likely to kill or mistreat their prisoners if they started to relate to them as people rather than seeing them just as targets. But Ganesh wanted Richards to remain afraid of his captors and for that reason he remained silent and continued to wear his balaclava whenever he went to see him.

The tour of the house was interesting. Lucy and Harry pretended to be a couple looking to relocate from London. Hemraj was introduced as a security expert, invited along by the couple to give a view on the house's security. The agent asked a few questions but seemed to accept their story. 'Why wouldn't he?' suggested Harry when they had discussed the plan earlier. 'He wants to sell the house and he has no idea whether or not we are genuinely interested.'

The house had been beautifully renovated by the current owners who, it transpired, had recently moved to the Cayman Islands, presumably, thought Lucy, for tax reasons. Hemraj asked a few security related questions and then disappeared off with the agent's permission to check perimeter security. This gave him an ideal opportunity to study Highworth's house. He took several discrete photographs of the rear of the house and of the woods that backed onto the garden. Content that he had seen enough, he rejoined Harry and Lucy on their tour of the house. For plausibility, he suggested to the agent that, with a few minor modifications, the house could indeed be made very secure.

They spent the rest of the afternoon and the early part of the evening discussing how best to approach and then get into Highworth's house without being seen or heard. The photographs that Hemraj had taken were invaluable, as were the images that they were able to download from Google Earth. Google's Street View, in particular, reinforced their initial impression that the house was too visible from the main road for them to try and approach the front door undetected. After several hours of exploring every possible option, they agreed to have an early supper in the town of Fleet before making their move. About thirty minutes from Farnham, Hemraj knew the town well and took them to one of its many Nepalese restaurants. He explained that when the UK Gurkha Battalion had been based in Church Crookham, Fleet had been the nearest shopping centre. Though the battalion was now long gone, a fair number of ex-soldiers and their families had settled in the area and it therefore retained something of its old Gurkha identity.

After supper, they drove the car to the far side of the woods that backed onto Highworth's house. It was already dark and there was little chance of them being seen but all three wore black fatigues, balaclavas and web belts. Harry and Hemraj had the Glocks whilst

Lucy had a short length of rope over her shoulder. Hemraj led the way through the woods until he came to a slight rise in the ground. He stopped, checked his bearings and, kneeling down, indicated that they had arrived at their destination. He'd identified the spot on an Ordnance Survey map that afternoon. Harry was impressed with Hemraj's selection. The slight hill provided a reasonable amount of cover as well as giving them a clear view of the back of Highworth's house. They settled down to wait.

Highworth arrived home late evening. From what the three were able to see, he was alone in the house with his wife. They had dinner in the large kitchen that faced the garden and then watched TV for a few hours before going upstairs. There were no signs of dogs but they made the assumption that the doors and windows would be alarmed. When they were viewing the house next door, Hemraj had noticed that one of the upstairs windows in Highworth's house had been open. It had frosted glass and Hemraj had assumed that it was a bathroom. Perhaps surprisingly, the window was still ajar. When they had discussed it they had agreed that there was no way that anyone could get access to the window without a ladder unless, Lucy had suggested, they were an exceptional climber. After much discussion, they had agreed that Lucy should try and climb up to the window. If this failed, then they'd decided that they would simply skirt round the side of the house, knock on the front door and, when it was answered, force their way in at gun point. 'Crude but effective,' Harry had said.

'Provided we're not seen from the road,' Hemraj had added with a slight smile. 'In which case it won't be at all effective as someone will no doubt call the police!'

They waited another hour to give Highworth and his wife a chance to fall asleep. Harry looked at his watch. 'Ready?' he asked Lucy.

'As I'll ever be,' she replied, slipping her balaclava over her face. Harry watched her as she checked her equipment. The combats were loose fitting. This and her height helped disguise her female shape. She was wearing climbing 'stickies'. They had bought these in Aldershot at a specialist climbing shop. Their sole was completely smooth and rigid but they gave tremendous grip, enabling the wearer to use even the tiniest feature as a foot hold. She put chalk on her hands to absorb the fine film of sweat that had formed and, with a final wave of her hand, she sprinted out of the woods, neatly jumping a small fence and landing on all fours in Highworth's back garden. She paused for a second to get her bearings and then sprinted for the rear wall of the house. Harry and Hemraj watched with their hearts in their mouths.

'She moves like Ganesh,' whispered Hemraj. 'Like a cat.'

'Yes,' replied Harry, 'only she's much prettier!'

Hemraj looked at him out of the corner of his eye. He knew Harry well and he thought he'd sensed something between his old friend and Lucy when they were at Ellie's house. He was pleased. From what he'd seen of them together, they were a good match.

'Good luck!' he said to Harry.

They watched as Lucy leaned her back to the wall below the open window and uncoiled the rope. She clipped one end of it to her webbing belt, turned round and started to climb. The wall was made of red brick. Though it appeared to be smooth, the pointing between the bricks had weathered over the years and she was able to find enough gaps to pull herself up. Slowly, she began to ascend. At one point, one of her hands slipped and she hung by one arm. Harry gasped and Hemraj started to move forward but she swung the free arm up and was soon putting her hand through the gap in the open window. A few minutes later, she had the window fully open and had tied the rope to something inside the room. She waved at the boys, the signal for them to follow her.

Harry went first. Again, he jumped the fence and then sprinted to the wall. Within a few minutes, he had joined Lucy in what turned out to be a very large and well appointed bathroom. He noticed that the rope was secured to an old fashioned cast iron radiator. 'Thank goodness they don't have under-floor heating,' he said to himself as Hemraj's head appeared in the open window. When they were all inside, they pulled up the rope and closed the window. It was dark but there was sufficient light for Harry to make out a door. He opened it slowly. Peering through the crack he could make out a large bed with two forms in it. He took out his pistol and unclipped a small torch that was attached to his webbing belt. Hemraj did the same. They opened the door and crept into the bedroom. Harry went down one side of the bed whilst Hemraj went down the other. On the count of three, they both turned their torches on and aimed them at the faces of the two sleeping people. Highworth woke up first. 'What the fuck's going on?' he shouted as he began to come to his senses.

'Be quiet Mr Highworth,' said Harry, 'or we will kill both you and Caroline.'

Caroline woke up more slowly but was equally surprised. 'Who the hell are you? What do you want?' she asked.

'If you do as I say, you will not be harmed,' said Harry in a quiet and menacing voice. 'Get out of bed, slowly.' They did as they were told. Both were naked and clearly terrified. Hemraj threw two dressing gowns on the bed. 'Put those on,' said Harry. 'Do it slowly. If you try anything, I will kill your wife. Do you understand Highworth.'

'Yes,' croaked Highworth. 'There's money and valuables downstairs in the safe,' he said. 'Take it all, just don't harm my wife.'

'Very touching,' said Harry. 'But that's not why I'm here.' They kept the torches aimed at their faces. 'Stand still and put your hands behind your backs,' he directed. They did as they were told. Lucy went behind them and fastened their hands together with plasti-cuffs. Hemraj then took hold of Caroline by the arm and led her into the bathroom, leaving Highworth alone with Lucy and Harry.

'What are you going to do with her?' asked Highworth.

'Shut up,' said Harry. 'You will only speak when I ask you a question. Sit down,' he said, dragging a chair over from the dressing table and putting it in front of Highworth. Highworth did as he was told. 'I am going to tell you a story and you are going to fill in the blanks for me. If you don't, my friend will start to hurt your wife. Do you understand me?'

Highworth stared at him. As if on cue, Caroline screamed from the bathroom. It was short and sharp, as though someone had covered her mouth as she screamed. 'What the hell is he doing to her?' shouted Highworth. 'I'll cooperate, just don't hurt her.'

Harry started at the beginning. He gave the impression that it was Richards who had told them everything in exchange for his life. He showed Highworth a few pictures of Richards trussed up in the cellar to encourage him.

'Where is the bastard now?' asked Highworth.

'I don't know,' lied Harry. 'He escaped. I'm surprised he didn't try and warn you.'

'I'm not,' spat Highworth. 'Self-serving bastard doesn't do loyalty.'

Harry spent an hour questioning Highworth. He was careful not to give any indication as to which of Highworth's many victims he was connected to, referring only to 'an interested party' who had cause to be upset with Highworth. Highworth gained in confidence as the questioning continued. 'Was it Knowles who put you up to this?' he asked. 'I knew Briggs would never be able to shut the old bastard up.'

'What do you know about Knowles?' asked Harry, trying to give the impression that he knew more than he did. 'Why do you think he would do this to you?' Highworth's answer was short and to the point.

'Because I screwed him and he didn't like it,' he answered.

'Surely there's more to it than that?' asked Harry. Highworth just stared at him.

'Aba!' shouted Harry. Hemraj heard the Nepali word for 'now' and pushed Caroline into the bedroom. Her face was covered in blood. The front of her dressing gown was open and there was blood at the top of her thighs.

'You bastard,' shouted Highworth. 'I'm telling you everything I know.' He strained at the hand-cuffs and started to stand up. Highworth was a big man and Harry was taking no chances. He hit him hard on the side of his head, knocking him back into the chair.

'Sit down,' ordered Harry. 'If I don't think you're telling me the truth, my friend will cut your wife into little pieces whilst you watch.'

Carline screamed again as Hemraj pushed her back into the bathroom. 'You've got to believe me, I'm telling you everything I know,' said Highworth. 'Please don't hurt her, she knows nothing about any of this.'

'OK,' replied Harry. 'Tell me about Fairweather and the artist girl,' asked Harry.

Highworth started talking. He explained at length about Bubble. com and his plan to start buying when the share price hit 300 pence. 'Fairweather deserved to die,' said Highworth. 'He was a nasty little self publicist who took all the credit for everything his team ever did.'

Harry continued asking questions until he was satisfied that Highworth had nothing further to tell him. He called to Hemraj who brought Caroline back into the bedroom. She was still covered in blood but this time also had a gag in her mouth. He sat her in another chair and used a roll of duct tape to fasten her to it with her arms behind her back. Highworth was about to protest when a gag was stuffed in his mouth and he was also taped to the chair he was sitting in.

'I suggest you don't move for an hour or so,' said Harry, pointing the torch in his face. 'I will phone the police tomorrow morning to come and release you in case you haven't managed to work yourself free by then. You can decide what you tell them.' Harry motioned for Hemraj and Lucy to go out through the window. Neither Highworth nor his wife could see anything other than the torches that shone in their faces. When these were turned off, it took several minutes for their eyes to become accustomed to the darkness. They heard the intruders go out through the bathroom window.

After an hour of struggling, Highworth managed to work his gag free. 'Don't worry darling,' he called out to Caroline, 'we'll soon be free.' Caroline grunted through her tears. The red sauce that had been smeared over her face to look like blood tasted awful and she could feel it drying on her thighs.

CHAPTER 57

Harry, Lucy and Hemraj were in the Range Rover heading back towards Dartmoor. It had gone far better than they had expected. Hemraj had been right. The trick was to go in hard and frighten the life out of the victims from the outset. It was the same approach he had taken with Richards and it had worked equally as well the second time round. Using tomato sauce to look like blood had been a masterstroke. Whilst they would have had no compunction killing Highworth given what he had done to others, they were reluctant to hurt his wife. Simple though it was, the ruse allowed them to deceive Highworth into thinking that they had tried to rape his wife and broken her nose. Not very pleasant but they had needed to persuade Highworth that they were serious. Her arms might ache from Hemraj pushing them up her back to make her scream but, beyond that, she was physically unharmed.

They had to decide what to do next. Richards was still in the cellar. Harry had called the police to report a break-in at the Highworth's house. He didn't like Highworth but he recognised that someone needed to release them. He wasn't worried about Highworth working out who had attacked him. They had been very careful not to use names and to keep the torches aimed at Highworth and his wife at all times. Harry would be surprised if they could describe their assailants at all other than to confirm that there had been two or three people wearing dark clothes and balaclavas. Harry was far more interested in what Highworth would say to the police when they arrived. He certainly wouldn't tell them what he'd told Harry.

They stopped for coffee mid morning at a service station. They had dumped their black combats and the rope in a skip in Aldershot. They had the weapons still with them but they were hidden underneath the spare wheel in the back of the car. There was nothing suspicious in the vehicle. Harry didn't expect to be searched but, ever cautious, he didn't want a routine police check, perhaps for speeding or a defective light, to be their undoing. They drank their coffee and ate a light breakfast of croissants and Danish pastries whilst they considered what to do about Richards.

'We can't just release him,' said Harry. 'He'll come after us and, as Lucy said, we don't want to spend the rest of the year looking over our shoulders.'

'What about just handing him over to the police with a copy of the two films?' asked Lucy. She had filmed the whole of Highworth's interrogation, standing behind Harry as he'd shone the torch in Highworth's face. Harry had done the same during Richards' interrogation

'We could but they would then know that your father had been involved,' replied Harry. 'We were careful not to name him in the Highworth interview but Richards knew him well and he would no doubt try and do some sort of deal with the police to reduce his sentence.'

'Why don't we just kill him?' suggested Hemraj. 'He is not a nice man. I suspect that he's killed a great many people in addition to your father,' he said, pointing at Lucy with his chin. 'I am very happy to see that Richards has a nasty accident.'

Lucy looked at Hemraj. She wasn't sure whether to be appalled or grateful.

'What about the body?' asked Harry, not sure that he liked the idea of killing someone in cold blood, even a man like Richards.

'There are plenty of ways to dispose of bodies,' said Hemraj slowly. Harry looked at his face as he said this. It was devoid of emotion. Hemraj saw Richards as the scum of the earth. He would have no hesitation in killing him, even with his bare hands if necessary.

They continued to discuss what to do with Richards. Eventually, Harry had an idea which he explained to the others.

'It might work,' said Lucy hesitantly.

Hemraj wasn't so sure. 'If it doesn't, then I will kill him for taking your father's life and for what he will do to us if we don't,' said Hemraj, looking Lucy in the eye.

She met his gaze. 'Thank you,' she said simply.

CHAPTER 58

Harry, Lucy and Hemraj arrived back on Dartmoor towards midday. It had stopped snowing and the snow ploughs had obviously been out clearing the major roads. Unfortunately, this didn't include the road from Moretonhampstead to North Bovey and they found themselves making slow progress for the final few miles. The Range Rover's traction control, which shifted power to whichever wheels could benefit most from it, had to work hard to get them up the last hill.

Sarah waved to them as they pulled up outside the house. 'Welcome back,' she said, shovelling snow off the path in front of the kitchen door. 'How did it go?'

'Fine,' said Harry, kissing her on both cheeks. 'We did what we needed to do. How's Richards?'

'He's been very quiet. I haven't seen him and Ganesh has only made the odd appearance upstairs to use the toilet and make tea. What are you going to do with him now,' she asked.

'We're going to try and do a deal with him. We have a lot of evidence against him, including a tape of his interrogation. We're going to suggest that we will let him go and keep quiet about his role in all of this on condition he leaves us well alone and forgets he's ever heard of Lucy or Camilla.'

'Are you sure that's a good idea?' asked Sarah, clearly concerned. 'You don't think he'll just wait until all this has passed over and then try and kill us to cover his tracks?'

'He might but we can give the evidence to someone and tell them to open it if anything happens to us.'

Sarah looked at Harry with genuine concern. 'You'll forgive me saying this but that is a crap plan. It will be no comfort to me as I take my last breath to know that my killer might, and I emphasise might, one day be held to account for murdering me. Can't we do better than that?'

'I'm open to ideas,' said Harry, irritated that Sarah was being so dismissive of his plan.

They followed Sarah inside. Ellie had made tea and they all sat around the kitchen table to discuss the next steps. Harry outlined his plan. Ellie and Camilla looked equally as surprised as Sarah had been.

'I don't think it will work Fish,' said Camilla after several minutes of silence. 'We have no guarantee that he won't just take us out one by one once we've released him. We know he's resourceful as well as ruthless. Even with the evidence we have, there would be nothing to stop him from killing us and then leaving the country and living somewhere that doesn't have an extradition treaty with the UK. We need to do better.' They sat in silence until Lucy suggested that they bribe him with some of the money that her father had left her. They kicked the idea around but decided that it could be the thin end of a wedge.

'There's nothing to stop him coming back for more,' suggested Camilla. The others nodded.

'I'm going to replace Ganesh,' said Hemraj, standing up and leaving the table. They watched him as he disappeared down the cellar stairs.

'Why don't we just let Hemraj kill him?' asked Lucy quietly.

'Because that would make us no better than him,' said Harry, surprised that Lucy seemed to have got over whatever reservations she had had earlier about killing Richards. Harry looked at her. 'Anyway, I thought you were against that?' he asked.

'I was. I've been thinking about it,' she replied. 'But the alternative doesn't appeal either if it means never knowing whether he's after me, waiting for an opportunity to kill me in some dark alley when I'm least expecting it, just as he did my father.'

'So what do you suggest?' asked Ellie.

'Well,' she said, 'my father is dead. Nothing will change that and what he did was wrong. I can't condone his actions. He took peoples' lives for money. I know he said that they deserved to die but did they? All of them? We recorded both Richards' and Highworth's interrogations. I know we considered this earlier but what if we sent both of the films to the police? I know my father's part in all of this will come out eventually but it can't harm him now. His reputation will take a few knocks and I might lose the money but so be it. It's better than the alternative: a lifetime of looking over our shoulders.'

They discussed Lucy's proposition for over an hour. The information in the films would be sufficient for the police to launch their own investigations. It couldn't be used as evidence because it was clear that both Richards and Highworth were under duress when they had been questioned. But equally, the police would want to act on the detailed descriptions of the murders and other illegal activities that both men had confessed to being involved in. It would take time but their own investigations would eventually corroborate what was in the films, allowing them to prosecute both men.

'What about Knowles and Briggs whoever they are?' asked Camilla.

'I think we can leave that to the police to work out,' said Harry. 'I don't think we want to get any more involved than we have to. We know who killed Lucy's Dad and we now know why. I think we let the police take the lead from here on in. Do we all agree to Lucy's idea?' asked Harry, looking at them each in turn. They nodded.

'OK,' said Harry. 'I'll tell Richards that we're going to release him as we said we would. I won't tell him about the plan to send the films to the police. I'll just tell him that, as far as we are concerned, we've got what we wanted. If he doesn't bother us, then we won't bother him.'

'What if he skips the country before the police get to him?' asked Camilla.

'It's a risk we have to take,' replied Lucy. 'They'll find him eventually.'

Harry went down into the cellar to talk to Richards. He pulled up a chair and sat opposite him, looking him squarely in the eye. He explained that they were going to release him on the condition that he forgot about them.

'Why are you doing this?' asked Richards, clearly suspicious.

'Because there has been enough bloodshed and we have the answers we were looking for. But make no mistake,' said Harry, 'my two balaclava wearing friends know exactly who you are. They will find you and kill you if anything happens to the girls or to me once we've let you go.'

Richards nodded. He wasn't stupid. He was taking it one step at a time. Once he was free, what he did was up to him. And if he could find out who the two men in combats were, then he could take them out at his leisure before killing the rest of them. None of this showed in his face. Instead, he feigned relief and thanked Harry.

'We'll cut you free and give you some clothes. We'll even drive you to your car. But then you go,' said Harry. Richards nodded.

'Cover him,' said Harry to Ganesh as he cut through the tape that held Richards to the chair. Richards stood up slowly, stretching his arms and legs. He winced as the blood started to flow back into his limbs. 'Put these on,' ordered Harry, passing him a set of the black fatigues. Richards held up his handcuffed hands. Harry gave him the key and stepped back as Richards unlocked them. 'Watch him,' he said to Ganesh, 'I'll turn the car round. Put the blindfold on him and bring him up when he's dressed.' Ganesh nodded, aiming his pistol squarely at Richards' chest.

Harry sat in the car waiting. Eventually, Richards appeared in the doorway. He was wearing the blindfold and his hands had been handcuffed in front of him. Hemraj led him to the Range Rover whilst Ganesh followed on behind with his pistol aimed on Richards' back.

'Get in the car,' ordered Hemraj. Richards climbed into the front passenger seat. 'Just so you know,' said Hemraj. 'I'm sat behind you and I have a pistol. Try anything and I will enjoy putting a bullet in you.' Richards nodded.

Harry eased the car down the drive and onto the main road. Richards had told them where he had parked his car and Harry drove slowly through the village, heading out towards Hay Tor rather than into Morton Hamspted. Ganesh had remained with the girls. He'd been up for twenty-our hours watching Richards and was dead on his feet. He needed to rest.

Five minutes later, they arrived in the village of Manaton. Harry could see Richards' Subaru parked near the church at the edge of the village green. He pulled in about twenty metres away from it. It was early evening and the deep snow was keeping people indoors.

'We're here,' he said to Richards, removing the blindfold. 'As my friend said, try anything and we'll kill you.'

'I won't,' said Richards. He was playing along but he was still suspicious. He couldn't believe that they were going to let him go. It just didn't make sense.

They got out of the Range Rover and moved slowly through the snow towards the Subaru. Richards held up his hands. Harry passed him the keys to the handcuffs. Richards undid them and then stumbled. Instinctively, Harry went towards him to help him to his feet. As he did so, Richards lunged at him. He caught Harry off balance and wrapped an arm tightly round his neck. He quickly removed the knife that Harry had strapped to his leg with his other hand and held it to Harry's throat.

'Drop the gun or I'll slit his throat,' snarled Richards.

'We've let you go, you don't need to do this,' said Hemraj.

'I don't trust you. I don't know what but you were going to do something,' said Richards, pushing the edge of the knife deeper into Harry's throat. 'Drop it now.'

Hemraj did as he was told, throwing the Glock over the hedge into the church garden. There was no way he was going to make this easy for Richards. Richards watched the pistol fly through the air. Harry seized his opportunity, forcing his head back, trying to smash it into Richards' nose. At the same time, he grabbed Richards' knife arm with both hands and pushed it away from his body. Richards reacted quickly, stepping back to avoid Harry's head and punching Harry hard in the temple with his free hand. Harry dropped to the floor, stunned by the force of the blow.

Harry was conscious but dazed. Realising that he needed to distract Richards before he used the knife on Harry, Hemraj shouted at him and ran towards him. Richards stepped quickly away from Harry and dropped into a crouch, the knife held out in front of him. He smiled thinly. He was a master at unarmed combat and he didn't doubt his ability to take the big Gurkha. He lunged at Hemraj. Hemraj twisted his body, the knife missing him by millimetres.

'Fuck this,' said Hemraj, taking off his Balaclava and throwing it to the ground. He adopted a similar crouch to Richards and the two men circled each other, looking for an opportunity. Richards darted in. Hemraj pivoted to avoid the knife and smashed the edge of his hand into Richards' outstretched arm. The knife fell into the snow but Richards recovered quickly. Amazed at how fast the big Gurkha had moved, he feinted with his right hand and then launched a rabbit punch at the Gurkha's neck. Rather than moving back to avoid it, Hemraj stepped in towards Richards, pushing the outstretched hand away and turning to land a powerful elbow strike in Richards' midriff. Winded, Richards stepped back. Hemraj's black eyes were locked onto his and, for the first time in many years, Richards started to feel afraid. He realised that, yet again, he might have underestimated his opponent. Hemraj launched a kick at Richards' groin. Richards jumped back but, as soon as he landed, Hemraj launched another kick, this time at his head. Again, Richards stepped back to avoid the blow. Recovering his balance, he charged at Hemraj. The two men fell to the floor, grappling for a hold. Hemraj managed to wrap a thick arm round Richards' neck. Richards struggled to break free but the Gurkha was too powerful. He wrapped his legs round Richards' thighs and then used every ounce of his immense strength to pull Richards' neck back. Harry heard a loud snap and saw Richards go limp. Hemraj had broken his neck.

Hemraj relaxed his grip, releasing Richards. He pushed the body away and then stood up, going over to Harry and helping him to his feet. 'Are you OK?' he asked.

'Yes,' said Harry. 'You?'

'Fine,' replied Hemraj. 'What shall we do about him?' he asked, pointing at Richards with his chin. 'We can't really leave him here.'

'No,' replied Harry thoughtfully. 'But I have an idea. Let's put him in the car out of the way and then I'll tell you what I think we should do.'

Hemraj did as he was told, easily lifting Richards' body and putting it in the rear of the Range Rover. Harry found the Subaru's keys hidden just inside the exhaust pipe. He cleared the worst of the snow off the car and started it up. He then got out of the car and explained his idea to Hemraj. Hemraj agreed the plan and got into the Subaru. Harry climbed into the Range Rover and led the way out of Manaton and towards the town of Bovey Tracy, a bustling market town that lies at the foot of the Moor. The roads were still covered in snow but there were a number of vehicle tracks that showed the line of the road.

It was dark when they stopped on the top of Trendlebere Down. They got out of their cars and looked down the steep hill in front of them. The road ran straight down towards the valley bottom before disappearing round a sharp corner. There were some vehicle tracks but it would be treacherous to try the descent without snow chains. Even then, trying it at night would be verging on suicidal given the ice that had formed in the vehicle ruts.

'Ready?' asked Harry. Hemraj nodded. He opened the boot of the Range Rover and took Richards' body out, carrying it over to the Subaru. They had dressed it in Harry's clothes and Harry, now wearing the black combats that Richards had worn, reversed the Range Rover and pulled in behind the Subaru. Hemraj positioned Richards' body behind the Subaru's steering wheel, turned the car's lights on and leaned over Richards to release the hand brake. The car started to move forwards slowly. It gathered momentum as they watched. It followed the line of the road but instead of going round the corner, it climbed the slight verge and disappeared straight down the hillside. Harry and Hemraj listened. They couldn't see the car but a few minutes later they heard a loud bang. The car had obviously stopped abruptly, smashing into the rocks at the bottom of the valley. 'With any luck,' said Harry, 'they won't find it until tomorrow. If it thaws overnight and the tracks melt away, they might not even find it for a few weeks.'

CHAPTER 59

Harry was in the shower, thinking through the last few days. Ganesh had edited the films of both Richards' and Highworth's interrogations, removing anything that might help the police identify who had carried out the questioning. They'd copied the films onto a memory stick and sent it to Jake, the policeman leading the investigation into Lucy's father's death in Edinburgh. It would be unlikely that the films could be used as evidence but the story they told could be investigated and, pointed in the right direction. The police would no doubt be able to unravel most of Highworth's illegal activities over the last twenty or so years. They'd agreed not to edit out the bits that described Lucy's father's role. There was a risk that this would lead to his reputation being tarnished but, without this part of the jigsaw in place, it would be difficult for the police to put the whole story together. 'And anyway,' Lucy had said when they had discussed it, 'the truth's bound to come out sooner or later.' Harry hadn't met Jake but he could imagine the surprise on his face as he started to watch the footage.

The shower was hot and powerful and he could feel the life returning to his muscles. He had just come back from running with Lucy. She was supremely fit and had taken a mischievous delight in watching him struggle to keep up. They had followed the same route that he had run with Sarah a few days ago. By the time they'd reached Butt Hill, he was ready to admit defeat but Lucy had punched him on the shoulder and raced off in front of him. 'Come on fatty, race you to the top,' she'd called over her shoulder as she'd sprinted for the car park. He'd charged after her but he didn't come close to catching up. Even Boot had been left in her wake. They'd jogged slowly back to the house and agreed that they'd have a quick shower before going out for supper at the Ring O'Bells. Sarah and Ellie had set off that afternoon to take Camilla back to London. The two Gurkhas had also headed home, leaving Harry and Lucy with the house to themselves for the next few days. They had been so busy over the last forty-eight hours that Harry hadn't really given much thought to what would happen next with Lucy. He still wasn't sure whether she felt as strongly about him as he did about her. He hoped so but he was still a little bit nervous about making the first move. He was thinking about this when he heard the shower door open. He looked round. Lucy stepped into the shower, dropping her towel to the floor and closing the door behind her. She was naked.

'So that's why she called you Fish,' said Lucy, patting the tattoo on his buttock before turning him round and putting her arms around his neck. 'We've got plenty of time to get to know each other properly now,' she whispered in his ear, arching her back as the hot water hit her.

'Yes,' replied Harry, putting his hands on her hips and pulling her close against him.

It had taken her a while to pluck up the courage to come into the bathroom. She'd sensed his apprehension over the last few days and had been worried that he might be shocked at such a brazen approach. But his body's reaction confirmed that it had been the right thing to do. It had been a long time since she'd been with a man and she was therefore surprised at how quickly her own body responded to his touch.

'Let's have a late supper,' he said, kissing her gently on the mouth as his hands slowly began to explore her body.

EPILOGUE

Harry and Lucy were having breakfast on the veranda of their hotel suit. They'd flown to Spain a few days before and had decided to stay in Javea. Lucy's father had mentioned it when he'd spoken to her before she flew out to Nepal to begin her expedition. He'd recommended the small resort as an ideal place for a break. They were staying in the Parador, one of a chain of luxury hotels set up by the Spanish government to breathe new life into historic buildings. Though the Javea Parador was relatively modern, it was located at one end of the main beach and had stunning views across the bay.

Isobel and Jake were due to fly out at the weekend to spend a few days with them. They had intended to come out earlier but Jake, as the police officer who'd received the films, had found himself at the centre of the Scottish end of the investigation. Recognising the opportunity to make his name, he'd been reluctant to leave Edinburgh until he was confident that the team that had been assembled had started to make progress. He and Isobel had been seeing a fair bit of each other since their first date in Tiger Lily's. They were an ideal match and Lucy was optimistic that the relationship would last.

It had been four weeks since they'd sent the films to Jake. To their surprise, the police had reacted almost immediately. Highworth's arrest, which appeared to come out of nowhere, had attracted a great deal of national media coverage. The Commissioner of the City of London Police, Sir James Briggs, had given several interviews suggesting that Highworth had been under investigation for a number of months and that his arrest had been the result of a recent breakthrough. He made no mention of the films but did suggest that a man who had been killed in a tragic accident on Dartmoor might be connected to the case. There were one or two desperate accusations that Briggs himself had been involved but these were dismissed as malicious slander. Sir Charles Knowles, the well known and widely respected city grandee, had been quick to support 'Straight Jim', telling the *Times* that the City was lucky to have such an incorruptible man in charge of its police force. Indeed, there were even rumours that Briggs might now be considered for the Met following the recent retirement through ill health of its commissioner.

Harry and Lucy watched the sun begin its climb above the horizon. It was a warm, balmy morning and Harry was feeling more relaxed than he had for years. He reached across the table and took Lucy's hand. 'Now that you are a rich lady and your PhD has been confirmed, have you given any thought to what you're going to do next?' he asked her.

She looked at him. 'I don't know,' she replied, smiling mischievously. 'I'm getting a great deal richer every day so, for the moment, I don't think I need to do anything other than enjoy being with you.'

'What do you mean?' asked Harry slowly. Interest rates were at an all time low and there was little chance of Lucy making much from the money her father had left her in his bank accounts.

'Highworth was right,' she said. 'Bubble.com didn't need Fairweather. Mymate is on track and it looks like it's going to be even better than he thought.'

'I still don't get you,' said Harry.

'Don't be angry with me but you know when we got back to the house after seeing Highworth?'

'Yes,' said Harry suspiciously.

'Well, I phoned my Dad's old financial advisor in Edinburgh and told him to take the money in the legal accounts, less the half a million for Kate, and invest it in Bubble.com shares. He refused at first, thought I was losing my marbles. Murdo McCleod had to convince him that I was sane and eventually he agreed to do what I asked. According to this morning's share prices, my three and a bit million has doubled over the last four weeks. And it's all legal.'

'No way,' said Harry, amazed.

'Yes way,' replied Lucy. 'And if Highworth's predictions turn out to be right, it should have doubled again by the end of the year.' Harry started to laugh. 'More coffee or would you prefer something stronger?' asked Lucy as she popped open a bottle of champagne that the hotel had discretely chilled for her.

'What are we celebrating?' asked Harry.

'Life,' said Lucy, pouring two glasses and handing one to him. 'And us. We're a good team, you and I. I think we owe it to ourselves to spend some of Dad's money on a team holiday. He would have approved of that,' she said, chinking her glass against his.

'Where do you have in mind?' asked Harry, delighted at the prospect of spending more time with Lucy.

'Not sure yet,' she replied. She'd given the matter a lot of thought. Although it was early days, she felt that for the first time in her life she'd met a man with whom she wanted to spend every minute of every day. Wherever they decided to go, she was determined that it would be a destination where this would be possible.

THE END